GROWTH

TAMING DESTINY

BOOK TWO: GROWTH

S. L. Winter

Podium

Copyright © 2025 by S. L. Winter

Cover design by Tommypocket Illustrator

ISBN: 978-1-0394-8240-1

Published in 2025 by Podium Publishing
www.podiumentertainment.com

GROWTH

CHAPTER ONE

Threat

"How did this happen?" The shock-filled query slips out without conscious thought.

But it's a valid question. I've just come back from a highly dangerous trip where I almost died multiple times—and, frankly, if I never have to see that kraken-squid-octopus thing again, it'll be too soon. I was hoping to get home, have a good meal, maybe indulge in my first proper wash with my new soap . . .

Instead, I find my landlady lying collapsed on the ground. Although Kalanthia's status as the most powerful creature I've come across so far might have been challenged by the beast I just faced, I certainly wasn't expecting there to be something capable of taking her down like this. Have I misjudged the capabilities of the creatures in this area? It's deeply worrying.

As is the fact that Lathani, her only cub, is missing—taken.

Ambushed, Kalanthia answers me. Even her mental voice sounds weak, as if it takes great effort just to project her meaning. *They shot me. Captured her.*

"But what kind of poison is strong enough to take *you* down?" I ask, almost disbelieving. It's only the evidence of my eyes that convinces me it's possible at all.

Stamina inhibitor. Instead of feeding me more words, I get a small "download" of sensation: the sense of constant exhaustion as my stamina is forcibly kept down to practically zero. I abruptly understand that there were, in fact, *two* poisons. One that made her use her stamina far quicker than normal, and another that's stopping it from regenerating.

Actually, the whole situation reminds me of how I felt when I was attacked by the black blob, the one that Spike saved me from. The thought once more sends a pang of regret through me at his senseless death even as I redivert my attention back to Kalanthia's issues.

I understand the problem now: even breathing is difficult with no stamina in the tank. Why that affects her mental voice too, I don't know, but clearly it does. I take a moment to review the memories I absorbed a while ago, which give me a basic understanding of the System I now have embedded in my being. What I learn there is alarming.

When stamina is first brought down too low, moving becomes difficult and the person can only sit or lie down and wait for it to regenerate. If it doesn't, or is immediately used again, the next step is difficulty in breathing. Kalanthia is already at that stage judging by how labored each of her breaths is.

The final step is the most dangerous and is fatal if not overcome. Organ failure. Having labored with a lack of stamina for too long, the vital organs of the body are put under increasing strain. If the low stamina continues, the organs will start failing one by one as health is consumed, little by little, to keep the body going.

I step forwards and reach out towards her before checking myself at the last moment. Unlike with Bastet, I don't want to overstep by casting magic on Kalanthia without her permission. While I figure the answer is self-evident, I'd better ask her first.

"May I try to heal you?" I ask anxiously.

Go ahead, she wheezes mentally, and I quickly touch her head.

Closing my eyes, I focus on my healing Skill, Lay-on-Hands. Feeding my mana into the massive leopard slumped in front of me, I feel like I'm pouring a bucket of water into a dried-up swimming pool. An Olympic-sized one. In short, by the time I've bottomed out my mana, I still don't feel like I've made a single jot of difference.

"I'm sorry," I tell her, shamefaced. "It's not much."

It's something, she reassures me, and I feel even worse; here she is, potentially facing death if she can't get her stamina up a bit, and she's helping *me* feel better.

"When my mana regenerates, I'll heal you some more," I promise.

No. Her voice, for all its weakness, is firm. *You must help Lathani. I will be fine. She is among enemies. If I wait until I'm recovered to seek her, it could be too late.*

"All right," I agree, though my heart is full of doubt. If these creatures were strong enough to take down *Kalanthia,* what kind of chance do *I* stand against them? Sure, I've come a long way since I arrived in this world, but my increased stats and new weaponry wouldn't help me much against Kalanthia; why would they serve me any better against her enemies?

Here, she tells me before dumping a whole load of information in my head. Like my previous experiences of knowledge dumps, it's painful. This time, though, it's not due to the sheer volume of memories suddenly needing to find space in my brain—or not entirely, anyway. The main reason for the pain is due to the *content.*

Kalanthia's memories are just simply too alien to easily fit in my head. Just like Bastet's impressions of scouting ahead in the dark were difficult to comprehend, these memories hold sensations that I simply don't have the faculties to process.

Kalanthia has much stronger sensations of smell and taste than I do. She has whiskers and fur, which communicate information, and two other senses that I cannot understand at all. One seems to be something to do with the earth; the other, some sort of sense that . . . expands beyond herself? That one's even more incomprehensible than the previous. In fact, the memory of the attack is so confused from her different senses being used in combat that all I get out of it is movement and bloodlust.

The pain comes from my own brain trying to wrestle with the new information and pummel it into some form that it can deal with. And the process is almost as agonizing as shoving the Lay-on-Hands Skill stone knowledge into my head.

By the end, though, I at least have more information than I started with, and I gain a sense for why she is hurrying me along. *I* wouldn't want to leave Lathani in the hands of the creatures that have taken her. Or should that be paws? Or claws? Anyway, she's right. I need to get going.

"Do you want to come with me or stay here with the cubs?" I ask Bastet. We've been through enough in the last couple of days that I'd better give her the choice. She thinks for a few moments before sending me a wave of emotion that expresses determination to be with me but also not wanting to leave the cubs alone. "Oh, I didn't mean to leave them here—I wouldn't trust Trouble near my pots," I tell her with a touch of humor. "I meant that if you wanted to keep them and yourself out of danger here, I'd understand." I wouldn't like it—I've learned *that* lesson multiple times over—but I would understand.

There's a clear sense of negation—I'm guiltily glad that Bastet seems to feel the way I do. Hopefully, the cubs will cope with being carried most of the time. We need to move fast.

No time to waste. I quickly refill my canteen with water and then look at Kalanthia a final time. She should be fine. She's got water here, and, hopefully, nothing will attack her in the time it will take her to regain at least some ability to move. I consider leaving her a carcass, but when I offer it, she rejects the suggestion kindly, but firmly. When I think about it, I realize why: a bloody carcass could easily draw predators to her vulnerable form.

My mana has regenerated somewhat in the last few minutes, so I give her another dose, allowing my mana to run out completely. Feeling suddenly tired, the sensation of emptying my mana completely almost as bad as emptying my stamina, I force myself to move. There aren't that many hours until dark and I want to make the most of the time.

As we move at a medium-paced jog, I go over the memories that Kalanthia sent to me. They're still difficult to parse, and there's no way I can gain as much information as she put into them—our senses are just too different. Still, I can get enough information out of them via sight, sound, and smell to know in which direction to head.

I could actually follow the river if I chose, as the lizard folk live not that far from it. That would waste unnecessary time, however, since the river isn't exactly a direct route. Hopefully, with my new knowledge of landmarks, I'll be able to find my way easily enough. Directions, though, are not my main concern.

That might seem a little surprising considering I have the natural directional sense of a paper bag blowing on the wind and my Map only helps me with places I've already been to. Despite that, it's more about *where* we're headed that concerns me. Specifically, into what area.

The lizard folk of the valley live exactly there—deeper in the valley. Technically,

I'm in the valley now since I'm not on the bare slopes of the mountain tops. But both valley and mountains are incredibly vast, the elevation of the peaks high enough to compete with several of Earth's highest mountains and their sides remarkably gentle for the vast majority of it. I already know that the further down into the forest we travel, the more dangerous the creatures we encounter will likely be.

Based on Kalanthia's memories, I can tell that the density of Energy is going to increase significantly; the density of animals and their danger level is likely to do the same. Which is not necessarily great news for me when I've struggled against several of the denizens around *here*.

When she walked through the area, Kalanthia wasn't particularly bothered by other animals around, but I have a feeling that that might be more of a perk enjoyed by massive predatory beasts rather than a feature of the area. I'm probably not going to be as lucky unless I can slip by using Stealth and Fade. All I can hope is that my new bow and upgraded weaponry will prove a match to the killer creatures I'm likely to face.

Not to mention the lizard folk themselves. From her memories, they look a bit like upright crocodiles, with long sharp-toothed jaws, though these jaws aren't as long proportionally as a real crocodile's. Actually, maybe it's more accurate to say that they look like humanoid T-Rexes. Or maybe a strange combination of the two.

They seem to often walk upright on their back legs, which have longer feet than their front, but when they want to run quickly, they lean forwards like a T-Rex would, their heavy tails providing a perfect counterbalance. Their heads are more crocodilian than a T-Rex's, though. They have spikes down their backs, which appear capable of flaring up and down. Unlike both T-Rexes and crocodiles, however, their front feet are far more capable looking and could be accurately described as arms with clawed paws on the ends. Paws that are rather obviously dexterous.

They don't look like easy targets, if I'm honest, with their clawed fore and back paws, their jaws, and their scaled skin, which looks better than most types of armor . . . Plus, though I can't fully decode the memory of the attack, the fact that Kalanthia was taken down by such powerful poisons indicates that they have some method of delivering it, whether through bite, scratch, or ranged attack.

Frankly, they make me wonder whether I'll actually be able to do anything even if we find Lathani. But I can't think like that. I've overcome so many odds so far; I can't leave Lathani to suffer and die, not when I know her mother isn't in any condition to rush to her aid. Not when I can at least try to do *something*.

I cast a glance over at Bastet. And I mustn't forget that I've got some firepower on my side too. One on one, I would put my money on Bastet. I'll just have to make sure that the odds stay in our favor.

CHAPTER TWO

Rematch

Although lacking useful detail such as how the lizard folk attack or what their capabilities are, Kalanthia's memories impressed on me their potential threat in an indisputable way: by making it clear that it was their specific threat that made her choose to move out of her previous den and travel up the mountainside. I've been wondering for a while why a creature like Kalanthia would be willing to live in an area with such relatively little Energy when she could easily carve out a territory in a more Energy-dense area. It seems I have an answer.

I do find it interesting that they merely disabled her and took her cub. Even if they expected Kalanthia to eventually die from the poison, it doesn't make sense when looked at coldly and objectively. Why would they dismiss the threat that they had clearly actively searched for—their stomping grounds are more than a casual day's travel away—but then take a creature that was clearly no threat to them?

Wouldn't it have made more sense to kill Kalanthia and leave Lathani alone? Or even kill Lathani as well because she could potentially be a threat in the future; nature is rife with examples of animals who instinctively kill the infant offspring of rivals in order to preempt threats in the future. And why take Lathani with them?

The answer: their approach makes no logical sense. At least, not if I'm looking at the animal kingdom. If I look at humans, however . . . Humans have been known to take the infant creatures of other species for a number of reasons, caring little about the adults if there's nothing in it for them. I've even got a whole Class centered around the taming profession and am currently helping raise some raptorcat cubs in the hope that I might be able to Tame them later. Could that be the reason?

But if it is, then that means the lizard folk might actually be self-aware . . . Nicholas said there weren't any civilized races here, but who knows what he classes as civilized?

I don't have enough information to know, but I can't dismiss the possibility that they might be more advanced than almost all the animals I've seen here so far. If so, it will make things harder. An intelligent enemy is always going to be more difficult to outmaneuver or defeat than a dumb one.

But that's for later. First, I need to actually get there.

Bash. My mace swings one way.

Thump. My mace swings back.

Each blow lands, and the larger and stronger cousins of the killer chickens let out coughing sounds of pain as my weapon cracks or caves in bone at each Strength-powered swing.

The first few hours of our journey haven't exactly been without incident, but I find myself surprised at how easily we tackle the threats. Stats and practice are really paying off. Even my bow skills have improved, my increased Dexterity helping with accuracy and a general feeling of fluidity.

That said, using a bow is a bit awkward with the cubs strapped to my chest, so I've been fighting with my mace whenever we get attacked before I can tuck them somewhere safe. I can really see my increased Strength coming into play as each blow has so much more effect than when I first used the knotted branch of wood. It helps for sure that I've also improved the mace itself. The chunky piece of stone fixed to the head with rope and pitch gives it a weight and heft that I very much appreciate.

Then, of course, there's Bastet. She's a whirlwind of teeth and claws and death, and few creatures stand up to her for long. Those that do generally have some sort of defensive feature that I'm able to overcome with my mace and Strength. We're a good team. She's quick and her claws are deadly; I'm significantly slower, but I have ranged options and my bludgeoning-type damage is deadly in a different way.

These older-brother versions of killer chickens are bigger and stronger, not to mention more numerous, but we're getting through them like a scythe cutting through wheat. It only takes me one or two blows to put the creatures down for good—even less than that for Bastet. In this particular battle, it's like a rematch with my previous foes. We've both upgraded, but the gap between us has only widened. The killer chickens are evidently outmatched, but for some reason they're still attacking.

A killer chicken darts forwards to snap at my throat, perhaps hoping for a lucky blow, but I just reach out to snatch at its neck and take the split second of surprise before it attacks me again to swing at its body. With such an easy target, it only takes one blow to cave in its rib cage on one side, leaving it down for the count as it struggles to breathe.

It's amazing how so many life-or-death encounters can inure one to the terror of mortal danger. And, frankly, these chickens are so far from that terrifying monster of the deep that it's almost laughable. I'd be dead if I had been snagged by even one of those tentacles, unable to cut through the skin as I was. These oversized farm animals are really just corpses walking.

That's not to say that the meter-and-a-half tall cold-blooded murderers couldn't do me in if I got too cocky; I'm fully aware that for all my improvements, I'm only a few steps away from disaster. It seems so long ago, it's hard to believe that I've only been in this world for a month or so. Still, the fact that I'm not even down to half my health by the time we dispatch the nineteenth killer chicken is heartening.

The fight over, I pull up my status screen to check my gains. There are no messages waiting for me—disappointing, but not overly surprising. I knew that after reaching ten in each stat it would become significantly harder to improve through effort, and that's proving true.

Name: Markus Wolfe		Race: Human	Class: Tamer
Level: 2	Energy to next level: 56%	Energy absorption rate: 19u/hr	Energy towards debt: 1%
Intelligence	12	Mana: 61/120	
Wisdom	12	Mana regeneration rate: 300u/hr	
Willpower	17+3 (+20%)	Health regeneration rate: 20u/hr	
Constitution	13	Health: 72/130	
Strength	12	Stamina: 16/60	
Dexterity	12	Stamina regeneration rate: 120u/hr	
Class Skills: Dominate – Beginner 4 Tame – Beginner 2 Fade – Novice 8		Non-Class Skills: Lay-on-Hands – Initiate 1 Stealth – Beginner 9 Animal Empathy – Beginner 8	

I'm pleased at the uptick in my Energy store; I started walking with nine percent and am now up to fifty-six percent. Most of that is due to the various battles we've engaged in, and almost half of it is down to this fight here. My Energy absorption rate has also been increasing as we walk further down into the valley. It doesn't seem to be a completely linear increase, either. It makes me wonder what the bottom of the valley is like if this is the Energy density of what's still very obviously a peripheral area.

My health, stamina, and mana are all down a fair bit, but mana and stamina start ticking up relatively quickly. I cast a couple more Lay-on-Hands and turn some of that newly acquired mana into health points. Bastet's looking a bit torn up too, so I channel some healing for her as well. Fortunately, it's all superficial stuff that would probably heal on its own within a short time anyway. Still, no point in going into a battle already wounded. Not to mention that walking around while bleeding is probably a good way of attracting more attacks.

Once we're both almost fully healed, I walk around and toss all the killer chickens XL into my Inventory, fortunately managing to fit them all in one slot. They're already missing their internal organs; Bastet and the cubs have been having a feast and now seem pretty satisfied.

Time to go—it's a-wasting and I don't know how much more Lathani has. Just because I've theorized she might have been taken for taming purposes doesn't mean I'm right, after all.

By the time the sun is heading towards the horizon and I'm starting to give serious thought to where to sleep tonight, I've accrued another thirty-three percent from encounters, bringing my Energy store up to eighty-nine percent. If this keeps on, I'll be leveling up in no time! And that's just from killing the creatures—I haven't been taking the time to dig out their hearts and cook them on the spot. I've collected a number of the most useful-looking corpses, but my Inventory is limited, so I can't take them all.

A wary growl from Bastet brings my attention back to my surroundings. We've strayed into an area where the foliage grows more thickly. It's hard to see very far as the trees are a strange type that seem to grow roots from their branches. Half-grown roots dangle everywhere, blocking my view.

In between, different plants flourish by seeking the light, which struggles to make its way through the canopy above. They're surprisingly brightly colored, or perhaps that's just because the trees themselves are so gloomy. It's like a strange psychedelic nightmare, frankly.

I'm wary because of the limited sight lines and Bastet's own instinctive response to them. I would have gone around the forest-within-a-forest, but I was concerned that I might lose the path.

We left the river a while ago to cut across one of the bends where it wends its way much more widely than we would prefer—if we get lost now, we could accidentally miss intersecting with the river again at the right point, or even end up going in circles. My Map is incredibly useful, but it only shows details around where I've been, and I can't see on it where the bit of river we're aiming for is. With little choice but to keep going forwards, we just have to keep our eyes peeled in all directions.

The leaves rustle ominously around us, and the vines sway in ways that are just not quite right with the wind. Eventually, we get to a point where the roots are growing so thickly that we can't get through.

When I turn around and look behind us, a sinking feeling goes through me. The way behind is impassable too; roots have grown with unbelievable speed to block the path we followed.

Looking around as fear begins to crawl in my throat and anger starts to warm my belly, I see no easy way through the cage of roots. We're trapped.

CHAPTER THREE

Close the Trap

I curse out loud. Despite suspecting it won't do any good, I pull my axe out and start hacking at the roots ahead of us. As I thought, as soon as I get through a single root, it's quickly replaced by another. Even worse, a root comes shooting at me out of the branches above.

Leaping aside, I look in shock at the arboreal spear, which is as thick around as my wrist. I didn't realize they could move that fast—I'd only seen them shift slightly. Perhaps now we're in its trap, it has no need to be stealthy. Though I reckon it's a bad sign if our attacker has the intelligence to make that sort of choice.

Backing up to where Bastet is looking at the trees around us, a growl rumbling in her chest and her teeth bared, I wonder what our attacker actually is. An animal mimicking the surrounding trees? The trees themselves? Can it be? I mean, I know Ents are a thing, but could there actually be trees capable of fast movement? Frankly, after everything I've seen, I can't ignore the possibility. Especially given the current evidence.

But if it *is* the tree—potentially *trees*—then how on earth am I going to deal with it? I don't think my knife or Bastet's claws are going to do much against wood. As for my mace and axe, I think that such an approach has already proved to be a failure. Fire might be a good option, but we're *in* the forest. It would be a literal Pyrrhic victory to burn down the trap and ourselves with it.

The tree isn't going to wait for us to make a decision about what to do. It shoots a couple of roots at us, which we both dodge relatively easily. I retaliate with my axe, and it's almost yanked out of my hand as the root quickly withdraws, my weapon stuck in it. I have to twist my wrist quickly to get it free before it's pulled out of reach.

A moment after, I have to dodge two root spears that shoot at me in quick succession. Could the tree be angered by my attempt to hurt it? I must look like I'm dancing a jig until the tree decides to give me a break and starts aiming at Bastet again.

The raptorcat has been trying to chew and burrow her way out to no avail. And as I see the evidence of her efforts, I realize something else: the space is getting smaller and smaller.

Watching for a couple of moments, I realize that the tree is actually sending down new roots straight into the ground on the inside of the wall and then withdrawing the ones behind, only moving three or four roots at a time. It's a good strategy to avoid leaving even the slightest gap, but it seems a bit inefficient.

If the tree can close the trap, I don't know why it doesn't do so immediately, but maybe it has some limitations I don't know about. *Or perhaps it just likes playing with its food,* I think darkly. Either way, we're done for if we don't get out of this mess before we run out of space to dodge the spearing roots.

What are we going to do?

Bastet fares no better in trying to attack the root spears—her claws and teeth are even less effective against them than my axe was. She can knock the roots off course, her weight and strength obviously enough to divert the piercing spears of wood, but that's where her capabilities end. Even when she manages to trap a root temporarily on the ground and chew it, all she achieves is getting a mouthful of splinters and another root shooting at her head.

While she holds the tree's attention, I try once again to find a way out of the cage, hoping that Bastet's distraction might be enough for me to create a small hole to exploit. No luck. The tree doesn't seem capable of directing more than two root spears at a time while it's also moving the ones forming the walls of the cage, but it retracts the spear it shot towards Bastet's head and then sends it shooting out at me. I dodge once more, my mind racing.

Can the tree only shoot the roots straight? Does it not have any ability to use them like tentacles? At the thought of tentacles, an involuntary shiver goes through me. Even in this desperate situation, that monster in the cave still has the power to send fear through me. Redirecting my mind to the current, increasingly pressing situation, I try to think of solutions. Other than setting everything alight around us, anyway. I don't really want to burn alive!

Direct attacks aren't working, neither are attacks on the cage itself, nor on the roots actively aiming for us. Digging our way out might be an option if the cage wasn't closing in ever tighter; climbing could potentially work if we didn't have the spear attacks to deal with. However, with the situation as it is, neither of those will be possible. With a feeling of dread in my stomach, I realize that I might have to use my last resort.

Of course, as soon as I decide to do that, another concern comes to mind. It would be great if I didn't accidentally cause a forest fire, but what if I can't cause *enough* of an effect? Green wood doesn't tend to burn very well, after all.

Well, I don't see any other options. I need to try it at least. The question, however, is how.

"Bastet, keep the roots off me," I tell her, sending a picture of her leaping at the roots to redirect them away from me. I hope that my observation earlier about the roots only shooting forwards and not being otherwise manipulable is correct. Otherwise, this is going to be even harder than it already is.

A wave of steely assent washes over me from her side of the Bond, and I crouch down to the ground. I pull out a torch and my fire-starter kit from my Inventory and tuck Trouble's head back into the sling—the curious cub poked his nose out to work out what was going on. I'd rather he doesn't get singed, though, so firmly tell him to stay put as I start using the flint and steel on the torch.

At first, nothing seems to change. The roots shoot at me, probably detecting easy pickings, but Bastet succeeds in knocking them off target. She doesn't try to bite them this time and just uses her weight to redirect them. Fortunately, it seems like my supposition was right: once redirected, the roots just bury themselves in the loam before they're retracted. The cage continues to tighten inch by inch.

Then I manage to get a spark, and the atmosphere suddenly changes.

I look up, alarmed, at the palpable shift in the air. From a patient watchfulness, the feeling of the area has suddenly taken on the heaviness of anger, and I don't think I'm imagining a sense of fear as well. Not things I would have ever noticed before, but I guess that's what a Wisdom score of twelve gets me.

And I reckon I'm not imagining it, because the roots suddenly start shooting at us with renewed vigor and the ones forming the cage increase their rate of movement. Where before it seemed like the tree was willing to take its time, believing in its inexorable triumph, now it appears to be in a hurry to catch its prey.

Heartened by the indication that perhaps this has a chance of succeeding, and more than a little trepidatious, I apply myself to my task. Unfortunately, the increased speed of the spearing roots means that Bastet doesn't manage to divert all of them.

One hits me in the shoulder and sends me sprawling backwards. Since it hits my chitin breastplate, though, it doesn't go *through* my shoulder. However, it's had another effect, one far more negative.

With horror, I watch my steel fly towards the edge of the cage, launched out of my hand as I lost my balance. Without thinking, I throw myself towards it, only barely remembering not to land on my chest and squash the cubs.

Instead, landing heavily on my side, I reach out to grab the piece of metal before it's snagged by a root aiming to restrict our space just that little bit more. Not quite fast enough to clear the space in time, I hiss as the root digs a groove into the back of my hand.

But I have my steel.

I grimly push myself to my knees and shift back to where I was trying to light the torch. Our cage has become a third of its original size, and the speed of its shrinking seems to have increased even more. Most probably it's because the reduced space means that the tree has to use fewer roots in each layer, enabling it to move faster. It's bad news for us, especially since the restricted space is making Bastet's diverting task even more difficult.

I need to work faster. I'm lucky that I was able to retrieve my steel. If I'd lost it, I could have probably used my knife, but this steel is the right shape to create a shower of sparks. The problem is that, for some reason, the pitch doesn't want to light.

It's not helping that my fingers are shaking as panic claws at me, meaning that few of the sparks are landing on the pitch itself as it is. I dart a look at the cage's reducing size and more fear curdles in my belly—we've got barely two meters of space in any direction now.

I stop, close my eyes, and take a deep breath. Giving into the gibbering hindbrain isn't going to help. I need to light this torch. There's no other option. Maybe I should use some fire starter as well. I didn't need it before, because the other torches had lit well enough without it, but this one is being stubborn at the worst of times. If the fire starter works, then great. If it lights without the fire starter, even better. Either way, the only way we lose is if I don't *get this bloody thing lit* before we have no space left to move.

I pull out some dried mosslike plant and pile a bit on top of the pitch part of the torch. The breathing and pep talk have reduced my trembling a bit, and I refuse to look at the progress of the cage.

Trying to calm myself, I strike my steel against the flint as I try to pretend that I'm in my cave. *Yeah, no rush here, just in my cave, going to make dinner. Nothing to it*, I tell myself.

Finally, I see the lick of flame from where one of the sparks landed in the moss. Refusing to let anything distract me, and trusting Bastet to do her best to keep the roots off me without me needing to look, I blow gently on the flame. It grows and I feel a similar flame of triumph light within my belly.

That's when I get hit by two roots.

The first knocks me onto my back, the second stabs me straight in the thigh. This time it manages to avoid the armor and goes a few centimeters *into* my leg. My mouth opens in a shout as pain radiates from the wound like a starburst.

It hurts even more as I have to move to avoid the strike of the next root, the one embedded in my flesh a pivot I have to shift around. Then it retracts, the rough wood dragging at my wound and forcing a hiss of agony out of my mouth.

Even once it's out, I immediately have to roll to one side to avoid the next strike, using my elbows to create a safe space for the cubs. They probably get a bit squished, though; I hope they're okay.

I quickly channel healing through my leg, and the magic closes the bleeding wound. Worse than the injury, the impact knocked me away from the torch at a critical time in the fire lighting. I push myself upwards as my eyes search out the torch, my heart in my mouth.

When I see the barest flicker of flame, I breathe out in relief. A quick glance at Bastet along with a touch of the Bond reveals that she's tired and hard-pressed but not injured past a few scrapes. At the moment, it seems like the roots only have the power to make superficial or relatively small wounds. That makes the prospect of being caught in the cage even more unappealing as it suggests a long, slow, painful death.

But fortunately, my flame is still burning; what's more, it actually caught on the pitch itself.

Within a few seconds, the whole pitch end of the torch is burning steadily. Just in time—the cage has reduced to just over a square meter of space and Bastet is actually already being confined to the point where she can barely move around anymore.

The next time the root shoots at her, I redirect it with the torch and tongues of flame catch briefly on the root itself. It catches surprisingly well, and the root has to stab itself into the ground to put it out.

I'm heartened. Clearly this tree is a bit more vulnerable to fire than even normal trees would be. Then that same thought sends a bolt of fear through me, and I steel myself. If I'm going to die anyway, I'd rather do it in a way that takes my killer down with me.

The tree doesn't seem to share my happy feelings and suddenly freezes mid-motion.

"Yeah, how do you like that, you rubbish excuse for a fern," I tell it savagely. "This is *fire*. And you'd best let us out or I'm going to burn you down." I'm not even bluffing and perhaps it senses that somehow.

The area is now suffused with fear and a sense of hesitancy. I take full advantage and move to hold the torch against a part of the cage wall. For a moment nothing happens, and then the bark starts to blacken and char. The leaves high above our heads rustle restlessly and the whole tree shivers. It doesn't move otherwise, though.

Then, as the wood on the roots seems about to catch light, the tree shivers more violently, and slowly, almost reluctantly, it lifts the roots on that side of the cage.

A space just about big enough for Bastet and me to squeeze through is revealed, almost like the tree is unwilling to lose its prey. But surely that's ascribing far too much human emotion to an unfeeling creature? Though, since when could trees *trap and kill* sapient creatures? Perhaps this tree can also feel regret.

Either way, I'm not sticking around here for longer than absolutely necessary. Eyeing the rest of the trees around me, which look all too similar to the one that almost got us, I wave my torch threateningly.

"If any of you are also thinking about making a quick meal out of us, I'm *very happy* to turn you into a blazing bonfire, understand me?" Unsurprisingly, there's no response except for the sound of the wind in the tree tops, but I get the sense of brooding dissatisfaction in the air around me.

Bastet and I share a look, both of us feeling reluctant to continue through this forest, but the only way is forwards. One thing's for sure, though: I'm not letting this torch go out for a moment.

CHAPTER FOUR

Quest

My knuckles are white as I clench them around the shaft of the torch. My eyes look suspiciously in all directions as I do my best to get us out of this wretched collection of trees intact. Though she sticks mostly by my side, from time to time Bastet ranges forwards a bit to scout ahead. Unlike before, she never goes very far ahead and certainly not out of sight. After all, we don't want to risk the trees around us daring to trap her simply because she's wandered too far from the fire I'm carrying.

I jog most of the time, preferring speed over stealth or caution. Unlike the journey up to this point, I don't use Fade at all and even turn off my passive Stealth just to save on stamina. Without those two consuming my resources, my stamina pool goes a lot further.

In fact, with my recent increases in Strength (Endurance), I only lose a bit more on jogging at a moderate pace than I recover. Interspersing jogging with periods of fast walking allows me to move as quickly and efficiently as possible. And frankly, it amazes me how long I can continue without stopping for breath—I'd never done much long-distance running before coming here, so it's a novelty for me.

The way I was traveling before the venus-human-trap trees used faster periods of running interspersed with slower periods of walking. I'd done it that way because of the cubs; they get restless if they're in the sling for too long, and it's not great for them to be trapped there all the time. The periods of walking allowed them to climb out and stretch their legs, and they could have a bite to eat and some water to drink. Then back into the sling for another period of running in order to cover as much distance as possible. Of course, that had also been interspersed with attacks from the various denizens of the forest, but the fights were generally over quickly enough.

None of that now, though. Not with how easily the cubs could be trapped and killed by the trees before we could do anything about it. Instead, we're having to make slower but steadier progress. At least with Bastet ranging forwards she's able to warn me about the terrain ahead. We've already avoided two places where the earth suddenly fell away thanks to her. I wouldn't have wanted to accidentally land on the cubs, even if I didn't hurt myself.

Despite our attentive wariness, the trees don't try anything more. The longer we go, though, the more worried about my spluttering torch I become. The pitch is very quickly being consumed. Though I do have at least one other torch in my Inventory, I don't have a limitless supply.

I'm thoroughly glad when I see the end to the trees appearing ahead.

It's surprisingly abrupt. Even the ground looks different in here, darker. I can practically see a line in the dirt where the forest ends. Looking back at the oddly uniform trees from a few paces away, I can see them all looming like shadowy reaper-like cloaked figures, arms held out to embrace those who seek death. But perhaps that's just my recent experience with them talking—I didn't notice all that when walking into the grove.

I shiver and turn away. Even if it's longer, I decide that we'll be coming back by the river route. After taking a moment to recover my bearings relative to Kalanthia's memories, I set off again. The cubs are wriggling impatiently. They've been trying to escape the sling for a good half an hour already, so I let them out as soon as I feel we've put enough distance between us and the trees to make it safe. Well, as safe as we can be in a forest that regularly almost kills us, even without murderous trap-trees.

Sighing in relief, I undo the sling across my chest, the cubs within beyond irritated with being stuck there. Once let out, the little fluffballs practically go mad as they bounce around the area. Trouble leaps over Ninja and then is tackled by Storm, who pins him to the ground for a fraction of a second before letting go and tackling Ninja, bowling her over her stubby little wings.

Ninja doesn't take this lying down and instead leaps back onto Storm. Or at least she tries to, but Storm hides behind me and Ninja instead lands on my leg, prickly claws bared.

"Ow," I complain half-heartedly as they dig in through my trousers—of course she hit a patch with no armor. "Are you guys hungry? Thirsty? Here." I dump a chunk of meat on the ground and then pour out some water from my waterskin into one of my bowls.

Bastet and I take the opportunity to eat and drink too as the cubs play. Though they drink the water thirstily, they pretty much ignore the meat. I'm not surprised, because I've been trying to keep them calm by feeding them scraps for the last few hours. We adults are hungry, though, and take it in turns to feed ourselves while the other keeps watch.

"Have you ever come across those things before?" I ask Bastet as we get going again with the cubs following at our heels. The adult raptorcat makes sure they don't go astray, nudging the cubs back into line if they start wandering elsewhere.

In response to my question, she sends me an uncertain feeling. Then a series of images follows, the interpretation difficult. I frown as I try to parse through the meaning carefully. It takes me a bit of work, and I realize why after a while. Not all the memories are Bastet's.

It's another clue indicating something I'd already suspected: raptorcats are capable of telepathic communication even without a Bond. Though whether they can only communicate with other raptorcats or develop the capability to do it with everyone as they get older or stronger, I don't know.

What's for certain is that one of the memories is from a male raptorcat who obviously traveled further than Bastet did. I know that because part of the memory is of him drinking from a much wider version of the river, his reflection showing a form that is significantly different from Bastet's. Through her eyes, the fact that he's male is immediately apparent too. Unless raptorcats are capable of changing their sex and appearance, that memory at least must be one she received telepathically. And if that one was, it lends credence to the idea that the others are too.

Anyway, the provenance of the memories aside, the fact is that, from what I can gather, normally these kinds of trees are found much further down in the valley. Closer to the Energy. And that's not the only weird thing I realize; I recognize the nagging feeling of a notification waiting for me and check my status screen in response.

Name: Markus Wolfe		Race: Human	Class: Tamer
Level: 2	Energy to next level: 95%	Energy absorption rate: 21u/hr	Energy towards debt: 1%
Intelligence	12	Mana: 120/120	
Wisdom	12	Mana regeneration rate: 300u/hr	
Willpower	17+3 (+20%)	Health regeneration rate: 20u/hr	
Constitution	13	Health: 130/130	
Strength	12	Stamina: 49/60	
Dexterity	12	Stamina regeneration rate: 120u/hr	
Class Skills: Dominate – Beginner 4 Tame – Beginner 2 Fade – Novice 8		Non-Class Skills: Lay-on-Hands – Initiate 1 Stealth – Beginner 9 Animal Empathy – Beginner 8	

I'm up to ninety-five percent in my Energy store. Considering I haven't killed anything since before entering the area with the trap-trees, I find that surprising. It suggests to me that the Energy density in the grove was significantly higher than the area around it.

I mean, that's a bit of an assumption: I certainly wasn't going to open my status screen to check at the time. Still, it makes sense to me. As far as I know, Energy only comes from either killing or Dominating a creature; we did neither to the trees. Therefore, the only Energy I should have gathered would have been from my general absorption.

With my current Energy absorption rate—well, with what it was before it increased to twenty-one units per hour, I was gaining a single percent every three or so hours. So, to have suddenly gained about six percent in only a few hours? Something else must be going on.

Checking my message box, I realize that the nagging feeling didn't come from having gained a point or the opportunity to gain a point by spending some of my gathered Energy. Instead, it's a new message entirely.

Congratulations! You have received a Quest.	
Quest: The Vine-Strangler Grove	Quest type: Regional
Description: You have encountered Vine-Strangler Trees in an unusual location, at an unusual stage of development, and with an unusual level of Energy in the area.	
Objective: Discover why Vine-Strangler Trees are growing in this location and the reason for the unusual level of Energy.	
Time to complete Quest: Unlimited	
Suggested difficulty: Initiate	Reward: Rare Bronze Chest

How interesting, I muse to myself. Apparently, this new System comes with quests, and somehow, I've triggered one. *How? Is it because I made note of something strange?* But there have been lots of strange things and I've never triggered a quest before. *Or is it something else?*

Another question to add to the list. By this point, I've amassed quite a few. It's a little strange that the memories I absorbed from the System stone have nothing to say on this point; is it that unusual? Well, I guess I'll find out when I get to Nicholas's world.

I suppose that I might have received this quest because I probably wouldn't have pursued my feelings of strangeness any further otherwise. After my experience in the forest, I was rather looking forward to putting it behind me and never thinking of it again, but perhaps I'll revisit it in the future. If a Rare bronze chest is worth risking going through that forest again, that is.

I look at the table hovering in front of me with a little more attention. Apparently, it's a regional quest type, whatever that means. Does it mean that if I leave the region, I'll fail the quest automatically? Or that I had to be in a certain region to gain it? I see I have unlimited time to address it, though the question mark next to that doesn't reassure me much. Either way, I'm definitely going to rescue Lathani before even considering investigating this wretched forest. It's a fairly vague objective too—it doesn't exactly give any clues. Not like the quest logs I remember from games.

The suggested difficulty is apparently for Initiates. That sounds rather similar to the way my Skills have been ranked so far. I've only got one Skill at that level—Lay-on-Hands, of course. It started at Beginner, ranked up to Novice, and then increased to Initiate.

All of those terms indicate that I'm still at the relative beginning of things, even after ranking up twice; an initiate isn't much further ahead than a beginner in most uses of the word. Does that mean that the quest is quite easy but not the easiest? If so, I wonder what reward chests I'd get for a Beginner quest. *A half-broken dagger for killing ten rats?* I ask myself sardonically. Whether a bronze chest is worth the effort, I guess I'll have to find out. Especially a Rare one.

I feel a nose press against my hand and close the screen to find Bastet nudging me. She sends a mixture of impatience and query. She's right; we need to get going again. I hadn't realized that I'd actually stopped while checking my screens, and we still have a good distance to travel. Plus, it's going to be dark fairly soon and I'll need to create a small shelter for us all. I reckon that we've got about three hours of travel time before we'll need to stop for me to create a small campsite.

I call the cubs over; they've been walking for a while, and we need to maximize our speed as much as possible. I want to get to the lizard folk's area tomorrow and hopefully find their den or wherever they've taken Lathani. To do that, we'll need to intersect with the river again today so I can make sure I have my landmarks correctly identified.

With the cubs tucked away in their sling again, we take off once more.

CHAPTER FIVE

And Then It Runs Into My Knife

I pull my bowstring back and train the tip of my arrow on the leader standing at the back. It's throwing rocks even as it exhorts its team to attack us with shrieks and chattering of its teeth. Breathing out, I release the missile and watch in satisfaction as it thunks into the monkey-like reptile, scoring a good hit in its exposed chest.

It's not a heart-shot, and its natural armor limits the damage, but it's enough to thoroughly distract the creature. Bonus: the strike has made it drop the rock it was about to throw. Even better, it was holding the rock above its head, so it's now got a headache as well. Always a great moment when the enemy does your work for you.

But this is no time for me to admire my achievement. Bastet's on the front line occupying the four melee members of their team. I need to take down the ranged ones before going in to help her out, if she hasn't already won against them by then. In addition to the four fighting in melee, there are three more acting as ranged backup, one of which is the leader I've already hit. Nocking another arrow to the string, I do my best to focus on hitting the beast somewhere painful and loose my arrow as soon as I feel confident in my aim.

The creatures are a strange amalgamation of monkey and reptile. Their skin is scaly and a gray-green that blends well into the forest. Their heads are big and ugly with bulging eyes on either side and a groove between them, which runs down to a slit nose and a mouthful of sharp teeth. They have ridges along their backs. The leader seems to have spikes running down that ridge; the others just have the protruding bone. Whether that's the result of some difference in social strata, or even a difference between sexes, I don't know.

They have wide shoulders and strong arms and legs on which the muscle is evident even beneath their thick scales. They don't have opposable thumbs, but that doesn't seem to stop them grabbing stones and throwing them at us with their clawed paws. Seeming to be comfortable resting in a crouch on two legs, they bob forwards to grab stones and then push themselves back into the crouch to throw them. I know that they can move both with two legs and with four after watching the way they ran towards Bastet.

Their tails help them when they're on two legs, almost acting as a third leg in the way it presses against the ground. Their tails are also able to curl around branches and help them reach further than their balance would otherwise allow. In general, they reach up to my waist when in their crouched position but can probably stand taller for a short time—I can't say for sure, though, as I haven't seen it.

Bastet is hard-pressed with them grabbing at her with their claws and using their strong grip to bite at her with their teeth. Of course, she's giving as good as she gets—her own claws are longer and sharper and so are her teeth. One of the attackers is already down, bleeding profusely. It's unlikely to last much longer, which at least relieves the pressure on her a little. The threat for her is more the rocks. Although the ranged fighters haven't been pelting her with too many as they don't seem to want to hit their own, each rock that does get thrown risks cracking one or more of her bones and changing the balance of the fight immediately. That's where I come in.

I don't aim for my targets' heads; I reckon that they're probably mostly bone and my flint arrows are more likely to bounce off than anything else, even with the full force of my bow behind the missiles. Instead, I aim for their large chests.

With my second shot, I manage to strike the monkile that's next to the leader, though I hit a fair bit lower on this one. I wince in sympathy when I see exactly where I've stuck my arrow—the creature's lack of clothing leaves nothing to the imagination. Though, that said, since they're reptiles, their genitals are mostly hidden away, so perhaps it's not as painful as I imagine it would be on me.

Still, it makes the monkile drop its rocks and bring both paws down to scrabble at the injury, all the while making high-pitched grunts. I continue shooting and whip off another arrow, which misses. Both my rate of fire and my accuracy have improved with practice. The three monkiles I'm shooting at are starting to look a bit like porcupines with at least three arrows in each. The leader, whose annoying shrieks are getting on my nerves, actually has five arrows sticking out of it—three in its chest, one in its leg, and one lucky shot in its neck. Unfortunately, it doesn't seem to have hit anywhere vital.

Apparently, I've annoyed them enough that they're now searching for the source of their discomfort rather than focusing on the fight. I'm exasperated. I was expecting them to get to this point a good five arrows ago. Frankly, if someone was shooting at me, I'd be on them after the *first* arrow. But maybe their scaly skin isn't particularly sensitive; it certainly doesn't seem like they've bled much from the hits.

Revealing myself by releasing Fade, I draw their attention.

"Took you long enough," I can't resist saying. Then I grin. "Good thing I'm here to keep you on the straight and *arrow.*" My ex, Lucy, would have probably groaned and smacked me for that one, but these monkiles have driven me to this point by being even less observant than I was when I first arrived here. Anyway, I've got the attention of the monkiles for sure now. Clearly, they don't appreciate dad jokes.

The leader lets out a new ear-piercing shriek and dashes towards me, quickly covering the small space between us. It runs really weirdly: its upper body stays absolutely still while its hips swing and its feet pad across the ground. Its tail is key to the movement as it counterbalances the shifts from side to side—maybe that's what I should have aimed for instead of its chest.

Then it's on me. Unfortunately for it, I'm ready; I've been ready since before shooting it the first time. The leader runs right into my knife. Then it withdraws and runs into my knife again. It must do it a good ten times, while I avoid blows from its claws, before I manage to hit something important and it drops to the ground, its lower body suddenly limp. It tries to snap at me weakly, but I just stab it in the throat. This time I definitely manage to hit an artery, as blood spurts out.

Backing up a little to get out of range in case it starts twitching violently as it dies, I warily watch the other two ranged fighters. The nagging feeling of a notification briefly distracts me. After drawing a quick conclusion, I focus on sending Energy to my debt even as I watch the enemies. Instead of taking advantage of my brief distraction, they stare at their downed leader, and I wonder if they might turn tail and run.

I'm not that lucky. Instead, they seem to exchange glances and then turn back to me, hissing like a pot boiling over. The next thing I know, they both launch themselves towards me. I quickly slot my bow into my Inventory so I don't risk it getting stepped on and grab my mace with my off-hand—with two-on-one odds, I'm going to need it.

Swinging in a backhanded swipe as they get into range, I manage to hit one with a hard blow, making it shriek in pain. Unfortunately, they're sturdy enough that even my Strength-fueled strike loses enough momentum to make continuing the swipe pointless. Instead, I bring my knife into play and score a strike across the other one's chest instead of managing to pierce its heart.

In return, their claws rake across me. Fortunately, my rough chitin armor is enough to turn their blows. My armor takes a beating, though, as one of them gets in a lucky strike that actually cuts through one of the ties holding my breastplate in place.

With the momentum of the fight back on my side, I use a strike from my mace to push myself back a little. This opens up enough space that I'm able to swing my weapon with enough force to crack the skull of the one on the right. It falls back, its paws going to scrabble at the wound. I think I might have damaged its eye too.

The other one lunges at me, but I get in a lucky hit: instead of it managing to bite my arm, it instead bites my knife . . . point first.

I press my advantage as it backpedals and grab its ugly mug so I can pull it further onto my knife. I hit something hard and my knife halts, requiring a flex of my muscles to continue its journey.

The pause must have been the tip of my blade piercing through its mouth and into its brain because a moment later it goes limp, the light leaving its eyes. After quickly finishing off the monkile that was still pawing at its eye and whimpering piteously, I look at my partner.

She's fine. Bastet's managed to down three of her attackers and is currently suffocating the fourth with a grip on its throat. She's looking pretty bloody, though, and I have a feeling that most of it is hers. That's partly because of all the rents I see in her coat, but also because our attackers have almost purple blood and most of what's on her is red.

I move swiftly through the battleground to cast Lay-on-Hands on her. As I stand with my hands literally laid on her bloody feather-fur to channel the healing, I scan the surrounding trees. Not finding what I'm looking for, I ask Bastet.

"Where did the cubs go?" They were following us when we were attacked by this troupe of monkey reptiles, and Bastet sent some sort of instruction to them that was too fast for me to catch. And then she'd leaped in to grab the creatures' attention and I triggered Fade. None of that left enough time for me to make sure the cubs were safe.

Bastet sends me a wave of uncertainty tempered with reassurance. I interpret it to mean that she doesn't know exactly where they are but thinks they're probably safe. Well, she should know, I suppose.

Once Bastet is in a better condition and I've managed to quickly patch my armor with a bit of spare sinew, we go looking for the cubs. Or I do, at least. The adult raptorcat just makes a few chirping sounds and suddenly—*poof!*—the cubs appear out of nowhere. That's how they make it seem, anyway. In fact, they just found a good spot at the base of a tree to hide in and their natural camouflage did the rest. Actually, *is* it just their natural camouflage? Given the new world I'm in, it *could* be magic. Perhaps they have the same ability that Bastet does; she disappears in plain sight all the time.

Either way, they're safe. I count one, two, and three, then sigh in relief. Fortunately, Trouble hasn't lived up to his name. Probably Storm kept him in line—I've been seeing her take charge more and more recently. Or maybe it's because the order came from Bastet. Whatever the reason, I'm relieved.

Cubs found, I begin clearing up the battleground. Or I start doing so until I realize that my Inventory is full. Damn. What with setting off after Lathani directly after exploring the cavern and gathering all that salt, I didn't have many squares in my Inventory left over even when I started the journey. A day and multiple encounters in and it's now completely full. I could take out my bow and sling it across my back to free up a space or . . . I probably have another option available if the nagging sense of a message waiting for me is anything to judge by.

I open my message box and see a couple of new messages, not just the one I was expecting.

Congratulations!
You have worked hard on your Dexterity (Agility) and have earned a point. This has been applied to your status.

Level up now / Close message

Apparently, I've done enough work on my Dexterity to actually earn a point outright. I'm not completely surprised; I did see a message not that long ago that offered me a point for Energy and I turned it down, wanting to save my Energy to level up. It seems that using my bow quickly levels my Dexterity. It's interesting that it's the Agility subcategory that's increased—I'll need to remember that.

As for the next message, I feel anticipation grow in my belly as I open it.

<table>
<tr><td>Congratulations!
You have gathered enough Energy to push your body to the next level. Would you like to level up?</td></tr>
<tr><td>Level up now / Close message</td></tr>
</table>

Yes! Finally! It feels like a long time since I last saw that message. I was expecting it; I was at ninety-eight percent before even starting the fight, so it was inevitable that it would happen during it. At least the distraction of me focusing on redirecting my Energy to my debt was brief and my enemies were too stupid to capitalize on it.

My heart actually dropped into my boots when I saw the first message was about Dexterity—until I spotted that there was another message waiting for me, that is. I'd been suddenly worried that I'd switched modes too quickly!

Fortunately, I was wrong. Well, I was right that I'd earned enough Energy to level up and wrong that I'd misinterpreted the nagging notification feeling.

Welp, time to get to level three! It's been a long time coming . . .

CHAPTER SIX

Choices

Having accepted the level-up, I'm presented with the same screen I've seen twice before now.

To level up, please choose the stats you would like to increase. You have 6 points available. Warning: if you do not assign all points now, you will be unable to use them later. You can choose to delay your level-up, but you will not store any further Energy until you do. Do you wish to continue to level up?

Level up now /Close message

I almost accept automatically, but the sudden thought of what happens after leveling up stays my hand. I eye my clothes, including my rudimentary armor. I don't want to walk around with my clothes stinking of the stuff that comes out of me during the process, and I'm sure as hell not taking off my clothes during it and then putting them back on after to just get messy again.

I reluctantly think *No* at the System, and the box disappears from my vision for now. Bastet looks at me expectantly.

"We need to get to the river so I don't end up stinking up the whole forest," I tell her grumpily. It's taken so long to get here; I was *really* looking forward to seeing—and feeling—my stats jump. Still, I suppose it gives me a bit of extra time to think through where I want to assign them. And if anything attacks us on the way to the river, at least I'll still be able to put some Energy towards my debt.

Suddenly worried that I might not have directed the Energy correctly since it was in the middle of the fight, I quickly open my status page and check. The number three sitting in the Energy debt box reassures me. Not wanting to leave the carcasses behind, I pull my bow out of my Inventory to free up the slot and pile the monkile corpses in. Fortunately, like all the corpses of the same species so far, they all stack, even the leader, despite it being a bit bigger. I do retrieve my arrows first, though.

Setting off towards where the river should be, I send a wave of gratitude to Bastet, thankful for her support, which made that fight so much easier. She replies with confusion. I don't know how to explain it, so I reply with the sense of "just accept it."

There are a few moments of silence from her side of the Bond before I get a response. It's an odd mixture of emotions and almost feels like a hug from a friend accompanied by a "you're weird" accusation. Ah well, I can live with my raptorcat companion thinking I'm a bit strange.

I'm just happy to have her here. I don't know where I'd be without her at this point, both on an emotional and a developmental level. I wouldn't have made it this far in the forest without her firepower by my side, or her acting as a shield to distract the enemies. I'm just . . . grateful. Once more I renew my vow to myself that I will never start treating her as some disposable tool.

Fortunately—or not, depending on perspective—our walk-slash-jog to the riverside is fairly quiet with only one attack. I barely even fight; Bastet almost manages to completely deal with it before I get a chance to step in. For once, it's not another strange reptilian crossbreed: this one just looks like a very big monitor lizard. Very big in the sense that it's actually slightly bigger than Bastet, who stands as high as mid-thigh on me. Still, it doesn't have her speed or long, sharp teeth. Failing to set its teeth into her, it signs its own death sentence. I only speed up the process by cracking its skull open with my mace.

After eyeing its carcass, I eventually sigh and just move on. Something else will have a feast tonight. Big and heavy as it is, it doesn't have as much meat as the total number of monkile corpses in my Inventory do. It also doesn't seem to have any other features that might make keeping it more useful than what I already have in my extra-dimensional space. No, better to just keep going. Once I've got ten more Inventory slots, I'll have a bit more leeway. Hopefully, I'll have a bit of time to deal with what's in my Inventory before the *next* crisis.

The cubs have been running with us as much as possible, their muscles clearly growing quickly. Before, they were only able to keep up when we walked slowly. Now they've started being able to walk reasonably fast with us. I reckon that in a day or two they should be able to keep up with us at a slow run, at least for a bit. Hopefully, we'll have found Lathani by then.

Still, I don't think taking a little bit of time to level up is a bad idea; not only is the river actually on our route anyway, but me becoming stronger gives us a better chance of survival overall.

We reach the river just as the sun touches the horizon. As much as I want to level up immediately, I know I need to build a shelter for us all before darkness properly falls. Deciding to recreate my dead-leaf shelter, only a bit bigger, I search for an appropriate tree and branch. Spotting both at a small distance from each other, I get to work.

As I prepare the shelter, I'm amused to see the cubs trying to help. Storm's the first one to get stuck in, with Ninja following shortly after. I guess Storm was watching me for a bit to work out what I was doing, but as I push dead leaves together to make a cozy mattress, I'm surprised when I start seeing her do the same thing. Or at least trying to. It seems like raptorcats aren't really adapted to pushing dead leaves around, as she's struggling to find a method that works.

In the end, it's actually Ninja who works out the most efficient way. She turns around and starts digging like a dog, kicking the leaves behind her with her front paws. When we've got enough of a mattress, I tell them to stop.

"I think we've got enough, girls, thanks." Then I hesitate. "We need sticks now. Do you want to help?" They look at me with heads cocked in confusion. Stupid—it's not like they understand words well enough to pick up something so abstract. Since I don't have the kind of Bond with them that I have with Bastet, they can't pick up my meaning mentally either. Plus, I'm not telepathic, so no chance of me just projecting my thoughts to them.

Instead, I just show them what to do, collecting sticks and putting them in a pile. The two cubs soon get into the groove, finding sticks and bringing them back with enthusiasm. It's just too cute to see them come running back with sticks in their mouths, their tails and stubby wings sticking straight up in the air in excitement. Or, perhaps even cuter, when they try to bring back sticks multiple times their own length and resort to dragging them backwards when they become too unwieldy to carry in their mouths.

I refuse to let myself become too distracted, though. I need to finish this shelter and I want to be able to level up before it becomes too dark and dangerous to do so. It's a struggle, though, especially when I see cubs tripping over their own feet, falling over each other's sticks, and generally being far too adorable for their own good.

Trouble doesn't really get into the whole shelter-building thing. In fact, living up to his name, he decides that shelter-*destroying* is more his jazz. Bastet eventually has to herd him away with nudges and nips, preventing him from causing things to take at least twice the time they should.

Eventually, I'm done. It's a bit darker than I'd prefer, and I bite my lip as I have to make a decision. Probably the sensible thing would be to wait for tomorrow . . . but I want to get an early start tomorrow; I'm hoping to get to the lizard folk's area before dark falls again to scout it out.

In the end, I decide that it's worth the risk. I light a torch—the fire should scare away some creatures and give me enough light to deal with any animals that are drawn to it—and tuck the cubs into the shelter as Bastet warns them to stay put. At least, that's the impression I get from her. Picking up my bow, I head to the river with Bastet at my side.

Fortunately, the shelter is actually within sight of the riverbank, so the raptorcat can keep an eye on it at the same time as watching for danger approaching me while I'm vulnerable. I restring my bow and put it on the riverbank just in case of something attacking. I'd take it in with me, but water and sinew don't really mix well.

Eyeing the river suspiciously, I throw rocks at a few spots that I'm not completely sure are just the river bed rather than some camouflaged crocodile.

Finally satisfied that there aren't any creatures waiting for me to venture close enough before ambushing me, I take the next step. Once more removing all my clothes, I wade into the river to mid-thigh level. I'll go in deeper to wash off, but I'd rather not risk the current—or something else—taking me away while I'm unable to move in the leveling-up process.

I don't need to open my status screen again; I just think, *Level up*, and the System does the rest. As before when accepting level-ups, I'm sent directly to my status screen with the pluses next to each of the stats. I've had plenty of time to decide how to spend my six points, so I quickly assign them, refusing to second-guess myself at the last minute.

Then, as I add the final point, the status screen disappears, and I have to make my choices for the stat that has two subcategories.

You have chosen to increase your Wisdom. Would you like to increase your Breadth or your Depth?
Breadth / Depth

You have chosen to increase your Wisdom. Would you like to increase your Breadth or your Depth?
Breadth / Depth

Deciding to hedge my bets, I choose Breadth for the first point and Depth for the second.

As before, pain quickly blasts through my body after choosing my points. In comparison to the agony I was in after the tentacle beast's attack, though, this is little more than a cramp. After the pain comes the feeling of bliss, which makes it all worth it. Finally, like every time so far, I double over and retch—all the impurities in my system seem to be working their way out of me.

I'm thankful to see that the trend seems to be holding true. The experience for level three is actually noticeably less awful than for level two, let alone the first time I leveled up. I vomit, but it doesn't feel like I'm puking my guts up along with the contents. And I get a sheen of sweat all over me, but I can still see my skin through it, something that wasn't true on the first two occasions.

Still, I'm grateful to be in the river and quickly take a couple of steps further in to wash up, glad to leave the spot that's filled with my vomit. It's already starting to drift downstream—I don't envy the fish that might come into contact with it. Bastet lets out a low growl as a sense of impatience comes across the Bond.

"I'm almost done," I tell her quietly while scrubbing myself with my rough soap. Bastet lets out another growl, this one more urgent. I open my eyes quickly, only to yelp and half jump, half fall to the side as a creature flies at my face.

Fortunately for me, the creature completely misses, and the sudden dousing washes off the rest of the nasty mess and suds on me. Less fortunate for me is the fact that I'm completely naked.

I stumble towards the riverbank and snatch up my waiting bow. Withdrawing arrows from my Inventory is my next move; at least I can still access the extra-dimensional space even when I'm not wearing a stitch.

Aiming, I get to see my recently gained point in Agility in action. I've discovered that while Flexibility helps me with small movements, Agility helps me with larger motions. Together, they help me to correctly line up my shot, and I manage to get the flying creature with my second arrow.

It tumbles to the ground, and I dart out of the water and grab my torch before approaching it quickly. As the light falls upon my attacker, I see that Bastet has already preempted me and is pinning the creature. Strangely, she's not going for its throat.

I send a questioning feeling at her, and she sends back a sense memory that is tinged with the slightest amount of reluctance. I'm surprised to recognize the memory, only it's from the other side of the battlefield. She's sent me the memory of that separate space in which we had the Battle of Wills.

"You're suggesting I Dominate this creature?" I ask her uncertainly.

She sends back another hard to parse flurry of emotions and images. Eventually, I think I've managed to work them out. I think what she's saying is this: *I miss my pack, but I have made a new pack with you. I wish to protect my pack, and we do not have enough members. I cannot fly and may never be able to, but I* remember *the value of a view from the air. If you are strong, you must take what you need to protect us.*

There's a lot in what she sends me, and several questions are raised by it all, not least by the memory she sends me of another raptorcat *flying*. Nevertheless, I don't have the time for that now; it's clear that she's deferring the decision to me as the pack "leader"—actually, I think the closest translation would be "matriarch," but that doesn't quite fit me for obvious reasons. Patriarch? I dismiss the thought—it's irrelevant.

Which leaves the main question: do I follow her advice or just kill the creature now for its Energy?

CHAPTER SEVEN

Mistakes Mean Death

The creature's not going anywhere for now, so I take a moment to gaze at it while I turn the question over in my mind. It's on its front, an arrow through its wing, and Bastet is pinning it down firmly. Unsurprisingly, it's squirming, but, unable to reach the raptorcat with its beak or claws, it's not got much of a chance of escaping.

The first thing I think of when I look at it is an eagle, but there are significant differences. It's got four legs that I can see, sprawled out forwards and backwards under Bastet's weight. Its wings are mostly leathery but with a fine coating of smooth almost-feathers, not all that dissimilar to Bastet's coat. It has hooks on the front joints of its wings, which look wickedly sharp, similar to the talons it has on its scaly feet.

Its tail is a fan of leather and almost-feathers, like its wings. Its eyes are reasonably big, though not to the point of being like an owl's, and each has a ridge of bone above that leads down to its snapping toothed beak. Its body is coated in what looks to be more like fur than feathers, unlike what is on its wings. It's about half Bastet's size and, although I can't make out the details of its coloring in the dark, I can tell that it would blend in very well with shadows. Not surprising considering it's clearly a nocturnal hunter.

None of which helps me to decide whether to Dominate it or not. For sure, it would be good to have some eyes in the sky, especially for what's to come; I'm not going to go into the lizard folk's territory with my figurative guns blazing. I'm going to need to get information first—about Lathani, about where she's being held, about the defenses around her. My plan was to send Bastet in, but a view from above would potentially be more useful and inconspicuous, especially if it's at night.

But is that a good enough reason for Dominating this creature? Since Spike's death, I've promised myself not to Dominate unless I'm sure that I need the creature. Do I? Well, an aerial scout would always be useful. Except underground, I suppose. A bird wouldn't have been much use when I was traveling through the tunnel to the salt cave, after all. But I'm not planning on doing that too much—one encounter with a giant squid monster is one too many in my life, frankly.

So, yes, I could use an aerial scout, even a nocturnal one, presuming it can still operate in the daylight to a certain extent. And while I've decided that it's immoral to just go out and Dominate everything because I can . . . this creature attacked me first. If I *don't* Dominate it, then I either release it or kill it. Or I suppose I could try to Tame it. Maybe that would work best?

Feeling heartened, I circle the creature until I'm in front of its head and kneel down. It tries to bite me as I reach towards it, but I was expecting that and succeed in avoiding the attack. Grabbing its head, I force it to look into my eyes—just in case that's also a necessary part of the process.

"Tame."

I feel a pulse of something go out from me towards the bird thing and . . . disappear. There's no notification, but I sense that my attempt to Tame has failed.

Great, I sigh to myself. *Back to my first question: Dominate or not?*

Releasing it just risks it attacking at another time, perhaps even grabbing a cub, who would be far more vulnerable. I can't see Bastet willingly allowing that risk. On the other hand, if I just kill it, then how is that any better than Dominating it forcibly? Killing in the middle of the battle is one thing; killing this creature in cold blood, pinned to the ground, feels different.

Perhaps I should decide to Dominate it in the way I did Bastet, rather than the way I Dominated Spike. With Spike, I pushed and pushed until he gave in because it was give in or be crushed. With Bastet, after showing her that I *could* force the issue, I negotiated with her until she agreed that a Bond with me would be better for her than the alternative. I can't help but think that the time I took in the negotiation set the seeds of the connection that we currently have, one that I'm grateful for.

And if the creature would prefer death over being bound to me, as Bastet would have had the cubs not been on the scene, I will respect its wishes. I can fail the Battle of Wills and let Bastet kill it while I'm in my vulnerable state. If it accepts, then I have another *willing* member to add to our unlikely pack.

"Dominate," I say, once more looking into its eyes.

As is now becoming more familiar, I fall into the liminal space of consciousness where these battles are played out. The pressure of water coming towards me is almost as strong as what I remember being directed at me in the battle with Bastet. Strange—I was expecting it to be stronger considering how we've traveled further down the mountainside. Then again, a raptorcat is definitely more dangerous to me than this creature is.

I force my way through the space towards the creature, which is fixed in place. Our eyes are drawn to each other like there's some sort of magnetism attracting them. I see an unbridled wildness in the orbs, a refusal to give in. I have a sinking feeling about my chances here but continue trying, nonetheless.

With either my increased familiarity or my increased stats allowing for it, I'm able to notice more about this space than the times before. For example, the closer I get to the creature, the more I understand of it. Almost like my approach isn't just entering its personal space but also in some way entering its mind.

"Come join our pack," I say to it. "We are stronger together."

I do not work with others, is the response. *I am alone and better for it.* It doesn't actually communicate with words, though my mind translates the experience into them. Instead, it's more of a wild cry, a sound hauntingly similar to a buzzard's mew. I remember going on holiday once to central France and hearing the raptors overhead as they circled the air. The sound became irrevocably linked to freedom—the birds soaring high above everything, free to do as they pleased.

"You are not better for it," I respond, determined to do my best to convince it. "You attacked a foe too powerful for you and lost. The price of that mistake is your life. In our group, you would have support, backup."

It is the Law. Mistakes mean death. I alone control my destiny.

"Don't throw your life away for nothing. Where there is life, there is hope. I do not wish to offer slavery, but companionship. A Bond, yes, but a reciprocal one where you gain as much as you give."

I feel the complete incomprehension and rejection of my words before the response even comes through.

I am alone. I live by my own successes; I die by my own failures. I am master of my fate, and I choose not to submit to another's leadership.

This is not a creature that yearns for companionship, like Bastet. Flashes of the creature's life come through with the last communication; my steady approach through the space between us has intensified our connection to the point where such things are effortless.

He has always been alone, even in his mother's nest. There is no evidence of a father, and every time he has been with a female of his own species, it has been an almost violent coupling, his four feet having to hold her in place to stop her from slashing at him. When the deed was done, he took his leave, never supporting the female nor encountering his offspring. Any other time he met one of his own species, he drove them off or was driven off in turn.

He's right: he's not a team player. I could force him to be through a Bond, but I won't. To do so would be to completely turn him against his own nature. Practically speaking, it would probably give me a Bound I'd have to monitor at all times to ensure his obedience. Morally speaking . . . it just feels *wrong*. Were my life on the line, I couldn't say whether I would make the same decision, but for now, I know what to do.

I probably should give him the death sentence he has earned, but after touching his mind and feeling the determination to make his own choices, which matches my own determination to live . . . I can't.

"Very well. Fly free," I tell him with heavy disappointment before giving a warning, "but if you attack either of us again, or the three cubs under our protection, you will die. My mercy only goes so far."

I don't wait for him to respond, and he doesn't look to be in a hurry to do so. Not exactly sure how to stop this whole thing, I make some guesses. Given that to "win," I have to push forwards until my opponent submits, then to "fail" I guess I have to be pushed back myself. Step by step, I move backwards with the pressure, reaching my starting point and then going beyond. As I keep stepping back, I lose connection bit by bit with the creature, eventually getting to the point where I cannot even see him beyond a blurry outline.

I start to wonder whether I've incorrectly guessed the way to fail. Not long after, though, as I reach the same distance behind my starting point as the creature is in front of it, the world suddenly blurs. I'm returned abruptly to my body, an immense weakness overtaking my limbs. I'm unable to move or even stay upright and fall heavily to the floor.

So, this is what the description meant, I muse to myself. A good reminder to never use this Skill in a situation when becoming this vulnerable would be fatal. Not unless I really have no other choice, that is. Fortunately, my Bond with Bastet is unchanged, and I communicate my regretful failure to her. She probably already knows the outcome given that I'm so completely vulnerable and the creature is biting and scrabbling with renewed vigor.

The wave of emotion I get back along the Bond is the equivalent of "Oh well," accompanied by what on a human would be a shrug. In the next moment a wave of killing intent billows from her, and I barely manage to send a rejection before she moves to bite down on the bird's throat, clearly intent on crushing it between her jaws as she has done so many times before.

Fortunately, I am in time. She pauses, her jaws literally around the bird's neck, the creature frozen in fear. Without shifting a millimeter, she sends a feeling of slightly wary curiosity along the Bond.

"I want to let him go." The curiosity is repeated, this time with a tinge of confusion. "We . . . touched souls. Or minds. Or something like that. I can't kill him when all he wants is to be free." Nor can I let Bastet do it, which is really me killing him by proxy.

She replies with more confusion along with an image of the cubs colored by a feeling of danger. I think she's trying to say that she fears for the cubs' safety with this bird flying around. And while she's right, that's why I gave the bird the warning while we were still able to communicate. Hopefully, it got through.

"We will protect them," I tell her, sending my certainty down the link. "Besides, I've told the creature that if he attacks us or the cubs again, we'll kill him, so hopefully he's intelligent enough not to even attempt it." My weakness from Dominate has faded, so I climb to my feet. The bird creature watches me warily.

After a slight pause, Bastet sends me grudging acknowledgment along with hints of what I reckon is a bit of contemptuousness towards the bird's intelligence. Which I understand; what kind of creature attacks something that clearly is far bigger, stronger, and better equipped? That said, I've been getting attacked by creatures that really should know better ever since I arrived here. It sometimes feels like the animals of this world lack a self-preservation instinct that those of Earth have in spades.

Bastet grumpily withdraws from where she's pinning the bird down. The bird creature doesn't take very long to try to avail himself of his renewed freedom, flapping his wings to take off. Unfortunately, his wing is still very much damaged by my arrow, so instead of taking flight, he just sprawls ungainly on the ground.

I can't leave him like that. Giving him his freedom back means nothing if I'm just setting him up for the next predator that comes along to have a good meal. I leap forwards and pin him once more to the ground. His eyes meet mine for a moment, and I see a deep rage and wildness in them. I don't know if he's capable of feeling betrayal, but if he is, no doubt he's thinking right now that my promise meant nothing.

"I just want to heal you," I tell him, my voice soothing. I doubt he understands my words; hopefully, he at least gets something from my tone of voice. If he does, it doesn't stop him from struggling. In the end, I actually have to get Bastet involved again to prevent him from hurting himself further by fighting against me.

The raptorcat obligingly pins him again, but she once more sends me the closest equivalent to "you're weird" that I think I'll get from her. This sort of thing is completely alien to her. Releasing an enemy is bad enough; actually *healing* it is beyond her ability to comprehend. It doesn't stop me from doing it.

Although I'm not sure that Lay-on-Hands will work on a creature that isn't bound to me, a creature that is actually actively hostile, I try it anyway. Fortunately for the bird creature, it seems like the healing Skill isn't only for allies, as I find my magic sinking into him without any hesitation. Not knowing more than the basics about birds' wings, and not willing to assume that this creature's wings even work the same way as those on Earth, I don't try to direct the magic. As a result, it takes a fair amount of my mana to heal his wing and the other smaller injuries that are a result of our scuffle.

This time when I release him and indicate to Bastet to do the same, the bird creature explodes into flight, winging his way past the circle of light cast by my torch and disappearing into the shadows.

CHAPTER EIGHT

Achievement

As I watch the four-legged bird fly away, I . . . feel good. I know he's a potential future threat to the cubs that we'll have to keep our eyes out for, but I'm glad I released him.

Somehow, it feels like I took a step away from the darkness, which would be all too easy to give in to. I can't ignore that I could use Dominate to make life so much easier for myself. I could take and take and take without giving anything in return, and as long as I never attacked a creature that could properly defend itself, I would get away with it.

Yet, I've already experienced what it's like to be someone who just takes—even when I thought at the time that I was being generous. Giving someone something they don't want isn't generosity: it's a sop to the conscience.

But this . . . I could have taken the bird's life very easily. Logic would say I *should* have. Or forcibly bound him to myself to turn him from a threat to an asset. But he truly had little chance against me; killing him would have gained me nothing but a bit of Energy, and Binding him would have just made me even guiltier than I was with Spike, acting with full knowledge against his wishes. His life, his *freedom* is all he has—and all he truly wants. Releasing him . . . Well, we'll see. For now, I don't regret it. After musing over the encounter for a moment longer, I turn to my companion.

"Are you hungry?" I ask the raptorcat. She sends eager agreement through the Bond and licks her lips, so I pull out a couple of the monkile corpses. "Well, go on then. Join us at the shelter when you're done." We should be far enough from the shelter itself here not to have too much of an issue from her leaving carcass scraps behind when she's finished.

Not needing to be told twice, she digs into the belly of one of the creatures with gusto, eating its entrails and organs first. I don't watch; I'm not exactly squeamish—how can I be after all I've seen in this place?—but I'm still not particularly keen on watching her tear a corpse to pieces.

Walking over to the shelter, I take the burning torch with me. It's not like Bastet needs it, after all. The cubs are snuggled into the leaves under cover of the branches and foliage of our temporary shelter. They're half awake as I ease myself inside *after* putting the torch back into my Inventory—I don't want to accidentally set light to our bed for the night.

Making cute sleepy noises, the cubs shamelessly take advantage of my body heat and press their bodies in close to mine. I try to say to myself that I'm just virtuously letting them take their comfort from me, but I know it's a lie. I'm getting as much out of their unhesitating signs of trust as they are from my body warmth.

It's odd that the fate of a creature that tried to kill me and that I didn't spend longer than five minutes with could affect me this much. The description of Dominate didn't say anything about prolonged emotional effects; it only talked about a short period of vulnerability as I recover from the Battle of Wills. But then, maybe not everyone does Dominate the way I just did, as a negotiation more than a show of strength.

Each time I use Dominate, it seems like the creature and I connect on a different level. I don't know if souls exist and that's what's happening here, or if it's that I gain an in-depth sense of the creature's life and motivations. Either way, I don't know how other Tamers push through it to forcibly Dominate creatures. Or maybe they don't. Maybe it's an acknowledged fact that Dominate is a negotiation rather than a true battle despite the name. I don't know.

I stop myself there. Like so many other questions that I have, I'm not going to get any answers until I speak to Nicholas and see his world. And I have to get through this year in the wilderness first. Without anyone to guide me, I have to make my own decisions. I have to somehow compromise between what will keep me alive and what will keep my sense of self-worth intact.

What happened with the bird felt like a good compromise for that specific situation. If the situation changes, my decision will probably have to change with it. At this point, I can't make contingency plans for situations I don't even know about.

With that settled for the moment, I bring up my status screen to check on the results of my level-up.

Name: Markus Wolfe		Race: Human	Class: Tamer
Level: 3	Energy to next level: 0%	Energy absorption rate: 21u/hr	Energy towards debt: 4%
Intelligence	14	Mana: 140/140	
Wisdom	16	Mana regeneration rate: 400u/hr	
Willpower	19+3 (+20%)	Health regeneration rate: 22u/hr	
Constitution	15	Health: 150/150	
Strength	12	Stamina: 60/60	
Dexterity	13	Stamina regeneration rate: 130u/hr	
Class Skills:		Non-Class Skills:	
Dominate – Beginner 6		Lay-on-Hands – Initiate 3	
Tame – Beginner 3		Stealth – Beginner 9	
Fade – Novice 9		Animal Empathy – Novice 2	

It's less of a drastic change this time than the previous two times. Six stat points to distribute looks a lot better when I have less than six points in most stats than when I'm already over ten in each. Still, it's a nice step forwards.

I decided to put two points each into Intelligence and Wisdom because of how difficult they are to train in this environment and how regularly I seem to run out of the ability to cast Lay-on-Hands. So far, I've mostly managed to keep myself and my companions alive and unmaimed—Spike being the most obvious exception. I'd like to avoid losing any more of my Bound and having the ability to heal them seems a key factor in that. It's been far too close to the knuckle sometimes.

My four points mean an automatic extra two casts with my increased mana pool in addition to a faster regeneration rate. By this point, I'm earning more than five mana points per minute, meaning that it takes about ten seconds less than before to regain the mana to cast another one. That may not sound significant, but when it comes to poison or a persistent hemorrhage, it really could be.

Besides those points, I dedicated two points to Constitution, reasoning that increased health points can't hurt. I hesitated for a while over the temptation to put a point in Dexterity for the increased stamina regeneration. I also considered a point in Strength (Endurance) since adding a point there would directly increase my stamina pool as well as help refine my muscles further.

In the end, though, I decided that both Dexterity and Strength are still relatively easy to train—the point I got in Dexterity earlier was a key factor in my decision. I may revisit the issue later because if I can get my stamina to the point where my regeneration rate is equal to, or even outpaces, my use of it, it doesn't really matter what my actual pool is. At least, that's my reasoning.

What is confusing me is that I've actually gained four more points than I was expecting: I have two more points each in Wisdom and Willpower than should be there. Why, I don't know. Perhaps something in my messages will explain it? I don't think there is anything special about level three that would account for it.

At least I've been able to answer a query I had about the percentage increase to Willpower. It only works with whole numbers, so I still only have three points in addition to my base points. I should get an extra point every five points I have in there. It actually makes me seriously wonder whether to dedicate one of my six points to it next time, even though it's my highest stat—that way it'll almost be a two-for-one deal. *Hmm, for later consideration.*

Before switching across to check my messages, I first scroll down to the bottom to see my Skills. Another surprise is waiting for me: the number of levels Dominate has increased by. I was half expecting it to move from Beginner four to Beginner five, even though I was wondering whether failing the Battle of Wills would even increase the Skill. Instead, it's leaped to level *six*. Not that I'm complaining, but it would be good to know why so I can try to repeat it.

Animal Empathy is another unexpected change. It's actually ranked up from Beginner to Novice. Is this because of the way the flying creature and I seemed to link minds—or souls—in the Battle of Wills?

Other than that, Lay-on-Hands is slowly but steadily improving with use as expected. Tame is a surprise, though. Considering that my attempt to use it earlier failed, I'm surprised to see that it's increased in level. Perhaps it was my intentions that counted there.

I switch across to my messages tab and access the first new message.

Congratulations!
You have advanced a Skill past Beginner. Animal Empathy is now Novice 1. You are now able to interpret some communications between animals to which you are not directly connected with a Bond. Increased familiarity with the animals in question will improve the accuracy of your interpretation.

Next message

Well, I guess that answers my question. This might be linked to the bird, but it's more likely to be connected to me understanding Bastet and the cubs more, even when I'm not using the Bond. The fact that it's sitting at Novice two rather than Novice one implies that the communication with the bird increased it after it ranked up.

I often wish that the System was a little more explicit. I don't always know exactly what caused the increase to happen, which means I have to stumble in the dark when it comes to repeating it. Still, I'm grateful to have the System at all, all things being equal. I move to the next message, and my eyebrows shoot up as I read it.

Achievement awarded: Steadfast I
Your principles were put to the test and you stood by them, even when putting them to the side would have lead to benefit for you. For your resolve and sagacity, you have been awarded +2 points to Willpower and +2 points to Wisdom.

Close message

That also provides an answer, this time to the question of the mysterious additional Willpower and Wisdom points. It's an answer, however, that poses more questions, not least because the memories I've absorbed from the System stone don't mention Achievements at all. Not even tangentially. Either it's something I lost when I absorbed the stone or it's rare enough that it's not included on the stone.

I close the screen down and lie there in the dark, thinking. Too many questions without answers for my liking. Still, with the evidence so far on this journey, I think I've at least definitively answered one of my long-held questions: what happens with the Energy of the creatures Bastet kills.

From what I've seen, my Energy store has increased even when I haven't been involved in the fight, which almost certainly indicates that she's feeding me at least some of the Energy she receives. Whether it's some, most, or even all of the Energy, I don't know yet. The lack of clear numbers makes it hard to guestimate. Also not yet confirmed is whether it only happened because I was so close, or whether the Energy would somehow be sent along the Bond if she went out hunting without me.

Then another question that's raised is about Bastet's own progression. If she's sending Energy to me, how is *she* getting stronger? Actually, how *do* beasts get stronger? I have to assume that they improve by killing other creatures, at least. But how does that work practically? They don't have a Class, I imagine, so how do they grow? How do they end up like Kalanthia, capable of telepathically communicating with others and commanding the very earth to move? Or is that just because of her species? Maybe she was always able to do that.

I guess that if—when—I get Lathani back and return her to her mother, I can ask the giant nunda. Maybe her gratitude will even get her to answer.

Because, honestly, there has to be a way to help my companions improve. My Class can't be all about just using creatures and then discarding them when they fall behind the Tamer's level of advancement. That just doesn't make sense. And if I can help my companions to grow, there will be less of a requirement for me to continually Dominate new creatures, thus removing that moral dilemma. Plus, it will make joining me more attractive if I can help them get stronger.

I fall asleep while musing on the possibilities and only briefly wake when Bastet joins us, using her own body to shield all of us from any potential threat coming in from the open end of the shelter. My sleep is a lot better than the first time I used this kind of shelter. I feel safe with her around. Or saf*er*, at least.

Tonight, sleep. Tomorrow, the lizard folk.

CHAPTER NINE

Sense of Urgency

There's no lollygagging in the morning. As soon as it's light enough for me to see, I get up. The cubs complain a little as I move, but they quickly fall asleep again. Two of them, anyway. Storm keeps an eye on me, her eyes glinting from within her pile of down and limbs. She doesn't deign to leave the warm nest, though, and abandons me to shiver a little in the dawn chill. The sooner I can get a fire going to boil some water, the better.

It's slightly misty, but I know from past experience that that will clear up. The mist seems to be the only thing keeping the smaller plants alive in this ongoing drought—it still hasn't rained since I got here. I'm glad of it in many ways, but I can see that there are a number of plants that could do with a bit of soaking.

Waiting for water to boil is often a frustrating waste of time, but this time I take a moment to relax and appreciate the forest in the early morning. If the impression I got from Kalanthia's memories is accurate, we're due to reach the lizard folk's village by the end of the day.

I take my pot off the fire once it's bubbling, then let it cool a little before drinking some and transferring the rest into my empty canteen. I put the canteen into my travel satchel—if I put it in my Inventory, it'll stay practically boiling hot, which I don't want, since I don't have any tea or coffee with me. After chewing on a bit of meat and a cooked potato, I'm ready to go.

By this point, Bastet and the cubs are also fully awake and eager to get moving. We set off, once more following the river. We walk together as a pack—the cubs need to have a chance to stretch their legs. While we move, I muse over my plans for today.

Ideally, we'll reach the lizard folk's territory by lunchtime, though attacks are likely to hold us up a bit. We'll need to gather a lot more information before barging into the village, though. It's a pity about that bird last night; a dedicated scout isn't a bad idea, really. Bastet is stealthy, but she's quite big and she's also become an essential part of our combat strength. That, plus the fact that she's the cubs' main caregiver, makes it a bad idea to send her off for any length of time, but that's what I'm going to have to do, I think—she's far stealthier than I am.

The weasitors or those baby crocodile things I encountered in my first few days in this world would have been pretty perfect scouts—unless they were weak enough to be easily picked off, which is a concern, or too small to cover ground quickly.

Unfortunately, I was just so overwhelmed by everything new around me, and the thought of using my freshly gained Dominate Skill really didn't occur to me at the time. I'll just have to keep my eyes out for something that might be suitable and not *quite* as against the idea as the bird was.

The journey is fairly peaceful to begin with. The cubs tire after a while, and I tuck them back into the sling. Fortunately, that happens before our first encounter of the day.

The creature sees us before we see it; our first clue that it's there is when we hear an offended bellow and the sound of plants cracking to our left. A large mass comes barreling out of the thick undergrowth straight at us almost before we have time to react.

We split apart as Bastet dodges one way and I dive the other, and the beast thunders harmlessly through the gap. Fortunately, it doesn't seem to change direction very easily, as once it skids to a halt it is quite ponderous in turning around.

It seems to be a grumpy herbivore, as indicated by the plants still hanging out of its mouth. In appearance it's similar to a triceratops with only one horn. Fortunately, it's also a lot smaller than a real triceratops: its head only reaches my shoulder level when it's raised high. The downside is that this means there's still a good deal of animal to provide momentum to its charges. We'll need to make sure not to get caught—getting hit by this thing would probably be like being hit by a truck.

How are we going to approach this? Bastet's already slashing at its hindquarters, to little effect; it's pretty well armored with skin that probably rivals that of the crocodile I fought. The same technique I used on that particular creature is unlikely to work here, though. Seeing that the creature is distracted by Bastet's mostly ineffective strikes, I back away a little and scan the area. *There!*

I make a beeline to a sturdy tree and tuck the cubs away behind it while warning them to keep still. Hopefully, they'll be sufficiently protected from the fight, but I need to go and help Bastet.

Flipping mentally through my weapons as I hurry back to the action, I decide that my mace is unlikely to have too much effect: the creature is just too bulky and my weapon too weak. If I could bash through its skull that would be one thing, but as it is, I doubt I'll do much more than just annoy it. Instead, I reach backwards and retrieve my bow and arrows from my Inventory.

I'm going to have to be careful here. Fortunately, I'm out of melee range, so I shouldn't have an issue with injuries unless I don't keep a sharp enough eye out for its charges. As most of the creature's body is well armored, I'm going to have to really put my new Dexterity to the test. And with the practice I've had since making my bow, I'm a *much* better shot than I was on that ill-fated test run.

As often seems to happen, since she's the biggest damage dealer and also has better stats in general than me—in particular, more health—Bastet is the main distraction. Although her claws and teeth aren't that effective against its armored skin, she is still managing to pierce through and cause pain, if nothing else. When she hits a soft part, she does a fair bit more damage. The mini triceratops is far too distracted by her slashing at its nose, targeting its eyes, and trying her best to bite at its throat to pay attention to me.

My part of the strategy is to target its other weak spots and use my arrows to pierce the softer points where its scales aren't quite as thick—mostly behind its joints. I'm out of its strike area, but that still means I'm shooting at pretty close range. My arrows hit with significant force and several penetrate by a good couple of hand widths.

The wounds slowly take their toll as my attacks to its major joints make it slow down, even if they don't cause much bleeding. Every time the creature starts trying to turn to get at me, Bastet is there to lay on more pain and grab its attention. It tries to charge a couple of times, but we just dart out of the way and restart our attack when it stops again.

Its other attacks are not fast, but neither of us escapes without injury. Bastet takes the worst of it as she's far too close to the business end of its horn, and I accidentally get hit a couple of times when I'm not fast enough to get out of the way. The main thing, though, is that we survive and the creature doesn't. Once I've damaged its joints enough, it becomes unable to move around properly and ends up slumped on the ground.

Though tempted by the thought of using this creature as a mobile tank, I dismiss the idea after a moment. It's too slow outside of its charges and will only slow us down. I can't help feeling that speed is key right now. If I knew that it would come down to a fight, I'd take the chance, but I'm hoping that we'll be able to sneak Lathani out some way without causing more conflict. I have a feeling this beast is the opposite of stealthy. Ultimately, I don't even try.

Bastet grabs onto its throat to suffocate it, but in the end it's me who gives it the coup de grâce as I stab its brain through its eye with my spear.

We take twenty minutes or so to recuperate, during which we eat our spoils. For a herbivore, it's worth quite a bit of Energy: six percent from the animal itself and another two percent from its heart. Bastet digs into its organs with eagerness and encourages the cubs to do the same. For once, the cubs were actually exactly where I left them, Trouble included. Perhaps they're slowly learning that this place is dangerous . . .

Of course, there's far too much meat to finish, or even make proper inroads into, the corpse. Not wanting to waste such a large quantity of meat, I pack it away in my Inventory once we've eaten the most Energy-dense bits. Nothing shows my improvements in Strength better than being able to heft this dead weight, which can't be less than half a ton. After putting out my small fire and washing off in the river, we get going again.

In the end we get another two hours or so of peace before the next encounter. This time we're attacked right next to the river in a section where the trees have retreated a bit further away, leaving a rocky, sandy area clear of most plants. There's a strange rumbling, cracking sound from behind us and we turn to see a small group of strange rolling boulders quickly following us. At least, that's what they look like as they come closer. I consider running, but they're too fast for the cubs to escape.

"Trouble, Storm, Ninja, *move!*" I tell them forcefully, and Bastet underscores my instruction with a sense of urgency. To the cubs' credit, they obey without question, putting on a surprising burst of speed. Unfortunately, they don't all run in the same direction. Ninja runs to Bastet, who picks her up and runs quickly to the nearest tree to deposit her in its roots. Storm also runs to a tree and actually climbs up to the first branch, where she sits, trembling and wide-eyed.

Trouble, on the other hand, goes in the opposite direction—straight into the water. By this point, the river is reasonably wide and as deep as my waist at its center—far too deep for a raptorcat cub to cope with. Running into the river without a thought, I grab him and keep going, then find a large boulder just on the other side. Depositing him there at about my shoulder height, I tell him firmly not to move. I'm already running back to the fight as I try to work out what's going on.

Bastet is grabbing the strange boulders' attention and trying to keep them away from one cub in the roots of a tree and another holding onto a branch rather precariously. She's doing a good job with that, but she isn't having much effect on them. They aren't all that big—about knee height on me—but big enough to have a decent impact. Add to that the fact that her claws and teeth appear to be having even less of an effect on them as on the previous creature, and she's in trouble.

We're going to have to be smart about this. As I'm still at range, I first try my bow, but my arrows are just deflected straight off. I nod absently; nothing unexpected, though it's annoying. Perhaps if I were an expert archer, I'd be able to aim for a tiny chink in their armor, but I'm not that good—yet, anyway.

After tucking my bow away safely, I grab my mace and spear. Wielding one in each hand, I try my luck. Both of them manage to knock the creature off course briefly, but otherwise have no visible effect.

This isn't going to work. Can I grab the cubs and then signal Bastet to follow? Maybe, but I sense that she's already getting tired—having to avoid being hit by five different creatures all moving at different speeds and in different directions is exhausting. We did well against the creature that was almost my height and multiple times my bulk, but this group of much smaller creatures is threatening to overrun us.

Taking a step back from the situation, I look to see if there's something I can use against them. Maybe we could all jump into the trees and get out of their reach that way? It'll waste time, but better to waste time than be knocked off our feet and squashed by these guys. Or what about the water? They're staying away from it. Could we just walk in the water and avoid them? They have to stop chasing us at some point, and ultimately, our aim is to find Lathani, not to get into fights.

Then I notice something.

The creatures are fine while they're in motion, but if they get stuck against anything, they have to uncurl, shift their position, then push off into that ball again. Frankly, they look rather like massive woodlice, with many legs, oversized mandibles, and a segmented shell. They're armored even in their uncurled positions, much as a turtle is, but my eyes still light up.

Seeing a possible opportunity to end this on our terms, I send a quick mental image to Bastet. It takes a moment, but I soon get back a response of weary assent.

CHAPTER TEN

Crystals

Bastet's an absolute trooper. She gains a second wind and pulls the couple of woodlice that had diverted to me back into her orbit. While she once more plays distraction, her own agility far superior to my own, I grab a spear from my Inventory and another good-sized stick from where it was lying. With judicious blows, I manage to corner one of the creatures. *The monster version of hockey,* I think to myself with grim amusement.

Using the branch and the roots of a nearby tree to form a triangular "cage," I stop the creature from just rolling away. Stuck, it reacts by uncurling, and its head and legs partially emerge from underneath the shell.

As soon as I have a target, I attack it with my spear, my improved accuracy enabling me to strike it directly through its suddenly vulnerable head. It lets out a high-pitched shriek as its legs desperately scrabble at the earth. It tries to curl up again, but its head is pinned to the ground, preventing it from doing so.

I twist the spear, conscious of my partner's tiring state. The shriek has grabbed the attention of the other woodlice and Bastet is having to work much harder to play interference.

The creature makes a final effort to escape, but it's for naught; a moment later, it goes limp. Success!

I don't waste any time as I pull my spear out and grab the branch again. I manage to corral another of the woodlice after Bastet intentionally allows it past her guard. A similar scenario plays out—two down.

As I twist the spear free, I abruptly realize I have a problem. The sinew binding holding the flint tip to my spear didn't like the twisting motion, especially while damp—it's come off and gotten stuck inside the oversized insect's head.

My kills have earned me the attention of the rest of the woodlice. I don't have enough time to do more than frown and drop the stick of wood that used to be one of my two spears before they attack me.

Once more having to dodge out of the way of large, rolling objects, I barely have a moment to retrieve my knife from my belt. Unfortunately, the woodlice are intelligent enough to adapt and the same technique doesn't work again. However, they aren't intelligent enough to pick a *winning* strategy to combat mine. Instead of continuing to roll and leaving themselves vulnerable to my corralling, they preempt my actions by uncurling and going on the attack.

With three converging on me at once, injuries are inevitable. One latches onto my leg at an unfortunate moment, and I'm left off balance, ripe for the next to knock into me and send me thumping gracelessly onto my butt. The third quickly strikes at my vulnerable back.

Their mandibles are strong and sharp; the one on my calf is digging in deeply and sending agony up my leg. It completely distracts me from the one attacking my chitin-covered back until that one actually manages to cut through the armor and nick the skin beneath.

Growling in pain, I stab at the one that currently has its mandibles digging deeply enough into my calf to hit bone. Once I've sunk my own knife in to the hilt, I twist and wiggle my blade until the creature goes limp, all the while trying to fend off the one that's not managed to land a hit yet. Not easy with my range of motion so constrained.

Dealing with the one gnawing at the flesh of my back would normally be the next priority—and a difficult one at that, as I've experienced before. Fortunately, this time I'm not alone here; Bastet deals with it even as the one that tried to bite through my calf twitches in its final death throes.

Lacking my knife, she goes for a simpler solution: chewing off its head. Trusting in my partner, I attack the final one, using my full Strength to hold it still for a moment while I jab my knife through it. I look around quickly in all directions, but everything is suddenly calm.

The fight over, I gingerly pull the two sets of mandibles out of my body, then quickly cast and channel Lay-on-Hands to stem the blood flow from the holes they made in me, my stomach roiling uncomfortably with the pain and blood loss. Bastet has slumped to the ground in exhaustion, her eyes closed and her breath coming heavily through her mouth. I send her a wave of concern, but she just replies with a feeling of tired reassurance.

"Are you hurt?" I ask next, but she replies in the negative. Apparently, it's just low stamina that's her issue right now.

I'm tired too, but I'm better off than she is since I didn't have to keep doing acrobatics throughout the fight. Deciding to gather the cubs together to make sure they're safe, I limp over to the spots where we stashed them.

Ninja almost gives me a heart attack—again—because she's not where Bastet left her. Instead, she's gone to join her sister; I look up to find the two of them perched like little birds in the crook of a branch, their claws fully sheathed into the wood.

It takes a little bit of coaxing to get them down, and when they eventually jump onto my shoulders, I wince at their claws digging in. Still, that they're fine is the main thing. I go searching for Trouble next and find him not far from the boulder on which I left him. He's courting danger, though, poking at the river with his scaly talons, looking inches away from jumping in again.

"If you go in there, you'll drown," I warn him. "And that's only if you don't get eaten by something that likes little cubs for lunch." Despite my sage advice, he still looks aggrieved when I pick him up and take him away. Carrying him back across the river, I grunt as the water threatens to take me off my feet in my weakened state.

I'm struck by the idea that we could potentially have won the fight by knocking the woodlice into the river—they'd probably have drowned without nearly as much effort as we needed to expend fighting them. Ruefully, I consider how I still have a *lot* to learn when it comes to combat.

Bastet has recovered a bit by the time I get back with the cubs, and she insists on inspecting and licking all of them, despite their squirming. Pack socializing done, we then investigate the carcasses.

Insectile as they are, there isn't anything in the bodies I want to eat, though I might be able to use the shells as containers for something—I'm not sure how watertight they are, but I could do with some storage containers. Bastet has managed to find something, though.

After doing a bit of digging in the bodies, she pulls out odd crystals from three of them—the big ones that attacked me at the end. The crystals are small, only about the size of a marble, and a murky brown. When she nudges one towards me, though, I notice that it gives off some strange sense of energy—or Energy, perhaps. I don't know what to do with it, so I hand it back to her.

She nudges one crystal towards each of the cubs. The cubs don't seem to know what to do with them either, so she demonstrates. She licks up the one in front of Trouble and bites into it, crunching it happily. How she happily crunches a hard crystal, I don't know, but she does.

An interesting sensation comes down the Bond: a sudden wave of energy, almost like she's drunk a Red Bull or something. Her lingering fatigue from the fight disappears and she suddenly feels ready for anything. She also feels . . . healthier? Like we might feel if we ate a nice salad after only eating pizza for ages. It's not easy to describe—all I know is that she feels qualitatively better after eating the crystal than before.

With her encouragement, the cubs copy her. Trouble looks accusingly at Bastet and tries to bully Ninja out of her crystal. Storm leaps to defend her sister and Ninja quickly eats her own, then grabs the last and takes it to hide behind Bastet. When Storm saunters back to butt heads with her, leaving a defeated and disgruntled Trouble in the dust, Ninja reveals the crystal she's been hoarding. Storm takes it as her due and crushes it happily.

Apparently, they like the feeling or taste or whatever because they start asking her for more, while Trouble sulks off to the side. Unfortunately, it doesn't seem like there are any more to be found, so, in true hoarder style, I just dump the rest of the corpses in my Inventory, then we get going, three of the four raptorcats fully refreshed.

As we walk, I allow my curiosity to take over.

"What were those crystals?" I ask her. She doesn't answer for a moment, but it's not because she's ignoring me. I get the idea that she's not sure how to answer and is trying to work out a way of explaining.

After a pause, she sends me a series of images. They show raptorcats killing different creatures, most of which I've never seen before. Several of the creatures seem capable of using the elements to fight with, and others have attacks that I would consider supernatural. After the raptorcats kill the creatures, they dig into the bodies and find crystals, then give them to a single raptorcat in the pack. The crystals are a variety of sizes and colors, and the bigger and more vibrant colors seem to come from the most dangerous opponents. In fact, one of them looks rather like what Kalanthia once asked as payment for potentially babysitting the cubs.

Over time, the raptorcat gets measurably, though imperceptibly, bigger and stronger as it eats more and more crystals. Then comes a day when the raptorcat writhes in pain and grows visibly, its wings growing and developing too. When it finishes its transformation, it's almost twice as big as when it started and its wings look fully developed. It opens its eyes, jumps into the air, and starts to fly. That's where the images stop.

"So, you eat the crystals and they make you stronger?" I summarize. A wave of assent comes at me from Bastet's side of the Bond. A thought occurs. "Can *I* eat them?" This time her reply is full of uncertainty.

She sends another flurry of images wrapped up in feelings. Parsing through them, I understand that when she sees a crystal, her whole body tells her it's something good to eat. She expresses uncertainty in my case—if my body doesn't do the same, then maybe it's not good to eat. It's a valid point. Maybe when we get back to Kalanthia after rescuing Lathani, I can ask her.

Anyway, maybe I shouldn't take the crystals away from the raptorcats even if they *would* be good for me; the stronger they get, the better off we all are. It's good to know that they *do* have a way of leveling up. It raises another question, though. I get to choose where I assign my stats on level-up. Do they have similar options or is it chosen for them? Something else to ask Kalanthia.

Of course, that depends on us actually rescuing Lathani and getting back to her, but since if we fail in those two aims, it'll be because we died trying, I might as well talk about "when" rather than "if."

We keep walking following the river. Fortunately for our travel time, we don't face any other foes until I begin seeing the landmarks Kalanthia indicated as the start of lizard folk territory. Reluctantly, given that we have no other option, I send Bastet out to scout. We need to get an idea of the lay of the land.

I'm waiting.

It's been a few hours since Bastet went to scout out the lizard folk's base, leaving the cubs with me, and I'm getting worried. I can't help it. We haven't been this far apart for quite a while now, and she's become indispensable to me in such a short time. Not only useful for combat, but . . . a friend. A companion.

Although I'm still nominally "in charge" and she follows my lead, it feels a lot more like it's because she acknowledges me as the leader of the pack rather than because she's compelled to follow my orders. But because I am the leader, I feel the responsibility of making the decisions, even when we both agree with the choice.

It was a mutual decision that she was the best scout option between the two of us—her stealth and my stealth are really incomparable, even with my Skills helping me. But in a way, the fact that I didn't Dominate the bird last night heaps even more weight on my shoulders. If I'd just pushed past my principles and forced it anyway, Bastet wouldn't now be in danger. If she dies like Spike did, and once more the price is paid for a poorly made decision . . .

No, I can't think like that. And besides, temporarily ignoring principles for expediency is the start of a very slippery slope. If I start just forcing random creatures to join me, will it end with me just using them as suicide troops? Treating them like not-very-valuable means to an end? No, I did the right thing. The right thing for me at least. I just have to hope that it doesn't cost Bastet.

I'm confident that I would know through the Bond if she were truly in a dire situation, but knowing that in my head and believing it in my heart are two very different things. I'll be grateful when she gets back, if only to know for sure that she's okay.

I hear the sound of something quietly moving towards us and tense, my weapons at the ready.

CHAPTER ELEVEN

Civilized

Fortunately, even before I see her, I sense my Bound raptorcat close by. Though waiting impatiently, it's objectively probably not that long before I see her sleek form slinking through the bushes. A quick glance over her has me breathing a quiet sigh of relief. It's good to see that she's uninjured and, from the lack of noise or movements, not being followed either.

"How did it go?" I ask quietly and warily. "Do we need to move?" Her first response is that of reassuring negation. She doesn't think she was detected either, which, considering her powerful senses, probably means she wasn't. She then sends a rapid stream of images. I close my eyes to improve my ability to focus on them. Fortunately, my significantly improved Intelligence seems to have an effect on both my speed of processing and my memory. Even when Bastet is finished sending me the images, I can still hold them in my head for evaluation.

As I look through her memories, I try to block out, for the most part, the extraneous sensory data and focus on sight since that's the easiest for me to make sense of. Through her images, I almost relive her experiences, though it's mostly a series of still images with emotion and other senses sometimes attached rather than continuous, like a video.

She started off by heading through fairly thick forest, searching for a trail or some other indication of exactly which direction to head in. There were a number of promising trails she came across but none of them went anywhere useful. Still, every dead end helped to highlight which scents to *avoid*. When she came across the thick scent of reptiles along with a number of prints in the soil, she followed them.

Eventually, she ended up reaching an area where the density of that smell grew greater and greater and the occasional footprint became less occasional and more frequent. I take a moment to pause the image to pore over the footprint. Although there are some differences between the prints, they are invariably long with four claw marks at the front and another small one at the back. It's hard to work out how long, considering I'm seeing them through the eyes of a creature significantly lower to the ground than me, but I estimate them to be between two and four times the length of my own foot.

As the footprints started to become dense enough to actually overlay each other, she realized that she was getting close to the main gathering point of the lizard folk. The images at this point gain a heavy sense of caution even as she continued moving forwards. It wasn't long before she encountered her first lizard folk—a small group of three walking along the trail.

At least, that's what I assume they are. They look similar to the images Kalanthia fed me, though seeing them "in person" makes it a somewhat different experience—here I actually see a sort of video. In the moving image, the lizard folk are wary, but they move with a confidence in their environment that I've only seen from the raptorcats before now. That alone would make me cautious, never mind all the other warning signs I see.

Just like with the footprints earlier, it's hard to get a proper size estimate. They look big to Bastet, but it's hard to know exactly *how* big they are. Still, I can see that she would probably reach between mid-thigh and waist level on them. That's pretty big—almost my height, probably. They're tough looking too, with corded muscle visible even underneath their scaled skin.

The lizard folk are bipedal, with tails that sweep behind them and large clawed feet. Their hips must be a lot more like mine than a normal lizard's, though, as they walk in the same way I reckon I would if I had a third limb on my lower half. A tail, that is.

Adding to the danger they individually pose are their jaws. Kalanthia's memories were right: they look rather crocodilian with reasonably long jaws and teeth that fit together. They don't seem to have lips that seal, so even when their jaws are closed their teeth are still visible. Their skull is a bit taller than a crocodile's, though, perhaps indicating a larger brain. Certainly, a larger brain might explain some of the other things I'm seeing that Kalanthia didn't give me any indication of.

For a place that is not supposed to have any civilized races, I'm surprised by the amount of civilization visible here. The lizard folk not only walk upright, but their forepaws—we should say *hands*—look rather dexterous. The fact that they're capable of craft is unfortunately made obvious by the adornments they're wearing.

I can't exactly call it clothing, but each is wearing at least one woven necklace. The necklaces are decorated with what look to be bones, stones, and other items they've no doubt found in their environment. Some are wearing woven strands around their arms or legs too. They don't have loincloths, and I guess they don't need to; their lack of obvious genitals is very much a nod towards their reptilian heritage.

Once the three lizard folk moved on, my Bound continued her stealthy approach. Eventually, she found the center of their activity, then hid in a bush and observed from there in order to stay unnoticed.

Lizard folk were everywhere. As the Bastet in the memories slowly makes her way around the area, peering through the undergrowth, I notice even more signs of civilization. Or relative civilization, that is.

They have houses. Huts, really, that are not much more than beehive-like mounds of mud. Some of them have carefully balanced leaves over the top, but they look sturdier than my temporary branch and leaf shelters for sure. I don't see much of the inner workings of the place. Bastet was rightly too cautious to get close, but I would hazard a guess that there are further signs of a community in the encampment itself.

There are even hints that the lizard folk might be using weapons: a couple of branches leaning up against some of the huts look more like spears than supports for the building.

After Bastet did a full circle of the place, she slunk back through the bushes, then made a straighter line on the way back than she had on the way out. It makes sense: she knew where I was in the forest, and she hadn't known where the lizard folk were.

Having finished going through the images Bastet sent me, I lean back against a tree, a sigh leaving my lips. Bastet looks at me expectantly even while the cubs climb her like a tree. The fact that the cubs are playing a game of king of the rock where she's the rock rather does detract from her dangerous and mysterious aura, but I know she's still a badass.

"It won't be easy," I tell her frankly. "An enemy with numbers is bad; an intelligent enemy is worse. Put the two together . . ." I trail off. I don't even know how many lizard folk there are; all Bastet's memories told me was "a lot." "Do you know if Lathani's even there?"

She looks thoughtful for a moment and then sends me a sense memory. This time it's much less of an image and more of a smell. I feel like sneezing even though my nose isn't actually involved in this at all. After sending me the first memory, which is a strong musky scent, she sends me a second. Even I can tell that they're the same smell but that the second one is a lot fainter. After a short pause, she then sends me a complicated mix of emotions, images, and more esoteric senses.

It's at times like this that I wish she could *talk*. I think she's telling me that the first scent was from Kalanthia's cave and the second was from near the lizard folk's village. It also feels like she's trying to say that she detected Lathani's scent near the village, drifting from one area of the village in particular. It was faint but not too old. Much easier to say in words than the crazy mix of things she sent me, but beggars can't be choosers. At least I can communicate with her at all.

"So, Lathani was there fairly recently," I say, checking with her. She replies with a clear sense of agreement. "But do you know if she's still there? Do you know if she's . . . alive?" Having to actually ask that gives me a swooping feeling in my gut, but I need to know. I'm not taking Bastet and the cubs into that mess unless I'm at least fairly convinced that Lathani's alive.

The raptorcat's response isn't entirely reassuring. She sends me a feeling of uncertainty but offers me another sense memory as well. This one is a different sense, one that I don't have any name for. It's the same one that somehow feels the hint of Energy in the world, and I'm not sure if I actually have it myself, or if I'm just getting it purely from her memory. Like being able to see in the dark with an infrared camera.

This memory makes me shiver. It feels like hopelessness, like grief, like depression and giving up on the world. In short, it feels far too like I did before arriving here. I reject the feeling violently and actually stand up abruptly and start to pace to get rid of the lingering emotions. My attempt to cleanse myself of them is helped by Bastet sending a wave of warm concern, which washes away the lingering coldness.

"What was that?" I ask her almost accusingly, even though I know she wouldn't have done that on purpose. In return, she sends me a flurry of other emotions and images, which I once again have to parse through.

If I've interpreted things correctly, she's telling me that this was something she felt when she was on one side of the village, the one where Lathani's smell was strongest. It's not clear-cut, not at all, but it could be an indication that Lathani is still there. Certainly, the emotions could fit how she would be feeling at being ripped away from her mother. And that the sense is so intense indicates that she's probably still alive, though apparently the imprint can last a while, especially of strong emotions.

"In short," I summarize with a sigh, "we need more information." In fact, we need a scout who could get further than Bastet into the village without being detected. Or perhaps . . . a mole.

Sure, I could go guns blazing—figuratively—into the camp with no information, but I reckon that would be tantamount to suicide. I wouldn't be willing to risk taking on that many creatures, not even if they were unintelligent, with their strong builds and natural weaponry. With the clear signs of sapience I've seen so far, I doubt I'd even get a few steps in before they took me down, healing or not.

No, it's time for me to leverage my Class. I'm a Tamer; that's going to be my way in. Sure, I could try to Tame a smaller animal that would be unnoticeable to go and scout for me, but finding information is only half the job. If Lathani is still alive, I need to get her out of there; that will take a lot more than a small scout could offer.

All things being equal, I think my best chance for success is to successfully Dominate one of the lizard folk. All I can hope is that my Willpower will be up to the job—and that, somehow, I'm able to convince them to give in to me. If not . . . my resolution to not Dominate another creature without their consent may be put to the test sooner than I thought.

CHAPTER TWELVE

The Great Predator

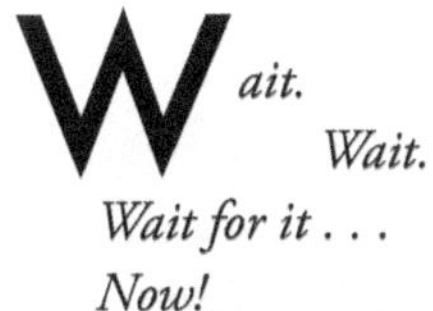 *ait.*

Wait.

Wait for it . . .

Now!

I haul on the bark-fiber cord with all the raw power I can muster. The creature's foot is snared and pulled up towards the canopy, and the rest of its body helplessly follows after. I don't pull it up high, nor do I let it dangle for long. The whole trap is more to disorientate than to hold, after all. Once its head is a foot off the ground, I let the rope go, hoping to stun it. Fortunately, my hopes prove true and its neck and head are sufficiently protected to not crack on impact with the ground.

As the creature lands on the ground with a thud, Bastet leaps onto it. Already disorientated, the creature doesn't seem able to muster any defense against an angry and snarling raptorcat. I understand; having something not all that dissimilar to a forest-colored panther with wings and taloned feet snarling *that* close to one's neck is not an experience I would recommend.

The distraction combined with the disorientation works. The lizard-kin doesn't even react as I start binding its legs and tail together using the cord that trapped it in the first place, still snared around one foot. It's not particularly secure, but hopefully, it will do the job. After tying off the first cord, I pull a second one out, which I use to bind its jaws shut. Bastet shifts slightly to give me enough space to work, but when the creature resumes moving in response, she takes her snarls up a notch, drawing her lips further away from her teeth, and I see the lizard freeze again in fear.

Once the creature's forearms are bound to its torso, I reckon we're as good as we're going to get with the equipment I have at hand. With a quick mental command, Bastet steps off the lizard creature, now bound practically head to tail. She starts mussing up the area around us as she does her best to disguise the signs of the brief struggle.

Meanwhile, I haul the creature over my shoulder in a fireman's carry. I let out a small grunt from the effort required—I may have significantly increased my Strength, but my burden is only slightly smaller than me and is solid muscle. Plus, it's starting to *wriggle.*

Casting an eye over the area, I send a short feeling of appreciation over to my Bound for her work. Even with my tracking skills, I would be hard-pressed to say exactly what had gone on here, though I would be able tell *something* had. That's as good as it's going to get, I reckon. Besides, this operation is supposed to be quick and quiet; every second longer that we spend here means more chance of discovery.

Turning tail, I start running, and Bastet first follows behind me to cover any tracks, then ranges ahead to check for threats. She repeats the process, her speed significantly faster than mine considering the weight I'm carrying. By the time we're far enough that I reckon we're probably safe for now, I'm panting and my stamina has almost bottomed out. As I've learned all too recently, letting my stamina completely deplete is not a good idea, so I slow to a stop.

Pulling the lizard off my shoulder, I let it drop to the ground with a bit of a thump, not even trying to be particularly careful with my burden.

"Right, let's find out what's going on," I say to my Bound. "If it tries to attack me, kill it." She sends a grim wave of acknowledgment across our Bond. Crouching down by its head, I meet the lizard's eyes and see the roiling mass of anger, helplessness, and fear within them. I almost feel bad . . . but these guys started it. "Dominate!"

I'm dropped into the normal space that accompanies the Battle of Wills, triggered by activating my Class Skill. By this point, I'm getting rather used to it. The humanoid lizard is standing across from me, glaring with all the force it can muster. A difference between this battle and my previous ones is immediately made apparent: if I want to win this, I'm really going to have to focus.

There are always two forms of pressure on me during these times: the amorphous pressure, which feels like the space itself is rejecting me, and the pressure that is aimed directly at me, presumably by my opponent. During this time, it's like we're both holding fire hoses and our wills determine the force they can impose.

The force projected by Spike and the bird creature was neither strong nor well directed. That is to say, it's like the fire hose was more of a dribble than a jet, like it was being held by the hose instead of the nozzle itself. Anyone who's tried to hold a garden hose like that knows exactly what happens next.

Bastet's force was significantly more powerful, but it was also not particularly well aimed. I only realize the difference now that I'm facing an opponent where the fire hose is both powerful and well directed. This attempt is like chalk and cheese with my previous experiences; it's different enough that I already feel doubt about winning.

Then I chide myself. If feeling cold or fear is enough to weaken one's will, feeling doubt about success is surely going to do the same. I can't fail here; I can't fail Lathani. My mind set, I metaphorically put my head down and get on with it, pressing myself into the pressure that is trying its best to push me back, and direct my own "fire hose" at the lizard standing on the other side of the space.

Bit by bit, inch by inch, sometimes even centimeter by centimeter, I make progress. It's exhausting work—a bit like forcing myself to do one more rep on the gym equipment, though purely mental rather than physical. But I refuse to give up.

I kept going at the gym. I kept going when my girlfriend left me. I kept going when my father died. I kept going despite being in a world where everything is trying to kill me. I kept going when my arm was broken and I was faced with pre-historic killing machines. I'm going to keep going now. If I only make a centimeter of progress, even if I only make a millimeter of progress, it's still progress. It's still moving forwards, and every move forwards gets me closer to my goal.

I hit halfway. I barely even realize it, so focused am I on just pushing, forcing my way forwards. When the humanoid lizard starts communicating with me, it actually makes me lose my focus and pushes me back a quarter of an inch. Despite the frustration this literal backstep causes, I welcome the communication.

Although I'm making progress, I feel like my Willpower has a limit and like the clock is ticking both on the Battle of Wills and for Lathani. If I can succeed in convincing the lizard to give in to me, it will both make things easier and satisfy my principles. If I can't . . . I push that thought to one side—I'll cross that bridge if I come to it.

Why are you doing this? The lizard-person roars at me. And yes, "person" is the only description I feel is accurate because of what this communication has just revealed: he is capable of language. The realization hits me like a bucket of cold water to the face. This proves that he is both sentient and sapient beyond a shadow of a doubt.

I'm very familiar now with both Bastet's and Kalanthia's telepathic communication. Bastet does not communicate in words at all. She has no true understanding of language and instead sends images, emotions, and sense memories. It's me that has to put the effort in to translate all of that to words when needed.

Kalanthia, on the other hand, has a much more sophisticated telepathic communication, though I've come to feel the limits of it more as time goes on. I had a suspicion that Kalanthia's telepathy was actually just a much more advanced version of Bastet's, and this communication from the lizard-person confirms it.

Instead of using words as a human would do, Kalanthia instead projects extremely focused thoughts, images, and emotions that say exactly what she wants to say and nothing more. My mind then interprets these as words because that's the way my mind works. I've been brainwashed into using language since I was in nappies; it's not going to change now.

Unlike my two animal friends, the lizard-person is communicating in words directly. There is none of the blurred touch of image or emotion that happens with Bastet or even slightly with Kalanthia. These communications are crystal clear. Of course, that's not to say he's using English, but I can feel the difference between him projecting his thoughts in words compared to Bastet or Kalanthia.

It's startling enough that I almost lose ground again, though I shouldn't really be so surprised. All the other hallmarks of civilization were there in the weapons, buildings, and adornments; why wouldn't language be present too? It's still a shock. Hopefully, that will make convincing him easier.

I can tell that it would still be very difficult to lie in this space, perhaps impossible. Although he's using words, I can still feel his emotions—the anger, confusion, and fear that are fighting inside him. If his emotions start telling a different story from his words, I'll know he's lying. If he can feel the same in me, he'll realize when I'm being sincere.

He'll also feel exactly how angry and determined I am, how I'm *going* to get Lathani back no matter what I have to do. As long as I'm not too late already. The thought centers me, fills me with a grim certainty. My eyes narrow at the lizard-man in front of me, and the pressure holding us apart feels ever so slightly less intense.

I'm doing this because your people attacked two beings very special to me and took one away with you, I snap at him. Just because we're communicating with words doesn't impede me from also using images. I send an image of Kalanthia as I left her and Lathani as I saw her last. I don't even try to divorce my emotions from the images.

The lizard-man's crest of dark-red spikes loses color and wilts. I feel fear overtake the anger in his emotions.

You are allied with the Great Predator, he replies, his projected words weak and whispery. *Is it with you? I thought it was dead!*

If by "it," you mean the mother of the cub you stole, she's not with me, I tell him grimly, feeling the relief fill him. *She sent me ahead. If I do not succeed in bringing her cub back, I strongly suspect that she'll come seeking answers herself.* The relief turns once more into fear and he projects, I think accidentally, the memory of finding another member of the tribe torn to pieces, their remains more than half eaten. The image shocks me out of my own anger a little. Here I was thinking that the lizard folk had driven Kalanthia out of her territory. And maybe they did, but maybe it wasn't completely unprovoked . . .

The images themselves are as sobering as coming across the pack of raptorcats torn apart by her was, and for a reason I still haven't worked up the courage to ask her. Seeing the aftereffects of one of her attacks on the lizard folk is a reminder to me that I don't want to get on her bad side. It renews and strengthens my determination to succeed here in this space—as if I needed any further encouragement.

Perhaps it's just due to my state of mind, but the pressure pushing against me once more seems just a little less forceful. *Why did you take the cub, and is she still alive?* I demand. Maybe even a failure here in the Battle of Wills could be worth it if I could at least get some information on Lathani.

Why should I tell you? The lizard-man's response is obstinate, his fear turning into angry stubbornness. I feel my own emotions rise once more to match it. The fact is that even if Kalanthia *did* attack the lizard folk first, they didn't kill her; they took Lathani, who's an innocent in all this. And I highly doubt that it was for any benevolent reasons. So how dare he feel angry that the consequences have come home to roost? *I can feel what you are doing. You seek to oppress me, to chain me far more successfully than your pitiful vine bindings could ever do.*

Funny—those "pitiful" bindings were enough to take you down, I retort. *You realize that even if you win this, you'll still have to fight your way out past my companion and me?* I'm bluffing a little as I know I'll be hit by a vulnerable condition for a few seconds after the battle, but I reckon that Bastet will easily be equal to the task of occupying a disorientated lizard-man for that time. Then the two of us together should be up to taking him down. Hopefully, he can't feel the uncertainty through my emotions. Either way, he's silent for a short while.

The lack of provocation allows me to calm down a bit, something sorely needed. I must remember that now is not the time to allow my emotions free rein. For all that I'm angry about what happened to my . . . friends while I was gone and worried about what's happening to Lathani now, the most efficient way of getting her out is still to convince this lizard-person—or another—to help me. Forcing a Dominate on him would be better than nothing, but, principles aside, it would be better if he agreed to help me—he will know better than I what information I will need.

I take a deep breath to force myself to calm down a little more. I decide to try a bit of negotiation.

Look, I don't want to kill you, I tell him as I focus not on my anger at the situation, but on the fact that if I kill him, I'll have potentially lost a way to get to Lathani. *I don't even want to force you into a Bond with me if you're completely against it. First, I want information about the cub, and then, if she's still alive, I need to get her out of there. Believe me, it's in your interest to cooperate.*

Really, the lizard-man scoffs.

Yes, really, I say completely honestly as I hit on a tactic that might actually work. I genuinely think that Kalanthia's going to want blood for this, especially if Lathani is killed. And frankly, in that case, I'd be willing to help her. *If you give me information now, but you don't agree to help me otherwise, I promise we will not kill you immediately. If the cub's alive, we'll keep you tied up until it's all sorted out.*

And if she's dead? His tone gives nothing away, nor do his emotions—the fear and anger are still very prevalent and could mean anything. At the same time, they've calmed down a little, and the beginnings of curiosity are growing in him.

If she's dead, I think that's the worst possibility for all of us. Kalanthia, the Great Predator, isn't going to be happy to know that her beloved cub is dead. She's most likely going to take that out on everyone around—especially those who killed Lathani.

Then we are doomed either way, he says finally, his mental voice full of despair, the façade of anger falling away to reveal the deep fear beneath.

What do you mean? I ask, curiosity cutting through my own emotions.

If we keep the cub, we are doomed when the Great Predator comes to seek it out. If we kill it, we are doomed when the Great Predator decides to destroy us for our actions. However, if we give it up to you, we are doomed all the same.

Lathani's alive! *Why would you be doomed if you give Lathani to me?* A good portion of the fight has gone out of the lizard-man, and I find myself taking significantly larger steps forwards, indeed even arriving within arm's length of the creature himself, if I could reach out my arm. And if I did, I sense that it would push through his final resistance and form the Bond forcibly, without consent.

But I don't do that. I'm not going to do that. Not just because of principles, but also because I'm curious about what he will say.

There was a reason we dared the wrath of the Great Predator, that we sought to kill it and steal away its cub.

Tell me, I order softly. I don't have any true power over this lizard-man, not without a Bond in place, but I can tell that he has very little resistance to offer me now.

Do you know of the forest that has grown up above us on the mountain side? he asks, a hint of defeat in his voice.

You mean the, uh—here I hesitate, trying to remember what the quest message had called them. Suffocator? No. Ah, I remember. *The vine-strangler trees? The trees that move and trap creatures?*

Yes, the lizard-man acknowledges. *Those. They have grown significantly in a short space of time and are beginning to threaten even our closest hunting grounds. It won't be another great cycle before they reach our village itself, and several of our number have already been lost to them. When he realized the threat, our leader sent some Warriors to destroy them—none came back. A second set were sent; only one returned to tell of his experiences. It is from him that we know of the trees that trap and kill.*

They were rather tricky to come through, I agree, thinking back to my own experience with those damn trees. If it wasn't for my ability to use fire, Bastet and I would be tree food now. I'm a little surprised that the lizard folk have had so little success with them considering how powerful they seem to be.

You made it through the Forest of Death? The lizard-man seems rather surprised, the emotion temporarily overtaking the others emanating from him. It also seems like he, at least, likes his drama—this is the second overly dramatic name I've heard from him.

I did, I confirm, but add no more. It's just occurred to me that possibly the difference between my success and their failure may lie more in the torch I bore rather than any higher skill on my part. Is it arrogant of me to think that perhaps they haven't yet discovered fire? Still, whether they have or haven't, I don't want to give potential valuable information to creatures that are currently my enemies.

The anger and fear in the lizard-man's aura has mostly gone by this point. It's been replaced by something that feels like a mixture of determination and tentative hope.

Do you know of a way to combat the traps of the predator trees? The question is direct and straightforward. My answer, however, is less so.

Possibly, I admit, not wanting to commit too fervently.

If you will swear to remove the threat of the trees from our upper-side border, I will serve you willingly. My eyebrows shoot up in surprise. Now that I wasn't expecting.

So easily?

Is the task of defeating the Forest of Death so easy? True. In addition, I'm not exactly inclined to *help* the lizard folk after what they did. But I do already have a quest to find the cause of the vine-stranglers' growth. Perhaps it won't be that much of a jump between finding the cause and eliminating it . . .

I will not be doing anything to help your tribe until Lathani is safe, I warn him. The feeling I get back from that is acceptance.

If you follow through with your promise, we will not need the cub, and so her loss will only positively impact the village, he replies with equanimity. I frown.

What do you mean by that?

Pathwalker Shaman determined that the Forest of Death is a great threat to us. She also decreed that we would need a Great Protector to combat it. I heard her talking with my master, our herbalist. They decided that the spirit of the cub of the Great Predator would be sufficient to the task.

The spirit *of the cub,* I repeat as a feeling of horror grows within me.

Indeed. We do not have your abilities to subdue our enemies in life, but Honored Shaman has some power to convince and command the dead. I do not understand the process, but she has said that by feeding the cub certain herbal concoctions while alive, she will be able to eke out more power from its spirit and make up for the fact that it is but a cub and not fully grown. My master asked whether it was not better to compel the spirit of the Great Predator itself, but Shaman was uncertain whether or not she would be able to direct it even after death.

The sheer casualness that the lizard-man uses when talking about the whole idea of killing Lathani and then enslaving her spirit is chilling and puts my own moral dilemmas in a comparatively better light. At least when I Dominate creatures, the Bond is broken by death. I'd never seen that as a *good* thing, but suddenly I do.

I'm seized by the almost undeniable savage urge to just push forwards and crush his own spirit the way he is so clearly comfortable with the idea of crushing Lathani's. I hold myself back by a force of will even greater than what it would take to just press on and complete this battle. If I force this lizard-man to Bond to me simply because his people want to enslave Lathani's spirit, which hopefully hasn't happened yet, then what does that make me? How can I claim to hold the moral high ground in that case?

No, I've got to be better than that. Which starts here and now by completing this negotiation with words rather than with a flex of Willpower and disgust. I have to remember that decisions made in anger are usually followed by remorse when calm. Still, it takes all my effort to stop myself from lashing out.

I see, I reply evenly instead, though I know that he can feel the boiling anger in me by the way his own aura flinches and his fear reappears as a sourness I can sense. Trying to take the mental equivalent of a few deep breaths again, I forcibly calm myself down a bit. Our time together is coming to a close, decision made or not.

It's an odd feeling: the space around us is always amorphous, but it's slowly gaining solidity to my senses, like fog that's being burned away by the sun. The pressure pushing at me from the lizard-man has become but the barest trickle—no impediment. At the same time, the pressure from the environment has only increased throughout our conversation. I can feel my mental energy flagging, like I've been through three difficult exams back-to-back. I think that's probably the reason for the Skill starting to disintegrate, though I've never been within it this long before.

While interesting, it does mean we need to come to a conclusion. Knowing what I now do about their plans, I am even more convinced that I need to get Lathani out of that place *yesterday*. As I start to speak, I'm pretty sure my determination is as clearly detectable to the lizard-man as my anger was earlier.

Here's my offer: You accept my Bond and help me successfully get Lathani out alive. If you succeed, I will then do my best to help you and your tribe solve your vine-strangler tree problem. Deal?

The lizard-man takes a moment to consider the ramifications of my proposed deal. I don't blame him, but I can't help but feel impatient and not keen on him taking too much time.

And what if you cannot help? It's a fair question, but due to the time limit, it does nothing but irritate me. I take a long deep breath again—after keeping it throughout our discussion, losing my temper *now* would only be counterproductive. Negotiations 101: it's often the one who keeps the coolest head who ultimately wins.

If I cannot help in the end, I will release you, and you will be free to help your tribe try other possible solutions. Like Kalanthia probably wiping them all out so that they don't have to worry about vine-stranglers or anything else. See how they like trying to kill and enslave innocent baby nundas *then*.

But this is *our solution*, he points out. *If I help you retrieve the cub, and you then fail to eliminate the threat, we will be left worse off than before, with no solution and less time before it engulfs us.*

Listen, I tell him, bringing all my resolve and fury to bear. *You came to my friend's home, hurt her, stole her cub, and are now planning on torturing, killing,* and *enslaving her. Believe me*, I say as I reenergize the scraps of Willpower that remain in me through sheer determination and focus my full will on him, *that I will be getting Lathani out of there. I'm already offering you a deal instead of just forcing you because I don't want to stoop to your level. If I have to do it without your help, I will. Even if that means going through your tribe one by one. And remember: even if I leave them alive, I'm willing to bet that the "Great Predator" won't if a hair is harmed on her cub's head. Are you willing to risk all of that when you have another option here?*

He quails a little, his aura weakening under my will, then calms. He is silent for a few moments, moments during which I feel the space around us tearing itself apart just that bit more. If the space is a fog bank, the sun is already visible and close to spearing through it.

Very well, he capitulates eventually. *I will throw my bones in with you and hope that you can achieve what the Warriors of my people cannot.*

CHAPTER THIRTEEN

The Control You Have

At the moment of his acceptance, the space finally completely ruptures. I'm dumped back into my body with the biggest headache I've ever had. Well, at least one of the top five. I close my eyes against the sunlight and even put my hand over my eyelids when just the light filtering through my skin is too much for the sensitive orbs.

"Ow," I moan. I'm not stuck in place like I was after I intentionally failed the Battle of Wills with the bird, but I'm certainly not feeling great. When I eventually manage to open my eyes without feeling like being sick, I notice that my health bar has actually decreased. My eyebrows shoot up in surprise, and I quickly check my status page.

Name: Markus Wolfe		Race: Human	Class: Tamer
Level: 3	Energy to next level: 37%	Energy absorption rate: 23u/hr	Energy towards debt: 4%
Intelligence	14	Mana: 140/140	
Wisdom	16	Mana regeneration rate: 400u/hr	
Willpower	19+3 (+20%)	Health regeneration rate: 22u/hr	
Constitution	15	Health: 134/150	
Strength	12	Stamina: 60/60	
Dexterity	13	Stamina regeneration rate: 130u/hr	
Class Skills: Dominate – Beginner 7 Tame – Beginner 4 Fade – Novice 9		Non-Class Skills: Lay-on-Hands – Initiate 3 Stealth – Beginner 9 Animal Empathy – Novice 4	

The first thing I notice is that, sure enough, my health points have actually taken a hit—apparently, pushing myself too hard in the Battle of Wills space can have a detrimental effect on my health. Just as well to know . . .

The second is that Dominate has increased. That's expected. That Tame has *also* increased again is not. Is it because of the way I'm conducting the Battle of Wills? Because, despite using the nonconsensual Skill, I'm still seeking willing agreement? Well, somewhat coerced willing agreement, anyway. Not that I care much about that right now. Maybe I will later, when Lathani is safe. Animal Empathy has gone up too.

I notice that I have a new message waiting for me in my message box. I click over to it and am unsurprised to see that I've earned a status point. After pushing my limits like I did there, I damn well should have.

> Congratulations!
> You have worked hard on your Willpower and have earned a point. Would you like to apply this to your status?
>
> Apply point / Refuse point

I willingly accept the point and check back on my status page to see how it's changed. To my delight, I see that I've now jumped from twenty-two points in Willpower to twenty-four; thanks to the twenty percent increase from Kalanthia's gift, I've received a two-for-one deal on points here. Definitely worth the sixteen percent of Energy it "costs."

That's probably the last of the points I can earn "naturally" in Willpower, though, now that it's reached the twenty-point threshold. I suppose I'd better be glad that the twenty percent bonus from Kalanthia obviously didn't count towards the threshold.

I dismiss my status screen and quickly channel Lay-on-Hands to help my health go back to normal. Most of the energy travels to my head, so I guess that's where the damage happened. Did I actually give myself brain damage?

Perhaps immediately coming from a successful Battle of Wills should mean that I have better things to do than go through my status screen and notifications, but I frankly needed a few moments to recoup. It was rather strenuous. Feeling up to the task now, though, I push myself to a sitting position and meet eyes with my new Bound.

The lizard-man is staring at me, still wrapped in my bark-fiber cord. Unlike before, his eyes aren't filled with rage and fear, though there is still some trepidation present. I can feel the Bond between us: it's thicker than any other I've formed so far, though it's not as . . . dense as the one with Bastet. Is dense the right word? All I can say is that if the Bonds were boxes of files, the lizard-man's would be the A3 one that's empty, while Bastet's would be only A4, but packed full.

I have no idea how to start communicating with him. I've never had such a contentious Battle of Wills, nor one with a being able to discuss abstract matters, things such as enslaving souls after death in order to protect a group of lizard folk from the encroaching threat of a forest of killer trees. And if *that* thought didn't prove I'm on a different world, nothing will.

"Hi," I say eventually, then curse at myself mentally for such a dumb start. I've engaged in a deep mind to mind—or soul to soul—communion with this creature, threatened him and his family, coerced his help, and "Hi" is the best I can come up with? "How are you feeling?" I ask quickly.

As an attempt to cover up my awkwardness it fails rather miserably. I suddenly itch to get moving—Lathani's in terrible danger and here I am trying to work out what small talk to use with my new Bound. I push myself to my feet abruptly and only consider as I start pacing that perhaps the lizard-man won't actually understand anything anyway. My words, I mean—he should be able to understand the impression of my thoughts in the same way Bastet does.

I admit I am feeling a little . . . out of sorts, the lizard-man responds cautiously, answering the question of whether he can understand me. It's odd, though. Perhaps this is what he experiences when I talk, but he's not speaking English. Actually, it would have been far stranger if he suddenly *had* started speaking English with a full-on British accent.

What he's using to communicate is not even something that I would have recognized as a language had I just heard it randomly. He snaps his jaws together, clicks his teeth, grunts deeply in his throat, and uses the crest on his head to flash different colors—yes, he apparently has color-changing spikes. However, I guess due to the Bond, the various signals are interpreted by my mind as English words.

Suddenly, I wonder what would happen if I couldn't see him and his colorful spikes. Would it impede my understanding or not? What if I couldn't hear the vocalizations? That could be a problem if we have to rescue Lathani under the cover of darkness or we get separated during the attempt. Then again, maybe it wouldn't make any difference; I'm getting the meaning of his words across the Bond rather than the visual and audio cues, after all. For now, though, I'm just glad that we're able to communicate with more ease than I experience even with Bastet. It should make planning Lathani's rescue significantly easier.

"Disorientated?" I ask.

A little, he admits. *It feels very . . . strange to have my core values overlaid by the desire to obey and protect you.* Huh. The first time Dominating a creature that is all too clearly sapient was bound to be a thought-provoking experience, but his very first words are already causing guilt to pool in my stomach.

I push them aside as much as I did my earlier questions; we have more important things to do. And I mustn't forget that he was at least party to the idea of killing and enslaving an innocent cub. Who I'm sure is also sentient and sapient, or at least could be so if her mother is any proof. That thought makes all remorse for my actions flee swiftly.

"I'll get those ropes off you," I say, then move towards him and match my words with efficient action. I'm not rough, but I don't try to be especially gentle either. "Do you have a name?" I ask shortly as I unwind the ropes. The lizard-man sits up and rubs at a few places where the cord dug in, managing to slip under his scales in a couple of spots.

I am called Runs-with-the-river. It was the first thing I did on my name-day,
according to my brood-mother, the lizard-man answers promptly. Then he hesitates.

"What?" I ask slightly suspiciously. Is he trying to hide something from me?

It is only . . . You do not want to name me yourself? he asks cautiously as he looks
up at me from his seated position. *It would advantage you—I sense it would tighten
the Bond between us and, subsequently, the control you have over it.*

I stare at him thoughtfully for a moment as I lean against a tree. *Why would he
volunteer information like that?* I wonder to myself. Logically, it would make more
sense for him to keep it to himself. Maybe this is a consequence of his "core values"
being "overlaid" by desires to obey and protect me—particularly the latter since a
stronger Bond means less danger to me. Or perhaps he's trying to show himself as
being obedient or acting in good faith according to our agreement? But then, if
that's the case, is he *actually* acting in good faith, or is he just *pretending* to do so to
gain my trust?

And then there is the question itself. Turning the new information over in my
mind, I have to admit that it makes a certain amount of sense—and holds some
attraction. I wondered at the time whether giving Spike his name had made a difference; it appears that it did. Bastet too, probably. Here, though . . .

It may be more advantageous to tighten my control over this new member of
our group in any way I can, but . . . a name is an important part of us. Nothing
makes us react as quickly as hearing our name does. It's part of our personality, and
renaming this lizard-man just because I can feels . . . wrong. I wouldn't want someone to come along and decide that my name should be Kevin; my parents named
me Markus, and that's what I'll stay. Same for this guy.

"I don't want to take your identity from you and replace it with another," I say
finally. "If you hadn't had a name, I would have given one to you, but since you
already do, I won't take that from you." It's hard to tell how the lizard-man feels
about that—I can't read his expression. "That said," I continue, "Runs-with-the-
river is a bit of a mouthful. Do you mind if I shorten it to River?"

Well, it's a mouthful in English at least; who knows how he says it in his language—
it might just be two teeth clicks and a grunt for him. Although I've tried to pay a little
attention to how he actually says things rather than just what I'm interpreting, I'm
completely lost.

Being a language that's developed completely independently from any Earth
one, it is likely to have completely different rules from anything even vaguely familiar. Heck, it may not even have recognizable words or syntax that conforms in any
way to Earth languages. And that's not even taking into account the physiological
differences between a humanoid crocodilian and a human.

River, he muses. *Yes, very well. Symbolic in many ways. I am not the same under
your rule as I was before, but I have not entirely been made anew.* That . . . wasn't
exactly what I was intending, but I'm not going to argue. He's a lot more verbose
in person than he was in our Battle of Wills. Again, that raises more questions. Is

it because of the nature of communicating through thoughts and emotions, or is it more to do with the context of the conversation? But those are questions for later. There's a more pressing situation right now.

"Okay, great. So, River, tell me everything about Lathani's situation," I order him grimly. "I need to know where she's being kept, what condition she is in, who's caring for her, what's being done to her to prepare her for your shaman's . . . thing. Everything."

My foot catches in a tree root, and I almost trip; the hobbling vine wrapped around my ankles is not helping me keep my balance in the slightest. I take several stumbled steps that threaten to have me on the ground at any moment.

Keep moving, I hear growled from in front of me as a clawed paw pulls at the vine around my neck. The binding around my wrists bites into my skin as I automatically try to balance myself with my arms. Unfortunately, with them tied behind me, that's not possible. I regain my balance only to almost tumble again as another hard pull tugs at my neck.

For what feels like the umpteenth time in the last twenty minutes or so, I touch the Bond between me and River to ensure that it's there. He's the one dragging me along by the neck, his actions rough only to sell the fiction. Or what I *hope* is fiction, at least.

I comfort myself with the thought that even if River actually betrays me, Bastet is staying close enough to us to swoop in and help me if it becomes necessary. I can feel her presence through our own Bond, though I don't even catch a hint of where she might be with any other sense. She's got the cubs with her since there was no way I would let them get caught up in all this with me and there was no safe place to leave them. Fortunately, we're not moving fast—my bindings ensure our slow pace.

After finding out all the details I could from River about Lathani, we came up with this plan. Well, I did. Needless to say, none of us liked it. At least, neither Bastet nor I liked it. River is a mess of contradictory emotions, even now; that's one reason I'm finding it difficult to completely trust him.

At the same time, I *know* that if worse came to worst, I could order him to do something and he would be forced to obey. Even if I was gagged for some reason, I could order him through the Bond. We tested it just to make sure. I have to hope that that's enough of a safety net because I'm genuinely going into the hornets' nest here—or a congregation of crocodiles, rather.

While perhaps the most sensible thing would have been to let River carry out the whole of the rescue, I couldn't bring myself to agree to that. I don't know him; a Battle of Wills doesn't exactly grant me the knowledge of a person that years of acquaintance gives.

Even if I disregard the possibility of betrayal, of him acting against my orders in a way that I'm unable to refute because I'm not present, I don't know how competent he is. He could be a complete dunce, only so easy to capture because he was already prone to falling over his own feet. Or claws, or whatever. I'm not putting Lathani's life in his hands any more than I absolutely have to.

Sending him in for more information occurred to me, but then I wondered how more information would help. I already have a Bond with one of the three who have definitely been involved in Lathani's ongoing imprisonment captivity. Lady Luck was clearly on my side in that. I also considered trying to Bind more lizard folk, but in the end decided that it was too risky.

The more I attack, the more likely it is that one will get away and raise the alarm. Though River couldn't give me a head count of the whole village, it's definitely more than I want descending on me in force. If I'm captured, Lathani is lost. Unless Kalanthia recovers in time and comes to get her cub herself.

But I can't rely on that. No, even if it means me putting myself in more danger, I'm willing to accept that risk if it increases the likelihood of us successfully rescuing Kalanthia's cub. To that end, I allowed River to wrap quickly woven vine fetters around my wrists, ankles, and neck. At his suggestion, I also gave him my only remaining spear, my mace, and a roughly crafted pot, which I'm not using for anything.

I tucked my bow and arrows away in my Inventory along with everything else, including my armor. While it might seem counterintuitive to go into a dangerous situation without the protection of my armor, I don't want to risk it being taken from me and then not being able to retrieve it when escaping with Lathani.

The reason why I let him take any weapons at all was the whole basis of the plan. He recognized their form and function, but the construction of both the flint head of the spear and the pitch holding the stone in place at the head of the mace were completely unfamiliar to him. He assured me that the other members of his tribe would be as curious as he was—the crafting-focused ones even more so. Enough, at least, to consider my survival more beneficial when compared to the nourishment my corpse would offer the village.

According to him, it's happened before when the tribe has managed to catch a sapient being who presents the opportunity to learn new crafting. Sometimes this has been another lizard-kin from a rival tribe; sometimes it's been another creature entirely. In each case, either the leaders of River's tribe learned what they could from the being and then killed them, or they kept the being in servitude to craft for them if it was something they couldn't learn for themselves. I guess I should have expected that kind of behavior from a race who would steal a cub, feed her herbal concoctions, and then plan to kill her and enslave her spirit.

As a result, the plan is simple but still fraught with danger: Allow myself to be "captured" and enter the village that way. Hope that the curiosity about me and about the weapons keeps me alive for at least a night and allows River to work behind the scenes to free Lathani. Then, as soon as possible, get the hell out of Dodge. It's a fairly bare-bones plan, but there are too many factors to account for to plan for everything.

So far, the guards we've encountered along the route have let us pass with a couple of grunts. Hopefully, that's because they believe our story, not because they know that we've got no chance of doing anything anyway.

After stumbling through partially worn tracks, which still manage to have enough ground cover to threaten to trip me every couple of minutes, we make it onto something a little easier for me.

We seem to have reached some sort of path. The ground has been worn down to bare earth and the littering branches have been cleared by the passage of many feet over time. My balance now easier to keep, I raise my head to look at more than just my next step. My eyes narrow as I see the mostly camouflaged huts ahead of me.

Showtime.

CHAPTER FOURTEEN

Guarded

It's different from what I expected. I suppose that's inevitable; I'd seen almost the whole area through Bastet's eyes, but I'd assumed that it was a bit like watching a video taken by someone else. I was wrong.

Due to her size, some of my estimates were way off: the huts are smaller than I thought and the lizard folk themselves also generally a bit shorter, though with some glaring exceptions. Then there are the things that she hadn't noticed. Like the fence.

For me, it sticks right out, a clear divergence from the natural growth of the forest. Bastet didn't even see it. Or if she did see it, she didn't notice enough about it for it to stand out in her memory of scouting the place. There are also more huts than she had seen or noticed.

I return my attention to the fence as I realize that it potentially presents a complication in my plan if it goes all the way around. The fence itself isn't massive, reaching perhaps a little above my waist. Still, it's like the big brother of the trap I created for the lizogs: sharpened stakes stuck in the ground and pointing outwards. Other sticks are braced against them in X shapes to create another barrier as well as strengthen the leaning stakes against whatever dares to charge them.

There's an entrance through the fence centered on the worn path we're walking. Well, in my case, shuffling. On either side of the gate are two guards. Unlike the rest of the lizard folk we've seen, who seem to be a bit smaller than I'd estimated through Bastet's eyes, these ones are bigger. By a fair bit.

I'd estimated that the tallest lizard-kin was a bit shorter than me; these are taller, even if not by much. They're not skinny, either. Though not body-builder buff, these guys still look like they could wrestle with that mini triceratops Bastet and I encountered on the way down—and win. And that's just looking at their muscles and ignoring the sharp-looking claws on the ends of their digits and the long jaws full of sharp teeth that extend from their skulls. My stomach drops just a bit, and I feel sweat bead on my temple. Maybe this wasn't such a good idea . . .

There's no way I can vocally communicate with River right now . . . but maybe that's not a problem. It's not like we're really communicating with sounds anyway—it's the Bond that does all the translation for us. I've sent messages to Bastet without needing to speak; surely it would be even easier with someone who's actually used to speaking with words.

It takes some concentration, but I've had a bit of practice at sending my thoughts to others ever since coming to this world. I'm unable to stop my nerves from making my hands shake a little. It might help if I focus on the escape plan for a bit.

River, are you sure we can get out of this? I ask him. I know he's received the message first from the surprise and then the acknowledgment that emanates from his side of the Bond, and also the small automatic turn of his head towards me.

He disguises his movement with a rough tug on the vine to make me stumble and another growled order to move faster. At least, I *hope* it's meant as a deception for the guards up ahead. Then again, it may be his revenge for how I tied him up and carried him around like a sack of potatoes.

I believe we have a good chance. He hesitates. *Do you want me to turn around now?*

I steel myself. We can't back out now. The guards on the path have clearly noticed us. If River suddenly diverts away into the forest with a captive, then returns with no captive, there will be questions asked. No, I've got to own up to my lack of asking the right sorts of questions and deal with the consequences.

No. It's fine. How far does the fence extend around the village?

There are four exits to the fence, though this is the biggest, comes the answer a moment later. He is physically silent, though I notice colors playing over his spikes still. His mental tone is a bit nervous, a bit uncertain, but with the sense of trying to stay forcibly calm. Hopefully, the nerves are because he's worried about whether our plan will work or not, rather than about how I'll react when he betrays me . . .

Are there guards like this on the other exits? I ask. Really, we should have worked this out before, but I hadn't realized that there was a fence, and River didn't mention it. Most of our attention was spent on working out how to get in and get Lathani free. The escape plan was pretty much just that—escape.

For a moment, I despair. How could *I* be the guy Nicholas was sent to recruit? Wouldn't someone who has more fighting experience be a better choice? Like an ex-military person or Bear Grylls or *anyone* other than a recently fired HR paper pusher? Surely, *they* would have made sure that the exit strategy was clear before committing to the plan?

A moment later, I take a deep breath and force myself away from that train of thought. Lathani is counting on me. *Kalanthia* is counting on me. I won't fail someone else I care about. Not again.

The two big exits are guarded, River informs me. *The other two exits are small— only a single person can travel through them at a time. They are also kept barred when not in use.*

How long does it take to unbar them? And how often are they checked? I ask, my mind racing.

It takes little time to unbar them. They are merely small structures of wooden stakes, which are moved out of the gap and then back into it. They are not checked, exactly, but anyone noticing an unbarred gate would likely re-bar it and then check with the brood-mothers as to whether any of their charges had gone missing.

So, the alarm would be raised, I muse mostly to myself, though maybe projecting it accidentally to River in the process. Any response he might have made is interrupted as we draw abreast of the first gate. The guards there start talking to him, but I immediately realize that I can't understand any of it. It's all just flashing colors, body language that includes their tails, and short sounds made by their mouths. Clearly, it's only my Bond with River that allows me to understand *him.*

The Bond . . . I risk taking a moment to pay less attention to the world around me and try to focus on the connection I have with the lizard-man in front of me. I've used the Bond to communicate with him; I've used it to get a sense of his emotional state. Now, can I use it to gain an understanding of his language?

It takes a few long moments before I get something, and what I succeed in doing is not exactly what I was intending, but that's okay—what I manage to do is good enough. Hopefully.

I don't tap into River's understanding of his own language, but I *do* get access to his understanding of what he's just heard. Then, probably thanks to the Bond, his understanding translates into words for me. I "tune" into his conversation with the guards just as it's ending.

. . . take it to the Pathwalkers. They'll give you further instructions.

Oh joy, more uncertainty. I'd like to dig into the rest of the conversation River had with the guards, but I don't know how. Or even if I should. Because that feels a bit too much like nonconsensual mind reading to me.

What I'm doing right now is probably skirting the edge a bit, but I can soothe my own conscience by telling myself that it's no worse than using a translation app. Digging into his memories without him sending them to me is an invasion of privacy, which might be crossing a line I should leave alone. If I can even do it, anyway.

Asking him to share his memories voluntarily or to tell me what he discussed with them is pointless: if I can't trust him to keep to his word to serve me willingly, I can't trust him to tell me truthfully what he was discussing. Or send me accurate memories. No, I'm just going to have to trust him . . . much as that leaves me feeling like I'm walking to the gallows while hoping that it's just a strangely shaped tree.

I just start shuffling forwards again as River tugs at the vine rope, and we move towards the huts. I focus on my surroundings, trying to take in as many of the details as I can. It's interesting how much this settlement resembles small tribal villages I've seen in pictures.

Most of the huts are round and made out of mud, their tops covered with leaves. They aren't tall, but the glimpse I get through one of the open doorways hints that they are partially dug into the ground. Unlike a building back on Earth, the entrance to the huts is not right down on ground level. Instead, it seems like they crawl through a space at about waist height, just below the level of the leaf roofing.

Is it because of floods? Or a leftover from whatever they evolved from? Either way, there are a lot of huts. At least thirty that I can see in just this small space and probably plenty more that I can't. That's what the sound I can hear from elsewhere in the village indicates, anyway.

The odd hut here or there is made entirely of mud with only a small entrance at the very top. I only know that there's an entrance because I see a lizard-kin climbing out of one. Once it's out, it moves a sort of capstone into place, which sits almost flush with the rest of the construction. Now that I know what to look for, I can see these types of seals on several other buildings.

Although these facts are interesting to note, they do present a bit of a problem: getting in and out of a building clearly isn't something that can be done as quickly as dashing through a doorway. If River or I get caught inside one of these, we could be trapped very easily. Then again, mud walls . . . Possibly, we could get out by *making* a doorway. Better not to rely on that, though—who knows what kind of reinforcements are present inside the hardened earth of the walls?

Lizard folk are everywhere, too many to count. There are few the same size as the ones at the gate, thankfully. Most seem to be fairly similar to River, though I can't say I notice any clear differences that could denote male or female. None of them wear any sort of covering to hide genitals; they don't need to, because there *aren't* any. Or not visible ones, anyway.

The only other clearly differentiated group are the ones we're walking towards. They're all smaller and slimmer than River; interestingly enough, they also seem to wear the most adornments. Is that an indication that they're female or that they're important?

Probably the latter, I decide as we stop in front the group of seven lizard folk, all of them wearing at least five woven adornments. Three of them even sport stereotypical claw or tooth necklaces, giving them a savage air. Not that such an adornment is even necessary considering their sharp-toothed jaws, bronze eyes with slit pupils, and clawed paws and feet. They are crouched around a carcass, casually ripping pieces off the still-bleeding corpse. My eyes track the movement as I watch them use their claws to tear off strips of meat, toss them into their mouths, and flick their jaws up to gulp the raw meat down.

I suddenly realize what I *haven't* seen any evidence of: fires. There are no firepits, fireplaces, campfires, torches, or bonfires. I could argue that maybe the fires are only lit at night, but there is no sign of even the existence of a fire—no charred or blackened ground or branches.

Is my suspicion from earlier right? Can the lizard folk really not have discovered fire yet? Of course, there could be another explanation. Maybe their biology means that raw meat is more nutritious than cooked, so fires are reserved for crafting or religious rites or something and are kept out of sight.

I push the thoughts out of my head; they may be important later, but right now I'm in front of a group of carnivorous lizard folk, all staring at me, and I really ought to pay attention.

CHAPTER FIFTEEN

Trapped

We come to a stop. In preparation for the communication that's surely about to happen, I repeat my translation strategy. Now having more of an idea of what I'm doing, the process is a lot shorter. This time I manage to tune in before much of the conversation has elapsed. River is speaking, perhaps in response to a question one of the lizard folk in front of us has asked.

. . . when I was searching for the herbs my master sent me out for. I saw its curiously crafted weaponry and thought it might be useful to you, Honored Pathwalkers. The Pathwalkers, whatever that means, are clearly interested—clearly to River, that is, though even I would be able to interpret their body language as them paying attention. The fact that they appear to be eyeing me hungrily isn't reassuring, but according to the interpretation in River's mind, that's just interest rather than a desire for me to replace the carcass they're crouched around.

One of the slim humanoid crocodiles stands up and looks at me as it twists its head slightly from side to side. I realize that it must be to get a better look at me; the lizard folk *do* have binocular vision, but their eyes are more set to the sides of their faces than mine are. Their binocular vision may not be as acute as mine.

It's a curious prey-beast, the lizard-kin says as it turns back to its brethren. *I have not seen its like before. Have any of you?*

Most of the others now straighten and come to inspect me. Two actually touch me: one using a clawed paw to prod at my cheek and then feel my hair; the other squeezing me in several places, fortunately avoiding the area I would most assuredly *not* want those claws anywhere near. I seethe with outrage at being handled like a piece of meat but manage to push it down and settle for balling my fists until my knuckles whiten and clenching my jaws until my teeth almost crack.

The vine fetters are not much of an obstacle, really. I could have probably broken them with a bit of straining when I arrived here as a baseline human; all the extra Strength that I've gained means that I almost have to put effort into *not* breaking them. However, fighting back right now is likely to get me hurt or killed, not to mention put them on the alert. For my plan to work, they need to see me as a curiosity, not a threat.

Apparently, the consensus is that none of them has seen one such as me before. Big surprise, since I'm apparently the only human on this wretched world. After deciding that, they seem to lose some interest in me personally and move to look at the items River "took" from me. These attract a lot more attention, and several wordless exclamations rise from those poking and prodding at the tools. One of the lizard folk turns around to speak to River.

You have done well, young Runs-with-the-river. Put the prey-beast in the cage and stay here for now. We will decide how to reward you after we have properly investigated these new crafts.

Yes, Honored Weaver, River says as he raises his chin high in the air for a moment. Perhaps it's their version of a bow—that would certainly match the respectful feeling that drifts over the Bond as he does it. The Pathwalker turns back to the huddle and the group momentarily ignores us both.

River hesitates as he looks between me and the cage. I follow his gaze and swallow dryly. It's small, clearly designed for creatures half my size. It's bigger than the average dog crate, though not by much—I'll be rather squashed. My mind races. Can we do something now? The Pathwalkers are distracted by the items I made, after all.

I shake my head involuntarily as I decide against the plan. The Pathwalkers may be distracted, but what about all the other lizard folk around here? They're unlikely to look away as one of their own and a strange, unknown creature start raiding their huts and then trying to escape.

No, we need to wait until the area is clearer, probably until nightfall, maybe even later. Unless the lizard folk decide to kill me. Then all bets are off and we'll have to fight our way out. At least, I hope it would be *we,* not just *I.*

Do it, I tell River grimly as I try to psyche myself up for getting crammed in a too-small space, which will completely remove all possibility of defending myself from the group of carnivores surrounding me.

But—

The longer we hesitate, the more suspicious we look, I snap back at him, interrupting whatever argument he might have. I force myself to calm down; it's not River's fault I'm particularly sensitive to enclosed spaces after my spelunking experience. Though, it's kind of his fault that I'm here at all, if only indirectly.

Still, none of that is useful right now. *Unless you have an idea that* doesn't *end up with us fighting half or more of this village?* I manage to ask reasonably neutrally. He hesitates for a moment longer, then starts moving towards the cage, pulling at my neck with the vine, though more gently than before.

No, I don't, he admits glumly. *There are too many others around,* he adds, echoing my own thoughts. We reach the cage and River moves behind me. I brace myself and prepare to be pushed into it. He doesn't do that—not at first, anyway. Instead, I feel my wrists part as he slices through the binding holding them together. I quickly rub at the red marks and intentionally don't send healing magic to them; the fewer aces I reveal, the better, even when it appears that River is the only one watching.

The vine binding around my neck is the next to be cut through. River then puts a hand on my shoulder and, more gently than I was expecting, pushes me down and forwards. Breathing through the panic that rises as I start to crawl into the enclosed space, I feel him cutting through the hobble stopping my feet from moving too far apart. When I pull my legs in and start to shift into a hunched sitting position, I see him shut the door.

Closing my eyes, I battle with my fear. I hadn't realized how much my experience in the tunnel to the salt cavern had impacted me; claustrophobia has never been something I've particularly struggled with. Though, maybe this isn't just because of the small space, which isn't even remotely dark. It's also the feeling of intense vulnerability, unable to defend myself as I am, surrounded by enemies who could turn on me at any moment.

Idiot, I tell myself. *How is this any better than Plan A?* I'm having to trust River either way; at least trusting him to get Lathani out of here by himself would have meant I could wait with Bastet rather than in a *cage.*

I'm sorry, River says, sounding miserable.

For what? I ask, using the conversation to distract me from the impulse to just start clawing at everything I can reach and struggling against the cage until I burst free—and then having to fight the rest of the village without even getting to Lathani.

For this. I can feel your fear. I . . . I just want to get you out of there—out of here. You're not safe, and the knowledge tears at my insides.

Why do you care? I demand, my curiosity actually pushing away some of the panic. *We were enemies when the sun rose today. If I hadn't created the Bond with you, you'd have happily killed me*, I point out. There's a short pause before River responds.

I mentioned before about how my core values were overlaid, he says slowly, his own emotions in a tumult. *Once, my highest priority would have been following my master's commands and pleasing and protecting the Honored Pathwalkers. Now they have been replaced by you.* He hesitates a moment. *Or rather, you have taken a higher place in my priorities than them. To intentionally put you into a position like this . . .* He shakes his head and stops, but the maelstrom of feelings within him says more than his words could.

We lapse into silence as our conversation dies out. I allow myself the time to think through what River has just revealed. The Pathwalkers are communicating quietly enough that River can only pick up vague parts of their conversation from the colors flashing on their spikes. They're interested, curious, and excited, which, frankly, is as good as we could have hoped for at this moment in time. Other than that, there's not much to distract me from considering River's situation.

I suppose it makes sense. It's why Spike protected me all the way at the start from the black blob: his core drive to survive had been made secondary in importance to ensuring my survival. The same with Bastet. I've never felt even remotely unsafe with Bastet ever since she accepted my Bond, despite her having been part of a pack that had literally tried to kill and eat me not that long before. And this, clearly, is why: her core drive to work with and protect her pack was realigned to do the same with me.

River's situation seems different, though, and it takes me a few moments to work out why. A frown creeps onto my face as I dig more deeply into what my subconscious is telling me. At least it's distracting me from my panic about feeling trapped.

After some deep thought, during which I stop paying attention to the Pathwalkers, I think I've managed to hit on what feels different: sapience. Bastet is smart, there's no doubting that, but she's still an animal. She's driven by instinct rather than thought. While she can be surprisingly analytical at times, it's purely about how to best approach a situation, not whether she *should* approach it.

Take our first day together, for example. I was worrying that she would be upset about sharing space with the killer of her pack; she turned out to be worried that I was going to feed her and her cubs to said killer. At no point has she sought to get revenge for her pack. Even though she misses them and the bonds they had, she lives in the present, not the past. Her pack is dead, and we are her new pack.

I've come to realize that she sees me as the leader of her pack, nothing more nor less. The Bond is perhaps almost irrelevant: I suspect that as long as she sees me as the leader, she will continue acting in exactly the same way.

River is a different story, though. He's clearly a thinking being, as are the rest of his tribe. Perhaps I'm making too much comparison with humans, but if he's anything like we are, he's capable of overcoming base instinct and choosing to do something different. We might be driven to protect someone, but if we think that the situation in general will be better if we don't, we can choose not to. Is it the same for him? Probably—that's exactly what he's doing now; though, he *is* doing it at my insistence, which may make a difference. He's admitted that he's torn because, essentially, his drive to serve me is warring with his drive to protect me.

I can sense that he would still be compelled to obey to the letter if I gave him a clear instruction, but I'd rather avoid needing to order him to do every single thing. So far, he's been helpful, offering suggestions and taking the initiative. I don't want that to change, but what if being back here in the village makes him decide to go back on his word?

Just because he agreed to help me during our Battle of Wills in exchange for my help later doesn't mean he'll stick to it—humans are notorious for making promises that we don't later fulfil. And he himself has admitted that his desire to serve and protect the Pathwalkers isn't *gone*, it's just bumped down in his priorities.

I'm suddenly more certain that choosing to be part of the plan to rescue Lathani was the right thing to do, regardless of the risk to myself. After all, if River is capable of defying the Bond in any sort of way, then leaving the whole rescue plan in his . . . claws seems the height of stupidity. At least if he betrays me, I have options; if I'd left the rescue to him, I might have been stuck waiting for him to come to me while Lathani was being sacrificed ahead of schedule. Worst case scenario, sure, but it's serious enough that I wouldn't dare to risk it.

Well, I guess that if ever a situation were to be the crucible of our Bond, this is it. He's being directly confronted with the beings who have been his world for probably his whole life, and yet, he is having to operate according to my orders in opposition to them. I resign myself to hoping for the best—and preparing for the worst.

Which starts with working out how to get out of this cage without his help if I need to.

CHAPTER SIXTEEN

Motivation

At first glance, the cage appears to be a series of rough branches bound together, like I would do if I was trying to create a trap. However, closer examination proves that the branches are in fact *grown* together. The only weak spot of the cage is its door, and even that would prove difficult for most creatures to deal with, considering that the vine bindings acting as its hinge and latch are difficult to reach from inside the cage. Difficult to reach for a creature trying to use its own claws, that is. Fortunately, I have a knife.

It calms my panic down to know that I have a way out if necessary. And then when out, I've still got a number of decent weapons available to me.

I want to ask River about the cage's construction, but my thought is interrupted before I even properly form it. One of the Pathwalkers beckons River over and he obeys, albeit with a quick glance at me first. I dig back into my Bond with the lizard-man to make sure that I don't miss anything.

Tell us more of this prey-beast. Where did you find it? Were there any other items with it that were left at the site? Fortunately, we've already discussed what to say—the bare bones, at least.

It was resting near the river, my Bound starts. *I saw it using the bowl to drink water, and I was curious, as the bowl seemed to be made of earth and yet was clearly not falling to pieces.* There is a flurry of interest.

It is an Earth-Shaper, one of the Pathwalkers says, its spikes flashing triumphantly. *What an excellent find. We have missed our Earth-Shaper's skills since she passed.*

If it is an Earth-Shaper, why would the spear have such a construction? snaps another of the Pathwalkers. *It could have simply Shaped the head onto the shaft, rather than using . . . what it used.*

Then how did it succeed in Shaping the head at all? argues the first Pathwalker.

Sisters, a third slim lizard-kin interrupts. This one is the most ornately dressed, its neck barely visible for all the woven vine necklaces encircling it. Sisters . . . Maybe they're important *and* female, then. *We have already discussed this matter and come to no conclusion. Further conversation seems unlikely to yield a satisfactory answer without more evidence. Runs-with-the-river, please continue your story.*

Yes, Honored Shaman, River says as he lifts his chin again, higher than the last time. My focus narrows on the creature that has just been identified as the mastermind behind the plot to attack Kalanthia, steal Lathani, then kill her and enslave her soul. My fury, stoked even hotter because of my current feelings of impotence, rises within me, and the vine bindings creak as I unconsciously put pressure on the door. River darts a look back at me and concern flows over the link.

I probably only feel it because I'm still deeply within our Bond in order to understand the conversation, but his concern cuts through my rage. I push it back down, reminding myself that there is a time and place for it, and this is neither. River is speaking as I tune back into the conversation.

. . . so I thought that it would be better to capture the prey-beast rather than kill it and potentially lose important crafting secrets for the tribe.

You chose well, the shaman says again, her spikes rippling with color in a way that denotes pleasure. *Are you not proud of your apprentice, Herbalist?* This last is directed at another lizard-kin nearby.

I would be prouder if he had managed to gather the herbs I sent him out for, the herbalist grouses, though her crest is rippling with yellow and orange, revealing the lie to her words and indeed showing pride. *It seems your prey-beast gave you some trouble,* the herbalist continues, raising a clawed paw to gently trace one of the cuts on River's face. We'd decided that us both appearing pristine might arouse suspicion, so we intentionally gave each other a couple of marks, which were more show than anything else; nothing a quick Lay-on-Hands won't cure if they prove burdensome when we make our escape.

River shrugs the comment off with a flick of his tail.

Mere scratches, Master. The prey-beast came off worse.

Nothing that could impede its ability to replicate these items for us, I hope, another Pathwalker says pointedly.

I was careful to bear in mind the uses I suspected you would wish to put it to, Honored Wood-Shaper. It was surprisingly easy to subdue; it does not seem to have any natural weaponry of its own. No claws, blunt teeth . . . Once I separated it from its weaponry, it was practically helpless. I glare at River. That wasn't part of the script.

Whether I accidentally project that to the lizard-man or he picks up on my emotions through the Bond, I don't know, but a moment later he sends a wordless thought to me. It's an image of a Warrior approaching a small snake in the grass . . . only to be surprised by the fact that the small snake is actually the tail of a much larger and more dangerous beast.

I interpret that as something about underestimation being a good thing . . . Perhaps, though the knowledge that without my weapons I *am* pretty defenseless doesn't sit well. I suddenly wish I'd taken Stun as my level-one Skill. What use is Fade when I'm in a cage in the middle of a lizard folk's village?

Does it understand your words, Runs-with-the-river? asks the shaman as she looks at me curiously. I grit my teeth and glare at the lizard-kin, who is first on my "to kill when I get the chance" list. River hesitates, also looking at me.

Tell her no, I say, feeding him the answer silently through the Bond.

I do not believe so, he says finally. *Though, it proved most docile once I subdued it.* He shrugs with a wave of his tail again.

Perhaps it could learn, muses one of the Pathwalkers who spoke before.

Any creature can learn given the right . . . motivation, the Shaman says with a tail-shrug. *Leave it there for a few days; when it feels the bite of hunger and thirst, it will be properly motivated to please its new masters.* I hadn't thought I could dislike the shaman any more than I already did after finding out her plans for Lathani, but I've just been proven wrong. If looks could kill, the shaman would be dropping dead, but unfortunately, I haven't learned that Skill yet. The heavily adorned lizard-kin watches me for a moment with a predatory look in her eyes, then turns back to the others.

Runs-with-the-river, you have brought the tribe a gift, the shaman says, her tone shifting to something with more formality. *What reward do you desire?* River hesitates for a moment and darts a look back at me.

My weapons, I tell him. He sends confusion back to me. *Ask for my weapons to keep. Then bring them with you when we escape. And stop looking at me, for heaven's sake!* He quickly obeys and instead looks at the weapons consideringly.

May I have the prey-beast's weapons for my use? he asks finally. Seeing the shaman hesitate, he quickly continues. *If the Honored Pathwalkers wish to investigate the weapons more at a later date, I will of course yield them to you. It is merely that I do not think such tools should be languishing, covered in dust and grime from lack of use.* The shaman's tail waves gently from side to side.

What say you, sisters? she asks finally. There's a chorus of responses, some ayes, some nays. More of the former than the latter, fortunately. Turning back to River, the shaman indicates for the other Pathwalkers to pass the weapons to him. *Very well. Your reward is to have this spear and stone-headed club. We shall keep the earthen bowl for further inspection; knowing whether the prey-beast is an Earth-Shaper or not is important.*

Thank you, Honored Shaman, River says, his tone grateful, his mouth almost pointing towards the sky briefly as he shows his throat.

Remember, we shall need the weapons present in order to indicate our wishes when we instruct the prey-beast. That will not be for a few days yet, I suspect. Plenty of time for you to test their power. River's crest flashes in submissive agreement and he once more lifts his chin high. The shaman flicks her claws in dismissal. He tilts his chin just a fraction higher, his throat going completely taut, then walks away with my spear and mace held tightly in his paws.

He doesn't look at me, but I sense his attention turning clumsily to the Bond, to the sense of my presence within him.

What do you wish me to do now, Master? he asks as he pauses near one of the round thatched huts to "inspect his reward." He's better at pretense than I would have expected. My mind ticks over the possibilities.

Actually, we're probably in the best position I could have asked for, considering everything. River has my weapons and has been dismissed. I'm in this cage, which isn't ideal, but from what the shaman said, I'm likely to be ignored for at least the near future, which is great. It's significantly better than being attacked the moment I walked in or being kept under heavy guard. Hopefully, that will all make the rest of the plan much easier.

Do you have any duties you'll be expected to do now? I ask my Bound. He takes a moment to think them through.

It's too late to go into the forest for herbs now. My master—former master, he corrects himself with a pang of regret and guilt that I ignore, *will expect me to help her prepare herbs for a number of concoctions. I will need to feed the cub later. Other than that, not much.*

Through my discussion with River earlier, I discovered that Lathani is being held in the herbalist's hut. She's given food and water in the morning and evening and a herbal concoction four times a day. This latter is apparently supposed to make her spirit easier to bind and more powerful than it would otherwise be.

Being only the assistant and not the master, my new companion isn't completely familiar with all the details—apparently, making the concoction itself is beyond his skills—but that's what his master said it would do: something about drawing on Lathani's future potential to enhance the present. Either way, the idea of her being force-fed *anything* has me gritting my teeth in helpless rage once more. I push it away with the thoughts of how we're going to get her out—tonight.

Right, then, I tell him, the plan gaining details in my mind, *this is what I want you to do.*

CHAPTER SEVENTEEN

Meditation

I shift for what has to be the thousandth time in the last few hours, unable to get comfortable. I grimace. When I get out of here, I'm going to have to cast Lay-on-Hands just to deal with the muscle spasms from being stuck in this cramped position or I won't even be able to walk. My stomach is grumbling; my mouth is dry. I will admit to taking a sneaky leak, though—aiming as far out of the cage as I could manage.

I fought against the shame of doing it in plain sight with anger. Fortunately, I have plenty of anger boiling inside—from their treatment of Lathani to them treating me like I'm a dumb animal. At least I haven't needed to deal with a full bladder on top of everything else.

It's been a long time since I was shoved in here. I don't know how long, but it was only mid-afternoon when I entered the village and night is starting to fall now. My initial fear subsided after some time, perhaps thanks to the lizard folk essentially ignoring me. I still tense again any time I see their eyes on me, but in between, I'm able to relax. As much as I can, considering my physical discomfort, anyway.

Once I stopped battling my fear all the time, I found boredom creeping in. Without River nearby to be my translation app, I can't understand the vast majority of the lizard folk's speech, but I can watch and observe. I also distracted myself with going through my memories, both those I had before I came to this world and those I gained from the knowledge stones. When I got bored of that, I focused on meditation. At least my forced inactivity has proved productive in its own way.

Although it was a bit difficult to actually begin meditating, considering the situation I've gotten myself into, I found that the longer I kept it going, the more my fears and worries subsided and were replaced with calm. This last hour, I've done little else but meditate, feeling that, finally, I've made some sort of breakthrough with it. Instead of just being a way of feeling my surroundings while maintaining some sort of inner peace, it's now having a real effect on my mind and body.

Despite the physical discomfort from my cramped position, as well as the hunger and thirst that threaten to intrude, I can find peace in my surroundings. Time itself also feels more amorphous: minutes sometimes seem to stretch out like honey from a spoon, and at other times the sun appears to leap across the sky in a great bound. Perhaps it's because I seem to become slightly detached from my body when meditating—the more I sink into the state of stillness, the more I feel connected to everything around me, some sense of self spreading out to touch my surroundings.

When I start feeling connected even to the lizard folk walking past me, I pull myself out of my trance. Perhaps logically I can accept that they're part of the natural environment, but right now, I don't want to feel any sort of connection with them.

Not when they hurt beings I care about.

Not when I'm shoved in a cage of their making.

Not when I might be faced with killing them before the night's over.

As I recognize the shaman's ornate adornments on the lizard-kin striding past me now, I feel my eyes narrow and my fists clench, the remnant sense of peace from my meditation melting away like ice in the sun. I don't think I'll have any problem killing *that* one, no matter how "connected" I might feel.

Deciding to take a break, I check my messages, feeling the nagging sense that there's more than one waiting for me. When I look, I feel a grin pull the corners of my mouth up and immediately conceal it. Not that these lizard folk are likely to be able to understand my body language any more than I can understand theirs, of course. I still choose to bury my face in my knees to hide it, the dark caused by my covering arms no hindrance to reading the messages.

<table>
<tr><td>

Congratulations!

You have worked hard on your Intelligence and have earned a point. This point has been added to your status.

</td></tr>
<tr><td>

Next message / Close messages

</td></tr>
</table>

Nice, I think to myself. A point I don't even have to spend any Energy on. The next isn't quite as good, but I'm still happy with it.

<table>
<tr><td>

Congratulations!

You have worked hard on your Intelligence and have earned a point. Would you like to apply this to your status?

</td></tr>
<tr><td>

Apply point / Refuse point

</td></tr>
</table>

Is that some sort of record? One and a half Intelligence points gained in . . . what, six hours? Not that I'm complaining. Clearly my efforts to analyze the situation and make connections between my memories have paid off. I accept the point and move to the next message.

<table>
<tr><td>

Congratulations!

You have worked hard on your Wisdom (Breadth) and have earned a point.

</td></tr>
</table>

Would you like to apply this to your status?
Apply point / Refuse point

Another point! Clearly down to my meditation, this one. I'll need to figure out Breadth and Depth sometime, but so far it seems like I get Breadth when I meditate and feel the connectivity of all nature to others and to myself. Though what that means in practical terms for me, I don't know. Once more, I accept the addition and move on.

Congratulations! You have earned a Skill: Meditation
Read Skill description? Y / N

Meditation You have discovered that by sitting still and calming your mind, you are able to feel your connection to the world around you. Due to your receptivity to your surroundings while in Meditation, you increase your Energy absorption rate by 5% for each level that you have in this Skill. This will be automatically diverted into refilling your mana pool at a rate increased by the same percentage as your Energy absorption rate. As a result of using this Skill to relax in difficult circumstances, you can also use this Skill to replace some need for rest. For every four hours spent in Meditation, gain the same benefit of an average hour of sleep. This benefit may improve as the Skill's level increases.
Close messages? Y / N

Not, perhaps, the most exciting of Skills, since five percent of my current Energy absorption is approximately one more Energy storage percent per day. Better for my mana regeneration, though, since that's another eighteen units per hour, which lets me pull off almost two more Lay-on-Hands if necessary. Still, I'm sure I'll find that the small increase shows its worth in the long run.

Being able to replace my need for sleep, at least partially, is probably the most immediately useful, though; I'm tired, but I can't imagine daring to fall asleep in this environment. But with what's likely to happen later, I really ought to get some rest. But first, stats! I close the message showing my Skill and pull up my status page.

Name: Markus Wolfe		Race: Human	Class: Tamer
Level: 3	Energy to next level: 16%	Energy absorption rate: 29u/hr	Energy towards debt: 4%
Intelligence	16	Mana: 160/160	

Wisdom	17	Mana regeneration rate: 425u/hr
Willpower	20+4 (+20%)	Health regeneration rate: 24u/hr
Constitution	15	Health: 150/150
Strength	12	Stamina: 60/60
Dexterity	13	Stamina regeneration rate: 130u/hr
Class Skills: Dominate – Beginner 7 Tame – Beginner 4 Fade – Novice 9		Non-Class Skills: Lay-on-Hands – Initiate 3 Stealth – Beginner 9 Animal Empathy – Novice 4 Meditation – Beginner 1

My Intelligence score is looking *significantly* healthier than it did when I first arrived. I don't *feel* a lot more intelligent, certainly not three times as much, but I have to admit that I do find it easier to make connections with things now. From watching the passing lizard folk, I've found that since I piggybacked on River's understanding of the Pathwalkers' conversation, I can actually pick up certain things they're saying to each other, though I can't actually *understand* them, exactly.

It's nothing complex, and it's more based on their color-changing crests than anything else, but I can imagine that if I spent much longer here, I'd learn their language pretty quickly. Or be able to understand it, at least. Pronouncing it would be a whole different story. Possibly my Animal Empathy is helping me, though I don't know if it has any effect on my interactions with sapient beings, since it is *Animal* Empathy. Then again, we're all animals, technically speaking. Does that count . . . ?

I haven't yet gotten a proper count of how many lizard folk there are; it's hard for me to tell them apart, so if a lizard-kin passes by my cage, I don't know if it's the same one who's passed by several times before or if they're all different individuals. I have noticed some differences, though. The slimmer and smaller Pathwalkers seem to be limited to the ones River spoke to, for one. The bigger guards also seem to be pretty limited, though more numerous than the Pathwalkers.

But even if I can't get a proper head count, I managed to get a better idea of their numbers—as the sun descended towards the horizon, the denizens congregated in groups around carcasses for dinner. Most of them, anyway. There was one group that didn't seem to eat for some reason. That was one of the largest groups, composed of more lizard folk than I'd seen in a single place previously. Frankly, even if I wasn't able to count them, the village would clearly be *way* too big for me to take on alone. Just as well I decided to go with a subterfuge tactic. At least, I hope it will turn out better in the end.

I push the doubt from my mind as I try to settle back into a Meditative trance. A couple of hours' worth of rest is better than nothing, and I don't have any idea how long it will take for River to give me the signal. I told him to come at a moment when the village is as quiet as it's going to get. That could be when true dark comes, or it could be even later than that.

But for now, I have more urgent concerns. My belly thinks that my throat has been cut, and my mouth feels like the Sahara has taken up permanent residence. I reach into my Inventory and pull out my waterskin, then gratefully deal with the most urgent of the two concerns. I gulp down several mouthfuls before slowing down.

After my thirst has been quenched, I sneak handfuls of grilled meat and "potatoes" out of my Inventory, scarfing them down to feed my grumbling stomach.

While I could have refreshed myself before now, I didn't think it would be wise—that first-on-my-kill-list shaman maliciously ordered me to be left without food or water; obviously, contravening that didn't seem like a good idea. However, the lizard folk are clearly not nocturnal, as with the falling of night their work evidently comes to an end. Few are now outside their huts, and those who are aren't paying attention to me.

Once I have satisfied my own needs, I clean my hands and face of the evidence, then close my eyes and return to Meditation. I need to make sure I'm in as good a condition as possible for later, and at least Meditation is a decent use of my time, all things considered.

One moon has passed overhead and the other is only just cresting the horizon before I surface from Meditation again. I've been vaguely aware of the activity around me reducing more and more until the last while, which has been almost completely still. It's because of the contrast that I am disturbed; my surroundings are shifting in a way they haven't for quite a while. It hadn't been easy to notice specific movements when there were so many lizard folk around; now that the whole village is still, the change is noticeable.

I open my eyes and strain them to look into the darkness. Fortunately, although the first moon is no longer overhead, it's still sending some fingers of light through the canopy above, otherwise I'd be completely blind. My night vision has improved a little since I came to the world but not enough to see in the darkness of a moonless night.

For a few moments, I see nothing. Then one of the beams of moonlight is broken, and I whip my head to the side. My ears focus on the area, and I hear a slight shift in the earth, the faint scrape of a claw. A figure looms closer, odd shapes sticking out of it. I touch the Bond, and the instinctive fright of a silhouette in the night calms as I detect the presence of my Bound.

Relief sweeps through me, ridding me of the majority of the worries that had run rampant whenever I stopped Meditating: That he'd thought better of our deal and decided to betray me. That something had gone wrong with the plan and he wouldn't be coming at all tonight. Or even that he'd just fallen asleep and lost track of time. I reckoned that if he got caught, I would hear the fracas, so I hadn't worried about that. Much. But his presence here indicates that the plan's still on.

Crawling forwards, wincing as my muscles protest the movement after hours of inactivity, I shove on the door. Along with sneaking some food and water, I also prepared for this moment by quietly slicing through the hinges with my knife. Mostly slicing, anyway—I didn't want there to be any indication of my actions for any sharp-eyed lizard folk to see. I'd have done the latch as well, but I couldn't quite reach it, even with my knife. As it is, I didn't need to: a quick shove and the hinges break. The door almost clatters against the opposite side, but I stop it by wrapping my hand around one of its bars. With the village so still, any noise could potentially alert someone.

Climbing out of the cage, I hold up a hand as River starts forwards towards me.

Give me a moment, I tell him grimly, then send a Lay-on-Hands through my body. *Ooh, that feels better,* I moan to myself as the healing energy washes through the muscles, loosening them and increasing the blood flow around my body. It even heals a couple of areas that were cut off by my crunched-up position. I send a quick glare at the cage. If it wouldn't be a red alert for everyone around, I would light it on fire and dance merrily in the glow. As it is, though . . . *Okay, I'm ready,* I send, looking at my Bound.

Here, he says as he hands some items over. First of all is my mace, second is my spear, and third is a thin vine, which I use to tie the weapons to myself. My spear goes onto my back and my mace onto my waist, though tied in a way that ensures it won't constantly get tangled with my legs and trip me. Straining my eyes, I examine my Bound. He's still got a strange shape on his back.

Is that . . . ? I ask him. He sends a feeling of agreement, and I nod unconsciously. *Okay, then. Let's do this.*

CHAPTER EIGHTEEN

You Can't Be Serious

We creep through the darkness. I've got both Stealth and Fade active, aiding my ability to slink through the area unseen and unnoticed. Good thing too: the night is so quiet that I would be easily discovered otherwise. Even the noises I'm used to hearing from roaming—and occasionally dying—night-time animals are barely audible. Perhaps it's because they don't dare enter the encircling fence of the village, so any noises I hear are from the forest beyond and are therefore slightly muffled.

I follow River as he heads towards a hut that's off to one side of the village and has a smaller hut directly next to it. Actually, it's separated from the rest of them by a comparatively large margin. As we reach it, I look beyond to see the gate. The sight sends hope through me, only to be chased by a frisson of fear as I see a small shift of movement near it.

Closer examination reveals what I'd hoped not to be the case: the gate is still guarded by two of those big lizard folk. I guess we'll be heading out by the side gate, then. However, that means trekking back through the village again, which is not without its risks either. Still, we need to get Lathani first.

We pause next to the hut, near its gaping black hole of an entrance. River pauses for a moment, and I hear him take a shaky breath. Concern rising, I'm about to communicate with him when he turns around and backs into the hut with practiced ease. There's a reason he's doing this part of the plan and my job is to stand guard.

To that end, I pull my mace from its vine tie and hold its handle with both hands, the wood creaking ever so slightly as my grip tightens. I put my back almost against the wall to reduce my profile if anyone were to be watching and look around myself attentively. I try to minimize the movement of my head by looking more with my eyes and only occasionally shifting my head around slowly to more closely examine what is otherwise just the peripherals of my vision. Movement catches more attention than stillness; moreover, it risks noise. Neither is something we want right now.

A few quiet noises emerge from the hut, but I'm confident they will not go far, even in the stillness of the night. After all, even though I'm standing so close, *I* can barely hear the faint sounds. Despite straining my hearing to the utmost, I can't identify exactly what he's doing. At least, I can't hear any of the sounds I've come to recognize as lizard folk speech. When movement from the dark hole catches the dim light, I almost startle.

A shape emerges from the shadows, and I quietly lay my mace down in order to help pull it through. I see the outline of ears, a head, and rosettes of black spots, barely visible in the low light level but still there. My heart wrenches as I smell the familiar musky scent of nunda cub, my poor sense of smell only just catching it at this distance. Her fur is warm and less fluffy than I remember.

As I gently pull her through, I realize that she's also heavier than I recall, not to mention longer; her body is at least three times as big as I remember. Maybe more. By the time her back paws have made it through, my eyebrows are attempting to reach my hairline.

What . . . ? I absently send to River. I must send my question through well enough, despite not vocalizing it properly even to myself, since he responds.

The herbal concoction. Oh. My teeth grit together in anger. This must be "drawing on the future to enhance the present," as he described it when we had our discussion in the forest. If this forced growth has done any permanent damage to her, I'll take it out of the shaman's hide. I realize that there's something else wrong too. She's completely still, silent. Her eyes are closed.

What's wrong with her? I demand from River, my fists clenching. *Why is she not awake?*

It's another concoction, Master. I told you about this earlier, the lizard-man reminds me, uncertainty and slight fear coming through the Bond. I breathe deeply, forcing away the emotion that will only cause me to make mistakes.

You did, I acknowledge, remembering it as he said it. I should have known—we'd agreed that River should continue to act normally, which included giving her the sleeping draught, though only pretending to give her the shamanic potion. Besides, I'd thought it would probably be easier to get her out if she was asleep. Though, now I can see she's so much larger . . .

I dismiss the thought and lean down to lift her over my shoulders like a particularly furry stole. With her larger size, her front and back paws both drape down past my hips.

Should I not take her? River offers.

No, I tell him, almost a growl in my mental voice. *I'll be fine.*

Between the two of us, River is likely the stronger; the wiry muscles he has going on probably beat out my recently improved ones. However, even with everything he's done so far to prove he's on my side, we're not out of the village yet, and I'm loath to trust Lathani with someone who could suddenly deviate at the absolutely wrong moment. It does mean that my ability to defend us is reduced, but since the main plan now is to run, that's okay. I can still wield my mace one-handed and keep a steadying hand on her if necessary. *Let's go.*

We tiptoe through the village huts as we head for the unguarded side gate. We start to relax as it comes into view—too soon, it turns out. We round a hut, only to bump into one of the lizard folk coming the other way. It's one of the Pathwalkers! Shock causes a moment of stillness that holds both parties like statues. Then the Pathwalker clicks loudly and frantically, raising the alarm.

I curse as I bump into River; I turned to dodge around the Pathwalker, only to find my Bound still rooted in place.

"Move!" I order him harshly. No time for niceties right now. And no point trying to be quiet: they all know where we are right now. He stumbles out of the way, his legs almost seeming to propel themselves. "Come on, we need to run!"

Not waiting to see if he is following, I run off in the direction of the gate, only to stumble over a branch suddenly in my path. I regain my balance, then lose it again as a wooden bucket slams into me from the side. I fall heavily, landing badly to avoid crushing Lathani's legs. *What . . . ?* I whip my head around wildly, even as I push myself back to my feet, my hip and thigh aching from the impact.

I see another branch come flying at me. No, a spear, I realize as I throw myself to one side to avoid its sharp point, my eyes going wide. But who threw it?

The only other figures around me are River and the Pathwalker, and neither of them were at the right angle to throw the spear. Or the bucket, now that I think about it. Judging by the commotion around us, we won't be alone long, but for now, I can't see my attacker. Even if I can't see them, though, they're clearly determined not to let me get away.

Then it all becomes clear as the same spear lifts into the air and flips over to aim at me, point first, once more: the *Pathwalker* is controlling it from a distance, its clawed paw moving in unison with the spear. I dodge the shot once more and feel its sharp tip open a slice in my cheek. A moment later, I leap forwards. We haven't got much time, since this lizard set off the alarm, and now it's stopping us from leaving.

With one hand steadying Lathani, the other goes to my mace and rips it from my belt. I swing at the lizard's head. It dodges the first fury-filled swing and attempts to attack me with the bucket. I bat the bucket away and swing again, the movement too fast for the Pathwalker to avoid this time. The heavy flint ball sinks into its skull with a crunch, the bone clearly not even as resistant as that of the crocodile I fought. I use the momentum of the swing to help spin me around to face the exit.

River is frozen, his mouth open, horror blasting through the Bond at me. I know it's unfair, even as I open my mouth to say it, but we *don't have time.*

"Snap out of it," I shout at him. "Either come with me now or stay here and face them." I point at the figures approaching us; the hulking mass of the guards makes my bowels quiver. Not waiting for him to reply, I take off, fear lending wings to my feet.

Heading for the side gate, I pump my legs as quickly as I can. There's a time to take it slow; that time isn't now. I've even dropped Fade since I don't want the stamina drain—it's not like they don't know I'm here, after all.

As I get closer to the gate, relief fills me when I see that the section that usually bars it has been shifted away. River did exactly what I told him to do. Managing to get through the hole without encountering any more lizard folk, I briefly pause as an idea hits me. Grabbing the loose section, I heave it around so that it's pointing its spears inwards. About to shove it into position, I pause as River runs out, his eyes wide and glinting in the growing moonlight.

There's no time to check if he's okay, no time to do *anything*. I shove the section into place and grab a big stick from my Inventory and wedge it through the bars, hoping it may delay the lizard folk chasing us, if only by a fraction. The sight of the five crocodilian shapes barely a few meters away makes my stomach clench, especially since two of them are massive hulking creatures who could probably tear me limb from limb.

Nope. Not like this. I'll come for you arseholes later, I promise darkly to myself even as I turn tail and run.

River and I are neck and neck as we dash through the trees, a thwarted roar rising from behind us. Despite the situation, a grin tugs at my cheeks. What a rush! Fear and victory are a heady combination.

Bastet! I call down our Bond. She responds with a sense that I can only translate as "here," and a dark shape emerges out of the forest to give me a near heart attack.

"Don't *do* that!" I growl at her through gritted teeth. I'm on edge enough as it is! Still, no time. The lizard folk aren't going to be delayed for long. "Where are the cubs?" She sends me a sense of "not far" and darts away. I follow quickly and sense River doing the same.

She's right—the cubs aren't far. I temporarily put Lathani down and mentally apologize to her when I'm rougher than I'd like to be from sheer haste. After yanking the sling out of my Inventory, I quickly tie it and pop the cubs in. They mewl and yowl in complaint at the abrupt treatment, wanting instead to greet me. I apologize under my breath to them, too, as I stoop to pick up Lathani again. A clawed paw on my arm stops me, and I shoot my eyes up at River.

Shall I carry it . . . her? he asks, his tone unusually subdued, his emotions flat. I hesitate for a precious moment as I consider it while my instincts shriek at me to say no.

But I am more than my instincts. I'm already carrying three raptorcat cubs, and he's probably stronger than I am, anyway. He's done everything I've asked him to do so far; it wouldn't make any sense to disobey me now. Not when he just stood aside as I killed one of his precious Pathwalkers and fled with me when the big lizard folk came. At this point, if he does betray me, is he likely to have a much better reception from his kin than I would?

"Okay. Thank you," I say instead, nodding once. I can hear the crash of branches carrying through the quiet night forest. We need to get going. River hoists Lathani up onto his shoulders and we take off running again, following Bastet.

Since my plan involved both River and me being tied up in the village for the rest of the day—well, *caged* up in my case—I'd set Bastet the task of working out our escape route. Trusting her to have done that, I focus on putting one foot in front of the other. And not tripping over any of the half-seen branches in my path.

Fortunately, as time goes on, that becomes easier and easier to do since the second moon's light illuminates our path in the first part of our journey, and then the rising sun lights it as the moon is going down. River must have come and got me not long before dawn.

I suppose that makes sense, I acknowledge with what brain power is not being used to keep moving quickly through the forest; there's more available than I'm used to since my recent increases in Intelligence. If the books and films I used to watch are anything to judge by, the period shortly before dawn is when people sleep the deepest and guards are the least likely to notice something. Unfortunately, thanks to an insomniac Pathwalker, our escape was rather louder than I'd have liked.

There's more bad news: our pursuers are catching up.

I wasn't sure at first; the increase in the volume of the sounds could have been attributable to other causes. But when I checked with River, he agreed with me.

We are most likely being chased by Warriors. Their strength and speed are far above that of any other tribe member. And they train for this. He continues with a glum prediction, *There's no hope that they will miss our trail; a blind hatchling could follow it. They will be on us before the sun rises far above the horizon.* My heart sinks.

Great, I say sarcastically, not caring if I project it to River or not. *Any ideas?* This time I include Bastet in the communication, sending her a few images and emotions to explain the situation. If River and I can hear our pursuers and draw conclusions from that, I'm sure she can too.

For a few minutes we just run in silence. Finally, it's the raptorcat who replies with a single image: the lizogs we killed together soon after our Battle of Wills. I frown even as I run, my stamina heading down towards two-thirds empty. What does she mean?

Spears? I ask her. *I've only got one, though.* I get a wave of negation from her. Not spears, then. She repeats the image, this time showing the lizogs running towards the wall of sharpened bits of wood, then them getting crushed by the rocks. Oh, I think I get it. *Are you suggesting we trap them?* I ask. She replies with a wave of agreement. Okay, sounds good. Only one problem. *But we don't have enough time to prepare a trap. The lizog trap took* hours.

She responds with the feeling of grim resignation and a single image.

"You can't be serious," I respond, my incredulity making me speak aloud despite really needing to save my breath for running.

CHAPTER NINETEEN

Gamble

Apparently, Bastet *is* serious.

You think going back into the area that definitely *wants to kill us is the best way to escape creatures that* probably *want to kill us?* My mental tone is incredulous, but who could blame me?

What is disturbing you? Despite seeming to have semi-resigned himself to being caught and killed, my other Bound is curious. That doesn't mean there isn't a hint of apprehension to his mental projections. I don't blame him—I probably don't seem like I've come up with a great plan that'll get us out of trouble. That's just as well because I haven't. Unfortunately.

Bastet is suggesting we go here, I tell him while sending the same image she sent me. I feel him recoil in shock.

The Forest of Death? He sounds as reluctant as I feel.

Precisely, I reply.

We're not going to do that, surely? He's as incredulous as I was when she first suggested it. And a lot more fearful; the emotion is cutting through the muffling that's been in place ever since I caved in the head of that Pathwalker. Probably shock, now that I think about it.

Bastet is insistent, though, and sends me the image again along with one of me holding a torch and then another of the lizard folk without.

She . . . has a point. I want to deny it because those trees almost killed us before, but if we can get through them and the lizard folk can't . . . It would take them longer to go around the forest than it would take us to get through—if they even want to pursue us that far. If we could avoid being trapped by the trees and stabbed to death . . .

It's a big if, but assuming it's possible, we'd have a good head start, which should allow us to get back to Kalanthia before the lizard folk catch up with us. And who knows, they might even give up the chase when they see us disappearing through the Forest of Death. That's probably just wishful thinking, though.

Alright, I've more than half convinced myself. While I run, I dare to open my Inventory quickly to check my stock of torches. I've got two half-burned ones and one fresh one. If we don't stop, that should be enough to get us through the forest with more to spare.

The cubs aren't going to be happy, but we're going to need to hotfoot it again through the area. At least we've already covered a fair bit of ground with our rapid pace. I'm going to need to stop soon to recoup my stamina a bit, though. Maybe I can walk for a bit instead in the vine-strangler forest.

As I close my Inventory, I almost run into a tree and dodge at the last minute. Amusement comes along the Bond from Bastet. *Laugh it up, devil-cat,* I think ruefully at her. Not literally—I don't try to project it along the Bond. I have a feeling that she catches an echo of the emotion anyway, as her amusement just grows.

After a moment, I let myself relax, the tension of the last half day and night fading slightly. Sure, we're not out of danger yet—heck, we may be about to jump out of the pan and into the fire—but at least I'm not still in that cage. We've got Lathani, I'm with Bastet, and for now we're free.

I look backwards and realize with a frisson of fear that I can now see the lizard folk chasing me. In the growing morning light, they look even bigger than I remembered: five big bastards crashing through the forest.

I gulp; if my mouth hadn't already been dry, it would have quickly become so at that sight. I mean, I've faced some steep odds since arriving here, but five muscle-bound crocodilian T-Rexes taller than me, carrying a variety of weapons including spears and shields made of half a tree trunk . . . No. Not without a decent trap or some other advantage, at least. They're still a fair distance away—my view of them is still often obscured by tree trunks—but not nearly far enough.

Can you direct us to the forest? I ask Bastet after deciding that the Forest of Death sounds like a *super* idea, assuming that we can get there before getting shish-kebabbed by our pursuers. I would check my Map, but I have a feeling that I really would ring my bell by colliding with a tree if I did that. Sure, I could stop, but with the lizard folk already so close, I'd really rather not. Bastet, thankfully, answers positively by adjusting her direction just a little.

After a while, River notices the slight change and sends a wary thought at me.

We seem to be heading for a certain place I thought we weren't going to visit.

Is that a question or a statement? I can't help poking at him a little despite the situation. Or maybe because of it—I need to get my laughs where I can find them, just like Bastet. Even if any actual laughs would probably be more hysterical than humorous.

Feeling pity for the lizard-man who's already been through a lot today, I continue.

We managed to get through safely last time; if we can do that again, we'll gain a large lead on your kin. If we can get back to Kalanthia before they catch up with us, we'll have a much better chance of surviving all of this. If they follow us at all.

If the trees don't kill us first, he replies gloomily. I don't blame him. I'm not a hundred-percent sure about this plan either.

After that we just focus on putting one foot in front of the other without tripping. Ever since I gained more points in Dexterity, particularly its Agility subcategory, I've found traveling through the forest a lot easier; I don't catch my feet in roots nearly as much. At speed, it's far harder, and I don't have any attention to spare for trying to make myself quiet. I crash through the forest like an elephant. Actually, elephants are surprisingly quiet—maybe more like a bull. Stealth would probably help, and so might Fade, but they're both deactivated to save all my stamina for running. Though, it's still running out quicker than I would like.

True to my prediction, the yellow bar in my vision is starting to get pretty low before I see the dreaded, yet also anticipated, shapes of the vine-strangler trees ahead of us. Our pursuers aren't far away. The fierce roars coming through the trees sound like they're almost on our heels; I don't dare spare the attention to check. Something else is absolutely obligatory before we enter the forest, though.

I need to light the torch, I tell my Bound grimly as we reach the edge of the trees, which have spread across the forest like a blight. *You may have to hold them off or distract them somehow.* So saying, I stop abruptly, pull the least used torch out along with my fire-starter kit, and start frantically creating sparks. I wish that the torches could stay lit in the Inventory, but that's how this barely used torch got put out: slotting it into the Inventory without extinguishing it first.

Bastet crouches by me, growls rumbling in her chest as she keeps a watch out for any attack. River, on the other hand, seems to disappear. I haven't got the eyes or the attention to spare for him as I desperately attempt to light the torch, feeling almost as under pressure this time around as I was while in the forest itself.

Finally, a flame leaps up from the dried moss that I'm using as kindling, and I gently nurse it until it catches on the pitch of my torch. I hiss in success and push myself to my feet as I look around to work out where River and our pursuers have gone—I was expecting them to catch up and attack us even as I tried to light the torch. Putting together the pieces of what I can see and hear, I realize that River disappeared to draw the other lizard folk off.

We're ready, River, I project to him mentally. Fortunately, he hasn't gone too far to communicate with him through the Bond, and I feel him turn back towards us.

As he breaks into view through a bush a few meters off to the side and runs towards us, I see that the other lizard folk are really hot on his heels—perhaps only a few tree trunks between them. I'm a little surprised that none of them try to communicate with River or River with them. Perhaps killing a Pathwalker is serious enough for no discussion to be possible.

Up this close they seem even bigger than before, though that's probably just an illusion because of the difference between them and River; I remember what size they really were when I saw two of them yesterday.

I consider sending a couple of arrows their way but quickly dismiss the idea; it'll take too long to get my bow out and strung. By the time I'm able to actually shoot an arrow, River will probably have caught up to me. Even loaded down with Lathani, he's moving quickly.

The Warriors are quicker, though, and with their prey in sight, they seem to have the wind in their heels. Turning tail, I start running again with Bastet at my side. Despite all five of the Warriors having spears, they haven't thrown them yet. Long may that last.

We enter the forest, and I hear the roars of the group kick up a notch. I verified with River earlier just in case, but he confirmed that there's no real message being conveyed in the sound—no message I hadn't already understood, anyway. They want us to know that they're coming, that they're gaining ever more ground, and that we should be afraid.

Underneath my anger, I *am* afraid. I doubt that we could take on the five of them at once, not with only Bastet and me fighting. Probably not even with River helping too. That's why we're running into the part of the forest that we barely escaped from with our lives.

But I make a promise to myself that I'll be back—and next time I won't be the one to run.

River catches up with us as we go past the third tree into the grove. We run alongside for a few steps before he vanishes from my peripheral vision.

I turn my head to see him collapsed on the ground. Perhaps I was premature in saying that the lizard folk weren't throwing their spears: one of them has done just that and got a lucky hit in. Without thinking, I switch directions immediately and run back to my fallen Bound even as the other lizard folk close in.

I yank the spear out and drop it, then slam both my hands onto River and cast an undirected Lay-on-Hands. Then, without daring to see how close the other lizard folk have gotten, I haul him to his feet. He's still carrying Lathani draped over his shoulders, so I have to cope with both of their weights at the same time. It's not beyond my increased Strength, but their weights are extremely awkward to manhandle.

Fortunately, River isn't fighting me; in fact, he's clearly motivated to do his best to work with me. I guess it's confirmation that whatever awaits him if he falls into his previous friends' hands is nothing good. Using my shoulder as a crutch, he limp-hops quickly. I channel another Lay-on-Hands, taking advantage of the fact that he's in constant contact with me. His gait eases as his wound heals, and we pick up speed.

I expect to feel a spear in my back at any moment, but it doesn't come. When I finally dare to glance back, I see our pursuers halted at the edge of the vine-strangler trees. The red in their spikes shows how angry they are at losing us, but apparently, they're not willing to enter the Forest of Death. Good. At least that gamble paid off. Now I just have to hope that the forest won't live up to its name.

CHAPTER TWENTY

Magnificent

A couple of hours later, I'm tentatively hoping that we'll get through this without incident. By this point, we're deep enough into the forest that we can't see anything but vine-strangler trees. In fact, we can't see the forest for the trees, hah. My torch seems to be keeping the spearing roots at bay. For now, at least. We've all been looking at every movement in this unnatural place with suspicion.

River is the worst, jumping at every sound and flinching at every shift. I don't blame him, though: we've actually been here before; he's only ever heard horror stories of the place. His leg is as good as new, at least. I kept a steady stream of Lay-on-Hands going until it was healed.

The trees are as ominous as ever, their vines swaying in a breeze that doesn't ever seem to touch our skin. The vegetation below is incongruously bright and looks more like something that belongs in a jungle than the dark forest it is actually in. I eye that in suspicion too; although it seemed completely innocuous the last time we came through, I'd rather be too paranoid than dead. At least I've managed to recoup a good portion of my stamina while we've been walking instead of running.

I hear a cough and there's an unusual movement from River's direction. I whip my head around and scan around and behind him to try to work out what moved. There's another cough, and I see the origin of my alarm. Thankfully, it's nothing to fear.

"Lathani," I breathe as I indicate for River to stop. He does, and we gently shift the nunda cub off his shoulders. Down on the ground and in the light, I can see how much she's changed. She's got to be at least three times as long, maybe more. "Lathani," I say again with a mixture of elation and fear as Bastet approaches to lick at her head. Even the cubs cradled in the sling against my chest make encouraging sounds as if they want her to wake up too.

Slowly, her eyelids slide open, and her gaze is focused and intelligent.

It's a relief. I was worried that the shaman had done something irreversible despite River's explanation of a sleeping draught. Or that the Lathani who woke up wouldn't be the same as the Lathani we'd lost.

Carer, I hear in my mind, a warmth of relief and gratitude shading the mental tones. My eyes go wide. Did she just . . . ? *I am glad to see you.*

Raising her head, she turns it to look around. Suddenly, her hackles go up and she pushes herself to her feet quickly, though stiffly. A growl rumbles through her chest, the tenor version to Kalanthia's bass.

Why is he *here?* She looks to be a step away from attacking. I follow her gaze to work out the reason for her sudden anger.

When I see the cause, I feel exasperated at myself for not connecting the dots quicker. Of course she's going to be concerned seeing a lizard-man next to me. Particularly since he's one of the lizard folk who were deeply involved in her incarceration.

"It's okay, Kal—Lathani," I reassure her while almost confusing her with her mother. Understandably so, surely: I have an association between talking leopards and Kalanthia. Lathani suddenly talking is confusing me. "He's one of my Bound now. He helped me get you out. He won't hurt you."

Your Bound? She sounds a little confused. *Like the spiky one and the smaller carer? And the little fluff balls who are fun to play with?*

"Spike and Bastet, yes," I tell her, amused by her ways of describing the various creatures that hang around her. "The cubs aren't actually my Bound, I'm just helping take care of them, like I do with you. Anyway, how are you feeling? And how come you can *talk?*" The last one is really bugging me, though my rampant curiosity isn't enough to pop the balloon of joy at finally having her with me alive and well—apart from being three times or more her previous size, that is.

But she's here, she's *talking*, and we're not being chased by lizard folk. *No, just magical and homicidal trees*, a little voice says in the back of my mind. I ignore it, determined to be happy for just five minutes that my latest half-baked plan was actually successful, despite all odds.

Her initial response isn't so much words as it is a wall of emotion bludgeoning me. It's similar to when Bastet sends me a message purely composed of emotion, but not quite the same. The main difference is that with Bastet and River's mental communications, I always have the sense that I could cut it off if I wanted to—a bit like a flip phone. With Lathani, it's more like she's standing next to me and shouting at me; I feel like there's nothing I could do if it all became too overwhelming. A bit disconcerting, I have to admit.

Hungry, angry, sad, mournful, relieved, fearful . . . The range of emotions she's feeling is impressive—and strong. Even my buoyant mood is briefly brought down by association. I don't really know where to start except by pulling out a corpse from my Inventory, one of those monkey-reptile hybrids we killed a couple of days ago. I hesitate before putting it down.

"Can you eat this now? I know I've fed you some cooked meat before, but you were drinking milk a couple of days ago . . ." The way she tugs it out of my hands and digs in tells me everything I need to know. Bastet indicates that she'd appreciate a snack too, so I pull out another of the corpses from the same fight.

It's not a bad idea to pause for a break, despite our surroundings. Between Bastet, River, and me, none of us has had more than a few hours of restless sleep in a full day and a half, and we haven't eaten properly in a good while. I would say we're running on fumes, but actually, with the improved stats, we're all coping fairly well. Still, we could do with some food, the cubs too.

I'm a bit reluctant to let the cubs out considering where we are, but they've been cramped up in the sling since before dawn and are past the point of wriggling. Frankly, I don't think I'll succeed in keeping them in there for much longer. We just have to be very careful that they don't get caught by any of the moving tree roots. Releasing the three cubs, I put them next to the same carcass Bastet's munching from, and they dig in happily.

"Are you hungry too?" I ask River. He takes a moment to answer.

I could eat, he says finally; his tone is effectively flat, though it's the stillness of a pond with a maelstrom of currents below the seemingly calm surface. I eye him but ultimately don't ask what's wrong—I have a feeling I know anyway. I tell myself it's because engaging in such deep matters while we're traveling through a dangerous area of the forest is a bad idea. In reality, it's because I chicken out. While I have a feeling it will be necessary to discuss eventually, I'd rather procrastinate exploring the fact that River has just betrayed all the people he's probably ever known and was party to me bashing in the skull of a villager he had shown deep respect for.

Then again, I could be completely misreading it. That could be a lizard-kin's Tuesday for all I know and he's in turmoil over something else. Regardless, there's only one thing to say.

"Do you want cooked or fresh?"

Cooked? he asks, a sense of confusion cutting through the other emotions drifting over the Bond from his side.

"Transformed into a different state by fire," I explain as I gesture at the still-burning end of my torch. He still looks bemused, so I just hand him a bit of cooked bird meat as a demonstration while quietly celebrating how well the distraction seems to be working. River takes the meat delicately from my hand with clawed fingers.

He sniffs it first, then puts it in his mouth. I watch his reaction as he chews. His crocodilian teeth don't seem to chew very well—he gnaws on it a bit at the side of his mouth near the jaw connection, then tips his head back and swallows. He makes a bit of a face.

It tastes strange. Not bad, but not good either. It's also very dry. I think I'd rather have what they're eating, he decides finally, pointing at the fresh meat the raptorcats and nunda are enjoying.

"No problem," I say with a shrug. I pull the final monkey corpse from my Inventory and give it to him. He stays standing and keeps an eye out even as he rips pieces of meat from the carcass with his claws and tosses them in his mouth. Ah well, I may not have made a convert to the ranks of the cooked meat eaters, but at least I don't have to defend my supply either.

It'll be easier to feed him, too, if he can eat fresh meat. Sometimes I wish I dared to as well. I'd rather not risk catching a disease or eating a tapeworm or something, though. Actually, I don't know if Lay-on-Hands could even deal with those. I'd rather not find out the hard way that it can't.

Once we're all sated, we keep going. I pick the cubs up and tuck them back into the sling despite their protests; I'm not willing to let them wander around by themselves right now. Besides, we need to move quickly and they're not that fast yet. Fortunately, Lathani apparently feels well enough to travel on her own paws.

While she was eating, I spent some time cataloguing the differences between her previous cub-self and her new juvenile-self. She pretty much matches Bastet for size. She's a little shorter than the adult raptorcat, but she's longer. Lathani's definitely not an adult yet, though: her features are still a little cub-like, even if they've definitely gained more adult definition.

I can see the nunda she's going to become, and she really is beautiful. Her coat is also more adult than before, as I noted in the dark when River passed her out to me. It's still a bit fluffy, though, and the markings are not quite as clearly defined as they will be. In short, although she's still a sight to see, she's less adorable and more magnificent.

"Are you feeling a little better, Lathani?" I inquire as we jog quickly. At this speed, I can still talk at the same time as I run. When we switch to a higher gear soon, I'll have to save my breath. Still, I've already earned a point in Strength (Endurance) in the last few hours, so clearly, this headlong rush is doing me some good.

Slightly, she replies. *I am no longer hungry. Where are we going, Carer? This is not a good place to be.* I'm curious about how she knows. Can she sense the murderous intentions of the trees around us, or the number of other creatures that have died here? Or is it something different? Either way, I already know that this place isn't a great spot, so it's not exactly news to me.

"We're going back to the cave, to meet up with Kalanthia," I tell her.

Mother is alive? Her whole voice brightens with hope and burgeoning joy. *I thought . . .* She doesn't finish, but I can guess what was in her mind, especially considering the emotions she hit me with soon after waking.

"She's alive," I confirm, my heart breaking at the thought of how she must have felt; kidnapped, taken away from everything familiar, then terrible things done to her, all the while thinking that her mother was dead. "They hit her with some sort of stamina-dampening poison. If not for that, she'd have been way ahead of me in rescuing you."

I had hoped . . . She trails off. *I thank you for coming for me, Carer. You are still so weak and puny that it took great bravery to follow me.*

"Thanks?" I reply a little dubiously, not sure if it's really a compliment. I want to ask what happened to her while she was with the lizard folk, but I figure that it would be pretty insensitive to do so right now. "How come you can talk now?" Hopefully, that isn't too likely to bring up bad memories.

I could always talk; you just weren't very good at listening, she accuses me cheerfully.

I frown. Is that right? Is it because I've increased my Wisdom that I can now hear her? Or Willpower? Surely that's not the answer . . . They've definitely done *something* to her.

"And nothing's changed about you?" I question her dubiously. She squirms a little, an odd look for a leopard.

Well . . . I suppose something's changed. I got bigger.

"I saw that," I acknowledge with amusement.

And speaking to people is easier. At least, speaking to you is easier. And the smaller carer. I never used to be able to speak properly to her either. But the scaly creatures couldn't seem to hear me. I never succeeded in speaking to them, even when they hurt me. My heart, already sore from her earlier revelations, breaks again at the innocent confusion and emotional wounds in her mental projection.

I also have a sudden urge to go and slaughter all the lizard folk I can find. I glare at River, and he has the grace to look away as shame comes across the Bond between us. Returning my gaze to Lathani, my burst of anger drains away to be replaced with compassion at her unhappy mien.

"I don't think they would have listened to you, anyway," I tell her gently. "I'm sure you did the best you could. And now you're not there anymore."

No, she agrees, once more hitting me with a wave of emotion—there's much more relief and gratitude in this one than the previous, though the undercurrents of hurt and fear are still there.

We pick up the pace soon after, which renders speech impossible—for me, anyway. Since I don't have a Bond with Lathani, I can't conduct the same kinds of mental conversations with her that I've been having with Bastet and River.

It's a while later that something happens. We've been traveling through this forest for a couple of hours, and the sun is nearing its zenith, judging from the angle of sunbeams through the canopy. There's a shrieking cry and cracking noise that keeps coming from an area just off to the right of us. Without me asking her to, Bastet peels off and ventures a little closer to investigate, but keeps within view. Like when we traveled through this forest before, I don't want anyone going out of sight in case the trees take the opportunity to spring a trap again.

It's close enough for her to see the cause of the commotion. She sends back an image of a winged creature trapped by vegetation.

This time it's not a tree that has caused a trap but one of the vibrantly colored plants that make up the undergrowth between trees. It seems to have thorny vines and has dug these into the wings and body of a creature not all that dissimilar from the one that attacked Bastet and me—the one with whom I chose not to forcibly complete the Battle of Wills.

Just like the other one, it has four legs, two wings with claws at the front joints, and a toothed beak. Unlike the previous one, it's much more brightly colored, mixing reds and yellows together in a beautiful display. Though, with the thorns that have dug into its body, there's rather more red than I suspect there should be.

I hesitate; we need to get through this forest before I run out of torches, and this one's already burning up. We don't have time to stop and help some random bird. But on the other hand, how can I just leave a magnificent creature like that to be torn apart by some overambitious weeds?

I sigh at the thought of the delay, but it's still not a hard decision to make. After signaling my intentions to my companions, we turn towards the noise.

CHAPTER TWENTY-ONE

Lumberjack Is My Name

As we move, I notice that River isn't carrying any weapons, though our pursuing lizard folk were. I send him a mental message.

Do you use weapons or are your claws enough? I ask. Regret comes through the Bond to me.

I lost my spear in the rush. I pause and frown to encourage him to explain further. *The vines binding it to my back were snapped when it caught on a tree. I dared not pause to retrieve it, not with the Warriors so close.*

Well, that sucks. With a tendril of guilt pulling at my heart, I toss him mine. He snatches it out of the air with his clawed hand and pauses to make a few test moves. *Adequate,* he judges finally, *though not as good as my personal weapon.*

Now I feel even more guilty—was it particularly precious to him? Then my guilt disappears as I remember that the reason for all of this is because the lizard folk attacked Kalanthia and kidnapped Lathani. The last traces of it vanish as I remember Lathani's plaintive confusion over why the lizard folk hurt her.

Giving my spear to River leaves me with my bow, mace, and knife. That's far better off than when I first landed in this world, admittedly, but I decide to make another spear as soon as I get the opportunity. *If these trees attack at some point, I might take one of their stabbing roots as a trophy,* I say to myself darkly.

It's at least half bravado—I'm not at all sure that we could win against *one* of these trees without fire, and we're trapped in a whole forest of them. Against the plant holding the bird creature captive, however, I reckon that we'll do fine.

Close enough now to properly assess the situation, I see that the vines holding the creature come from some sort of bramble. It's a thorny mess covered in tantalizingly colored fruit. I reckon I can see why the bird got too close. Who would have guessed that the plant would actually bite back?

The thorny vines wrapped around the bird's body are not very thick, perhaps about the width of my little finger, but they're clearly pretty tough. They're trying to drag the avian creature downwards—to some sort of mouth hidden beneath the rest of the brambles, I imagine.

The bird isn't going down without a fight, though. It's biting at the vines and seems to have the claws on the front joints of its wings hooked into a branch on the trees above. Even as I watch, however, one of the claws loses its grip, tearing through the bark on the branch, then dangles uselessly in space. Kept away from the murderous vegetation only by a single wing-claw, its fate looks bleak.

That's where we come in, of course. Seeing the opponent, I actually take a moment to swap out my mace for my axe—*Lumberjack is my name; overgrown weeds, I am your bane.*

I take a moment to put the cubs down. It's hard to know which option is more dangerous: keeping them on me as I engage in battle or separating them from the torch among these vine-strangler trees. I decide that the first scenario *just* outweighs the second on the danger scale.

Hopefully, they'll be okay. Not so close to the fight that they're within easy range of the thorny vines, but near enough that if the trees start trying to trap them, we can be there in a flash. That's if they don't go wandering, of course. Bastet tells them firmly to stay put—I hope they listen!

We dash into the fray.

I'll go for the vines holding the bird, I tell the others. They send acknowledgments over their Bonds and veer off to play distraction.

Bastet starts performing strafing runs, leaping in to make several lightning-fast cuts and then darting back out of range. She's not particularly effective—her claws don't prove much of a deterrent against mobile brambles—but she makes up for it by being a good distraction. Her speed is such that she avoids almost all return attacks.

River is a bit more effective and sends the spear lancing through the thorny vines to pierce whatever is in the center. At one point he seems to hit something important, as the whole bush freezes for a moment and then shudders before returning to the attack with renewed frenzy. After that, the bush or creature or whatever it is seems to see him as the main threat and concentrates most attacks on him.

Fortunately for him, his scales seem to be pretty good natural armor and most attacks just glance straight off. I do spot a couple that seem to dig in, though. He doesn't react and just continues to attack with determination.

As I indicated to my companions, I go straight for the bird and the vines gripping it. Holding my axe and knife in each hand, I swing at the vines pulling the bird into the mass below. The vines are tough: each takes at least two good swings of my axe, even when I manage to get it trapped against something hard.

My knife isn't any better and requires far too long to saw through a single vine. After a few attempts, I tuck my knife back into its holster on my leg and just concentrate on using my axe. At first the bramble doesn't take much notice of me and is more focused on my companions. As I get halfway through freeing the bird, though, that changes.

After that, it starts sending attacks at me. My armor does a decent job of deflecting the vines aiming for me, but since it only covers my chest and back, there are far too many places on my body where my only protection is my already damaged clothes. The vines just rip straight through the thin fabric, leaving painful welts and scratches in their wake.

As for the ones aimed at my head, I just have to do my best to dodge those. The amount of blood I feel trickling down my skin attests to how many I unintentionally let through. Still, it's only dripping blood, and while it's painful, I've had much worse. I just cast Lay-on-Hands and keep soldiering on.

Lathani, not having been part of the mental communication, doesn't even realize what we're doing for a few moments. When she does, she tries to copy Bastet's moves. Unfortunately, she's clearly not quite used to her new size and strength and keeps over- and underestimating her own prowess at critical moments. Her coat swiftly gains a red tinge, and I make the executive decision to bench her.

"Back off, Lathani," I call over to her. She looks like she's considering ignoring my orders, and I fail to dodge a couple of attacking vines as I keep more than half an eye on her actions. Then, just as I can see her summoning the determination to keep going despite what I said, I get through the final vine holding onto the bird.

Distracted by four avenues of attack, one of which is seemingly taking most of its attention, the mass of brambles has stopped sending new vines to wrap around the bird. It's still pretty badly trussed up, but now it's not being pulled into the center of the mass anymore. "Lathani, grab the bird and pull it out of range," I yell at her as I send Lay-on-Hands through my fingers and into its body.

This time, thank goodness, she perks up and quickly trots over, grabs the bird's back legs between her jaws, and drags it across the ground. I hope that it's not suffocating and that Lathani's rough approach isn't going to do it more damage; I'll have to worry about that later.

Do you know what this is, River? I send to him. *Can we kill it?* I ask because he went unerringly for the parts of the mobile bramble tangle that had the greatest effect—surely he's encountered it in the past?

I've seen it before. Not anywhere near this big, though. It has a vulnerable part within the brambles: a combined mouth and stomach. Damage that enough and we'll win, he answers quickly.

Right. I think fast to myself. Should we keep going or should we just back off? It's not a fight we have to continue. But we do have to earn Energy, and we're already half done with this battle; if we back off now, we lose the Energy we could have gained if we won.

I glance around at my companions. Lathani is the most visibly injured by far, but even for her it's basically just scratches. Some deep scratches, for sure, but nothing that won't heal on its own. Even my own injuries are really just rips in my skin from where the thorny vines dug in.

We'll continue fighting, I tell my companions decisively. *River, keep doing what you're doing. Bastet, I'll clear a path for us to the center. You keep playing distraction.* The message is accompanied by images of what I imagine us doing in the next few minutes, and my Bound understand immediately and send back their agreement. After taking a moment to pull out my mace again from my Inventory, I start swinging at the bramble with both hands as I shout out to Lathani.

"Guard the bird! Make sure nothing eats it while we're killing this thing. And keep an eye on the cubs, please." I add on the last as an afterthought. I only hope she'll listen.

My mace isn't the greatest of weapons against this particular foe, which is the reason I put it away in the first place. However, what it doesn't have in terms of cutting ability, it has in crushing power, and it forces the brambles to the side. Unfortunately, even when the brambles are crushed to the ground, they start moving again a moment later. That's where my axe is by far superior: the bits that it cuts off stay cut off. Still, the mace offers me some breathing room and ability to choose more carefully where to swing my axe.

Slowly and painfully, thanks to not being able to avoid all the brambles flailing wildly in the air, I make progress. As I get closer to the center, the rate of attacks increases; the mobile bramble clearly considers me to be the greatest threat now. All I can do is grit my teeth, use the arm holding my mace to protect my eyes, and keep going with my axe. Thanks to the arm covering my face, I'm mostly blind, but it doesn't take much skill to hit vines, not with such a high density of them so close to its core.

When I break through the final defenses, I actually stumble forwards, the lack of resistance putting me off balance. Bastet leaps past me and starts savaging the "body" of the bramble creature. When I see her scaly talons sizzling a little and feel her send pain down the link, I realize that the surface we're standing on is actually acidic. Truly a mouth-stomach.

"Back up, Bastet," I tell her urgently even as I quickly do the same, already feeling the beginning burn of acid through the holes in my shoes. "It's just going to hurt you." She doesn't argue and backs up all the way out of reach of the vines, mincing like she's been walking on hot coals. I wince both for her and for what I'm going to do.

I swing my axe and start savaging the mouth-stomach, practically ignoring the thorny vines it sends to tear at me. This thing is going to die *now*. I'm vaguely aware of River at my back warding off some of the attacks by using his spear as a staff, but my main focus is on my own actions.

I just hope that I'll still have an axe after this. The flint should be okay, but the pitch and the bark-fiber cord? Well, I've gone too far now to back out—I'll have to repair any damage later. It's a stupid thing to worry about right now.

After what feels like an age, the bramble creature gives a final shudder and its vines flail around one last time before they collapse to the ground, finally immobile. I'm breathing heavily; the effort required to take this thing down was much more than I expected.

I turn around to find River looking at me unreadably.

"What?" I ask him a little self-consciously.

You do not seem to feel pain, he remarks. I frown and he gestures to my head, then hesitatingly to everywhere else. I touch my head and look at my body, my frown deepening.

"What do you mean?"

He clarifies. *You are bleeding. Significantly.*

"Well, so are you," I point out.

Not anywhere near as much you, he returns. I shrug.

"Well, I don't have natural armor like yours. Only my crafted armor offers me any protection, really, and that doesn't cover much of my body. Vines that hit anywhere else cut through my skin and made me bleed."

Then this is normal for your kind? he asks, now sounding a little intrigued. I shrug again.

"I mean, it still hurts—don't get me wrong—but . . ." I shrug. Actually, now I'm thinking about it, shouldn't it be hurting more than this? The patches of skin not covered by my armor look like I've been dragged through brambles. *I wonder why,* I think sarcastically to myself.

Lines of angry red cover my skin, and I can feel an uncomfortable stickiness beneath my clothes. Still, my health bar has only decreased by a sliver, and there isn't nearly as much pain as I might expect. Is this the effect of increased Constitution?

A question for later. For now, I just give another shrug to River and slap a Lay-on-Hands on him to help heal his wounds. Striding over to Bastet and Lathani, I trigger an undirected Lay-on-Hands to bring my own health up closer to maximum, then apply one each to them. Lathani needs a second since her wounds are worse than those of either of my Bound, but she soon looks worse than she actually is. Clearly uncomfortable with the blood matting her fur, she starts grooming herself, aided by a motherly Bastet.

Now, to see how our rescuee is doing. Hopefully, the bird is still alive.

CHAPTER TWENTY-TWO

A Partnership

It's alive. That's the first thing I note, and I feel a little relieved that the object of our rescue attempt did actually survive it. I can tell because the bird creature is moving slightly: its beak opening and closing a little, its eyes blinking. Those are the only parts of it moving, though; the rest is all wrapped in thorny vines. I wince—the thorns must be painfully digging into the bird's flesh. I empathize, largely because I've so recently been literally fighting my own way through the thorn bush.

Not wasting any more time, I crouch down to start releasing the bird from its bonds. I have to work carefully—any tug at the vines just means the thorns dig more deeply into its body. I do have to tug at them a bit when I saw through the vines, but the alternative is unfeasible. Trying to find the ends of each individual vine and then untangling them, like the bird is a kitten caught in a tangle of wool, would make me explode with impatience. My kingdom for a pair of secateurs.

Piece by piece, the vines fall away, and the feathers of the bird's body are revealed. By this point, it looks completely red despite me having seen yellow on its body earlier; the blood has just stained everything. It's weak, that's clear. Even when I gently pull the final thorns away from its flesh, it barely moves. It raises its head, then tries to push itself upright but fails to do much more than twitch.

"Hey, take it easy," I say to it soothingly. "Here—have something to eat while I heal you up." So saying, I pull a chunk of uncooked meat out of my Inventory. It looks at the meat but ignores it. Then I feel like slapping myself for my idiocy. If it was a meat eater, why would it have been attracted by that fruit on the bramble creature to begin with?

Then again, why would it have such a serrated beak if it *didn't* eat meat? Still, it's worth offering it some berries. "River, could you find a few pieces of fruit from the bramble thing we just killed, please?" The lizard-man grunts in assent, pushes himself to his feet from where he's been resting, and walks back to the scene of the fight.

While I'm waiting, I start pushing healing magic into the bird's body. Its flesh is pretty lacerated, honestly. Its wings are particularly bad; the tender skin connecting the bones was especially vulnerable to the ripping thorns. One wing is worse than the other, probably the one that was under attack for longer.

If left to heal naturally, I'd guess that this creature would never fly again. Fortunately, with the power of my healing Skill, I watch from both "inside" and out as the flesh slowly knits together, leaving smooth skin behind. It doesn't regrow the feathers, though, and leaves a good few spots with little to no feather coverage.

By the time River gets back with a clawful of cherry-tomato-sized fruit, the bird is well on the way to being fully healed. Halfway through the healing, it pushed itself to its feet. It could actually choose right here and now to just take off, assuming that the missing feathers won't impede it in any way; I'm more than half surprised that it doesn't do just that. Instead, it waits calmly, if still a little nervously.

I'm not at all surprised at its display of nerves—standing on the ground between several predators, all much bigger than it is, has to be more than a little uncomfortable.

As I offer it some of the fruit River hands me, I'm pleased when it doesn't just fly away and instead starts picking the fruit delicately out of my hands. I run my eyes over the bird's form as it eats, gently holding each orb in its front claws while it chews at the flesh with its beak. Apart from color, it's fairly similar to the dark-colored beast I chose not to Dominate before we got to the village. There are some physical differences, but they're small; perhaps these are cousin species?

I've been calling it a bird creature because it flies, but it's not easily confusable with a bird from Earth. Principal among the differences is the fact that it has four legs. The front set are noticeably bigger and stronger and look more like the grasping claws of a bird of prey—another strange feature, considering that the bird disdained meat.

Its back feet are little more than simple supports. They have three long toes with small claws on their tips, two facing forwards, one facing back. They do a decent job of holding the bird stable on a flat surface but seem good for little else. The bird's weight is concentrated mostly in its front, and the wings are attached just above and behind its front legs.

In fact, its position reminds me of a human's plank position if the human was resting on their hands rather than elbows. And if they'd seriously been concentrating on arms while skipping leg day every time. And if the human's neck was significantly longer. And it had wings. So, nothing like a human, really, but I can't think of anything on Earth that it's truly like. Either way, it looks significantly more comfortable than I would be if I tried to imitate its position. *Actually, wouldn't my new Strength help with that?*

I brush away the random thought. Considering that my exercise these days consists of running through a forest to avoid getting killed, or fighting creatures to *also* avoid getting killed, the length of time I could hold a plank position seems rather irrelevant. I'd be better off doing exercises to help me fight. Hmm, now *there's* a thought, though not one for now either.

I continue looking at the bird. Its beak is fairly straight and quite short with sharp protrusions of bone imitating teeth. It's these that make chewing the fruit so easy, though it seems to be chewing with the ones on the side towards the back of its beak, which are reasonably blunt; the ones at the front are sharper and some are even *hooked*. My flesh crawls at the thought of them digging into me.

Otherwise, it has proper feathers covering the skin that stretches between the bones of its wings and proto-feathers covering its body, which are similar to those that cover the raptorcats. It also has a hooked claw at the front joint of each of its wings, the joint that would be a wrist on a human. I don't know if the claws are supposed to be more weapons or utility options, but they were certainly instrumental in clinging onto the branch above the bramble bush. Without it using them to hold on, I doubt we'd have had time to save the creature from being pulled into acid and digested while still alive.

When the bird finishes its fruit, it looks up at me questioningly. In its gaze I see nervousness, but also a strange sort of invitation. Something is nagging at me. I frown as I try to tease out what has caught my attention. Then a memory comes back to me: Kalanthia's anger when coming home from a hunting trip to find me feeding Lathani. *I wonder . . .* Maybe it's time to try out that other Skill of mine again. It didn't work last time, but I have a good feeling about it right now.

"Tame," I invoke seriously. Not sure what the requirements for this Skill are, I err on the side of caution and choose to look it in its orange eyes. They're the first with round-shaped pupils I've seen in this world, I realize with a start. Then the Skill takes hold. I don't know exactly how I know when the Skill starts—there's no feeling of being pulled into a separate space like there is with Dominate. The world doesn't fade out around me, and I'm still completely aware of the small movements and noises of my companions and the eerie forest surrounding us.

Instead, it feels like a dialogue has been opened. No, not a dialogue. More like . . . a trade window in a game—a mental version, not a literal window opening. It feels like I've offered a trade to the bird and the bird has accepted it and is now waiting for me to actually make the offer.

Feeling completely at sea, I default to the way I've been approaching the Battle of Wills these days. I project my thoughts and emotions towards the bird as if I already had the link of a Bond or the temporary connection of a Battle of Wills. Then I offer it companionship and the protection of working together in a group.

I can't offer it much more, unable as I am to guarantee even my own safety, let alone that of others. I'd like to be able to offer it food and shelter, but even that is something I cannot promise, not without knowing its needs. Equally, I can't offer it strength, since I don't know how beasts develop, but I can promise that I will work towards the betterment of the group, not just my own betterment. After a moment more of consideration, I also tentatively offer healing if it is hurt.

In return, I need a team member, one who will work *with* the team, not in opposition to it—I've seen how one bad apple in a team can rot the group from the inside in the corporate world. Like it or not, I am the leader of this team, thanks to my position as Binder. Any new additions need to recognize and accept that. And, most importantly, be willing to take directions from me—or my other Bound, in the right contexts.

The nature of the Tame Skill means there's no way to tell how my "offer" is being received. The physical demeanor of the bird doesn't give any clues either; it's been observing me with the same curious wariness ever since I freed it from the vines and started healing it.

The seconds multiply, and I start to wonder if this is going the way it's supposed to or if something's gone wrong somewhere. Then, just as I'm about to try doing something different, there's a shift. It's the mental sensation of the other party putting their cards on the table. The bird recognizes what I can offer it and is giving its counteroffer.

It expresses its desire to always be free to fly, never caged. While this should be an obvious one, I sense that the bird isn't imagining a physical cage—perhaps it doesn't have a reference for that. What it does know how to express is a desire to be free mentally, to cooperate with a companion rather than obey a master. It expresses the need to have its expertise listened to and respected, the need to be able to reject any decision that it feels puts it in undue danger. It agrees that it doesn't need to be the decision-maker, but it will not accept being offered as a sacrifice for others. It draws the line under being able to leave the relationship at any point if it feels these needs are not being met.

All of this, of course, is not being expressed in words; the bird would have to be the most intelligent one I'd ever heard of to be able to express thoughts so abstract in such a way. With this kind of mental connection, however, words are unnecessary. Feelings, emotions, sensations, all of these combine to translate the message I believe the bird is trying to convey. I might be wrong—misinterpretations are, of course, possible—but I don't think I am. There's a solidity to my impressions, which I can't help but think the Tame Skill is the source of. Either that or my increased Wisdom or Animal Empathy are stepping in to help me here.

I give the offered counterproposal the time and deliberation it deserves; we have a time limit here in terms of the duration of my torchlight, but I can't rush this. In the end, I accept the trade with the feeling that it's nothing I wouldn't agree to even without the Tame Skill structuring the offers on each side.

After accepting it on my side, I immediately feel when the bird accepts on hers. A Bond immediately snaps into place; the sensation is far more intense than the almost unnoticeable one of the Dominate Skill. It's very different too—although the sense of being able to communicate mentally and detect the other party is present, the control is not.

In my Bonds with River and Bastet, there is no doubt that I am the dominant one. I instinctively sense that, at a moment's notice, I can shut down the Bond on my side and block communication and feelings from my Bound; they cannot do the same to me. I can also remove the Bond or enforce my will through it, taking away my Bound's ability to disobey—all completely unilaterally. I haven't done any of these things intentionally. Not yet, anyway. It doesn't mean I don't know what's possible, though; the higher my level in Dominate goes, the more understanding of my capabilities I gain.

This is not like that. It's what the bird asked for in the first place: a partnership. Neither of us can act unilaterally on the Bond; we have to agree for the connection to be modified in any way. Neither of us can oblige the other to do anything either, and the Bond can be broken by either of us at any time.

The lack of control does mean that I don't even have the safety-net which ultimately led me to be willing to enter the killing-zone of the lizard-folk's village with only River's presence to aid me. As much as I struggled to trust him, at least there I knew that I could order him to do something and the Bond would enforce it. Here, if the bird decided to attack me, there is little I could do with the Bond that would stop that. Our agreement feels more like a written contract than the chains of my Dominate Skill: the Bond will not stop either party from contravening the agreement, but it will enforce consequences, such as breaking the Bond if I send the bird on a knowingly suicidal task.

It leaves me vulnerable in a way; I can't imagine doing this with River and then immediately going into the village with him. Only the knowledge that I could order him and compel him to obey allowed me to go through with the plan.

However, in some ways, I like Tame much better than Dominate. Not only are contracts a lot more familiar to me than chains, but when it's an equal partnership, I need bear no guilt about forcibly engaging the creature's allegiance. Moral concerns can be dispensed with when there's a consensual agreement between myself and another party.

My torch flickers for a moment. I look at it sharply. The pitch is more than half used up and we still probably have a long way to go. We need to get moving again.

CHAPTER TWENTY-THREE

Salamander

We're being herded.

That's the only conclusion I can come to, at least. My Map tells me which direction we need to travel in to get back to Kalanthia, but our surroundings aren't letting us. We consistently run across blockages: here the trees are growing so closely together that only the feline-types would be able to squeeze through; here it's so thick with undergrowth that we'd spend far too much time hacking our way through to make it worth it.

Recently, the trees have gotten even less subtle: the last two blockages were made from the tree vines actually making a wall. Add that to the naturally rocky and uneven terrain and making headway is slow going enough to be nonexistent.

I've considered hacking through the tree vines to clear a path but, just like with the other vegetation, that approach would take far too long. We're on a timer. My barely used torch has already gone out, and I'm down to two half-used torches, one of which is starting to flicker. If we run out of torches while we're still in the forest . . . Yet, I fear that "threatening" the trees by using some of their deadwood to create more torches would prompt them to attack, regardless of the risk. If it's a choice between letting the torch go out completely or using it, I'll obviously do the latter. For now, though . . .

Of course, I've also considered going through with my threat and burning away the obstacles in my path. The thing is, though, I'm still wary of causing a forest fire while I'm still *in* said forest, especially considering how slowly we're making progress. We're deep in the middle of vine-strangler tree territory and getting away from a fire we caused could be a dicey prospect.

For now, the trees haven't actually been threatening us, they've just been blocking the way. I've therefore made the decision each time I've considered it to maintain the uneasy truce that we have going on until I have more idea of the lay of the land.

Bastet and River are as ill at ease as I am. They've both had enough experience of life to know when things aren't right. Lathani, despite her older appearance, is still as much a cub in personality as she always was. We've had to work hard at times to keep her on track instead of wandering off to investigate the surrounding vegetation. At least there aren't other animals to attract her attention, even if the lack is a bad sign on its own.

Speaking of cubs, the baby raptorcats really aren't happy with the situation, and we've had to let them out at various moments to get some exercise, even though that's just contributed to the delay. At least at those moments we've been able to convince Lathani that it's her job as the elder to keep the other cubs in line and together. Well, I say "we," but I actually mean Bastet. Experience from raising many generations, I guess.

As for my new companion, she doesn't communicate much. From what I've been able to work out, her intelligence level is somewhere between Spike's and Bastet's. She's capable of responding to communication with emotions but not in the same directed way as Bastet. I've been trying to offer her names, but she's rejected all of them so far, so for now she's still "the bird."

She's currently sitting on my shoulder. We decided that flying wasn't the best option, given the trees that can shoot wooden spears in all directions. Her front two feet are gripping carefully onto my shoulder, her back two providing stability by bracing against my shoulder blade. She seems comfortable, and at least her talons aren't biting into me.

The only good thing that's come out of all this walking so far is that both my Dexterity and Strength have increased by a point—the Endurance subcategory for Strength, of course.

Name: Markus Wolfe		Race: Human	Class: Tamer
Level: 3	Energy to next level: 42%	Energy absorption rate: 23u/hr	Energy towards debt: 4%
Intelligence	16	Mana: 160/160	
Wisdom	17	Mana regeneration rate: 425u/hr	
Willpower	20+4 (+20%)	Health regeneration rate: 24u/hr	
Constitution	15	Health: 150/150	
Strength	14	Stamina: 80/80	
Dexterity	14	Stamina regeneration rate: 140u/hr	
Class Skills: Dominate – Beginner 7 Tame – Beginner 5 Fade – Initiate 1		Non-Class Skills: Lay-on-Hands – Initiate 4 Stealth – Novice 1 Animal Empathy – Novice 4 Meditation – Beginner 3	

Tame increased too—that's somewhat expected but gratifying, nonetheless— as did Animal Empathy and Lay-on-Hands. I guess that healing another type of creature was good for my only purely magical Skill. Fade and Stealth are annoying, though, and refuse to rank up.

Wait, hang on.

I frown at my Skills list. When did Fade rank up? And Stealth? I don't remember seeing messages about that. I navigate back to my notification history and mentally flick through them until I find the ones that I—somehow—glossed over. Perhaps I accidentally closed my messages after seeing my Strength point earlier without noticing that there were further notifications to see? Anyway, I have a look at them now, trusting my Bound to tell me if something is wrong.

Congratulations!
You have advanced a Skill past Beginner. Stealth is now Novice 1. Due to your use of this Skill in an unfamiliar environment, you have developed a new aspect of it. When at least half your body is in shadow or the surrounding light level is at 50% or less, Stealth is doubly effective.

Next message / Close messages

Interesting . . . So, it's not just using a Skill in a different way that can help it rank up. It can also be from using the Skill in a different context. I haven't moved around much at night; it's always seemed like too much of a risk considering my lack of vision. Last night I had a good reason to be moving around then. It seems like the risk has paid off in multiple ways.

I move onto the next message and look at the description of the second of my Skills to move up to the Initiate rank.

Congratulations!
You have advanced a Skill past Novice. Fade is now Initiate 1. Due to your use of this Skill in a new environment, you have developed a new aspect of it. Where Fade confuses others' eyes, it sharpens yours. While in Fade, gain 2.5% clarity to your gaze per level past Initiate in the Skill. This is doubly effective in dark conditions: when in low-light conditions, gain 5% clarity of gaze instead of 2.5%.

Close messages

Feeling a little excited over the new effects, I close my status screen and immediately activate Fade. The new "clarity of gaze" isn't terribly blatant. I don't know whether the murky light within the vine-strangler grove counts as low-level light conditions or not. Still, I do notice a difference: some details are sharper, especially ones further away, which would normally be slightly blurry.

As I look ahead, I frown as something catches my attention. The light is different on the route ahead of us, brighter. I hadn't noticed it before. There's also a funny smell in the air, a smell I associate with fire. Has there been a lightning strike or something?

I connect to my Bound and indicate the change. They'd already noticed it, less distracted than I was. We move in the anomaly's direction warily, figuring that anything other than more trees is worth investigating.

As we get closer, it becomes clearer that it's indeed a break in the persistent ground cover of trees and the light source is the sun, far brighter here than at any other place in this thick forest. Reaching the tree line, we see that it's a large vaguely circular clearing. Funnily enough, it's not covered in the vegetation that we've been seeing everywhere else, either.

I frown as I note the differences and, in the back of my mind, try to work out what caused them. The whole area is black, and there is a small bowl-shaped crater at the center of the clearing. *A meteor?* I wonder, though dismiss the thought after a moment—nothing else I can see fits with that explanation.

I venture forwards a couple of steps and touch one of the patches of blackness.

My fingers come away covered in dust. Ash. Well, that explains the strong smell of burning. Was there a forest fire? Possibly, but I somehow doubt it; there are no stumps of trees, and the clearing is far too delineated. What kind of forest fire consumes some trees perfectly and then leaves their neighbors practically untouched? An unnatural one.

Though, that said, the trees are oddly combustible even when green, so them burning down to the ground might not be outside the realm of possibility. Then again, that leaves even *more* questions about why the neighboring trees would be untouched.

Are there creatures who know how to use fire like humans? Maybe I've underestimated the lizard folk . . . But no, River hasn't seemed to recognize the fire of the torches, so it can't be something he sees often.

A moment later, I have an answer to my questions, but I'm not happy with it.

A creature climbs out of the hole in the middle of the clearing. As the only thing in the area that isn't completely black, it's easy to spot. At first, all I see is red and yellow outlined with black. Then, as it clambers out in an ungainly fashion, I see that it appears like another type of reptile, only different. Its body is long, and its head is relatively small, though not flush with its neck like a snake's. It has four legs and a long whiplike tail. It also seems to be *eating* the ash.

By itself, that doesn't say anything except that the beast likes eating ash. However, it doesn't stop there. After munching a bit, the creature wanders across the area towards the tree line. Fortunately, it doesn't aim itself directly at us, but it's not really heading away either. As it reaches the nearest tree, it *breathes fire* at the oversized plant.

The vine-strangler tries to protect itself by shooting out spearing roots towards the salamander—because what else can it be but a fire salamander, only this weird world's version? Sadly for the tree, the salamander isn't bothered. It dodges a few of the strikes, tanks some more, and then actually bites back at the others. It spits out the wood, though—apparently, living wood isn't to its taste.

All the while, the fire it breathed on the tree has been eating away greedily at the vine-strangler. Either it's a special type of blaze or the particular vulnerability of vine-strangler trees to fire really works against it, as it goes up in flames much more quickly than green wood normally would. It's not long before the salamander is happily munching the charcoal remains of what was a healthy tree not long before.

Let's go before it notices us, I send to my Bound while tapping Lathani on the shoulder to indicate that she should back up. Unfortunately for us, backing up doesn't appear to be an option.

While we were watching the salamander, the trees behind us quietly built a wall of roots. Growling at the trees, we start sneaking sideways as we try to move away from the over-large amphibian without attracting its notice while simultaneously looking for a way around the wall of roots.

Of course, it's not that easy. As quickly as we move, the trees are quicker in blocking our way. If I didn't know better, I'd suspect that the forest was trying to set both its threats up against each other in the hopes that they'll kill each other off.

Heck, what am I saying? This is a completely different world; maybe I *don't* know better and trees *are* capable of strategic planning and execution.

Either way, we appear to be stuck in a clearing with a fire-breathing salamander . . . which has finally noticed the interlopers in its territory.

I curse as the salamander bellows in rage and starts charging at us surprisingly quickly for its bulk. As it comes closer, I realize that I significantly underestimated its size. I thought it was the size of a large cow, but it appears to be more the size of a horse. And a big shire one, at that. Still, it has quite a bit of space to cover, so we have a few moments to prepare.

We need to fight, River tells me grimly even as Bastet projects a calm question about our plan of attack.

"I know," I sigh. Swiftly, I pull the sling with the cubs in it off my chest. The bird is disturbed and flaps up into the air before alighting on River's shoulder instead. I don't pay her much attention and instead focus my attention on the nunda cub. "Lathani," I say to her seriously, "I need you to protect the cubs."

You're trying to keep me away from the fight, she accuses me.

"Partly," I admit, but press on quickly—we have no time to lose. "Your mother would kill me if I survived this and you didn't, but also there's nowhere safe I can put the cubs, and I don't want to take them into the fight with me. I need you to do this for me." I hold her eyes for a long moment, willing her to understand. The salamander is past the halfway mark and gaining swiftly on us.

Okay, fine. She gives in with a mixture of bad grace and pleasure—annoyed at being kept out of the fight but pleased to be given the responsibility, I'd guess. She's agreed and that's all that matters to me right now.

Without more than a quick nod of acknowledgment, I run off to the side, and my Bound follow me. With the cubs now under supervision, we need to make some space between us. That this will delay the salamander just a little more is a bonus.

Any ideas? I send to my Bound as we run.

I am most comfortable with the spear, River replies. Bastet sends a similar agreement, only replacing the spear with her claws and teeth. The bird offers wordlessly to circle and attack from above.

"Okay," I say as I come to a halt. We've got a bit of space between us and the young ones, though not so much that I can't see them. The salamander is nearly upon us, but we have a few seconds before it reaches us. "Dodge its charge, then River, you stab it, and Bastet, go for its belly. Bird, try to get its eyes. I'll see what I can do." The salamander skids to a halt and opens its mouth. "Damn! Avoid its—" I'm cut off by the wave of fire that comes billowing at us.

CHAPTER TWENTY-FOUR

Grilled

I fall flat to the ground, mouthing swear words, and the fire rushes over my head instead of hitting me full force. It's close enough to singe my hair with the heat but not actually catch me on fire, fortunately.

When the wave ends, I push myself to my feet as quickly as I can. As I get out of the way of the salamander's mouth, I glance around myself to see where my companions are. Bastet managed to dodge to the side, her speed and reactions serving her well, and looks unharmed. River is another story.

Not as fast, he instead obviously dropped his spear to the ground, hunkered down, and protected his head with his arms. The scales on his shoulders, the back of his head, and the backs of his arms are blackened and cracked, but still mostly intact. If his scales can shrug off even just *some* fire damage, he's in a better position than I am.

As for the bird, a quick glance upwards proves that she was quick enough to fly up and out of the way of the deluge of fire. She's actually quite high above the battle. Absently, I wonder if she was able to catch the updrafts caused by the sudden heat. She's already descending, though, in a dive towards the salamander's head.

After a brief pause caused by our collective disbelief at the fact that we survived the first attack, we all spring into action.

As we planned, Bastet immediately goes for the salamander's underbelly, raking at it with her claws and biting with her teeth. At points she even disappears underneath the creature—I hope that thing doesn't think of lying down, or she'll be easily squished under its mammoth bulk. A salamander as tall as a shire horse is significantly wider than one, the proportions of a salamander being the way they are.

River runs at the amphibian, his spear held at the ready. He stabs at its neck, at the join between shoulder and throat, and at its front leg. If he's lucky, he'll hit an important artery or its trachea, but even if not, wounds there should impede its mobility. It's a good choice of attack. He's slower than usual, though—the burned scales across his shoulders are clearly paining him.

I dart in after him, keeping a wary eye on the salamander's head as it snakes around biting at anything within range. Laying my hand on River's back, I send a wave of healing magic into his body. Before Lay-on-Hands has had time to finish its work, the salamander's biting mouth forces me to jump back.

River's shoulders look a lot better; the minimal damage is easy to heal. I've noticed that as Lay-on-Hands has leveled through the Initiate stage, it's been healing more points at once for the same mana cost. Clearly, my efficiency is improving. In this case, it means that River's burns are almost healed, making movement significantly easier and less painful for him.

River sends me a wave of gratitude down the link as I hurry out of range, and he returns to his job of stabbing. He's aided when the bird drops down onto the salamander's head and starts raking at its eyes to distract it from the lizard-man making holes anywhere he can reach, not to mention the raptorcat threatening to disembowel it. It would help if we knew where this thing's heart is, but that's going to have to be a trial-and-error approach.

Even as I pull out my bow and arrows and prepare to shoot, the salamander whips around to bite at Bastet. River takes advantage of that to start stabbing behind its foreleg, clearly hoping that maybe he can hit the heart or lungs from that angle.

Bastet, of course, is too quick to be caught, and the salamander closes its teeth on nothing. My heart still leaps in fear as the sharp fangs click together a hair's breadth from one of her wings. Fearing that I'm too slow to risk melee, I shoot at the salamander and get mixed results.

Where the arrow hits head-on, it pierces, but not deeply; even with my increased Strength lending power to the arrow's flight, the salamander is clearly heavily armored with those scales. Where the arrow doesn't hit head-on, it just skitters off and lands somewhere in the battlefield. I keep going, though, and continue aiming for the probable weak spots—I may get lucky and hit it in a vulnerable spot. I doubt my mace would have any better luck, frankly.

The bird takes advantage of the big amphibian's distraction to swipe at its eyes again, and it bellows angrily as it swipes back, its own clawed paw twice as big as the bird's whole body. It opens its mouth once more to fire its incinerating blast. That's my cue. I shoot directly into its open oral cavity; my accuracy is good enough to have more than a decent chance of hitting such a large target. Best-case scenario, I pierce its brain by going through the roof of its mouth. Worst-case scenario, I merely interrupt its fire breathing.

The arrow hits the salamander clean in the mouth and pierces its tongue.

It snaps its mouth shut on its own fire, and flames leak out of the sides of its mouth for a fraction of a second. Its eyes go wide—clearly, that's not a sensation it appreciates.

The attack also serves to make it a bit more wary of opening its jaws again for a short time, and it tries to use the weight of its head to knock into River instead of biting at him with its teeth. It also uses its claws more and steadies itself on three feet while using the fourth to strike at my companions.

Without an easy target, I pepper it with arrows, aiming for points that I think might have the potential to cause damage. I shoot at its joints, the soft spots at its jawline, and its eyes. The main problem is that my arrows simply don't pierce deeply enough. My arrows pierce a few inches in at best, but when the skin is probably an inch or more thick to begin with, that doesn't do much.

I need to get at its eyes or mouth again to do much. I get another chance when it opens its mouth to take a bite at the bird; her efforts at raking its eyes are more annoying than effective, but they serve their purpose as distraction.

The angle isn't great for me, but I manage to slip an arrow between its jaws again and pierce one of its gums.

The salamander bellows once more, this time in pain. It lowers its head to the level of its forepaws and uses one to scrub at its mouth in a clumsy attempt to get rid of the annoying pinprick.

Not having the dexterity to pluck the second arrow out, it doesn't succeed in doing more than presenting a tempting target for Dominate.

Making eye contact with it, I quickly activate my Skill. However, for the first time, I am so clearly outclassed, it isn't funny. The pressure on me is less like that of a garden hose and more like a firefighter's.

I resist as much as I can, but it's futile. I lose ground quickly and am blown backwards like a pebble in a strong current of water. I land far beyond the starting point.

The Battle of Wills shatters.

I slump to the ground, paralyzed, as the backlash of losing the battle hits me. The salamander bellows and takes a step forwards, its angry eyes fixed on the being who dared try to Dominate it. Fortunately for me, River rides to the rescue as the salamander's sudden focus on me gives him a good opportunity.

The lizard-man stabs at the base of its head, probably attempting to go for the brain like I was earlier. A flurry of movement on the other side of it reveals that Bastet is also trying to take advantage by going straight for its throat.

The two coordinate so well that I wonder whether they're able to use the Bond to communicate with each other without going through me. Or maybe they're both just that good at reading combat.

The salamander reacts unpredictably, though. Its head snakes out quicker than expected and digs its teeth into Bastet before the raptorcat can jump away.

My heart rises into my mouth as it lifts her into the air. It shakes its head and blood flies everywhere. I'm paralyzed with agony; the seconds it takes for me to regain control of my limbs seem like an eternity as one of my Bound is savaged.

Fortunately, River is once more there to help. Using his spear, he stabs into the base of the salamander's neck as hard as he can. The wooden shaft sinks in deeply, and the large amphibian opens its jaws to bellow in pain again.

Bastet falls out of its open mouth and lands heavily on the ground.

Fear runs through me as she doesn't make any effort to break her fall. My heart leaps as the weakness from my failed Dominate fades from my limbs. As soon as I can control them, I scramble to my feet and run over to Bastet's limp body.

My eyes are only on my oldest companion as I slide to a stop next to her. I slap my hand on her side and immediately channel healing into her.

She's alive, but only just. The blood is running out of her almost too quickly for my healing to compensate. I curse myself for being greedy—if I hadn't tried to Dominate the salamander maybe Bastet wouldn't have been so badly injured.

Master! River's urgent tone grabs my attention. I look up to see the salamander's jaws aiming at us, the flicker of flame already kindling at the back of its throat. I know instinctively that any more damage will be the end of my loyal companion. My friend. My family member.

With a leap fueled by desperation and the strength of an Olympic jumper, I propel myself forwards and grab onto the salamander's head, then yank it forcibly off course. I almost manage to get my body out of the way of the fire that jets out of its mouth.

Almost.

Flames lick at my side like white-hot tongues, each pass singeing and charring my flesh. My armor is little protection, my other clothes even less.

My grip loosens involuntarily, and I drop from the creature's head like a stone, then quickly start to roll—as much to put out the fire that's caught on my garments as to get out of the path of the enraged amphibian. I send a quick Lay-on-Hands through my system to at least start to deal with the large portion of my torso that has just been grilled. My pain threshold rises to a new high. This is the worst physical agony I've ever experienced.

I'm screaming loudly, something I only realize a moment later. I manage to cut off the loud noise, but it's done its job to attract the attention of the salamander back onto me.

Healing.

I need healing . . . but Bastet needs it even more. I don't even know how my other two companions are doing.

But how can I do anything when it's taking all my Strength and Willpower to just avoid the attacks of the pissed-off salamander? A creature that is bleeding from innumerable wounds but still seems as powerful as it was when we first started fighting it. Worst of all, it seems to have its own healing power since even the wounds that River made in its neck don't seem as bad as they were originally.

Healing.

An idea comes to mind, a thought I half play with at odd times ever since I saw the rank-up message.

Do I risk it?

Do I have a choice?

My eyes narrow, and I wait for my moment. It comes when the salamander once more tries to bite at me. I roll out of its path and manage to avoid it in such a way that I'm in a perfect position to carry out the rest of my plan when it buries its teeth in the dirt. I grab onto its neck with arms and legs and am lifted into the air when it raises its head once more.

Of course, the salamander immediately starts trying to shake me loose. River seems rather confused about my strategy, sending me a questioning feeling down the Bond. I'm a little busy, though, and unable to reply with more than a desperate need for help as I cling onto the salamander's neck with a death grip.

At the same time, I send healing magic into the flesh I'm holding onto. Of course, I'm not actually trying to *help* the creature, so instead of just letting the magic loose to heal the numerous wounds we've dealt, I keep a tight control on it. Concentrating isn't easy, but when the salamander's attempts to throw me off reduce, it becomes a little less difficult.

Tightly gripping onto the magic, I guide it up through the neck and into the brain. There I direct it to make the vessels grow. I want them to swell until they burst, causing an aneurysm—a fatal one, preferably.

The healing magic bucks against my hold on it. There's some sort of blockage, an obstacle. But it doesn't feel like this is an impossible task. I grit my teeth and focus harder as I push with my twenty-four stat points of Willpower. I refuse to entertain the possibility of failure. Bastet needs me *now*, so this creature needs to go down *yesterday.*

The barrier or obstacle or whatever it is resists, but I just keep pushing with the faith of the desperate. Maybe the problem is that I haven't put enough magic into this. I channel more and more, throwing it all at the blockage. It flickers, then suddenly fails with a rush. Unhindered, my magic saturates the salamander's brain and, in an instant, causes innumerable blood vessels to grow and burst.

I drop heavily to the ground as the muscle I'm holding onto suddenly loses all power. I don't spare the dead monster more than a single glance, and that's only to make sure that it is truly dead.

The blood leaking out of its staring eyes and gaping mouth is enough proof for me. After pushing myself to my feet, forcibly ignoring my side screaming at me, I half run, half stumble over to my raptorcat friend.

"Please don't be dead, please don't be dead," I croak under my breath as I fall at her side.

CHAPTER TWENTY-FIVE

Between Bad and Worse

Placing my hands immediately on the seriously injured raptorcat, I channel my magic into her body, following it with my mind. I direct it to the deep wounds that pierce through her body; my earlier efforts slowed the bleeding but didn't stop it. I feel the healing magic pulling together flesh, connecting blood vessels, and—

My mana runs dry. Inside Bastet's body—mentally, at least—it feels like I've run out of air. Gasping for breath, I'm pulled back into my own body, the sudden return a shock. My body feels like an ill-fitting garment, like I've shrugged on the wrong shirt. A moment later, the sensation has gone and left behind a simple nauseous exhaustion.

"No," I croak as I try to trigger Lay-on-Hands again and again. Nothing happens. The exhaustion is joined by horror as I realize that my closest companion in this world, my *friend* is dying in front of me and there's *nothing* I can do about it until my mana regenerates. I must have used more than I thought to kill the salamander. Even my recent points in Intelligence haven't helped.

I slump back and stare at her, my eyes tracing the blood being absorbed into the blackened earth beneath. Two minutes is all it will take for me to regenerate enough for a new Lay-on-Hands; two minutes is a lifetime—and may be more than Bastet has left.

"No," I whisper again as I try to rack my brain to find a solution. Anything that can delay the otherwise inevitable is better than nothing.

I need to put pressure on the wounds, keep her blood inside her body in the non-magical way that's used all over Earth. I pull my backpack out of my Inventory and yank a shirt out, fighting past the lethargy that still tugs at my limbs and my nausea as I move. Leaning over Bastet, I press the shirt against the puncture marks and lean my weight on it.

Let me, River rumbles as he falls to his knees beside me. His hands are full of something. I immediately give him space; I don't feel any ill intent in the Bond, and he has to know that if he intentionally made the situation worse and killed her, I would kill *him* for it. Besides, the situation is already dire—what could he do to make it worse, bar slitting her throat?

He packs the contents of his hands into the wounds and tips a liquid in over the top. Pressing the fabric of my shirt to the mess, he swiftly flips her over so she's lying on that side. The wounds on her other side start bleeding more freely—the pressure from her body lying on them had been holding them mostly closed, but now there's nothing to stop the red lifeblood from pouring out.

I almost intervene out of anger at his actions, which have caused even more precious fluid to leave her body and reduced her chances even further. The lizard-man seems to detect something, whether it's from the connection between us or my body language, and he sends grim reassurance down the Bond.

The feeling settles me a little—I sense that he knows what he's doing and is trying his best to save my friend. Even as he communicates with me, his hands are not idle. He's doing the same on this side as he did on the other, packing the puncture marks with what look like bits of plant, which he's withdrawing from a strangely shaped box.

Once they're packed tightly, he tips some more of the liquid all over, emptying the container that looks like a large chunk of hollowed-out branch. After pulling the sleeves of my now blood-stained shirt through from either side of Bastet, he ties a knot over the wounds.

Done, he slumps. A wave of trepidation and hope crashes through the Bond.

"What did you do?" I ask him as I check my mana bar. A sliver has returned; not enough yet for Lay-on-Hands. I've become practiced at estimating how much the mana bar represents in terms of practical use.

I don't have the skills my master—my former master, he corrects himself with sadness in his tired voice, *has with herbs, but I have learned a few tricks and made sure to bring some supplies from . . . with me. I also always keep a few essentials on me.* He pulls at the woven strip of vines around his waist, and I realize that what I had imagined to be a decorative belt is more than that. Wound into the body of the belt itself are little hollows, and each holds a little carved chunk of branch with a wooden stopper or a load of shredded plant. However, that's not where he got the things he packed into Bastet's wounds from. That was from the box.

The box is oddly shaped, with an oblong, boatlike form. It's something I noticed in our escape but didn't bother looking closely at even once the light level got high enough to do so. Like the cage I was held in, it looks more grown than carved. It has two woven handles on it, which River was using to wear it like an oddly shaped backpack. I'd thought it to be a container of essentials, which I'd recommended he bring with us in our escape.

Now he has it open, the lid looking more like a large oval cork than something on hinges, I see how it's separated into sections, each one filled with dried parts of plants. Flowers, leaves, stems, roots, fruits . . . I'm frankly amazed at how much he's managed to pack in there. *I have packed in some herbs and poured in an unguent,* River explains. *In my kind, these herbs help Warriors avoid inflammation of their wounds and reduce blood loss. I am hoping that they will have the same effect on your companion.*

"You *hope,*" I repeat, my voice hard.

Yes, he replies, meeting my gaze without flinching. *I have never heard of nor seen them used on a creature such as she. Normally, we kill this kind of creature rather than heal it.* I concede the point with a grunt, irrationally angry.

I want someone to blame for this, but the only ones I can blame are the salamander for giving her such grievous wounds and myself for putting her in the position where she gained them.

I watch my mana bar out of the corner of my eye and immediately know when it's regained enough to cast another Lay-on-Hands. Without wasting any time, I place my hands back on my raptorcat and channel healing into her once more.

Focusing on dealing with the worst of her wounds first, I soon run out of mana again. Nonetheless, I feel a hint of hope flare in my heart: her condition hasn't really worsened since I last ran out of mana. It seems like River's stopgap measures have at least helped her maintain her previous state.

I repeat the process for the next six minutes, not daring to even look away from my desperately injured companion in case I miss the moment something goes wrong or I don't cast Lay-on-Hands the second it becomes available again.

At some point, I feel a nudge of soft fur against my elbow and see patterns in my peripheral vision. Lathani's here. Either River went to get her, or she came of her own accord.

I dare to look away from Bastet for a second and check that the three cubs are here too. They are. As I return my gaze to the raptorcat adult, I feel the lifting of a weight from my heart. I realize that I was expecting something to happen to the youngest and most vulnerable of our group while we weren't able to help.

Fortunately, for once things seem to have gone our way. It just took Bastet almost dying to get us there.

By the time I've cast my fourth Lay-on-Hands, I allow myself a sigh of relief. She's out of the woods. Not literally—we're still stuck in this damn forest—but the worst of her wounds are on their way to being healed and her condition is not worsening between casts. Bastet was even closer to death than she had been when we first met, but finally, she seems to have pulled back from the edge.

I dare to do more than just watch her attentively and take a look around as I absently reach out to stroke Lathani's head. When I realize what I'm doing, I pause. The headbutt she gives my hand says more than words ever could, so I continue. The motion is soothing, probably for both of us. I look over at River.

"Thank you," I say, heartfelt. He just dips his head, his expression unreadable.

She fought like a true warrior, he says finally, his tone faintly admiring.

"She always does," I respond fondly as I reach out to stroke her leg. It's cold; her blood is concentrated in her torso so as to keep her vital functions going. I take the opportunity to send more magic into her system, my mana having just about regenerated enough. I look at Lathani. "Were you safe the whole time?"

Of course, she replies, sounding insulted. *I agreed to look after the cubs, so I did.*

"I'm not questioning your commitment," I say, trying to soothe her. "It's just that I was worried something else might have appeared while we were focused on the giant salamander."

Oh, she replies, her hackles lowering. *Then no, nothing appeared. I kept an eye on that hole in the center, but nothing else came out.*

"Good," I reply, relieved. We'll probably have to investigate that hole, but not until we're all healed. I look back at River. "How are your wounds?"

Manageable, he replies stoically. I send skeptical feelings through the Bond, and he shrugs, wincing a little. *I shall be glad of healing,* he admits, *but it can wait until your companion is out of danger.* I nod.

Frankly, I feel the same. My own aches and pains are making themselves clearly known by this point, not to mention the painful burns still covering my side. Looking around, I wonder where my newest companion has gone. Not seeing her, I look towards River. He points up. I follow his clawed finger to find a dot circling around, making larger and larger loops.

"What's she doing?" I mutter, not really intending to speak aloud.

Scouting, River answers. I look back at him. *At least, that's my guess,* he adds. *It's not like I can talk with her, after all.*

"Fair," I admit. I guess that answers the question I had earlier—Bastet and River are just *that* good at reading a combat situation. Silence falls for a while, as none of us really has the energy to talk. Well, Lathani probably does, but she's unusually subdued, just pressing close to me and staring at Bastet.

Actually, maybe that's not surprising—the adult raptorcat has been a carer for her as well over the last few weeks. The other cubs are also subdued, squabbling a bit but not venturing far away from us. I wonder whether they remember the scent of blood and death and are affected by it as much as the rest of us, even if in a different way.

It feels like we're in a limbo of some sort, broken only by my regular casts of healing magic and the odd movement. We're attentive to our surroundings, River more than me, admittedly. Everything is calm and still. It's a little odd after so many hours of moving on eggshells, keeping eyes watching in all directions for the next attack. Here, in the ash-choked clearing that the salamander made, next to its huge body, we're safer than we have been in quite a while. As long as it doesn't have a mate or children wanting to avenge it, that is.

We all eat and drink, needing the nutrients and fluids. I even succeed in trickling a bit of water into Bastet's mouth; I'm sure she needs nutrition the most out of all of us, but we're not going to get meat down her throat until she's awake enough to chew. I'm out of water now and almost out of cooked meat. Fortunately, there's a massive body lying next to us, and the carnivores that make up the majority of the group don't waste any time in digging in.

"Save me the heart, would you?" I tell River. He acknowledges my request even as he starts digging meat out of the carcass with his sharp claws. Lathani and the cubs join him too. I stay beside Bastet and keep the healing going. In between casts, I look around the area, seeing its desolation anew.

The sun is already far on its way towards the horizon—the walk through the forest has taken longer than we wanted, thanks to this detour. Then add in the fight and the healing, and it's not surprising that we're only a few hours away from dark. Once more, I have a decision to make: Keep going and risk walking through a bunch of killer trees in the dark? Or stay here and risk being attacked by something coming up from the hole?

Frankly, I'd rather fly out of here like the bird did, but until we all develop wings, that's not going to work. Like it or not, I'm going to have to choose between bad or worse. But which is bad, and which is worse?

CHAPTER TWENTY-SIX

Tunnel

Honestly, with Bastet still significantly injured, it's too much to expect that we'll heal her and still get out of the forest while it's light. And frankly, walking through the vine-stranglers in the light is tempting fate enough, let alone in the dark. I'm down to my last torch, and that one's half-used. The torch I was using before is finished—I was too distracted by the salamander to put it out. Between that and the time I spent healing Bastet, the little that was left burned itself out. It's not a big loss; it was starting to flicker out anyway. But it still means just that little bit less time available to us.

I now only have a single half-burned torch stuck in my Inventory, and based on past experience, that's nowhere near enough to get us through the danger zone, light or dark. Not unless we're almost to the edge of the forest.

Not having enough torches isn't the end of the world by itself, though—I'm surrounded by trees that have proven to be vulnerable to fire. I didn't dare create more torches while actually in the forest, but we seem to be out of easy reach of their spearing branches here.

Of course, I'm assuming that they aren't capable of remembering that my torches are made out of their branches and taking offense at that when we return to the forest later. With them being plants, I normally wouldn't even consider it, but since they appeared to herd me here to face another of their threats? I'm suddenly questioning everything I knew about trees. Ultimately, though, I think I'll have to take the risk, as I simply don't have enough wood to create enough torches to be confident about seeing us through the forest.

Regardless, I reckon that waiting until the morning and then continuing through the forest is the best idea, if only because of how much more difficult I, for one, will find it to travel through the tricky terrain in the dark.

Staying here for the night should be fine, but much longer isn't really an option. We have plenty of food between the salamander carcass and the load of corpses I have in my Inventory, but I've finished the water I had in there. And that's not counting the fact that there's really nothing here. Even if the trees can't get at us, we'd be prisoners all the same, still relegated to a slow death.

No, we'll have to brave the forest at some point. Though, it would be good to have an idea of how far we have to go, so I can make some plans. On that note, I wonder where the bird has gone. Has she taken this opportunity to fly into the clear skies and leave us permanently?

No, I can still feel the Bond—she hasn't broken it from her side, at least. She's far enough away, though, that all I can get from the Bond is a vague sense of direction and her steady emotional state.

I turn my thoughts back to the present situation. After casting Lay-on-Hands once more on Bastet, I find my eyes being pulled inexorably back to the hole that lies at the lowest point of this shallow bowl-like basin. I'm not quite sure why it seems so important to me, so I try to think about something else. Often, the harder I try to find something when I'm not sure exactly what I'm looking for, the less likely I am to find it. And then when I stop searching for it, that's when it comes back to mind.

Deciding that Bastet can afford me looking away from her for a time, I close my eyes. Maybe Meditation will help me out here. If nothing else, my new Skill means that I should regenerate my mana more quickly. I didn't dare to do it before: Bastet needed healing as quickly as possible and with the way time seems to slip away while I'm in Meditation, I couldn't be sure that I wouldn't just meditate her life away.

Besides, before now, it would have taken too much time to sufficiently calm myself to actually properly engage in Meditation and gain its effects; I would have been dropping out to cast another Lay-on-Hands almost before I'd managed to slip into the trancelike state. Now that she's more stable, though, I figure I have the time, and my emotions are a little more settled. In fact, if I allow more mana to accrue, it will also allow me to heal in a more efficient way. Just like how using Energy in bulk to raise stat points is more efficient, so is healing with greater quantities of mana.

Breathing deeply, I feel my eyes slide shut of their own accord. I reconnect to my surroundings and frown a little as I feel the differences. There's something . . . odd about this area. It's probably just the smoke I can smell, but it *feels* like fire. I try to push past the ghostly flickers of flame against my skin, the memory of the fire snatching at my flesh. I wrestle my thoughts under control before they snap me out of my Meditative state, then open my eyes and stare at the hole, all while I direct my newly regenerated mana into Bastet's body.

Thoughts percolate like water through coffee grains. I feel a realization slowly come closer. It's hard to just wait for it to come instead of mentally reaching out to snatch at it, but I know that's completely counterproductive. In hopes that it might spark something, I let my eyes drift around the area, where they alight briefly on the salamander's corpse and my Bound and other companions as they dig into it, then wander past to pass over the trees around us.

The realization I was waiting for hits. How did the salamander get in here? I mean, I'm assuming that the destruction in this area of the forest was caused by it, but based on what I saw of it attacking the tree, I think that my supposition is justified. And if that's what it does to the area around it, why is there no evidence of its path through the forest? I mean, I suppose that the trees could have regrown and eliminated all evidence of its passage.

That doesn't make a huge amount of sense, though. I can see what it's done to trees in this clearing, and there's really nothing but ash to indicate that they were ever even here. Besides, why would it have wandered through the forest, then randomly stopped and made a rough circle with a hole at the center? No, another explanation makes far more sense: it came *up* through the hole.

All of which indicates to me that there might be a way *out* through the hole too.

It's a tantalizing thought to not have to brave the vine-stranglers, where one foot wrong could lead to our deaths. Where I'm constantly worried that one of the pack will wander a bit too far and be trapped and killed before we can save them. Or where a lucky strike could kill any of us at any time. Not knowing when or if the trees will risk calling my bluff keeps me on edge at all times. And even if they do, now I've seen how easily these trees can burn, can I bring myself to cause a forest fire when I'm *still in the forest?* The trees' fear of fire is well explained.

On the other hand, if this hole is actually a tunnel, do I dare trust that it's any safer? Even if it is a tunnel to the outside, it could be infested with any manner of beast, other salamanders being the most likely.

If it's a tunnel infested with those fire salamanders, we'll brave the forest instead, but if it's not . . . They say that fortune is for the brave and that we make our own luck. Is it too late to find out if that's true?

Either way, before we can do anything like that, we need to all be mobile, and Bastet isn't yet. Besides, River said that he thought the bird was scouting; perhaps we should wait to see if she has any new information to add. I would hate to be only a half hour walk from the closest edge of the vine-strangler forest without knowing it. There's something else I can do now, though . . .

"River," I start, turning my head to look at him.

Master? Discomfort nags at me at the address, but I push it aside.

"Can you just walk down to that hole in the center? See whether it's just a pit or whether it looks like it goes somewhere." I feel his assent, and shortly after he departs, the spear I gave him held ready for any attack, I speak again. "Lathani," I say next.

Yes, Carer? she says, but since it's a mental voice, I can't use it to tell exactly where she is.

"Can you keep an eye on River, please? If anything moves anywhere near him, let me know."

Sure, she agrees, but there's something unreadable in her tone. Unfortunately, I don't have the connection with her that I do with the others, so I can't investigate any further. I miss Bastet and her cool efficiency. She wouldn't need to be asked: she would already be keeping an eye out. Pushing the thoughts away, I return to what I know I need to do to get her back on her feet.

I continue Meditating and intermittently emerge to heal the raptorcat. Her health point pool must be several times that of mine because she's already absorbed enough healing to almost fill my own and she's still significantly injured. Bit by bit, though, River's stopgap measure of herbs and unguent is pushed out of the wounds as healthy flesh takes its place.

Rousing from my latest bout of Meditation, I cast Lay-on-Hands again and once more follow the channeled magic into Bastet's body, directing it to heal the last of her serious wounds. She's still unconscious, but I reckon she'll wake up soon—the sense I get down the Bond is that of an exhausted sleep rather than deathly unconsciousness. There are still a few more wounds to heal, but they're little more than skin-deep. I'll Meditate to let my mana regenerate a bit more and then, hopefully, clear all of us of wounds.

Looking around, I almost jump as I see River sitting within arm's length.

"When did you get back?" I demand to cover the fact that my heart is now racing and my hand has automatically gone to my knife.

A few clicks ago. I tried to rouse you, but you were dead to the world. Huh. So *that's* what the latest upgrade message to Lay-on-Hands meant when it said that I would not be able to detect my surroundings. I might not have gone so deeply into Bastet's healing while River was out scouting if I'd realized that Lathani wouldn't actually be able to wake me from it if there was danger. I'll need to keep that in mind. But first . . .

"What did you find?"

It's a tunnel, River replies. I lean towards him, eagerness and hope running through me.

"What is it like? Could you see the end?"

It is a single large tunnel. It's large enough for the creature we fought to move through easily enough, but its end is around a bend. However, I strongly suspect that it has an exit outside the Forest of Death. My eyebrows shoot up at the certainty in his mental voice and the Bond.

"What makes you say that?"

There is a strong breeze that caresses the tunnel walls—it brings with it the faintest hints of the normal forest. I grin, hope igniting in my heart. I want to see what the bird has to say, but already the hole is rising to the top as an option for our escape. Then a thought occurs, and my grin shrinks a little.

"Did you see any signs of other salamanders?" He clicks his mouth closed twice as negation comes through the Bond.

It was clear of movement as far as I could see, he confirms. My grin widens once more. Excellent. No guarantee that there won't be critters waiting around the corner, ready to pounce, but it's a good sign, nonetheless.

I decide to wait until the bird comes back, just to confirm that it wouldn't be a better idea to go through the trees. I decide to go back into Meditation until my mana has fully regenerated. I never know when I'll need it next. After letting River know my intentions, I drop back into my trance.

CHAPTER TWENTY-SEVEN

As Much of a Burden

In Meditation, the world makes sense. The luminous connections spool away from me and give me the hint of a picture that's far too big for me to actually see. The peripheral links are barely there; only the ones that directly touch me have more presence than just a flicker of instinct, like something seen out of the corner of one's eye but invisible when looked at directly. My mind explores the network of connections linked to me.

Several of them are linked to my Bound, and I touch them in a different way than before, sensing the connection I have with them from the outside as well as the inside. I feel the links between the cubs, half detectable to the sense I only seem to be able to access when in this trance.

Far less perceptible is the network of links between them and everything else, but I am aware *something* exists in the space. For a moment, I even feel a flicker of emotion through the faint connections they have with me, but it's too brief to identify any more than that it was there. From my companions I move on to sensing the rest of the world around: the blur of connectivity of everything to everything else.

Hints of fire lick at my sense of self, not hurting but teasing, tantalizing me with secrets only they know. Even the trees have links that stretch out into the world around them, though theirs are hostile, rejecting the touch of mine. I feel their strong links to each other, the lines so powerful they stand out to my sense in comparison to everything else around. Apart from the strong connections to each other, there are also thick lines that plunge deep into the earth.

In curiosity, I reach out my sense, moving far more by instinct than thought. Deep, deep, deeper does my perception go. I wonder why the trees around me have such a thick connection with something below . . .

And then I'm yanked out of my trance by a touch to my shoulder—my physical shoulder. I flinch. The sensation is suddenly too much, gentle as it is. My body feels ill-fitting, both confining and loose in the wrong spots. I blink and swallow, and then the world rights itself. Like emerging from an immersive dream, I feel my way back to who I am. Not the trees, not the connections, not the fire . . . Markus Wolfe, human.

I rub a hand across my face. Maybe I need to be careful how far I go with this trance stuff. Then I chuckle dryly. I would have never thought I'd want to put a warning label on *Meditation* of all things. I check my bars: my mana is full, so it's probably just as well I was woken. There are other things to do.

As the first thing, I feed more healing magic into Bastet's body, pleased with her progress. In the end, I don't need all of it to heal the surface wounds that remain. Although I sense that she's not quite at full health, her body seems mostly healed to me. My hand falls away from her side, and I gaze at her head intently, hoping she'll wake up soon.

What do you want us to do with this, Master? River asks me, the sudden rumble and clicks of his voice breaking through the quiet that had taken hold. I twist around to see him holding a fist-sized crystalline structure. I push myself to my feet with a wince and head over to him. Before examining the thing he's holding more closely, I look seriously in my Bound's bronze slit-pupil eyes.

"You don't have to call me that, you know." He frowns—which, incidentally, on a lizard-man involves his mouth opening a little and his spikes flashing a dark orange.

What?

"You know . . . '*Master.*'" I hadn't cared before when my anger at the lizard folk—and River by dint of being their representative—was crushing any sense of guilt. But considering the situation, what he's done for me, what he's given up in pursuit of my objectives . . . The word makes me feel dirty now, like I'm the bad guy. "Just call me Markus." River eyes me uncertainly and with no little confusion for a moment. And is it just my imagination, or is there also a hint of . . . loss? Disappointment?

As you wish . . . Markus. Pushing away my bemusement at his reaction, I squint at the red crystal the lizard-man is holding. It's large, filling most of his hand. It looks like a rough-cut ruby or a chunk of red-tinged glass. Taking it from River, I tilt it in the soft light of the sun, the orb not far from the horizon.

The color isn't very strong, but it somehow renders the material opaque, nonetheless. Light acts strangely when it hits the thing—at times reflecting off it like it would a real gemstone, at others seemingly getting absorbed into a matte surface. I think I've seen something like this before, though they were a lot smaller.

"Is that a . . . ?" I don't know what to call it. I just know that Bastet ate one of the thumbnail-sized ones we found in those insectile things and gave the two others to the cubs. I shove the memory down the Bond to River and attach a questioning feel.

Yes, he confirms. *We call them Energy Hearts because they are what grow in us and are instrumental in our control of Energy.*

"You have them too?" I ask, curious.

Everything does, once they are strong enough, he replies. *But right now . . . no, I don't have one.* He seems a little ashamed, or embarrassed, perhaps.

"I don't want to pry, but if you're willing to tell me why . . . ?"

If you wish to know, he shrugs a little uncomfortably. *It is no big secret. I haven't accrued enough Energy or impressed the ancestors enough to cross the threshold. Once*

I do, I will either be able to direct my Energy into my body to strengthen it and grow bigger, or I will be able control some lesser form of Energy like Honored Pathwalker Shaman and my . . . our . . . Honored Pathwalker Herbalist. For a moment I war with myself. Should I . . . ? Finally coming to a decision, I sigh and brace myself. Whether it rocks the boat or not, it needs saying.

"Look, man, I . . . I want to say that I appreciate your help. You stood with me against everyone you knew. And I appreciate it." River is looking at me and, if the feeling coming down the Bond is anything to judge by, he's more offended than anything else.

I swore to serve you, he replies finally, his tone sounding like I just insulted his mother. Or whatever they have. I grimace mentally.

Why am I doing this? My ex made it clear that she considered my emotional intelligence to be the equivalent of a teaspoon's. *Just call me Ron.* But I'm doing this because ever since we left the village there's been this unspoken . . . weight in the Bond. And my history with unspoken negativity has proven that just ignoring it doesn't actually make it go away. No, it just makes it fester and ferment until it explodes one day and destroys something.

It's that thought that makes me continue.

"Yeah, you did," I acknowledge. "But I also recognize that you could have followed the letter of what you swore, and I appreciate you following the spirit." He makes a derisive noise as the sense of insult grows.

Prey must be coerced and threatened into fulfilling their tasks. The word of one of the People is our bond.

"Right," I say slowly. Different cultures, I guess. And if my experience in the lizard folk's village was anything to judge by, slavery or indentured servitude or whatever seems pretty normal. I kind of want to dig more deeply into that, but it's not the time. "Well, then, I just want to say that I'm sorry about . . . well, about what had to happen." He just looks at me, his spikes rippling with different colors. "You know, about the one that I . . . who died. It seemed like you thought they were pretty important and—" I cut myself off before I start babbling.

What is done is done. It doesn't matter, he says dismissively as he turns away and crosses his arms, his tail shifting uneasily behind him, pain coming through the Bond.

"It clearly does to you," I point out, unable to stop myself. He whips around to glare at me, his mouth open to bare his teeth, his spikes flashing a deep red.

It doesn't matter! he snarls at me.

I raise both hands in surrender and don't push further. The display is pretty intimidating, but that's not why I stopped—the benefit of being the Tamer in this situation is the certainty that I could stop him from attacking me. I stopped because continuing to press on what is obviously a sore spot is unlikely to take us anywhere productive.

Clearly, my attempts to point out the elephant in the room have been worse than useless. I should have known better than to try to broach emotions. When has it ever turned out well? Especially at a time like this. *Idiot*, I castigate myself. I turn away a little to give him some space and let the veil of silence fall back into place.

My emotional state is too disrupted to be able to easily relax back into Meditation, so I shove the Energy Heart into my Inventory and move towards the massive corpse stinking up the air near us. After pulling out my knife, I start digging into the side of the salamander myself. The Energy must be dissipating from the carcass already; I don't want to miss out on what I can get from the heart.

I still haven't found it by the time I'm elbow-deep in the body. I've probably got the wrong angle here or something. Muttering curses under my breath, I pull my arm out and try to look into the hole. Of course, I don't see anything—the light barely pierces the tunnel I've made, and what I can see is just red flesh, indistinguishable from any other bit of body.

Here, let me, River offers quietly; his tone is subdued as the meaning comes over the Bond. Wordlessly, I step aside. He sticks his clawed hand in, a look of concentration on his face. I see the blackened scales over his shoulders and arms and the clotted wounds that have ripped through them: the marks left on him from the fight with the salamander.

Without even thinking about it, I place my hand on his shoulder and channel the mana I've regenerated into him. Flesh knits together and grows anew to replace burned bits. In a few moments, he looks significantly better. Dirty, but uninjured. I let my hand drop, satisfied.

Suddenly realizing he's staring at me, I look away for a moment, embarrassed and not really sure why. Then I straighten up and look back at him with determination. Why should I be embarrassed? I didn't do anything wrong.

Thank you, River tells me, a hint of something I can't interpret in his voice. The emotions coming at me through the Bond are too complex to parse, positive and negative mixing together into an indecipherable mass. I shrug.

"You were injured, and I had the mana."

So were—are—you, he points out.

It's true. I shrug again. I'll heal myself in a few minutes' time—it's not like it really cost me anything. I've lived with the pain this long; I can live with it for a few minutes more. My own health regeneration has already started working on the wounds anyway. He looks at me for a long moment and then turns away to continue digging into the side of the salamander.

As he works, staring blankly ahead at the wall of flesh, the emotions within him stabilize a little, leaving loneliness and sadness to dominate.

I thought I knew what I was giving up when I agreed to your bargain. I thought that knowing I was doing my best to save the village would be enough of a justification for my betrayal. He's silent for a few moments. *I was wrong,* he adds finally, almost in a whisper. *It still hurts.*

I turn towards him, my mouth open to say something—anything—to help with the broken-glass pain I feel emanating from him. It's a familiar pain, one I've felt too many times before, and it's one I don't wish on my worst enemy.

I'm interrupted from whatever banal platitude I might have uttered by a shift in his emotions. Underneath the negative feelings is the hint of something else. Hope. He looks back at me, the same emotion evident in the hints of pale green that dance between his spikes. *But maybe my vow of obedience shall not be as much of a burden as I feared.*

Before I can respond, not that I really know how to, a new set of feelings filters down the Bond: confusion, fear, hope, and a determination to protect.

Bastet.

CHAPTER TWENTY-EIGHT

Life-Devourer

I scramble over to the prone raptorcat and meet her eyes. They're clear, focused, and contain very little obvious pain. I breathe a sigh of relief. It's not that I thought it likely, but there was always a possibility that something might have gone wrong in the process somewhere.

"I thought I'd lost you," I breathe, the words barely more than a whisper. Reassurance flows along the Bond along with a pointed question. "Yes, it's dead," I tell her, waving an arm at the corpse lying behind her. "Hope you're hungry."

The eagerness that comes over from her side reveals that, indeed, she's *starving*. It's not surprising: I've noticed that healing seems to consume resources in the body as well as mana; recovering from significant injuries leaves a body feeling like it hasn't eaten for days. "Do you feel well enough to stand?" I ask her anxiously. The wounds are healed, but I can't help remembering just how close she came to bleeding out.

Cautious agreement comes across the Bond, and the raptorcat slowly pushes herself to her feet as if she's also concerned that something might not be fully healed. I wonder whether Bastet ever gets the feeling that her brain is expecting there to be a wound where her body has already long healed, as I do. After checking herself over, she grows in confidence and pads over to the carcass, needing no further permission to dig in.

She's still a bit stiff—the healing regenerated a fair amount of flesh. It'll take some time for that flesh to start moving properly again. Lathani greets Bastet with an affectionate head rub, and the cubs scramble over each other to greet her too, adorable squeaky sounds filling the air as they press themselves against her.

I stand there gazing at the felines. It's a strange environment in which to feel contentment, but I do. We beat the enemy trying to kill us and are currently eating our spoils. We're temporarily safe from our other enemies, even if the situation isn't tenable in the long term. And now, the cherry on the cake, our little family is back together. It's intact after I feared for so many agonizing moments that it might be ripped apart like my first family was—twice. So yes, I feel contentment even standing in a field of wrath and tears.

A large form comes to stand next to me. I don't need to look to know it's River. I do so anyway: I'm curious about the feelings drifting through on the Bond. They're not visible on his face. Only the spikes that make up his crest show a faint patterning of different colors to indicate his tumultuous emotional state. In his hands is a large lump of flesh. We stay there for a few moments before he broaches his thoughts.

You really do care about her, don't you? About them. You didn't only come for the cub out of fear of the Great Predator. It's not really a question, even though the words indicate that it should be.

"Yes," I reply simply. "They're family." It feels strange to say. None of them is human in any sort of way, but we've made a family together, a pack. My recent foray into the world of connections has proven that without a doubt; the connections between us are far too strong to deny. Me, Bastet, the cubs, Lathani . . . I'd suspect even Kalanthia to an extent, though she's still more aloof than any other in our strange pack.

River is silent after that. Both his expression and emotions are still too complex to easily decipher. I don't try—I want to offer him a little privacy. He's earned that, at least.

"Is that the heart?" I ask after the silence makes it clear that he's not intending on coming out of his thoughts any time soon. He looks down at the organ, almost like he'd forgotten he was holding it.

Oh. Yes. Here, Mas—Markus. He holds it out to me, and I take it. The salamander heart is large, about the size of my head. I guess it would have to be, to pump blood around the body of the oversized amphibian.

"Thanks," I reply simply. When it seems like he's happy just to watch the felines play and eat, I shrug and look at the heart. Do I dare eat it raw? On the one hand, it's possible there are parasites and diseases that even Lay-on-Hands can't deal with. On the other, I'm limited on firewood unless I want to get more from a forest that already wants to kill me . . . Just as I'm debating, a shadow passes over me. I glance up warily.

A dot flies far above us, and I watch it with caution, remembering the last time I had a bird flying high above me. A brush over the Taming Bond in my chest reveals that, this time, the identity of the dot is that of an ally, not an enemy. The bird descends rapidly through the colorful sky, the sunset touching clouds with pink and orange. The sun is already below the level of the trees, though it doesn't look like it's quite dropped below the horizon yet.

With a flutter of wings, the bird banks to drastically reduce her speed and then lands on top of the salamander. She shrieks softly and then climbs down the corpse to find an opening, her front two feet moving separately, her back two bunny hopping forwards in a motion that looks both awkward and oddly efficient. So, she *does* eat meat? *Why did she turn it down in the forest, then?* In the end, I shrug to myself. If she eats meat, all the better: unlike the situation I can imagine on Earth, meat here seems to be the one thing I don't have much trouble getting hold of.

"What did you find?" I ask the bird impatiently as she tears shreds off the corpse. I receive back an admonishment via the Bond, a hammer of a feeling that is essentially "I'm eating—wait." I try to cross my arms, but I'm still holding the massive heart. Grumbling under my breath, I crouch and pull out the firewood I have left in my Inventory. I leave two long sticks that I could potentially use as torches but pull out the rest.

Perhaps it would be a better idea to save the branches, but I'm determined to eat this creature's heart. If the bird tells me that going through the forest would be quick and easy, I've got half a torch set aside, as well as those two long sticks. If we decide to risk the tunnel instead, I can grab a few chunks of deadwood without fearing that the wrath of the trees will be visited upon us later. Worst-case scenario, I don't cook the meat fully; if I can get it hot enough to roast any potential parasites, that's all I need.

Crouching down, I pile the sticks together and get out my fire starter. River kneels down to watch my actions when sparks start jumping from my starter to the pile of dry material. I'm aware of his eyes on my every move as I go through what are now the very practiced actions of lighting the fire, then building a spit for the heart above it. I use my knife to slice the heart into slices; at least if the meat is thinner, it will take less time to cook.

When the fire is ready, I use two sticks to hold the meat flat above the fire, watching the flames pop and flare as drops of liquid fall into them. I gaze up at the bird still gorging herself. I wonder what news she will give me. I don't actually know which I would prefer: that the edge of the forest is near and I should give up thoughts of exploring where the hole goes, or that it's far and, therefore, the hole is our best option. I glare at the bird as she chokes down a chunk of meat. Couldn't she have told me *before* she decided to fill her beak?

This is what you use on the sticks you've been holding while traveling through the forest? River's voice interrupts my thoughts. I look at him with confusion, and he indicates the fire with his claws.

"Yes. We call it 'fire.'" He tilts his head as confusion emanates from him.

Fire? he repeats as if it's a completely unfamiliar word. *I do not understand this . . . fire?*

Interesting. It seems there's a limit to what translation via the Bond can do if the concept doesn't exist in the other person's experience. Though, surely River has encountered *some* sort of fire before?

"What about 'lightning,' do you know that?"

The bright flash that falls from the skies accompanied by great sound, yes. We haven't had any recently, though Honored Wind-Whisperer has predicted a storm to not be far away. I make a mental note. Not that there's much I can do about it right now, of course, but it might be worth sticking close to Kalanthia's cave for a few days after we get back.

"Well, fire is something that is sometimes created when lightning strikes and everything around is very dry." River gives off a feeling of solemnity.

The life-devourer. I know of that, though it has only happened once in my lifetime.

I was barely out of the egg at that point, so my brood-mother gathered me up with as many of my egg-siblings as she could. We hid with the rest of the village in a specially dug underground shelter. It was very hot for a long time and hard to breathe for a short time. Many died, mostly those who could not make it to the shelter in time. I was fearful when I saw that our recent enemy was able to wield it, he admits.

I'm sobered by the reminder that my experience of so many things in the safe, civilized world in a capital city in a developed country is far different from what many others experience. On Earth just as much as on this world. When a forest fire is the only experience a group has had with fire, it's unsurprising that they would be wary of it. And it makes his willingness to go into battle more laudable considering his experience of the damage fire can do.

"Well, this is a small contained version of that, which I can keep under control so that it doesn't hurt us. Not if we're careful, that is," I tell him, trying to bring his thoughts away from past fears. I don't know about him, but I would have appreciated someone being able to do the same for me. I might not have ended up in this world if they had. That thought sends an odd feeling through me. I dismiss it and turn back to my explanation.

I see, River replies thoughtfully, calmer than I might have expected him to be. *And what is this . . . contained life-devourer useful for?*

"It keeps the vine-strangler trees from attacking us, for one thing," I explain. "Clearly, they're afraid of fire—for good reason, apparently, since they seem to be particularly vulnerable to it. For me, it's also useful for creating food. I can't just eat raw meat like you can. Then, beyond that, there's a whole world of infinite possibilities that all build off the ability to create and control fire. Possibilities you couldn't even imagine."

And you will build those? He actually sounds excited, his eyes gleaming and his spikes flickering with yellow, blue, and green.

"No." I laugh, then, seeing and feeling his immediate disappointment, modulate my answer. "Not all of them, anyway. And not immediately. The vast majority require equipment and tools that I don't have access to. Maybe one day I'll be able to build some very basic ones, but . . ." I shrug.

What I don't say is that I don't know how far I'll be able to—or should—progress along the path of technology. Anything electronic is so far out of the realm of possibility that it's not even worth considering. Not only do I not have anything like the right facilities, equipment, or materials for it, but I don't have the knowledge either.

The survival knowledge stones I absorbed right at the start had some information about basic blacksmithing, enough to create a mold for some basic tools and arrowheads, but little else. Whether I even go that far will very much depend on how things develop with my own abilities—if I pick up an offensive Skill at level five, there might not be much point in advancing my weaponry. Of course, I'd also have to find the materials. I thought I might have seen the glint of metal ore in the raptorcat cave, but I haven't been back to check—I might easily have been mistaken.

The first slice of meat is cooked enough for me to risk eating it. I pull it off the fire and replace it with another. Then, as I'm about to sink my teeth into the still-bloody flesh, there's a flutter of wings and the bird lands in front of me. She flips her wings back primly and looks at me, first with one eye then the other.

"Are you done eating?" I ask. Agreement comes through the Bond. Murphy is clearly on duty right now: she's done just as I'm about to start! Oh well, I've had many working meals in the past. I can eat and plan, no problem. "Then, what did you see?"

CHAPTER TWENTY-NINE

Uncertainty

I automatically accompany my question with a mental query down the Bond. The bird responds more to that than to my words and sends me a memory of a literal bird's-eye view of what surrounds us. It's not hopeful. Not if we want to make our way out via the trees, anyway.

The vine-strangler grove is so much bigger than I thought it would be, the trees obvious from above because of their much darker coloring and smaller size than the normal forest giants. From a bird's view, the grove looks vaguely like a large eye with our little clearing being the small pupil at the center.

The part that I crossed with Bastet and the cubs was like the corner of that eye, the point of which touches the banks of the river. Despite being one of the narrowest stretches of trees, it still took us hours to cross. To do the same with the thickest part would probably take more than a day, maybe two or even three depending on the terrain hidden by the canopy.

Fortunately, we wouldn't have to cross that section, as we are in the center of the eye, but it's still as I suspected: we're too far away from the nearest edge of the vine-stranglers to make it through before dark. Heck, even the thinner stretch we would have to traverse might still take more than a day's light, considering the small glimpses of difficult terrain I can see below the canopy.

I activate my Map and see with interest that the details of the vine-strangler grove have been added to it. Evidently, what one of my companions sees can also be considered what I have seen. That's useful to know for the future. I don't remember the same addition when Bastet went scouting . . . But then again, I suppose the lizard folk's settlement *was* added to my Map.

Perhaps it was just that there were no other notable landmarks to include. The addition from the bird also shows me that the route we took to the center was as meandering as it felt but, nonetheless, was always heading in a certain direction— the trees clearly knew what they were doing with their efforts to channel us here.

But despite all of that, is the known danger of the vine-strangler forest still better than the unknown danger of the tunnel? River was confident that it was a tunnel rather than a hole, but we don't even know if the whole length of it is passable by all of us. I decide to put it to my companions. After explaining the situation in simple terms, I wait to hear what the three most communicative members of the team think.

I want to go back to Mother, Lathani tells me a little unhelpfully.

"I know. I want to get you back too," I tell her earnestly. "But do you think it's better to go through the forest or try this tunnel?"

I don't know, she replies, sounding unhappy. *I just want Mother.* With a wordless mewl of complaint, she sinks to the ground and lays her head on her paws. I feel for her. She's still all too young, not more than a cub despite her size. I need to remember that.

I move over and try to give her some physical comfort by stroking her head and scratching behind her ears. After a moment, she shifts her heavy head onto my leg and closes her eyes.

Well, I think we should try the tunnel, announces River with determination flashing across his crest and through the Bond. I send his thoughts through to my other companions after remembering that they wouldn't have received the message.

"Why's that?" I ask, curious as to why he's suddenly so keen on the idea.

This is the center of the Forest of Death, you say? Then I wish to know what is in this tunnel. Perhaps it could indicate the reason for the explosive growth of the death trees that so threaten my village. Looking at the Map again, I see why the village is so concerned about the trees. While it hasn't yet been engulfed, the closest edge of the trees is not very far away from the village itself.

The only reason it took us a while to reach when we were being pursued was because we weren't running directly at the tree line, but instead aiming to retrace our footsteps towards Kalanthia's den. If we'd gone directly for the forest, we'd have probably hit it in an hour. Or less, considering that we were running.

With what River now knows about the sheer immensity of the forest—definitely a forest and not a grove, whatever my quest says—I can understand his urgency. I don't know what the rate of growth is like, but the lizard folk's alarm is enough to tell me that it's fast.

In that light, I suppose River's desire to explore the tunnel is understandable: the only reason he agreed to our Bond was because he wanted me to help him save his village. Whether that's the best idea for our whole group right now is another question.

"What do you think, Bastet?" Out of everyone's opinions, frankly, hers is the one I trust most. Not only is she the oldest—maturity-wise, at least, since I'm not actually sure how old River is—but she's also probably the most cautious since she has cubs to protect.

As usual, her response is in a wave of emotion, but I notice this time that it's more pointed, more defined. It's easier to interpret, which is good for me. She expresses caution, as expected, and highlights that our reason for being here is to rescue Lathani and get her—along with the cubs—back to the den. At the same time, she expresses uncertainty that traveling through the forest is a good idea: we are forever one step away from being caught in a cage we cannot escape.

Additionally, she raises a point that I hadn't thought of, being so concerned about the trees. There are other threats in the forest that may not be so affected by our torches. We came off well against the thorn bush, but what if we faced something else like that, only bigger and more powerful? Overall, she seems fairly neutral towards both options and prefers whichever seems the least dangerous.

Frankly, I feel the same way she does if I take my curiosity about the tunnel out of the equation. My conclusion is that we need more information before making a definitive decision either way. If the tunnel is now a completely clear and easy route out of the forest, I wouldn't want to miss it because I was too scared to set foot in it, but equally, if we got ambushed by the salamander's friends or some other dark-dwelling creature because I chose to go down it while missing information, it would be completely my responsibility.

"Okay, thank you for your ideas," I say aloud, knowing that my thoughts will be automatically projected down the Bonds. "Here's what we'll do. Bastet, are you feeling up to scouting?" I'm reluctant to ask her, especially considering how injured she was so very recently, but she really is the best choice for this kind of task. A wave of assent comes from her direction. "Great. Please check out the tunnel, then. Don't take any risks—at the first sign of danger, come back here. If you need help, let me know down the Bond."

The adult raptorcat agrees, though there's a hint of derision at the thought that she might put herself in danger unnecessarily. She's right—I'm probably projecting. But considering how close she was to death, I think I should be allowed a bit of leeway.

She nuzzles the cubs, and I sense a message passing between her and them, traveling along a connection that has nothing to do with our Bond. It's not with words, of course, but if I had to articulate it, I would say it was along the lines of "Be good and stay with the pack." Then she trots down the slope to the tunnel. Pausing at the edge, she's still for a few moments. When I touch the Bond, I get an impression of watchful observation, all her senses extended.

Then she shifts again and slips over the edge of the hole and descends into the tunnel. The tip of her plumed tail is the last we see of her.

Feeling restless, I finish eating the cooked heart. As it is, I have enough wood—just—to singe all the pieces of meat. They're rare, and a French version of rare at that, rather than my preferred medium rare, but I hope it's enough to avoid any possible negative consequences from eating completely raw meat.

The heart is actually surprisingly tasty—not like steak, really, but almost like a gamey chicken. I've never eaten a chicken's heart, but I imagine it would probably taste quite similar; the killer chickens don't count.

My meal over, and now feeling rather full even if still rather thirsty, I consider how to prepare for the journey ahead. The way I see it is that either we'll stay here tonight and set off tomorrow morning through the forest, since traveling in the dark through killer trees is a poor idea, or we'll make our way through the tunnel as soon as Bastet gets back. Day or night probably matters little there.

We could spend some time resting even if we take the tunnel, but I'm very aware that even though we have plenty of food, we have no water. My mouth is okay because I've just been eating some juicy meat, but it's going to be getting dry soon. My companions will probably be fine since they can eat the raw meat and partially hydrate themselves from it, but I can't do that. Ideally, we'll get going as soon as possible, regardless of the option we choose.

I try to think through our other needs. Whichever way we choose, we're going to need torches. In the forest they're needed as protection; in the tunnel they'll be needed as illumination. That means braving the edge of the vine-stranglers to search for deadwood since I'd rather be over- than underprepared. I need to regenerate my mana so I can heal the group. And I need to check my messages because they're almost causing me a headache with their insistent nagging. Now, which one to do first?

"River," I say as I hold my half-burned torch over the fire to light it, "take this." I hand the now-lit torch to him as he comes up next to me. He holds it like a snake that might bite him at any moment. I'd find it sad if I didn't know why he was so wary. "It's okay. Just hold the torch by the unlit end and don't let the fire anywhere near you. It should be fine."

He doesn't look particularly reassured, but evidently, the fact that it hasn't burned him just from holding the wood is enough proof, and he grips it a little more forcefully. "We're going to look for wood, okay? I'd like you to keep an eye out. If you see any tree even look like it might be considering attacking us, wave the fire at it threateningly, all right?" He assents a little reluctantly, but I'll take it.

I don't know how long Bastet will be away, but I know I need to get some torches ready before she comes back. My messages can wait for now—I doubt I have enough Energy to level up so soon since the last time, so any notifications about points earned can be dealt with later. If I'm lucky, further exertion will even turn them into points applied automatically rather than points I still have to "buy."

"Bird, Lathani, please keep an eye on the cubs, okay? We're not going far, just into the edge of the forest to look for wood. Cry out if there's an issue and we'll be back in seconds."

The bird agrees, disinterest coloring the message. Lathani is still moping, but she agrees too, shifting so that she can keep an eye on the three cubs, who are currently playing with one of the salamander's claws.

Satisfied that things are as under control as possible, I walk towards the tree line. We set up camp on the other side of the salamander's corpse, which by itself is several meters away from the trees. Still, that means that we're within earshot if anything happens. Even as we walk towards the forest, I see a few branches lying at the roots of the trees just beyond the tree line. This should be a cakewalk. Get in there, grab some wood, then get out. Simple.

What could go wrong?

CHAPTER THIRTY

Close to the Wire

River is nervous. I don't mind admitting that I am too. In the twilight as we are now, the shadows of each tree are deep and the whole forest seems even more threatening than it did before. The flickering of the torch doesn't help: it deepens the shadows even further and makes them move in my peripheral vision. It's a thoroughly unnerving experience that leaves me feeling permanently on edge. Then again, I probably would be regardless, considering the threat that surrounds us.

The lizard-man sticks right next to me, but I see him making the effort to watch our backs rather than always looking in the same direction as I am. I appreciate his efforts—hopefully, we won't be attacked, but if we are, at least we'll have as much warning as possible. I stoop down and collect the dry wood cracking with our footsteps.

Wanting to have enough for another cooking fire if necessary, I just collect any piece of dry wood that comes to hand and let my Inventory sort the pieces out according to size. Fortunately, with my level-up a couple of days ago, I still have several slots free. Unfortunately, there seems to be far less deadwood here than I was expecting—these trees don't seem to drop as much of it as the trees near Kalanthia's den.

We try not to go deep into the forest and stick to where we can see the clearing through the gap between only a few tree trunks. I can sense the forest's anger around us, though I don't know if it's because we're collecting wood, because we avoided its trap, or because we dare to walk with impunity within its bounds while carrying fire. Frankly, I don't care.

After a while, I even relax just the slightest bit—the forest doesn't seem quite as scary as it did before. *Why am I even so scared of it?* I find myself wondering. *I've already managed to travel through it once. With fire at my side, I'm safe.*

The thought seems wrong in some way, but I find it hard to work out how. Then I hear something that sends the whole thing out of my head: the bubble of water. *A stream?* My throat aches in its dehydration.

The fears I had seem to flee like shadows before the sun's light. I turn from one side to another as I try to identify the direction of the sound. It's deeper into the forest, of course, but I would guess it to only be a short distance away. Besides, I've already worked out that I have nothing to fear from the trees, not with that torch in River's hand.

I step towards the sound eagerly. I'm already thirsty, and the opportunity to refill my canteen and water pot would be most welcome.

Mas—Markus, are we not staying close to the edge of the forest? River asks, his tone uneasy. I glance at him. Where I have relaxed, he seems to have become even more tense. Something inside me starts shrieking at that, and my foot hesitates for a moment. Then the sense of confidence that's grown in the last few minutes pushes the rising fear to one side and I keep on walking.

"It's fine," I tell him. "You've seen that the trees are harmless as long as you hold the torch. And I want to get some water."

The lizard-man looks both confused and uneasy. His tail is swaying from side to side, his head constantly shifting to look in different directions.

I thought that we needed to be wary of more than just the trees, he ventures uncertainly. I frown—that's true, now I think of it. Why did I stop being wary of that? *And I don't think there's any water here,* he continues. *I thought we were here to collect branches.*

"Yes, but if I can collect water too, that would be a bonus," I tell him, then I pause again as the part of me that's shrieking inside gets louder despite my previous self-assurance. Is River's hearing not at least as good as mine? Why can't he hear it? "Can't you hear that stream?" I ask. Negation comes through the Bond even before he answers, and my foreboding finally sweeps away the sense of safety that had invaded my mind.

I can't hear anything but the wind in the trees, River confirms.

Too late.

As he speaks, the trap that I had so unwittingly walked into closes on me. The forest floor a mere foot away from where I'm standing shimmers, only to reveal a bulbous body and a gaping maw filled with teeth. Before I can react, tentacles snap out to wrap around my body. I shout as serrated edges bite into me. Why is everything in this forest either thorny or spiky?

The shock of being attacked wears off very quickly. I have had far too much experience of ambushes to be frozen for long.

Even as I grab my knife from my belt, thankful that the creature left my right arm free, River charges in with his spear held in one hand and the flaming torch in the other, bellowing in rage.

I'm not sure why he's so angry—is it because he now considers me the best hope for his tribe, because I was attacked under his watch, or because he has some racial hatred for this creature? Whatever the reason, it's clear he would like to teach my attacker the error of its ways—in a permanent fashion.

Between us, we manage to make quite short work of the creature. It's only after the thing has subsided to the ground that I realize I'm feeling more lethargic than I should be after such a relatively short fight. The lethargy is soon joined by nausea and dizziness, and I see that my health is dropping even as I look at it. Having already experienced something of this sort twice now, I have an idea of what's going on.

"I'm poisoned," I warn my Bound even as I cast Lay-on-Hands and channel my mana through my body to counteract the damage the poison is doing.

What are your symptoms? he asks, his tone urgent.

"Lethargy, nausea, dizziness. It's doing damage to my insides, I think," I tell him shortly. I'm worried that my health is still decreasing even with the amount of healing magic I'm channeling. My wounds are still bleeding too. They're small but painful, and the number of them means that I'm losing quite a lot of blood. I have to guess that the poison also contains something that stops my wounds from clotting.

I tell River this too. I hope it's a short-lived poison. If not, I may end up running out of mana before it stops affecting me. With the blood loss added in, that would probably be fatal.

I have herbs that will help back in the clearing, River tells me. I look up at him muzzily; at some point, I fell to the ground.

"I don't have the same physiology as you," I slur. "They may poison me instead."

I know the poison that affects you. If it's not stopped, it will ravage your body in a very short time. You don't have a choice.

"Great," I sigh. So much for a quick jaunt into the forest to pick up some wood. I try to push myself to my feet but lose my balance before I can. River holds out his clawed paws, and I gratefully use them to help steady myself. He starts off towards the camp.

"Wait," I murmur, a thought occurring. Confusion emanates from his side of the Bond, but he helps me as I return to the corpse of whatever it is, heave it just off the ground with a grunt—if River hadn't been there, I'd have fallen over again instead of succeeding—and stuff it in my Inventory. Such a poison sounds like a great one to add to my collection, and there's no way I'll be coming back to find the corpse later.

Of course, I have to survive first. "Okay, let's go," I tell my companion, and we stumble back to our camp.

River's on high alert in an attempt to compensate for my inability to defend myself right now. My stomach roils with every step, but somehow, I manage to keep it down. Fortunate, that—I wouldn't want to have to live with the nasty taste with no water to wash it out.

The trees shift around us, and I fear for a moment that they'll take advantage of my incapacitated state to attack. The torch still burns brightly, though, and clearly, that's enough to keep them at bay. We manage to make it to the clearing with no further attacks.

By the time we're sitting down with Lathani, the bird, and the cubs, my health is down to a quarter and my mana is almost out. I'm getting more than worried. It hasn't been all that much time since this was the condition Bastet was in, and we almost lost her. I don't want to die either!

River quickly leaves me as soon as we're in safety and strides to his little box of wonders. I slump to the ground and weakly bat away the cubs, who're crowding me, obviously sensing that something's wrong.

What happened? Lathani asks frantically, her hackles up and a growl in her throat. *Is there an enemy?*

"Not now," I tell her. "Killed it. Poisoned." Short phrases are easier to communicate than anything else with my increasingly numb lips. "Give River space," I urge her as he turns and strides back to me. She backs away, and he crouches down with a number of plant parts held gently between his paws.

Eat these, he tells me brusquely. I take them but hesitate.

"You're sure they won't poison me? More, I mean."

No, he replies grimly—the fear running through him says more than the words. Well, he's honest at least, but I would rather have a comforting lie at this point. But as he said earlier, I don't have a choice. Depending on luck is a poor strategy.

I stuff the plant parts into my mouth and chew on them. They're nasty, a mixture of bitter and sour. Though, there is one in there that I wouldn't mind having again, something that reminds me of mint. Without water to help me swallow, it's hard to choke the things down, and my continuing nausea doesn't help. Nonetheless, I manage eventually.

My stomach spasms a bit, and I'm convinced for a moment that the herbs are going to come right back up. I even turn over and retch a few times into the ash. Is my body rejecting them? With a final cramp, my stomach calms and the nausea mostly abates. With the nausea goes my dizziness, albeit more slowly. I cast another Lay-on-Hands and channel it until my mana is only the tiniest sliver—I don't want the severe nausea and exhaustion that comes with mana deprivation to make me feel even worse.

I bite my lip as my stomach roils from something other than the poison. My Lay-on-Hands helps: this time it actually pushes my health up a little, but only from about five percent to fifteen percent. When it stops working, my health starts ticking down again, bit by bit. My wounds are still bleeding sluggishly, but I think that they are starting to clot.

Slumped on the ground, feeling absolutely wretched, I watch as my end ticks closer and closer. Is this what it was like for my dad? It's depressing that even having access to literal healing magic isn't a sure defense against dying by inches.

Can you do anything else? I ask River, too exhausted to open my mouth and form the words. A sense of helpless frustration comes over the Bond. I know his answer before he says it.

No. I'm sorry. I close my eyes briefly in despair before opening them again. I can't see the number of health units I have left in numerical terms, but I would guess that it's only about seven or eight.

As I watch, another sliver leaves the bar. If it *was* eight, it's only seven now.

My mana is still almost drained, though it is regenerating slowly. The problem is that I'm losing health more quickly than I'm gaining mana. Like a drowning man clutching at straws, I close my eyes and try to calm my mind.

It's not exactly easy, as close as I am to dying, but somehow, through a force of will, I manage to do it. Perhaps it was all that practice in the lizard folk's camp. The fifteen percent increase in mana gain may not be massive, but if it can keep my health above zero units, then I don't care.

I think I once heard someone say desperation is the mother of invention. Even as my body fails around me, my mind races as it searches for some solution. Any solution. I touch the connections around me. Surely this can't be it for me? I pluck at the links around me, touching them with the sense that I cannot name. And then a thought sparks.

What did the Meditation Skill description say? Why does Meditation help my mana increase? I don't dare drop out of the trance to check. But wasn't it something about improving my connection to the world around? Isn't that why my mana regenerates faster when I'm in it? And are these connections anything to do with all that?

A gut instinct tells me that they are, that they're *integral* to the whole thing. And if the connections are the means by which I gain mana, could I do more than just passively absorb it? What if I *actively* draw it in? It's worth a shot.

Of course, conceiving of an idea is one thing; putting it into practice is something completely different. I'm sensing connections in a way I cannot describe and never felt before yesterday; now I'm trying to affect them somehow using that sense.

It's like trying to fish spaghetti out of water, except I'm not holding the fork— it's attached to a series of pulleys by a string and I have to control it like that. Blindfolded. With gloves on. And with no experience of pot, fork, or spaghetti. Impossible, right?

But never underestimate what a desperate person can do, and I sense that I am very, very close to the edge right now. I can't see my health bar in this state, nor really feel my body's physical state, but something about the way many of the connections around me are reacting tells me that I'm probably only a couple of health units away from death. Even a blindfolded and gloved pulley controller can get lucky once and pull a strand of spaghetti from the pot.

And, despite really not understanding what I'm doing, despite fumbling in the dark, I get lucky. A flash of heat travels into me and I feel a sudden pain from the Bond I have with River. I'm pulled out of Meditation.

Immediately, I register that my health bar is, indeed, almost entirely empty . . . but that my mana bar has enough of a sliver to cast Lay-on-Hands. Not wasting even a second, I pour the mana into myself without leaving a single unit in the tank.

I get hit immediately by the effects of mana exhaustion. Nausea returns, as does a cracking headache. My limbs already feel encased in lead, so nothing changes there. But my health bar has jumped up again, though not by much: my Lay-on-Hands has increased the number of points it heals, usually hitting twenty or so for a single cast, but with my larger health pool that means it's only filling a bit over ten percent of my bar at a time.

However, when the specter of death is raising its scythe over my shoulder, that's a massive difference. I still feel like I've got one foot in the grave, but I'm not quite as close to losing my balance and tumbling in.

However, whatever I did has consequences, if the look on River's face is anything to judge by.

CHAPTER THIRTY-ONE

Drain

What happened? Why are you looking at me like that?" I ask as I instinctively search around us to check for a threat. Seeing none, I turn back to him questioningly.

You . . . I felt a drain upon me through our connection. I receive his message with dismay.

"Did it . . . hurt?" He doesn't answer immediately, and when he does, it's full of uncertainty.

Yes . . . ? But not like a wound. More like a loss. I understand. Kind of. What I took must have literally been drawn from River. Maybe from his own mana pool, if he has one? I hesitate. The majority of me is screaming to just do it, to rip whatever I can from River—I'm *dying.*

Even now, the small amount of health I managed to regain is being stripped from me bit by bit. I'm probably losing a health point every four seconds, which is a lot better than it was before, but still unmanageable. I need to at least outpace the effects of the poison until they wear off, but my mana takes about a minute and a half to regenerate enough for another Lay-on-Hands. Even if I Meditate, that only increases the amount of mana I regenerate by one unit per minute or so—not enough to help me. Ideally, I could find a way of clearing the poison from my system, but to do that I'm going to need even *more* mana.

But if it means ripping something away from someone else? Something that maybe they need? How can I ask that of River?

In the end, I don't have to. While I've been sitting here silently with my thoughts racing to find another option, despite feeling the pressure of my impending end, River has clearly been going through his own thought process.

Do it, he says, his tone firm. I blink, a little taken aback. Is he really saying what I think he is? He must feel my question through the Bond, as he sends a wave of affirmation. *Take what you need to live and overcome this poison.* Despite the time pressure, I want to make sure he's certain.

"Are you sure? Even though it hurts you? What if it damages you permanently?"

If I can save you so that you can do what you promised . . . Those left behind in my village are more important than I am by far. I have faith that you will hold to your word to save them, even if I am rendered useless to you by this service. It's more of a desperate hope than a certainty, but I nod in acknowledgment as I feel metaphorical chains bind me in return.

For what he's done and is prepared to do, I will do my best to help his village, even if it means Dominating them one by one to make sure they leave the area before setting them free. For what River's offering me now, I'll go against my own principles if it's the only option left to me. I don't send the detail of my thoughts to him, but he feels my commitment. He encourages me again.

Then do it.

My health is back down to a sliver, so I don't hesitate for a second longer. After slipping into a trance—the state is becoming easier and easier to achieve as I practice it—I touch the Bond I have with River. It takes a few increasingly desperate attempts to copy what I did before, but I succeed eventually, even as I once more sense the connections around me withering away.

This time when River hisses and I feel pain come at me across the Bond, I don't stop. Guilt suffusing me, I continue to draw steadily on the link. When I sense that I'm right on the edge again, I drop out of the trance to quickly cast a Lay-on-Hands.

Now with a bit more leeway, I slip back into the trance and start drawing again, only taking two attempts to succeed this time. River hisses in pain again, and I stop when the flow seems to become harder to draw. Opening my eyes, I see that he looks worn out and haggard. His skin has lost color and almost sags on his frame, and his posture is slumped.

Guilt claws at me again, but I can't focus on that right now. If I waste the precious mana he's given me by wallowing in guilt, I'm only compounding my selfishness.

Instead, I note that I've regained about half my mana pool and immediately channel that into my body. Following the mana with my mind, I search out the poison in my system.

I soon discover that it's truly a nasty one: my brain, my liver, my heart, my lungs, my kidneys . . . most of my major organs are under attack. With my school-level ideas of anatomy and the knowledge I gained from the Lay-on-Hands Skill stone, I figure that the best thing to do would be to void the poison from my body. With the choice of opening a vein or pushing it through my kidneys, I decide to do the latter; I figure losing more blood is not a good idea even if it gets rid of the poison more quickly.

Working with haste, aware that the mana I have is limited and sensing that I won't be able to draw any more from River right now, I use my magic to push the poison around. Fortunately, it doesn't resist in any way, so the main job is making sure I don't miss any bits: I don't know if it's something that could self-replicate and don't want to risk it. The speed is a little limited by my pulse rate, but I keep the poison clumped up and direct it through the intricate network of my blood vessels until I get it through my kidneys, encasing it in mana all the while to avoid it damaging anything enroute.

When it lands in my bladder, I pull back until I'm settled into my body and no longer feel instead like a speck of light traveling through it. Just in time: my mana bar is back down to the merest sliver, probably only a couple of units away from running out. I fumble with my trousers, unbutton the fly, and reach inside to free myself.

Wishing I was strong enough to at least crawl away from where I'm resting, I instead just lean onto my side and try to aim my stream so that it's going downhill *away* from me. It's dark yellow and stinks, more than just ammonia polluting the air. With a sudden thought, I cover my nose with my off-hand and hope that the poison isn't effective when airborne as well.

After rearranging myself and doing up my fly again—this is no place to expose such a precious part of my anatomy—I lean back to lie down. I dearly hope that nothing attacks us now, as we'd be sitting ducks. Except for, ironically, the only bird of the group: she could just fly off.

It's pretty crazy that I'm in a worse state after fighting some table-sized ambushing predator than after fighting a horse-sized fire-breathing salamander. Then again, one of my other near misses was from a venomous trap-making spider. Being poisoned is really something I need to be careful about, clearly. Unbidden, the idea I've had before comes back to me. *If I could turn that power against my enemies . . .*

I take a couple of moments to verify that my health is no longer ticking down. It's not, but it's not above ten percent full either; after River's herbs did their job, I spent all my healing mana on clearing out what remained of the poison and only the barest minimum on repairing the damage it left behind to stop myself bleeding out. I open my eyes to look weakly over at River.

"How are you feeling?" He wordlessly sends a similar sense of weakness over to me, though his is more . . . drained. Actually, it's very familiar: the sensations are similar to the ones I get when my stamina or mana is exhausted. I resolve to check him over with healing magic when I can, but I don't get the sense that he's in danger. Right, that makes it clear what I need to do next, then. "Can you keep an eye out?" I ask my Bound—not that we could do a huge amount, but forewarned is forearmed, or so they say. He agrees, sending a feeling of tiredness and discomfort but readiness to do what he can.

On second thought, I send the same message to the bird, since she's actually in decent condition. She agrees too, though she demands some more meat in payment. Feeling like rolling my eyes, I point out the salamander corpse to her and tell her to help herself. She replies with a feeling of fullness: clearly, she meant later, not now. Sighing with frustration, I agree to feed her later, and she sends me back a feeling of satisfaction. If everything's going to be a negotiation with her, that's going to get annoying *fast*.

With that all sorted, I slip back into my Meditative trance. It's interesting, but since my frantic attempts to draw mana along the Bond from River, I notice that my connection with him is stronger and more obvious in this state, where connections are what define my environment far more than anything physical in nature. After noting that, though, I relax my focus and allow my mind to wander along the different links rather than trying to focus on any one in particular. My ability to affect the Bonds is something I want to experiment with, but not here, not now.

By the time I come out of the trance, my mana is almost full, which means that probably a little more than twenty minutes has passed. It's dark but the rising moon makes it possible to see outlines of things. My health has increased a little, but my regeneration rate for that is so slow in comparison to my mana that the fact it's climbed by a noticeable chunk means a fair bit of time has passed. I cast a Lay-on-Hands on myself and repair the damage the poison did. That's a lot easier to do without the poison working against me faster than I can heal myself—I still have half my mana pool when my health has almost climbed to its maximum.

Feeling *significantly* better, I push myself to my feet and go to check on River. I'm still tired; the kind of healing I've just been doing takes mental energy more than physical stamina, but that doesn't stop it feeling more exhausting than the marathon we ran to get down to the village. It's a relief, though, that my body feels pretty much back to normal otherwise. As I walk, I pull out a chunk of grilled meat. My mouth is dry, and I'd love a drink, but nothing would convince me to go back into that forest to search for water at this stage.

River twists his head to look at me as I approach.

"How are you feeling now?" I ask him.

Still drained, though it is less all-encompassing, he replies. I crouch to put my hand on his shoulder and send healing magic into him. As I continue pouring mana into the spell, I start frowning. There's . . . something there, but it doesn't appear to be anything I can affect with my healing magic. Even when I try to direct my magic to what I half sense is there, it just slips around or *through* whatever the thing is and doesn't affect it in the slightest. All I can do is heal a few small things here or there and then withdraw.

"I think it's just something you'll have to recover from in time," I say to him finally, trying to speak with a confidence I don't feel. At least, I *hope* that he'll recover from it in time, because if not . . .

At least he is starting to look better. His scales have regained some of their color, and his skin isn't looking quite so loose on his frame. He's still not moving with the energy I've seen from him so far, but hopefully, that will return too.

Now free of the worry that either River or I will die in the next few minutes, the nagging sense of messages waiting is getting on my nerves. Deciding there's no time like the present, I sit down and open up my message panel.

CHAPTER THIRTY-TWO

Way of the Healer

I open up my message screen and stare. Fortunately, it's possible to read my messages regardless of the light level around me. My message area looks a bit like an email inbox, but each entry is just labeled "Message" with no helpful subject line. Read messages are slightly gray and unread ones are highlighted white. I can scroll down to see all the messages I've received since the beginning, but these days, actually finding something in the list is a bit of a trial. It shouldn't really be a surprise considering how urgent the nagging feeling was getting, but I'm still shocked at the number of unread messages.

I mentally scroll down to the oldest message—there are so many messages that they don't all fit in the space immediately before my eyes—and select it.

Congratulations! You have gathered enough Energy to push your body to the next level. Would you like to level up?
Level up now / Next message

My eyebrows almost disappear into my hairline. *I can level up again? Really? But I only leveled like . . . two days ago . . .* That's *fast*. I choose to move on for now and navigate to my status screen, still half disbelieving the notification.

Name: Markus Wolfe		Race: Human	Class: Tamer
Level: 3	Energy to next level: 100%	Energy absorption rate: 72u/hr	Energy towards debt: 4%
Intelligence	18	Mana: 180/180	
Wisdom	18	Mana regeneration rate: 450u/hr	
Willpower	21+4 (+20%)	Health regeneration rate: 25u/hr	
Constitution	16	Health: 160/160	
Strength	14	Stamina: 80/80	
Dexterity	14	Stamina regeneration rate: 140u/hr	

Class Skills:	Non-Class Skills:
Dominate – Novice 1	*Lay-on-Hands – Journeyman 1*
Tame – Beginner 5	Stealth – Novice 1
Fade – Initiate 1	Animal Empathy – Novice 5
	Meditation – Beginner 7

I mean, the notification was right. I'm sitting at one hundred percent in terms of Energy gathered. But the surprises don't stop there.

Starting from the top, the first number that sticks out to me is the Energy absorption rate. That's a *crazy* number. Kalanthia's den is in an area where I get thirteen units of Energy per hour. More to the point, River's village is in an area further into the valley than we are now, but I was only getting twenty-five units of Energy per hour.

To have such a dramatic difference between absorption rates within just a few hours . . . There's got to be something wrong. Or right. Or maybe it's normal. What do I know?

Regardless, I mentally switch my Energy absorption to go towards my Energy debt; right now, I'm just wasting the opportunity. I wonder how long I've been at the point of being able to level up, and I curse myself for not checking my notifications sooner. I *really* wasn't expecting them to be about leveling up already.

Well, nothing I can do about it now . . . Next, I note that my Wisdom, Willpower, and Constitution have each increased by a point. My Intelligence has increased by *two*. I have to guess that it's because of my experience just now with the poison, but I might be wrong. Given that I didn't have to assent to the points, they must be ones I fully earned rather than needing to shortcut the System with a bit of Energy. And that makes this last half an hour more productive than any non-level-up half an hour *ever*. It even beats out that achievement I got. Or have I gained another one? I guess I'll find out.

Finally, I look at my Skills list and the number of changes there. Dominate has actually ranked up, interestingly enough. Considering that I haven't actually Dominated any creatures recently, I can only think it's linked with my current Bonds—maybe drawing mana from River is the cause? That'll be one of the messages waiting for me; perhaps whatever new feature of the Skill I've gotten will explain where I got it from.

I'm also curious as to why Lay-on-Hands is suddenly in italics when it never was before . . . I know I haven't lost the Skill or anything because I've been using it, so at least I don't have to worry about that. It's also ranked up, though that's not entirely surprising considering I've never cleared out poison in the way I just did.

Animal Empathy has increased a little and Meditation a lot—also not really surprising considering what I've been doing recently. Still, nothing groundbreaking there. I decide to clear out all my notifications before leveling up since there may be information in them that could change my allocation of stat points.

<table>
<tr><td colspan="2">Congratulations!
You have made progress on your Quest.
You have discovered the center of the Vine-Strangler Grove and encountered a guardian of unusual size and strength. Investigation of the guardian beast's lair may yield additional clues.</td></tr>
<tr><td>Quest: The Vine-Strangler Grove</td><td>Quest type: Regional</td></tr>
<tr><td colspan="2">Description: You have encountered Vine-Strangler Trees in an unusual location, at an unusual stage of development, and with an unusual level of Energy in the area.
You have sought the center of the Vine-Strangler Grove and have had an encounter with a powerful beast.</td></tr>
<tr><td colspan="2">Primary objective: Discover why Vine-Strangler Trees are growing in this location and the reason for the unusual level of Energy.
Secondary objective: Investigate the guardian beast's lair.</td></tr>
<tr><td colspan="2">Time to complete Quest: Unlimited</td></tr>
<tr><td>Suggested difficulty: Initiate</td><td>Reward: Rare Bronze Chest</td></tr>
</table>

Apparently, despite not being sure about attempting to complete this quest at all, and most definitely not wanting to do it before delivering Lathani back to her mother, I've been sucked into it, nonetheless. Could the quest have been given by the vine-strangler trees themselves? It seems strange to consider trees giving a person a quest, but it's also strange to think of trees herding me into battle with a giant fire-breathing salamander.

On second thought, though, that same salamander is clearly considered a "guardian" in the quest, which is something I doubt the trees would consider it. Unless it was guarding something else? I dismiss the thoughts with a shake of my head. Either way, it doesn't make much difference. The situation hasn't changed and that hole in the center of the clearing still potentially offers our best chance of getting out of here, since we can't fly like the bird. It just gives me a warning that the tunnel might be even more dangerous than I thought. Dangerous . . . or lucrative.

Being called a "guardian beast" really makes me wonder what exactly the salamander was guarding—and whether it might be any use to me or mine. Deciding to think about that later, I move on to the next notification. This one is pretty surprising too.

<table>
<tr><td>You have discovered a use of your Skill, Lay-on-Hands, which is not compatible with its originating school, the Way of the Healer. Skills from this school are explicitly focused on doing no harm. You have used your Skill in a combat</td></tr>
</table>

situation to kill your opponent. You therefore have a choice to either Evolve your Skill or Split it.

Evolve

If you choose to Evolve your Skill, you will gain access to a new area of magic: Flesh-Shaping. This will enable you to shape your own and others' flesh to your desires with or without permission. This Skill is not classed as healing magic and is, therefore, subject to different limitations and potential growth than your original Skill. Some potential aspects that you have not yet explored may therefore be lost. Functions that you have practiced and gained personal knowledge of will be retained.

Split

If you choose to Split your Skill, you will retain your original Skill and all previous progress will remain intact. You will also gain a second Skill: Body-Invasion. This new Skill will allow you to influence an opponent's body with either destruction or overgrowth by invading their bodies with your mana. Invasions with foreign mana are automatically resisted by the enemy, and this resistance must be overcome in order for the Skill to be used successfully. Intense concentration is required for this process, and mana can flow both ways over the connection.

Until you make a choice, you will be limited to the use of your original Lay-on-Hands Skill. This precludes combat applications.

Choose now / Next message

I stare at the message for a long moment, reading and rereading it. I still don't fully understand it. So, I *was* able to kill the salamander by invading its brain with my magic, but now I can't, because some people in this "Way of the Healer" school say I can't? How on Earth—or off it—can they enforce that? Illogical or not, apparently they can.

Is this why Lay-on-Hands was written in italics on my status sheet? Because I could lose it entirely and replace it with Flesh-Shaping? My being shrinks away from that option, especially since it says I could lose "potential" aspects of Lay-on-Hands, whatever that means. Lay-on-Hands has kept me alive, it's kept Bastet alive—twice—and in no way do I want to lose anything about it.

However . . . I can't say that Body-Invasion sounds very appealing. The last line in particular makes me leery. Needing to have intense concentration probably means I won't be able to do anything else, which could potentially make me as vulnerable as I am after a failed Battle of Wills. Not to mention that the warning about mana flowing both ways indicates that others could attack *me* through it.

In the end, I decide that I need to see what Kalanthia thinks about it. And maybe River too. They might have heard of either Flesh-Shaping or Body-Invasion before and have an idea of whether one Skill would be better than the other. I mentally choose to move to the next message.

> Congratulations!
> You have advanced a Class Skill past Beginner. Dominate is now Novice 1. Due to your unusual uses of this Skill, two new effects have been discovered.
>
> Effect 1
> You have used this Skill to negotiate with rather than crush your opponent during a Battle of Wills. Henceforth, you are able to impose a sense of peace on the Battle of Will's space. This sense will increase slightly with each level that you gain in the Skill and will calm and pacify strong emotions, allowing reason to prevail. Note that this effect can only take place when you are yourself calm and attempting to negotiate. If you aim to forcefully overcome your opponent in this space, the sense of peace will be replaced with a sense of aggression of equivalent strength.
>
> Effect 2
> You have discovered that more than just thoughts and emotions can pass along the Bond. You are now able to draw mana from your Bound's mana and health pools. Experiment with this capacity to discover new aspects. Be wary, however, of the effect this has on your Bound—and yourself.
>
> Next message / Close message

I click away, feeling a little troubled. The fact that negotiations will become easier is great; it's the second effect that worries me a little. That the System box even warns me about the consequences is a red flag for me. I'm going to have to be very, very careful with this, I decide.

But that doesn't mean I'm not going to investigate it at all. If I could draw on my Bound when I'm low in mana? That could be a lifesaver. Even better, what if it could be a two-way street and I could share my own mana or health with a heavily injured companion? I may be reading more into the possibilities than actually exists, but if any of these are potential discoveries waiting to be made? Game changer would be the least of it.

The next three messages are the expected notifications about having gained points in Wisdom, Willpower, and Constitution. It doesn't say why, but I can guess. The following message is what I was half expecting.

> Achievement awarded: Risky Innovator
> You have played with unknown energies and unknown methods, and yet, you

have somehow come out the better for it. +2 to Intelligence to make you better at doing it in the future.

Next message / Close messages

I wonder if it's just me or if that System message actually has a hint of personality to it that none of the other messages so far have. I also can't help but feel that it's a bit of a backhanded compliment: "Yes, you achieved it, but more out of luck than anything else, and if you were smarter, you wouldn't have done it that way in the first place." Oh well, the System message can say what it likes. The fact is that I was desperate and it *did* work.

Would I do the same thing in the future? Yes, probably. Though, I will try not to get *into* the situations in the first place. Almost dying could have been avoided by me not falling for the creature's trap in the first place. Or by having enough wood in my Inventory so that I didn't need to go into the forest again at all.

Lastly is my rank-up message for Lay-on-Hands. Clearly, until I make the decision about whether to Evolve or Split the Skill, it's considered business as usual. I suppose I should be grateful that not making the choice hasn't frozen my Skill's ability to progress or something.

Congratulations!
You have advanced a Skill past Initiate. Lay-on-Hands is now Journeyman 1. You have shown an understanding of the body's anatomy on multiple occasions. Healing magic that is directed according to the body's natural rhythms is now more efficient. For every Journeyman level in Lay-on-Hands, channeled healing that works with the body now uses approximately 5% less mana.

Close messages

Nothing particularly groundbreaking, but useful enough. Like the extra absorption of mana while in Meditation, it's the kind of thing that shows its use over time. However, by the time that I reach Journeyman nine, I'll have a forty-five percent reduction in mana costs—that's big. Given that my most recent issues have been to do with not having enough mana to deal with the gravity of injuries, it feels a little like an answer to my prayers.

Actually, how come I've had two Skills in two days offer me something that's effectively a percentage increase in mana? Is there a reason, or is it just coincidence? Sighing, I push the question out of my mind—perhaps I'll discover the reason later, but if another Skill suddenly starts affecting my mana, I'll conclude that it's not just pure coincidence.

With all the messages dealt with, it's now time to consider where I'm going to put my level-up points. I wasn't expecting to level up for a good while yet, so I haven't exactly put a lot of thought into it. Not that I'm complaining, of course: the quicker I level up, the stronger I get. But now, instead of just putting points wherever seems best in the short term, it's time to seriously consider what kind of fighter I want to become.

CHAPTER THIRTY-THREE

Making Decisions

Returning to my status screen, I consider the numbers carefully. I've only gotten to more than twenty points in a single stat: Willpower. Intelligence is at eighteen and so is Wisdom. Constitution is at sixteen, and Strength and Dexterity are at fourteen. So, the question is whether or not to add points to my physical stats to bring them more in line with my mental ones.

I consider what the scholars in Nicholas's world think about assigning points. According to them, focusing all my points into one or two stats and leaving the others to fall behind is not a good idea, but neither is treating all stats completely equally.

When considering stat allocation, two of the three main things the scholars highlight are having a baseline of twenty points in each stat and not letting the strongest stat get too far away from the weakest. The third is to lean into one's strengths. Not all Skills require the same supporting stats; not all people want to do the same things.

Up to now I've been mostly making decisions based on what I seem to need in the immediate future: more health, more strength, more mana. But my recent experiences have shown me that there's more to the stats than what's displayed by my status screen. My increased Intelligence has made things easier to think through, and solutions come with an ease I'd have envied back in my previous life.

I won't necessarily say they're always *good* solutions—it seems like I can't get away from the fact that I'm human and fallible—but my thought process itself is smoother, faster. If I'd waited to absorb the knowledge stones until I had twenty points in Intelligence, I can only imagine the greater understanding of them I would have received.

Then again, I'd probably already be dead.

There are stats that have proven themselves to have even more hidden depths—like Wisdom. Ever since gaining my Meditation Skill, I've felt like there's a whole world out there that I can only barely perceive. And though it doesn't explicitly say in the Skill that it depends on Wisdom, the fact that both Skill and stat are involved in mana regeneration indicates to me an implicit connection. Also, the fact that I gained a point in Wisdom after managing to do more than merely perceive the links around me indicates that any more work in that area is going to be improved by having more Wisdom.

Knowing that the connections aren't just features of the environment around me but are things I can actually touch, in some obscure way, has lit a fire of curiosity within me. There's nothing about these connections in the System lore stone. Did I fail to learn it when I absorbed the stone because my brain wasn't ready to receive the information? Or is it not something the scholars have explored? I promise myself I'll investigate the whole thing more when we're back home and safe.

For now, though, I take a long hard look at myself and my Skills. I have a Tamer Class. I've accepted that that means I'm strongest when surrounded by my companions, Tamed or Dominated. I'm a team player, not a lone wolf. A team leader, if only due to the fact that I'm the nexus of all the Bonds. But, as I know from my corporate experience, teamleader doesn't mean being at the front or even in the middle of the action.

In fact, it's often the opposite; if the person directing the project is also responsible for working on the details, they may lose sight of the bigger picture. I need to plan my progression based on the fact that, although I need to be able to take care of myself if I accidentally get separated from the group, my principal role is as leader.

Right now, looked at practically, we have two damage dealers, a scout, and a healer-fighter—me. That's a better team than we had on the way to rescue Lathani, when we only had one damage dealer apart from me. Of course, it's only a better team if we work together well, and that's my responsibility to manage as the team leader. If we find we have gaps in our lineup, it's also my responsibility to close them. I can only do that by recruiting others for the team, and I do *that* with my Class Skills.

Dominate is clearly dependent on Willpower as its primary attribute. There may be other underlying attributes, but if so, I doubt they're any of the physical ones. Tame isn't as clear. It talks about a beast of moderate or higher Intelligence being able to reject the Bond, but does that mean it uses *my* Intelligence as a modifier? The fact that it talks about "connections" makes me suspect it has a link to Wisdom, based on recent experiences.

Lay-on-Hands is heavily dependent on mana, and therefore, a bigger pool or faster regeneration would definitely improve my ability to use this Skill. In addition, I reckon that a higher Intelligence stat would help me think through problems and find solutions with more speed and efficiency. A higher Wisdom level would possibly enable me to connect better with the creature I'm healing, though that's very much a guess.

Of my other four Skills, Animal Empathy is based on Wisdom with future developments linked to Constitution. This Skill could be important for me to develop since it'll probably improve my negotiation skills, which will be essential to either Tame or Dominate. The way *I* do Dominate, anyway. Meditation, as I was thinking earlier, is not explicitly improved by any stat, but from the description, it seems to be at least connected to Wisdom; I doubt that improving the stat would harm it, at least.

My last two Skills are the only ones that are linked to the physical stats. Stealth relies on stamina to work and on Dexterity to be quieter when moving. However, even that one mentioned needing mana for later, more exotic effects. As for Fade, I need mana as well as stamina just to operate it. If I want it to conceal any more than just visual effects, it will then scale with Wisdom or Willpower. Briefly, I wonder how to actually make it do that, then put the thought aside; something to consider later.

While there is a question mark over whether having Skills that hide me from opponents' perception is even any use now that I'm part of a team, I'm still inclined to say that there is. First of all, Bastet's stealth abilities are still far better than my own. If I'm traveling with her, I'm the one who attracts notice. Second of all, even if I do have other companions who are less stealthy even than me, if I'm taking more of a back seat when it comes to the fights, an ability to conceal myself could be essential. It worked with the monkiles recently: I stayed in Fade and sniped at the other ranged fighters while Bastet drew their attention. That way I could control when I revealed myself and thereby control the pace of the fight.

Sometimes I feel a bit disappointed that I didn't take Stun instead of Fade; it could have proved the turning point of some fight. Then again, if I'd used it against the salamander, it could have either meant that none of us got hurt if the massive amphibian was Stunned for long enough that Bastet or River could have ripped out its throat, *or* that I would have been completely out of mana when Bastet was almost bitten in half. However, if I can seriously improve my mana regeneration rate . . . When I get to level five, I'll have to see if there's anything better than Stun on offer; if not, I'll pick that one.

In summary, it seems clear that Willpower and the mana-related stats are by far more important to me than the physical stats. As much as it makes me feel good to swing a mace and crush the skulls of my foes, leaning further into the melee-based fighter probably isn't my best bet. I still need to be able to defend myself, sure, but I don't need to put loads of points in my physical stats to be able to do that. Not right now, anyway.

My best effect on the fight will probably be by keeping the damage dealers healed, supporting them from a distance through ranged attacks, and returning them to full health afterwards—and maybe even during it if I can work out how to heal without touching my target, assuming that's even possible with a Skill named "Lay-on-Hands." Not to mention stacking the deck in our favor from the beginning by bringing the right fighters to the table.

The physical stats are therefore less important for me. I need to bring them up to a decent level—twenty, at least—but I'm probably better served by letting that happen naturally in my new labor-intensive life than dedicating level-up points to Strength, Dexterity, or even Constitution. Heck, on this journey already, I've gained points to Constitution and Dexterity without even having to dedicate any Energy to them.

It might be the wrong decision to make, but there are always counterarguments for every decision; I have to make a choice eventually. Adding points to

Constitution makes me feel safer: each point is ten health points extra away from dying, after all, but it doesn't actually do anything to improve my survivability beyond that. Besides, with enough mana, my Constitution stat almost becomes irrelevant. What does damage matter if I can heal it away? Though, I suppose if something like Kalanthia came along and bit my head off, I'd be done for, but I probably wouldn't survive that even if my Constitution stat was at a hundred points. Or would I?

Anyway, with the decision made to put two points in each of my mental and soul stats, I push myself to my feet. I'm happy about the opportunity to level up— of course I am. I just wish that it had happened while we were next to the river. Without even any water to wash my mouth out, I'm going to have the worst case of bad breath ever. Not to mention the body odor of that revolting liquid that comes out of me. Bastet, River, Lathani, and the cubs probably won't be all that happy about it either.

"Watch my back, would you?" I ask all and sundry before stepping a little bit closer to the hole. After looking up nervously at the sky, I quickly strip off. No point in having my clothes soaked in the stuff, right? Throwing a glance back at the group, I see River watching me in interest and feel a few moments of insecurity. Then I remember that he's a lizard-man, and he's probably more curious at seeing a body so different from his own than trying to check me out. With effort, I manage to get control over the flush rising up my neck.

The level-up process is the normal mixture of blissful and deeply unpleasant. As soon as I've regained full awareness, I quickly rub myself down with a shirt that's too torn to ever be repaired and do my best to spit out the rancid taste of my level-up vomit. Situation now improved, if not ideal, I reach for my clothes.

Wait, River says, and I pause, then look around myself warily, including above my head. Has he seen something? *Rub the dirt all over yourself*, he tells me. Okay, apparently it's not an attack. I turn around to frown at him, and my hand automatically goes down to cover myself; something about him being mostly humanoid elicits the reaction where Bastet hadn't.

"Why?" I ask, frowning, before my question actually sparks a memory. Not my memory—one I absorbed from the tracking skill stone. I answer my own question. "To reduce my scent, right?"

Yes, he agrees. *Yours is . . . strong right now.* I can't help but grin at that. I haven't had a proper bath in weeks and I just leveled up. I can live with "strong" as a description. Actually, maybe I can't; if my scent gives us away, none of us might live with it. With no further ado, I grab handfuls of the ashy ground and rub them all over. It feels weird to clean myself by putting more dirt on, but that's life now.

This time when I reach for my clothes, my skin now a mucky gray color all over, obvious even in the moonlight, River doesn't object. Even so, I bet Bastet would have turned her nose up at it. That makes me wonder where my raptorcat companion is. She seems to be taking an awfully long time over her scouting . . .

CHAPTER THIRTY-FOUR

I'm Not Her Little Cub Anymore

I try to work out how much time it's been since Bastet went to scout. She left before I went into the forest and that whole debacle, and she was gone for the entire recovery phase, not to mention me checking my notifications and leveling up . . .

I stand as I feel nervous energy running through me. What if she's in trouble? Then I remember that I can just touch the Bond and check on her, and I feel like an idiot. Doing so immediately, I get more information from the connection than I ever have before.

My raptorcat companion is absolutely fine. She's a little tired, but no more than that. Still feeling well-fed. Not thirsty, which is better than *I* am right now. As for her emotional state, she's wary and eager to get back to us, but there's also a significant amount of excitement. The last makes my eyebrows lift in surprise.

What could she be excited about? Food? Or maybe she has confirmation that there's an exit? That would be good!

Either way, she feels like she's still a fair distance away. Relieved of that worry, I open my status screen briefly to check things out. With my level-up, I've now reached twenty points in both Intelligence and Wisdom, which means that I'm not going to be organically earning any more in those. Willpower was already over twenty and is now sitting at an effective twenty-seven points.

Closing my screen, I find myself at a bit of a loose end. Until Bastet comes back, there isn't much I can do. Well, I suppose I could deal with the salamander carcass a bit; salamander armor sounds like a good idea. The hide dealt pretty well with Bastet and River's attacks, after all.

I step over to the salamander corpse and start skinning it in large sections, filling my Inventory with the large pieces of hide. After a while, River joins me silently and butchers the meat that I've revealed to the air.

We keep each other company for long enough that the sun fully goes down behind the horizon and the moon starts rising. We don't say anything, but it feels better for that. Like there have been too many words already.

Once I have enough hide to cover myself head to toe four times over, I bow out of dealing with the corpse and leave it to River. I'm tired—I've basically not slept in two days. Probably the only reason I'm keeping going at all is because of my new Meditation benefit, which means I have actually been able to get some rest.

Maybe I should sleep if I can? The thought tugs at me almost irresistibly, but I push it away with a force of will. Before I give in, I need to check up on my group.

I squint in the darkness as I struggle to see the cubs or Lathani. River's clear enough with his outline picked out in moonlight. Then I consider how this would be a perfect opportunity to use the newest rank-up of one of my Skills. I activate Fade and feel a sharpening and lightening of the world around me. It may only be two point five percent, but it makes a noticeable difference—unless the light level is low enough for the five percent, that is. If that's the case, the change would make more sense.

I'd say it's like the brightness has been turned up a couple of notches, but that wouldn't be quite accurate. At least I'm now able to spot the nunda cub—or juvenile, or whatever she is after all the changes. Even though she doesn't seem to have any magical stealth, her coat allows her to blend in well with the mottled ground. Having seen her, I next identify Storm cuddled up to her; the paler raptorcat is easier to see than her siblings, who are also nestled together.

I walk closer, trying to be quiet in case Lathani is sleeping. When I see her eyes glint in the moonlight, I realize she's still awake. The raptorcats are dead to the world, though, just bundles of fluff and feathers shifting slightly in their sleep. My eyes flick over the nunda cub, and something—maybe my Animal Empathy, maybe something else—tells me she's feeling miserable.

I release Fade a couple of steps away, not wanting to surprise her. When she only shifts her head to look at me with no surprise visible, I realize she already knew I was somewhere nearby. I really need to figure out a way of hiding my scent and the noises I make. Fortunately, right now it doesn't matter.

"Hey," I say to her gently as I crouch down next to her. "We'll get you back to your mom, I promise." She's quiet for a moment.

Do you think she'll accept me? What if she turns me away? Where would I go? What would I do? I frown.

"Accept you? What do you mean?"

Like this. Different. I'm . . . I'm not her little cub anymore. I'm quiet for a few long moments as Lathani's words inadvertently dig at a wound within me.

"I think you'll probably always be her little cub," I tell her in the end, "if she's anything like my mom was. And I don't think you're as grown-up as you think you are," I add a little pointedly. That makes her raise her head and growl at me. The whiny hint to the sound just proves my point, in my opinion. "Anyway," I continue, trying not to smile, "if she *does* reject you, you can always stay with us."

But you live with Mother, Lathani points out. I let my mouth pull up at the corner.

"Well, she forbade me from using either of my Skills on you at the start, but if she rejects you as her cub, then I don't see how she could complain about me offering you a Bond—if you want one, of course. Then she's *really* got no grounds to complain about you staying with us." I'm pretty sure it wouldn't actually be as clear-cut as all that; the possibility that, without the need for my babysitting services, my landlady might turn me out on my ear is the least of the potential consequences.

Since I don't think that there's much chance of Kalanthia rejecting her beloved cub, though, I don't bother Lathani with the details. Apparently, having a backup plan is enough to cheer her up a little, as she nuzzles me for a moment before putting her head back on her paws and closing her eyes. I'm sure that it hasn't soothed her worries completely, but if it allows her to get some rest, then all the better.

Checking on the cubs, I see that they're deeply asleep. Finally, I walk back over to River. He's still butchering the salamander carcass, piling the chunks of meat on top of a section of the salamander's skin. I quickly begin piling the lumps of flesh into my Inventory, glad to have ten new slots available. Without Fade sharpening my eyesight, and with the moonlight only barely lighting the area, I have to work mostly by feel.

"How can you butcher a corpse in this light level?" I ask River in curiosity. He certainly doesn't seem to be fumbling around.

He moves in the lizard-man version of a shrug, that gentle wave of the tail visible only because his scales catch the light.

The moon is sufficient for the task. Hmm. I straighten and look at him.

"River, how would you describe your eyesight in the dark?" I ask slowly.

Passable, he replies. *My people would never consider ourselves nocturnal. Communication becomes more difficult when we cannot see each other's visual cues, but as long as at least one of the bright eyes is in the sky, we can move without fumbling too much. And yourself?*

"Worse than that," I admit. "I'm struggling to see now."

Oh? he asks curiously. *This light level is a little dim for me, but I can still accomplish my task well enough.* I hum in acknowledgment. Good to know. I hope improving my Constitution will improve my sight in the dark in the long term since I don't want to have to use Fade all the time.

There's a slurping, squelching sound. River turns to me a moment later.

Do you know what this is? he asks as he hands me something.

It feels like a bag full of liquid, but he's holding it by what I guess is the outlet since no liquid is pouring over my fingers. I hold it in the moonlight and reactivate Fade so that my eyesight is maximized. It looks similar to what I was expecting: a bag about the size of a soccer ball, but more like a saggy tit than anything else. It's not full, whatever it is. Idly, I wonder about making a waterskin out of it: if I could cure the exterior walls, it would be perfect. Then I catch a whiff of the liquid and all thoughts of turning it into a waterskin flee my mind.

"Keep holding that, would you?" I ask River absently as I reach for some sticks from my Inventory; it's fortunate that I had already collected a good amount of wood by the time we were attacked. Then I wipe my damp and greasy-feeling hand on a cloth that was already ruined by my level-up, before quickly shoving it back into my Inventory as my nose scrunches up at the stink. When I run out of space, that cloth will be the first to go; for now, it's doing a good job as a disposable rag.

Starting the fire is only a matter of minutes, but I'm still impatient as I wait for the fire to catch well enough for my little experiment. Then, once the flames are eating hungrily at the twigs I've placed in a pile, I reach for the gland, or whatever it is. I tip a little of the oily liquid onto a stick, then toss it on the fire. It's only a few drops, but I'm glad I didn't use more.

The fire flares up brightly, and its foot-tall flames illuminate a shocked lizard-man. I don't mind admitting that I'm a little startled too. Well, I guess we just found whatever the salamander was using to breathe fire. A thought occurs, and I stare at the trees as a malicious smile creeps across my face. If Bastet comes back and says that the tunnel is even remotely dangerous, I think I know *exactly* what to do. Heck, it's tempting just to set light to the forest and then hide in the tunnel anyway.

It's only the knowledge that once I've done that, I have no control over what happens after that stops me. River agreed to help me in exchange for me destroying the forest to save his village; I doubt he'd appreciate it if that also means a "life-devourer" sweeping through his village and killing half of his people. No, if there aren't any better choices, I'll do it, but I must at least wait for Bastet to get back before deciding.

In the meantime, however, I've got another idea. I sacrifice another of my shirts by cutting it into four, then wrap the pieces around four branches and soak the ends in the liquid. That easily, I've managed to create some more torches. If necessary, I've got the items needed to create further torches, but the fewer clothes I need to sacrifice, the better. If it's a question of life or my clothes . . . Well, it's a tough choice, but if I lose my life, I won't be able to wear my clothes, so . . .

After dipping the head of one of the new torches in the fire, I test it—I've learned my lesson about leaving field tests until I'm actually in the field. The torch flares brightly for a few moments, then dies down significantly. Fortunately, it doesn't die out completely but starts burning the cloth and wood inside merrily. I'm not sure how long these torches will last, but with four and a half, it should be fine. Erring on the side of caution, I put all four of the new ones in my Inventory, the burning brand no doubt snuffing out immediately.

I hesitate. I should keep loading my Inventory with the chunks of flesh that River has returned to slicing off the massive carcass, but . . . I just want to sleep. I can't see the bird, but I sense through the Bond that she's resting at least. It's just me and River awake now.

"How are you doing?" I ask him. I want desperately to knock off but feel unable to do so without checking on all my companions. The ones within range, anyway. "How are you feeling after earlier?"

Tired but serviceable. He hesitates for a moment. *I don't feel like I have fully recovered whatever resource you took, but the aftereffects have largely eased. Now I just feel a little . . . drained.*

"Why don't you sleep?" I suggest, hating myself even though my guilt prompts me to speak. If he sleeps, *I* can't. Then my sense of shame deepens when I feel a wave of negation through the Bond.

It is fine. I do not think I could sleep tonight. Not given everything that has happened.

"I can understand that," I answer awkwardly. It was easier when I didn't think of any of the lizard folk as *people*. "But you need to sleep sometime."

I know, he answers, and I feel pain underlying the response. *But I cannot now. Rest, Markus.* A wave of renewed guilt runs through me at how transparent I must appear to him. It doesn't stop me from taking his advice. I'm out like a light as soon as I curl up with my back against Lathani.

It doesn't feel like more than a minute later when I'm nudged urgently. I mumble and try to bat the interfering hand away. My fingers touch rough, scaly skin attached to sharp claws. Moving up the arm, I feel feather-fur.

Opening my eyes wide, I see a familiar outline in the moonlight, the glowing orb having inexplicably advanced across the sky in the minute my eyes were shut.

A wave of amusement hits me through the Bond.

Bastet's back.

CHAPTER THIRTY-FIVE

The Most Promising Route

Bastet," I call quietly, snapping to alertness. "What did you see?"

She bludgeons me with a feeling of "Come on!" and even turns and takes a few steps down the slope as if too impatient to even wait for me to get up.

"No, really, what did you see?" I ask her firmly, then get up and move over to the pile of salamander meat chunks. Shoveling them into my Inventory in handfuls, I fill more than three spaces with the meat. In addition to what I added there earlier, I've now got almost five slots filled with this stuff. And the corpse isn't completely picked clean. I also grab some of its bones. Marrow would be a nutritious addition to my meals, and the bones may be able to be transformed into needles—something I desperately need if I want to stay clothed for even another month, let alone the rest of the year.

Bastet sends a feeling of irritation at me, but she goes over to the cubs and wakes them up along with Lathani. Darting a look overhead, I see that the moon, which had been shedding light before, is now almost directly overhead. It's probably only been two or three hours since I laid down; the thought makes me sad and seriously contemplate ordering the raptorcat to wait until I've slept myself out. Then I rein in my impulses. Once more, I ask Bastet to report back on her scouting, but this time I send it as a pointed mental message rather than a verbal one.

She replies back with what I can only describe as a mental sigh. Like she's going to humor me only because she realizes I'm not going to get moving until she does. She sends me a series of quick mental messages, like the ones from the tunnel to the salt cave: more sensation than visual image.

A tunnel, much bigger than the one we wormed our way through before. A hole into a narrower tunnel below, but still one with a fair bit of space to move. A hole above her head into another tunnel. Fresh air and light at the end of it. All great stuff, and not an enemy to be seen! Then she shoves another image into my mind, insistent in a way I've never known her.

At first glance it's beautiful: an opening into a cave of wonders, all rubies and reflected rainbows of light. But I don't get her eagerness. Sure, I'm happy to see it, but I would be happier if I had any use for rubies right now. But I don't understand *her* excitement.

Bastet shoves the image at me again, her eagerness now tempered with frustration that I'm not *getting* it. She tries to make me understand in a couple of other ways before giving up. It leaves both of us feeling frustrated, but perhaps she's right—I need to see whatever it is to realize exactly why she's so excited.

At least the tunnel has proven itself to be a better option for escape than the trees, even with my new flammable liquid. Part of the reason Bastet took so long was because she inspected every inch of the place to see whether there was any threat. She only went partway along the tunnel: she didn't want to take too long and, apparently, it's obvious enough by the volume of air moving through it that there's a wide exit. She found no signs of threat, though there's the possibility of something guarding the exit.

To that end, I tidy up the last of the salamander meat; we'll have to leave what's left on the corpse since there's no way I can lift the carcass enough to fit it inside my Inventory. Then, with a quick look around, I drop into Fade to make the most of my eyesight in the moonlight and follow my scout.

The cubs complain as we walk, not taking kindly to being disturbed. A couple of growls from Bastet are enough to shut them up, fortunately. Lathani is silent, moving like a ghost through the ashen field. As for the bird, she's claimed a perch on River's shoulder and seems to have gone back to napping.

We step carefully down the slope and soon approach the tunnel mouth. Having four sets of eyes looking around is far better than just one, and I feel a lot safer as part of this group than I did when I first arrived on this world. I'm sure there are plenty of threats flying around at night, but I feel confident that we'll be able to face them together if necessary.

Bastet and River both move with a practiced ease and alertness that speaks to their experience of surviving in a dangerous world. Lathani seems to be doing her best to copy the adults, though with limited success. Still, her natural instincts seem to be serving her well considering how often I lose track of exactly where she is.

As we get closer to the tunnel, I start to see a faint red glow emanating from it. At first, I wonder if I'm imagining things, but when I peer down into the tunnel itself, I realize I'm not. The tunnel is reasonably steep, but not so much so as to need ropes to descend or ascend. There may be a few places where I'll need to scoot down on my bum or go down backwards, though. I wonder how River will cope since he's bipedal as well—I doubt the cubs or Lathani will have any trouble.

At the bottom of the slope, the tunnel curves away just enough that I can't see exactly what's causing the light. Peering downwards, I wonder what the source could be. Torches from some other people Nicholas wouldn't class as "civilized"? Except no, it's not flickering the way torches would.

Considering it's a tunnel that's angled steeply down, I hope it's not something like lava—surely it would feel significantly hotter if we were close enough to see the glow of molten rock. It couldn't be the cave that Bastet saw, could it? The light didn't look bright enough to cause such illumination, but I suppose it wouldn't be the first time looking through Bastet's eyes turned out to be a bit inaccurate.

At any rate, Bastet can be relied upon to spot threats, and she didn't see any, so it should be safe enough. The raptorcat is already scrambling over the lip, encouraging the cubs to follow her. She *really* wants us all to see the rubies, it seems.

The entrance to the tunnel is steep; the tunnel itself is even steeper. As I thought would happen, I'm not comfortable walking down it and instead climb backwards using both hands and feet. The first few meters of the tunnel are the same rocky soil that composes the entrance, but the surface I'm climbing down soon becomes rock. River copes well enough with the rocky soil, but he soon starts copying my method as we get onto the rock, where his foot-claws can't get as much purchase.

My brows knit together as I try to work out what caused the tunnel. It's remarkably smooth for a natural formation, and my feet sometimes slip in spots where there are few knobbles or dips. It almost looks like it was . . . melted? I look nervously down the tunnel, *really* hoping that we're not going to encounter lava. Or worse: a creature capable of melting *stone*.

I briefly consider the idea that the salamander created this tunnel but soon dismiss it. The tunnel might be big enough for a large amphibian the height of a horse and width of a car, but I highly doubt it was capable of producing a flame hot enough to melt—no, *evaporate*—stone, especially in the quantities required to excavate something like this.

If it had been able to do that, River wouldn't merely have been burned when blanketed in its flame, he would have been immediately incinerated. Besides, the liquid from the bladder he found was highly flammable, but not to the point of melting *rock*.

Which, of course, means that the cause of this whole geological strangeness is still unknown. And if the past is anything to go by, that means it's going to bite us in the butt sooner or later. My only consolation is that Bastet wouldn't have led us into danger knowingly, and there was certainly no indication of lava in her memories.

We continue clambering down into the massive hole. Well, apart from the bird. I still need to find a name for her that she will accept—I can't keep calling her "the bird" in my thoughts. She's still perched on River's shoulder, awake now and looking rather miserable. I understand: she's a creature of the wind and sky, not dark underground tunnels. I'm sure she can't be anticipating this with anything but distress.

"Hey, do you want to meet us outside?" I ask her gently. I can sympathize: I don't particularly like tunnels either. Even less so after my salt-finding experience. I can't imagine how much worse it would be if my primary way of traveling was by flying and I had to go into a space where I couldn't do it properly.

I get a feeling of reluctant desire, like she wants to go, but she also doesn't want to leave us. "We should be coming out another entrance—where, I don't know. You should be able to feel our direction with the Bond." She sends a hesitant acceptance.

A moment later, she uses her wing claws to push off from River's shoulder, then flies dangerously close to the walls as she circles her way upwards. I think she only succeeds due to the updrafts coming from below—her wing span is almost a third of the diameter of the tunnel. From this angle, I'm able to see why she doesn't have a tail: her back paws actually link together to offer the same benefits a tail would in terms of steering.

It's not too long before she's out of sight—once she's no longer in direct moonlight, she disappears into the night. I hope she makes it out of the forest fine. I hope *we* make it out fine too.

River and I share another look and then, without needing to say a word, continue climbing down. Right now, this appears to be the most promising route out.

Lathani moves easily, her four paws and claws offering plenty of stability. In fact, she looks like she's rather enjoying herself, leaping from spot to spot, then running back up to urge us on. The cubs are similar, and their personalities are showing through in the way they approach the descent.

Trouble with his devil-may-care attitude is instantly identifiable, as is Stormcloud with her meticulous approach. Ninja is more hesitant but tends to follow in Storm's wake. River is rather more grim set. His claws offer more purchase than my fingers or shoes, but the whole motion looks a little odd with his elongated back feet. Still, like Lathani, his tail helps him keep his balance, even arching high over his head to push him forwards towards the rock when he accidentally leans too far back.

It's hard work, not that far from rock climbing at certain points. I feel my limbs become leaden as the long period since I last properly slept, the frantic battles we've fought, and the continued physical exertion all combine to bring me close to the limits of my endurance. If I don't get another point in Strength (Endurance) by the end of all this, I'll probably throw the closest thing at hand at the screen. Which, due to its intangibility, probably means I'll end up accidentally enraging a hibernating bear or something.

By the time we reach where Bastet is waiting impatiently for us, I'm panting and sweaty, and my muscles are telling me firmly that they've had enough. All my discomfort is wiped away, however, when I see what she's found. *It's . . . Is it . . . ?* I don't actually know what she's found. All I know is that it's *beautiful.*

CHAPTER THIRTY-SIX

Cave of Wonders

I suddenly feel like Aladdin in the Cave of Wonders. Like I've walked into some underground fairy realm. Bastet's memory wasn't a patch on the reality and, though I'm still not sure why *she* was so excited, I'm enraptured by its beauty.

We're in a cavern that's several times the size of the tunnel we've been traveling through. The walls around me are encrusted with fiery-red diamonds, their hearts shimmering with what almost look like flames. There's no question about whether this is the source of the red light or not: the stones don't just reflect and refract light, they actually emit it. There are dozens, hundreds even, looking almost like they've grown from the rock. Or like droplets of blood shed from innumerable small wounds.

The whole impression is one of magnificence, but why would a nonhuman be interested what looks like this world's version of precious gems? Bastet is almost bouncing in place as she looks around. Lathani seems curious; the cubs are just ignoring everything and rolling together as they wrestle something. River, however, is unusually animated, a palpable ebullience creeping over the Bond. It's contagious, and I start feeling an anticipation for something I don't even know is worth feeling excited about.

"What are they?" I ask River, deciding that he might be more able to explain than Bastet.

Look at them, he says instead, his tone admiring—and covetous. *What do they look like to you?*

What is with my Bound and being mysterious about these things? Exasperation running through me, I lean closer without touching—I know better than to touch something I'm unfamiliar with, no matter how my Bound are reacting. When I look at only one of the gems and mentally separate it from the cluster, I realize that River's right: they *do* look familiar. The fact that they're growing in groups on a wall rather than being extracted as single items from a corpse had put me off.

Frowning, I pull the salamander Energy Heart out of my Inventory and compare them. I was right—they are similar, though not the same. The salamander one is far darker, garnet instead of ruby, and its reflection is infinitesimally duller. It also doesn't actually emit light the way these appear to. Although it looked like a gem in River's hand, now it looks like barely more than some everyday rock in comparison to the rubies in front of me.

The salamander Energy Heart is smaller than most of the gems clustered on the walls, but it's not the smallest. No, the main difference is that it looks carved, shaped, like it's already been processed by some skilled craftsman. In comparison, the rubies all around me are rough and natural rather than carved. It makes their capacity to sparkle and reflect the world around even more impressive: if they are like this when rough, what would they be like when carved?

"Are these . . . ?" I ask out loud to no one in particular. River comes into my line of sight. He's more excited than I've ever seen him before.

Yes! They're natural Energy Hearts! I've never heard of them being found in such a large quantity! Do you know what this means, Mast—Markus? I don't, but from his reaction, and Bastet's as well, it's got to be a good find. *With this many Energy Hearts, I'll be able to Evolve in no time!* That catches my attention.

"Wait, what do you mean 'Evolve'?" It's got to be a good thing, right? Certainly, River seems to think so. A memory comes back to me of a raptorcat growing bigger and gaining wings. Is that what he's talking about? River ignores me and instead does his version of cooing over the Hearts.

That's an image I'm sure I'll never forget: a sharp-toothed, sharp-clawed croco-dile-man looking like he's halfway towards melting over a bunch of rocks. "River?" I ask a little impatiently as he starts stroking the Heart.

For a moment I think that it's rubbed off on his clawed fingers—the digits seem to gleam in the light very briefly. The next instant, the shine is gone, and I wonder whether I just imagined it, or if somehow River's scales caught the light in an odd way. My Bound is completely rapt, and it takes me putting an annoyed hand on his shoulder to get his attention.

Even then, he barely manages to tear his attention away from the Energy Hearts in front of him.

What? he asks absently, clearly only giving me half his attention. *I will do what-ever you wish, Master, only let me . . .* He trails off and I sense that even the fragments of attention he had given to me have slipped away again.

"Turn around and talk to me, River," I request. My unease grows as he doesn't even respond and his eyes slide shut. Something is wrong.

"I think we should step out of here," I say slowly, trying to push calming feelings down the Bond. I dart a glance to the others. Bastet looks to be much the same as River, almost nuzzling the rocks. This time I'm pretty sure something rubs off on her, as I see her feather-fur gleam. That can't be good . . .

The cubs seem more bored than anything else, though Lathani is poking with an interested paw at one of the rocks growing on the ground. "Yep, come on every-one," I order as I move towards the exit. Lathani and the cubs follow me with no issues, especially when I pull a couple of bits of cooked meat out of my Inventory to bribe them with. Only Lathani casts a look back at the rock she had been prodding. Bastet and River, however . . .

"Bastet, River, come here," I tell them levelly, making it very clear that I'm not asking. I don't like using the fact that they can't disobey a direct order on them, but I'm feeling more and more concerned about the situation. Maybe we should wait until morning and go through the forest anyway? My two Bound try to resist, but their limbs don't let them, and they get walked over to me regardless of their attempts to stay with the shiny red jewels.

As we move around the bend of the tunnel and the cave is blocked from view, I observe my Bound relax. They stop resisting my order and perhaps even start to control their limbs again. We pause there, and Bastet lies down next to the cubs. I sit on the stone floor and River joins me there. Both of them send over a sense of apology, and River's also thrums with shame. The lizard-man looks at the ground for a long moment before speaking.

Master, I'm . . . sorry. I was out of line there. I'll accept any punishment you feel fit for my rudeness in ignoring you. I shake my head before he even finishes.

"I told you, call me Markus. And it's fine, no harm done. I just want to know what happened. Why were you and Bastet so drawn to those things? Did they have some sort of control over you?" Of all things, that's my worst fear. Earth's legends have plenty of ghouls, ghosts, and demons in them. We've already come across carnivorous trees and fire-breathing salamanders; who's to say there's nothing that could exert mind control over or possess my Bound?

No, River responds immediately. *There was no control. There was just . . . desire.*

"Desire?" I ask curiously; I'm reassured a little but remain cautious.

My whole body—no, my whole being cried out for me to approach the Energy Hearts, to touch them, to consume them . . . to Evolve.

"You said that before," I note. "What do you mean?"

Do you remember what I said about Energy Hearts? River asks me, his voice taking on a lecturing tone even as his eyes are drawn back to the cave.

"You said they are something that grow in you, that they are useful for you in controlling Energy. You found one in the salamander." Which is now back in my Inventory. I meant to give it to Bastet, but between her being injured, eating, and then going to scout, I haven't had the opportunity. Maybe I should just give it to River since he's the one that found it . . . But only once I'm convinced these things are good for my Bound. What I saw in the cave is not exactly heartening. The lizard-man dips his snout in agreement, his attention now firmly back on me.

Indeed. We claim Energy from other creatures when we kill them—I imagine you have experienced this already. I nod. *Some creatures have an Energy Heart in them, like the beast we recently fought. These Hearts are rich sources of Energy, containing multiple times what we can claim from the creature as it dies.* My eyes light up.

"We can get Energy from these Energy Hearts? How?" Then I remember the tiny one Bastet crunched down. "By eating them?" Amusement comes across the link even as River makes a hissing sound.

Not generally. Beasts that know no better do that, but we don't. Over time, my people have discovered that eating Energy Hearts actually loses some of the Energy they have to offer. Instead, we meditate and absorb the Energy over time. Bigger Hearts we might spend days absorbing. Though, due to the rarity of those, only the most powerful of the tribe would be given the opportunity to do so. He pauses for a moment, thinking. *However, I did see my mas—Honored Herbalist adding slivers of Energy Hearts to her potions to improve their effects, so you could argue we eat them then.*

Interesting. But it doesn't explain anything about my original question.

"But what is this whole 'Evolve' thing?"

When we've absorbed enough Energy, we develop a Heart within us. It's a risky endeavor, and not everyone even manages to attempt it, let alone succeeds. One of our number successfully developing a Heart is always a cause for celebration. We gain access to more power, are automatically raised in status in our village, and also become able to mate. It's the dream of every hatchling to one day Evolve and either become a Pathwalker, who controls some form of Energy, or a Warrior, who gains physical strength and some other physical ability.

My . . . previous master has no ability with stone or wood, but she can combine different substances in water or other fluids and enhance their effects. Honored Shaman can commune with spirits and control them. Honored Wood-shaper can make wood flow like water into the shapes she wishes them to be. He reaches for a handle on his belt, draws it out, and hands it to me. I thought it was another of his containers, but it isn't. It's a knife.

It's completely made out of wood, and when I test the edge, I find it has significantly better cutting power than I would have imagined. Though not to the standard of my own knife, I still find it capable of cutting my skin with less pressure than I would have expected. Perhaps somewhere between a dinner knife and a kitchen one. Extremely impressive considering it is made purely of wood.

"One of the . . . Pathwalkers made this?" I ask, thinking about how one of the other Pathwalkers almost stymied our escape attempts with her powers of telekinesis.

Yes.

Pieces click together in my head. It's no wonder that they would be the leaders of the group, even if they were smaller than most of the rest. Magic is a great equalizer. Though, as the Pathwalker I killed proves, if you get close to them, they're just as vulnerable to a mace to the skull as anyone else. I hand him his knife back as a thought occurs. "Have you ever heard of Flesh-Shaping?" A sensation of River being deep in thought comes through the Bond before he answers.

No, I don't think so, he says finally. *Water-Shaping, Earth-Shaping, Wood-Shaping, yes. But not Flesh-Shaping.* Ah well. It was just a thought. I guess I'll have to ask Kalanthia about it after all.

"So, Pathwalkers have some form of magic. Do they choose it? Or does it choose them?"

River hesitates, appearing uncertain.

I do not know for sure, he answers slowly, *but I believe that the ancestors choose, not the newly Evolved.*

So, it's out of their control, in short.

"And what about the Warriors? You mentioned something about them getting a physical ability? Do the . . . uh . . . ancestors choose this as well?"

Yes. Most who Evolve are chosen to be a Warrior, not a Pathwalker, and among the Warriors, some are chosen to be scouts, who grow a little in body and a lot in agility and speed, while others are chosen to be fighters, who grow a lot in body. They each gain at least one ability. Perhaps size or strength, or more armored skin, or speed. Perhaps even better senses. It's rare, but I knew one who could follow a trail using his intense sense of smell. There was no escaping him once he had your scent.

River suddenly looks sad.

He was one of those sent to capture the Great Predator's cub. He never returned. Many of our Warriors did not.

I have to admit that I'm struggling to find sympathy for lizard folk who died while attacking Kalanthia and trying to take her cub from her. I decide not to say that, though, and instead try to steer the conversation away from that particular roadblock.

"Even if you can't choose your actual abilities, can you choose your path of Evolution?" I ask. "And if so, do you have a preference between Pathwalker and Warrior?"

If I could choose, I would become a Pathwalker. Our village always needs more egg-carriers and magic-users. That is why I was so grateful when my mas—when Honored Herbalist offered me the opportunity to assist her. There are some indications that actions prior to passing the threshold may make a difference to the Evolution itself. I hope—hoped—to gain an ability similar to Honored Herbalist's if I succeeded in ranking up. The village needs more healers. Then he looks lost. *But I suppose that is no longer my path.*

I barely hear what he says. My mind is still stuck on what he said at first.

"So, wait, you say that you only gain the ability to mate once you've Evolved? So, if I understand this correctly, if you become a Pathwalker, you automatically . . . become female?"

Confusion comes across the link, and I wonder if I'm going to regret asking.

Female? He tries to pronounce the word with as little success as "fire" earlier.

"Yeah, you know. The . . . the ones who carry babies or . . . well, I suppose in your case, eggs."

Oh! he says, understanding. *Yes, that's right.* He stops there, not seeming to see an issue with this.

"And right now, you're male . . . the one who, um, *sires* the babies or eggs . . . ?" Or have I been using the wrong pronoun for him all along?

I am Unevolved, he answers, seeming just as confused as I am. I consider giving up now despite my curiosity as I feel my face flushing at the awkwardness of the topic. Though, that mostly seems to be on my side of things. River just looks confused. But I know that if I drop it now, it will continue to eat at me until I open the conversation up again, which I don't want to do.

"Which means what?" I ask, pressing onwards. "Are you . . . the one who sires the, uh, eggs or who carries them?"

Neither, he answers as if confused at my confusion. *I have not Evolved. If I succeed in Evolving and I become a Pathwalker, I will be able to carry eggs. If I become a Warrior, I will be able to sire them.*

Great. Right. Obviously. I'm totally stupid to have not thought that having a *third* gender would be the answer. Which then raises the most important question for now.

"So, when you speak of each other, when you are Unevolved, do you use 'he' or 'she' or something else?"

I . . . do not understand the question, he answers. *If I speak of . . . Stung-by-a-bug, I will say that he . . . is a good hunter.*

Right, they use "he," then. Or this is a problem with mind-to-mind communication and they simply have pronouns that just don't translate into English. But most of my curiosity has been assuaged at least, and we have more important things to discuss. Unless I hear any complaints, I'll keep using "he" for River.

"So, are Energy Hearts dangerous in any way?"

CHAPTER THIRTY-SEVEN

Compulsion

*N*ot to my knowledge, River replies evenly. *All the Evolved of my village use Energy Hearts to make progress, and it does not seem to have any ill effects on them.*

"Then what was all that in there? How can you say they don't pose a threat when you and Bastet both couldn't seem to tear yourselves away?" I ask pointedly. This is an absolutely key question since it will determine whether we attempt to travel through the tunnel again or give up and head for the trees once the sun's up.

I believe it is just the sheer number of them. It creates a temptation to sit there and absorb them that is almost irresistible. Now I know what will happen, I'm confident that I will be able to resist it. I look at him for a long moment. *What?* he asks defensively.

"What makes you so sure?"

An uncomfortable feeling comes across the Bond.

If you've never felt the attraction, you won't know what it's like. It's . . . a deep, intense yearning to grow, to become stronger . . . to Evolve. Seeming to run out of words, he instead shoves a sense memory at me. All of a sudden, I feel exactly what he was describing. And I understand why it was so difficult to tear himself away.

It feels like . . . all my problems would be solved if I could only get closer, if I could only absorb the power floating around me. Like my destiny is just waiting for me to reach out and grab it. The sensation is dulled thanks to it being a second-hand memory, but even so, I feel its strength.

It doesn't reassure me that going back into that cave is the best choice; it does the opposite, in fact. Sure, having those Energy Hearts sounds like a great bonus, but not if it means my Bound lose their minds because of the sheer quantity of them. Actually, since I was able to put the salamander Energy Heart in my Inventory, does that mean I could break these other stones off the walls and put them in there too? Because if so, I could harvest some, and then, if my Bound can't handle the compulsion, we could go through the forest anyway at dawn. I decide to test it.

"Wait here," I say absently to the group. River, Bastet, and Lathani all make a noise ranging from reluctant to curious. I just wave their objections away as I stand up and walk around the bend and back into the cave. Pausing at the threshold, I take a moment to consider my own emotions. Any feeling of attraction? Any sense of that desperate need to possess?

Not really. I can feel . . . something. A . . . density? Like the air is thicker in here. But none of that all-consuming need that gripped River earlier, and Bastet too, I guess. Stepping over to the closest Energy Heart cluster, I examine the things. They shine in the light, a fire lit within their depths.

Leaning forwards, not touching it yet, I tilt my head so one of my ears is facing it, wondering if there could be any sort of sound. I listen to it for a good half a minute, feeling increasingly stupid at listening to what appears to be a *rock*, but either it doesn't produce any noise, or my hearing isn't good enough to detect the sounds it's making. Glad that no one's watching—I don't even dare to think what I must look like—I turn my head and lean even closer to give it a sniff.

Despite only doing it for the sake of being thorough, I realize that there *is* something here. A faint . . . spiciness? Or sweetness? It smells good, whatever it is, and I'm almost tempted to take a bite. I resist the temptation, not wanting to break my teeth. Then again, Bastet and the cubs *did* crunch up the cores we found in that posse of attackers. Does that mean cores are edible? Or is this a raptorcat thing? River did say that his people don't eat the cores directly, but he also talked about adding bits of cores to potions to enhance their efficacy.

I dare to touch one, but I'm ready to pull back the moment I start to feel any sense of needing to possess them. The crystal is hard and cool to the touch, yet not completely cold. It also leaves some sort of residue as I pass the crystal to the other hand. *It's almost like the whole thing is covered in a thin layer of glittery oil,* I remark to myself as I hold my hand up to the light. This must be what I saw on River's paw and Bastet's coat.

A moment later, the sparkly substance disappears—it's been absorbed into my skin. My stomach drops for a moment, worried that it might have detrimental effects. I only just got over being poisoned by that creature in the forest!

Nothing seems to happen, though, and there's no sense of any new status notifications. My health bar stays full, as do the other two. After opening my status screen, I stare at my Energy absorption rate value: well over two *thousand* units per hour! A couple of seconds later, though, that rate drops down to a still whopping one hundred and eighty-five. Absolutely insane! When that rate doesn't change after a good thirty seconds or so, I have to conclude that it's just due to the Energy density here.

I briefly touch the Energy Heart while keeping an eye on my status screen and see it leap up once more, this time to two thousand, nine hundred, and seventy units per hour, as soon as the oily feeling on my fingers disappears. The effect only lasts about ten seconds, but that's just enough time for my Energy store to increase by a single percentage point.

My excitement grows. Forget risking my life to kill beasts; if I can just absorb a load of these, I'll leap up the levels in no time!

I gaze around the cave with greed—if *this* is what Nicholas meant by "treasure trove," then I find I have to agree with him. However, it's a treasure we have to take away with us since there's no way I'll be trying to absorb all of these things at once. Heck, even if Bastet and River both absorbed them as quickly as they could, it would take us days to put a proper dent in the hoard. We don't have the supplies to stay that long, and who knows what might stand in the way of us getting back? Besides, Lathani needs to return to her mother.

So, using the pommel of my knife, I try to crack the Energy Heart. I start softly and work up to heavier blows. Still, it's not a particularly strong impact that creates the first visual change. Instead of the whole thing fracturing, as one might think should happen with a crystalline structure, a small splinter of a shard splits off. It's more like my flint knapping than anything else.

I hold the shard to inspect it. For a moment, I can see how the edges gleam, looking as sharp as a knife. Then the whole piece softens and *melts* like it's made of ice, the solid suddenly becoming liquid, and flows to pool in the palm of my hand. There, like the residue that coated my skin earlier, it is absorbed.

I freeze as I wait for my health to start ticking downwards or something. After a few seconds, I relax a little: so far, I haven't seen any negative effects. I reopen my status screen and see that it's jumped up to the same two thousand, nine hundred, and seventy units per hour.

The difference is that this time it lasts long enough for me to accumulate three more percent of Energy towards my next level. So, the rate of Energy absorption is the same, but the length of time varies according to how much of the Energy Heart I absorb at once . . . Good to know. *Very* good to know.

Next, I try to break the whole lump off the wall. It takes a few attempts before I succeed; most of the methods I use at first instead just break off other shards. Interestingly enough, the shards that fall on another Energy Heart end up being absorbed into the lump they land on. The ones that fall on the cave floor, however, remain intact as shards. I make a note of my observations and push them away to think about later.

In the end, I succeed in prizing the Energy Heart off the wall by chipping away at its base with my knife and then using a rock held in my fist to bash it off. Acting against all expectations, the Energy Heart that falls on the floor doesn't then burst into a load of different shards; it just sits there as the rough edges visibly soften and round. Within a short space of time, it strongly resembles the salamander Energy Heart, although significantly brighter, clearer, and "rougher."

Interesting . . . It's almost like the Energy Heart is molten glass, except it's not hot and is always attempting to arrange itself around the central point.

As I pick up the Heart, I'm intrigued to see that it doesn't melt into my hand like the shard did. There's still that oily residue, but the Heart maintains its integrity even after a minute or so.

My next test is the most important: I put it in my Inventory. A moment later, I take it out. I don't bother to wait any longer than that, since, from my experience with hot soup and burning torches, it doesn't seem to matter how long the item is in there: any change will happen immediately, and if there is no effect when it's put in, there will still be no effect a day or more later.

The Heart appears unchanged. That's useful. I was worried that it would be considered an "unstable" Energy source like the flesh of creatures I kill. Instead, it seems it might be more like the Skill and knowledge stones I used right at the beginning of my journey here. Excellent! Then the question is more about how many stones I can collect before I get too dehydrated, rather than how I'm going to carry them out of here.

It would *be useful if River could help me, though,* I muse to myself. A task shared is a task halved. Or perhaps it would be better to say that two pairs of hands double the number of Energy Hearts we can reasonably harvest. I'm still wary about the whole compulsion aspect, but it appears that River might be right about the Energy Hearts not having detrimental effects. In the end, I head back out of the cavern to where the rest of my party is waiting.

Bastet and River both look up at me hopefully as I approach. It seems that regardless of their species, the desire to grow, to Evolve is the same. I won't try to pretend that I haven't been gripped by the same urge, either, though the Energy Hearts don't seem to have the same compulsive effect on me as they do on my companions.

"All right," I say, holding up one hand as they eagerly get to their feet. "Hold on a moment." They do, though both are emitting a sense of impatience. I do the mental equivalent of crossing my arms and staring sternly at them until they subside a bit. River settles back on his feet from where he was practically on tiptoe—well, tip-*claw*—while Bastet huffs and sits down again, then looks away and casually cuffs one of the cubs, who is trying to chew her tail. It's Ninja, I think, but the darkness makes it hard to tell.

"I haven't noticed any negative effects from the Energy Hearts on myself," I admit to them. "And I accept that having access to a supply of them could be very beneficial—I'm willing to take River's word for it that they're not hazardous in the long term. And we would definitely be able to take more Energy Hearts with us if all of us work at harvesting them. However"—I give them a stern look as Bastet gets to her feet again and River even takes a couple of steps forwards—"I need to be confident that you two can keep your heads. So, if either of you start feeling like the urges are getting too much, I want you to leave the cavern and cool down. If I have to order *either* of you, then we'll have to leave prematurely via the forest. Deal?"

I get a hurried sense of agreement from both of them, and then they're past me, almost racing each other to make it back into the cavern. I'm left exchanging glances with Lathani, feeling a little bemused. Then, shrugging, I accompany the other four members of our current party back into the cavern to see Bastet and River already hard at work harvesting the Energy Hearts. All I can hope is that I don't have to carry out the threat of leaving the cavern behind before I've filled at least the three slots I have free.

CHAPTER THIRTY-EIGHT

Anything and Everything

To begin with, I keep an eagle eye on my Bound, both physically and though the Bonds, as they harvest the Energy Hearts. After a while, I start to relax—I can feel the strong desire both of them have for the Hearts, but they seem to be channeling that feeling into harvesting as many as they can. River is using his wooden knife, which is far more effective than I would have thought.

Bastet, conversely, is just using her claws. Again, not something I would have expected to have much effect on what appears to be gemstone, but whatever Energy Hearts are made of, they don't react like precious stones. Bastet is slower than River, but she's doing well enough. Out of all of us, I'm the slowest since I'm more than half watching the other two.

As for the others, Lathani seems to be trying to copy Bastet; she clearly understands that these things are useful in some way. I see her taking a couple of surreptitious licks. She seems a little undecided seeing as she doesn't suddenly start licking at one of them with eagerness, but neither does she appear to *dislike* them, since she keeps coming back for more at various intervals.

As for the other cubs, Trouble and Ninja are playing with one of the harvested Energy Hearts, batting it away and then running to pounce on it. They seem to have turned it into a bit of a competition—whoever gets to the Heart first wins, I guess. As for Storm, she started by intently watching Bastet and is now trying to copy her guardian. Not with a huge amount of success, I will admit, but at least she's trying.

Not wanting to compete with either of my companions, and wanting to have a good view of both of them, I move further into the cavern and harvest a section that's sticking out a little. It's truly *thick* with Energy Hearts, so it should occupy me for a good while. I almost whistle while I work, thinking about a certain iconic song. Well, if this is the sort of thing dwarves go for, no wonder they're happy to be off to work!

Is this why the salamander was identified as a guardian? Was it watching over this treasure trove? Perhaps it even evolved here; I can't believe that the fire-breathing amphibian could possibly have been born like that. Then again, fantasy often insists that dragons are a real thing. In a world of magic, how can I say for certain that they aren't? How cool would it be if River could become a dragon-man instead of a lizard-man?

It's probably a remote possibility, if possible at all. If we can get Bastet to be able to fly, that would be awesome enough. That leads me to the question of whether *I* could Evolve. I mean, I didn't have the reaction to Energy Hearts that they did, so does that mean I can't? Or is it that I need something else to do so? A question for a later time.

With my mind musing over such ideas and focusing on harvesting the Hearts, I don't realize there's something else present in the area. When I do see it, I forget about everything else.

Tucked around a corner so that I only spot it when I've shifted a bit to reach some more Energy Hearts, I see a shining pool of liquid. It can't be water—it glimmers and glistens far too brightly to be water. It looks like liquid diamond, the substance reflecting the light of our torches and refracting it to dance around the little alcove. Or perhaps, like the Energy Hearts, it *emits* light . . .

"What is that?" I breathe as I step towards the shimmering and dancing liquid. It draws me in, a whisper to my senses that promises anything and everything. When I stare into the rainbow refraction within its ripples, I almost believe that I can see my mom there. My dad. Lucy. Long-cherished memories of the past dance barely noticeably in the substance. I shuffle forwards, entranced.

I feel like I need only to reach out and touch the liquid and all my dreams will come true. I yearn for it; my body *thirsts* for this like nothing else. The dryness of my mouth is forgotten as it's surpassed a hundredfold by the deprivation I feel from only seeing this substance and not touching it. I take a faltering step forwards, then another.

A faint flicker of discordant trepidation sparks through me like electricity through my nerves. This situation feels far too familiar.

But of *course* it is familiar. Familiar by its absence. This, *this* is what I have been missing in my life. My eyes are fixated on the visions I only see flickers of. I want to see more. I *must* see more. I want to make the flickering images into reality, and I know that I *can* . . . if only I touch the mesmerizing substance.

A sudden sense of warning awakens within me. *Wasn't there a problem about . . . something . . .* I lose track of my thoughts and push away the caution. What is there to be wary of in having every single one of my dreams brought to life? In being able to do *anything*? Instead of being banished, the sense of warning turns into fear, like there's something inside me that's trying to pull me back even as the rest of me keeps my feet shuffling forwards.

Barely heard, barely registered, I hear a muffled voice in my mind.

Mas—Markus, what are you doing? Markus? Master! Stop!

Who is speaking? Why do they feel fear?

In response, a new wave of anxiety rolls over me, but the serenity of the joy, love, and acceptance emanating from the liquid drowns out the voices that speak of fear and caution. Somehow—I don't know how—I've crossed the cavern from near the entrance to the lapping edge of the pool. I'm close enough that I could just reach out and touch its surface.

The sense of warning, of something being wrong intensifies within me and I hesitate at the last moment. Why do I feel this way? It is so peaceful and desirable; why does part of me not wish to touch it? Everything is foggy and dreamlike.

I feel like I am waking with the traces of a dream still holding onto me even as I become aware that reality is different from my dream. I fight to question where I am and what I am doing. And why, with a feeling of dawning horror, my hand is reaching for an unknown substance.

Time elongates—I feel like I'm moving in slow motion. The sense of danger explodes in me; the feeling grows exponentially as my fingers descend towards the inviting liquid diamond. Yet it feels like I can't stop myself. Even as part of me screams to stop, the other part of me yearns for union. And that other part of me is stronger than my conscious mind.

Time stops as the tips of three of my fingers dip into the surface, covered up to the first knuckle in the dancing, shimmering liquid. The feeling is . . . indescribable. In one moment, it feels like air moving against my fingertips; in another, like a thick gel that resists my touch.

For one perfect moment, the world is bliss, like I'm connected to all that is, all that was, and all that will ever be. I feel infinite. I'm at peace because why struggle when I am everything? Why strive when I can will things to be made and unmade with a flex of thought?

Then the heavens crack and it's like hell has opened up and engulfed me.

An unfathomable *something* burrows underneath my skin—no, deeper even than that. Into my *soul*. I've never been so certain that I have one until this moment, when I can feel it being *shredded*. Or melted. Or dissolved.

The sensation starts at my fingertips, but it quickly moves up my fingers, into my hand. I realize that when I thought I was in hell before, I didn't know what hell was. My hand feels like I dipped it into the molten rock I was so worried about earlier and then decided to throw on some salt just to make sure. No, not salt, pure sodium. No, *potassium*.

I barely feel it as I'm tackled, and I hit the ground hard, crushed beneath a heavy body. My eyes are open, but I'm unseeing. My mouth is hanging wide in a scream that I cannot hear. All I can focus on is the sheer, impossible-to-describe agony that is my hand; the rest of the world might as well not exist.

Moments stretch like honey, cloying and sickly sweet. The agony in my hand doesn't improve; if anything, it gets worse. It feels like there was something in my hand before that isn't there anymore because it got consumed. Moment by moment, it feels like the molten heat is expanding just a little more, devouring my soul, my body, my entire *being* a fraction of an inch at a time. Should I cut my hand off?

If it will save my life, I'll do it, but I hesitate. Cutting my hand off is truly a last resort since, without both my hands, daily life will become infinitely harder. Better than no life, but not by much. I'm not at all sure that I'll be able to rebuild my hand. I might have been able to fix my eye, but that was more about repairing the damages to it, not rebuilding it entirely. I don't know enough about the anatomy of a hand to even begin to direct the healing! And without me directing it, what if it just cauterizes my wrist or something?

But I have to do *something*. Every moment I spend agonizing deliriously over what to do, I sense that I lose something more of myself. The all-encompassing pain makes it extremely hard to come up with possible ideas, but I have to fight through it. I *have* to. The other option is not acceptable.

Desperately, I try to use my Lay-on-Hands to fix the problem, but the results are not at all what I expected.

Strangely, despite all the molten fire rolling around in my hand, there doesn't seem to be any actual damage. Not physical damage, anyway. However, that's not to say that my magic doesn't do anything.

As soon as it makes contact with the mass of *something* in my hand, there's an immediate reaction. I didn't send much mana to the area, wanting to test the waters first, so I can't tell exactly what happened. However, the fact that it *did* react tells me something by itself: the mass has to be linked to magic or Energy. Why else would it be affected so directly? I latch onto the idea as my mind races to try to work out how to turn it into a solution.

Wondering whether I can just push the whatever-it-is out of me directly, I cast Lay-on-Hands again, this time using a channeled version. Painstakingly, I feed the healing magic down my arm and for the first time become aware of it emerging from some sort of warm glow somewhere inside my chest. Instead of flooding the area with healing, I try to do something similar to when I pushed the poison out of me.

It doesn't work—the molten mass of stuff in my hand refuses to budge. Worse, it actually seems to *grab* my strand of mana and *pull*. It feels like a hungry monster slurping at a string of spaghetti. The glow in my chest dims significantly as it sucks away at me, half of my mana bar vanishing in an instant. As more and more of my glow is pulled away with inexorable force, I feel myself become weaker and weaker.

When my mana runs out, I watch in horror as my health starts to drain along with my stamina, disappearing, fraction by fraction.

CHAPTER THIRTY-NINE

A Bad Idea

**o.**

No!

Something within me revolts against what's happening, at how inevitable it appears. It's not the first time I've raged against fate, not anywhere close. But it is the first time that I *might* be able to do something about it. I've survived so much, grown so far beyond the people I knew on Earth. I'm not going to let some life-vampire liquid ruin everything now.

But what can I even do? Lay-on-Hands didn't work. If anything, it just made it worse! I've been close to death before, even in the last few hours, but at least then I knew what to do: I needed more mana to heal myself. Now . . . the healing itself has turned against me.

I'm panicking, I know that. I *knew* I shouldn't touch the liquid. I *knew* it was a bad idea. Yet despite my increases in Wisdom and Willpower, I couldn't stop myself. What good are stats if they don't come through when I need them?

Calm down, Markus, I tell myself, trying to grip the reins of my own thoughts. *Calm down or you're going to die!*

Oddly enough, it doesn't help.

And what happens when this thing has consumed all of me? I've recently discovered that I can drain the mana and health from my Bound—will this spread to them too?

A new fear goes through me. I hadn't considered that. To think that Bastet or River could pay the price for my idiocy . . .

That centers my thoughts. The fear that I could be the cause of another of my loved ones' deaths overrides even the fear of this killing me.

There must be a way to deal with this! I tell myself desperately. *This* can't *be the end. Not like this.*

I focus once more on the mess within my hand hungrily devouring all my resources. My mana is emptier than I've ever felt it before, my stamina almost out, and my health getting that way too. The connection formed by my Lay-on-Hands is a tube in my veins, its suction undeniable.

But is it? I formed the connection; can I not affect it to my advantage? If my mana, health, and stamina can be drawn out of me, can I not draw it back? If I had more time, I'd probably curse at myself for not thinking of it sooner.

Focusing on the connection, I try to use the same type of metaphysical hands that I used to draw mana and health out of River. Though it still feels like trying to take spaghetti out of a pot with a complex contraption at a far remove, I manage—desperation has lent me competence. Once formed purely of mana, now it's a strangely slippery cord woven of health and stamina. After finally managing to engage the Willpower that I've increased through gift, level-up, and sheer bloody-mindedness, I grip onto that cord and refuse to let go.

The drain slows, and then it stops. Mentally doing the equivalent of setting my teeth and feet and leaning back, I put all the force I can muster into tugging on that cord. I don't know where the force comes from. At this moment, I don't care. All I know is that, somehow, I can hold the cord; somehow, I can exert pressure on it. Somehow, I might be able to save myself, and with me, my Bound.

For a moment, it feels like the world is holding its breath. Nothing moves, nothing changes.

And then, so slowly—glacially enough that, at first, I think I'm imagining it— the flow reverses. In the beginning, it's just a sense that I get from the metaphorical hands holding the metaphysical cord. Then, I actually see results as my health and stamina bars tick back up bit by infinitesimal bit.

The success emboldens me, and I pull with even more force, using reserves that I didn't realize I had, not even in my sheer desperation a moment ago. The flow quickens as my stamina and health return to full, and then my mana bar increases once more. It increases past half, then three-quarters, and then is full again.

But the flow doesn't stop there. I'm no longer tugging, but the cord is still present, providing a route from my hand to my core. Triumph turns into horror as I realize that all I've done is invite the molten substance to skip all the intervening space and go straight for what feels like the center of my everything.

I start panicking as the thick heat moves up the cord like concrete through a pipe. It's slow, but nothing I do seems to be able to stop it.

I try to push the cord away, to cut through it, to redirect it. The cord, despite being merely a metaphysical or metaphorical construct, might as well be made of steel and fixed in place by solid rock for all that I'm able to affect it. Perhaps I could do something if I used my mana, but after the last round, I'm not keen to try *that* again.

All I can do is helplessly watch as the impossibly hot substance crawls towards me. By this point, cutting my hand off is probably not an option. Heck, cutting my *arm* off is probably not an option either: the molten substance has already gone through my shoulder joint. The only good thing is that it doesn't feel like it's devouring me anymore. With a path for it to follow, it doesn't need to create one itself by destroying every bit of me in its way.

In fact, although the substance in my hand is as hot and agonizing as ever, the part of it traveling towards the core of my body is surprisingly innocuous. Of course, I don't expect that to remain true when it comes into contact with the glow of mana where the cord has its anchoring point.

Preparing myself tiredly to put up a fight once more as it tries to consume my health, stamina, and mana, I'm surprised when the substance doesn't actually do that at all. Instead, it almost eagerly trickles into my core. At first, it's a relief. I don't dare to relax, but I do dare to hope.

The molten substance is still hot, but somehow, it doesn't burn me—not here in the center of my being. After a short time, however, it does start feeling uncomfortable. A bit like I've consumed rather too much at an all-you-can-eat buffet restaurant.

Then the discomfort worsens, like even after eating too much, I continued shoveling it down, and for some reason I didn't become nauseous and vomit; instead, I just continued forcing my stomach to expand past what it should have been capable of. Only, it's not my stomach that's being affected, but something else entirely.

The overexpansion soon becomes an agony of its own, which almost overtakes that already raging in my hand. Worse, it feels like whatever is being forced to expand is at the limit of its capacity and might break at any moment.

There's been the nagging sense of a notification ever since I first started feeling "full." I didn't dare shift my attention enough to check it out. Now, though, I can only hope that it might possibly offer me a solution.

Honestly, I've racked my brain to think of a way of cutting off the flow and I'm losing hope of being able to affect either the substance in my hand or the part of me that feels like it's an overfilled water balloon on the cusp between being intact and popping. Feeling that I'm a drowning man clutching at straws, I quickly open the message, somehow going directly to the one that is most relevant despite the others I see waiting for me.

Congratulations!
You have gathered enough Energy to push your body to the next level. Would you like to level up?

Level up now / Close messages

Wait, what? I think, flabbergasted. *Is it . . . ? Could it be . . . ? Surely . . .* No. I can think about these things *after* I've prevented myself from decorating the walls à la Markus Wolfe. That's what it feels like I'm on the verge of doing, anyway. If leveling up will help, that's what I'm going to do. I can think about the whys later.

I assent to the level up and quickly assign my six stat points to Intelligence, Wisdom, and Willpower like I did before—perhaps even if leveling up doesn't help, they'll make the difference so I can figure a way out of the situation I'm in. When the usual messages about Breadth and Depth come up, I choose to put one point in each, continuing my usual strategy of spreading them out.

I feel bliss take over my body, but this time isn't nearly so all-encompassing considering the agony I am in still. In fact, I feel like it rewires my brain a bit to feel so much pleasure and so much pain all at once. When the wave of discomfort comes afterwards, it's oddly not nearly as powerful as usual. I would have thought that the sensations of pain would add to each other, but perhaps the soul-deep agony from whatever is happening to me is just too strong to allow bodily sensations much space.

Following my level-up, the feeling of having eaten far, far too much is significantly improved. I still feel "full" in a way, but it's not threatening to explode me all over the walls. Some of my suspicions strengthen, but I have no time to think through them or the implications of them: the molten substance is still coming up through the tube from my hand and I'm beginning to feel overfull again.

This time, as soon as the nagging notification feeling comes, I just think to level up immediately. Again, I dump my six points into my mental and soul stats because I think they did help me feel a little better. Once more, the bliss is less overwhelming, but so is the pain that follows.

The flow keeps coming, seemingly almost inexhaustible. I'm a little concerned, though: the substance, which I'm almost certain is somehow liquid Energy, has turned from concrete to milkshake in consistency and is coming quicker. Or maybe the cord has widened. I don't know. The center of my body becomes oversaturated once more shortly after I complete the level-up process. Of course, I accept the level-up again, once more choosing the path that seems to be working for me.

The Energy comes quicker and quicker as one level-up happens immediately upon the heels of the previous. I lose count, honestly. My whole world is a wash of pleasure and pain, both blending into each other so that pleasure becomes pain and pain becomes pleasure and both become neither.

I've lost my sense of normality; this is the new normal. I've become somewhat accustomed even to the soul-deep pain that at first felt like I was being dipped into lava. It doesn't vanish, but it . . . impacts me less. *Impairs* me less.

Slowly, both pleasure and pain hold less sway on my mind, and I become more able to think through even those moments when one of them is at its peak. All I am able to do is keep going, grimly forcing myself to level up again and again.

But it isn't sustainable. When I finish one level-up process only to immediately find myself once more on the cusp of another, feeling like I could explode at any moment, I acknowledge that I need to find a different strategy. There's only so quickly I can activate the level-up, mentally direct the System to place the points in the stats of my choosing, and choose which subsections of Wisdom should be increased.

I consider briefly *not* adding points to Wisdom and instead just put them in Willpower and Intelligence, but then dismiss the thought—if anything, I need as much Wisdom as I can get. No, there's a deeper problem here. Not only is this clearly not sustainable in terms of the speed of Energy flow, but I feel . . . fragile. Something inside me feels like it's shattering a little more every time I push myself to the limit, and the limit is coming faster and faster.

I can't stop the molten mass coming, and I can't push it out of my hand . . . but maybe I can change the destination. If whatever this is can be used to level up, surely it can also be used for something else: repaying my debt.

CHAPTER FORTY

Unanimous Agreement

My method worked. It's gone, finally. The Energy in my hand has vanished, all sucked up through the tube to the core of my being. That doesn't mean it's the end of the matter now, though. The substance might be gone, but I can tell it has left behind significant damage. I'm going to have to investigate that more closely, but for now, I start trying to force my eyes open—I need to find out what's happening around me first.

They're sticky, clogged with the salt from my tears of pain, but I can tell there are no sounds of combat around me—at least my screams haven't caused other creatures to come investigate. Once my eyes are open, a wave of relief goes through me: my companions are safe.

Despite the low light level in the cavern, which turns them into silhouettes, I can see their concern and even anxiety. Bastet is nearly standing over me, and River is on high alert as he guards us, sending glances over to me. When he sees I'm awake, he hurries over.

You're alive, he says, relief evident in his voice.

"You know what that was?" I ask. Well, I *try* to ask it—my screams have wrecked my vocal cords and they haven't yet recovered. I reflexively try to send a tendril of healing magic to them but don't even succeed in drawing it from that glowing center before an exceedingly sharp pain strikes through me like a lightning bolt.

I flinch and abandon the attempt. Fear goes through me at the thought that, in my stupidity, I might have somehow destroyed my capacity to heal by touching something I didn't know anything about. Fortunately for our communication, however, my companions aren't actually listening to my spoken words anyway.

I believe I do, he replies, then hesitates. *But among my people, it is nothing more than legend: the river that mortals enter to rejoin the ancestors directly.*

Lovely—I interpret that as instant death. And after my recent experience from just dipping the tips of three fingers into it, I can't deny that it's probably accurate.

It's Energy, right? Pure Energy, I say, sending the message to him mentally to give my voice a break. Considering everything I observed during the last frantic and desperate time, I'm fairly confident in my guess.

I believe so, he agrees. *Which, if the legends are correct, may explain both the strength of the guardian beast and the speedy growth of the Forest of Death.*

They're feeding off this? I ask, frowning a little. Did the liquid have such a bad effect on me because I'm from another world or just because my level is too low?

Not directly, I would imagine, he replies, *but the legends say that while stepping into the river is a direct path to joining the ancestors, being close to it offers unparalleled opportunities for growth. Though, that growth is not always in a desirable direction.* Well, that tallies with feeling on multiple occasions that I might explode. *How are you feeling?*

I use a few moments to take stock. If I thought I stank to high heaven when I leveled up last time, it's nothing to how I smell now after who knows how many level-ups. My body feels like it was stretched on the rack, then crushed under stones, and then finally twisted into a pretzel and baked—no, microwaved: it's worse inside than out.

Closing my eyes, I instinctively reach for Meditation, only this time I don't reach *outwards* but *inwards.* Something about my battle within myself has opened a whole new world to me, and I'm now aware of some glowing core at my center. As I observe with some sense that is somehow both completely new to me and completely familiar, I realize that my body has come off lightly compared to my insides.

The glow at my center is spluttering, flaring and dimming at odd moments, its shape fluctuating subtly in a way I sense that it shouldn't. It's also incredibly tender in a way that's indescribable. I feel like . . . a glass vase full of cracks, ready to disintegrate at any moment. Frankly, all that's keeping me together is hope and a prayer; I dare not even press too hard with my metaphysical presence in case it causes everything to finally shatter. Now I understand why trying to heal myself earlier hurt so much: it must have been like pressing my fingers into that shattered glass and struggling against the shards.

If my center, which I'm increasingly convinced must be the equivalent of an Energy Heart, is bad, then my hand is even worse. Although nothing looks damaged to my physical eyes, to my mental gaze, it's like a black hole.

I'm not an expert; I've only just discovered how to "look" at myself in this way, after all. Still, I hadn't even realized how much my whole body glows—and not just the center of it. If the glow of the Energy that was there was the molten heat of the sun, then the glow of my Energy Heart is that of the moon. Before looking at my hand, I thought the rest of my body was dark, but in fact, it's more like a dim twilight, evenly diffused across the whole of me.

My hand, in comparison, is a black hole: a darkness so deep that it seems to suck me in as I observe it. I swiftly pull myself back to my own physicality to break the pull, settling my consciousness into my body and its aches and pains. My mind is also tired; a mixture of lack of sleep and the strain I put it through in the last while is making concentration difficult.

I'm alive, I finally answer River, not even trying to keep my sense of exhaustion and pain from him.

You need to sleep, he tells me.

I know, I admit it. But we also need to get out of here.

We do, he agrees, *but there is no guarantee that our passage out will be without conflict. For now, we are undisturbed. Sleep.*

I struggle with myself. Part of me just wants to push myself to my feet and get out of this place where I've almost died twice. But a much larger part of me yearns for the rest he offers—I was exhausted before we entered this death trap of a room; now, I'm barely managing to keep my eyes open.

All right, I concede. *You guys keep harvesting as many of the Energy Hearts as you can. Unless you need to sleep too.*

We will rest for a bit, he reassures me. *But at least one of us will be on guard at all times. Sleep.*

I lie down but am determined not to sleep yet. I feel the mass of notifications waiting for me like they are a physical presence in my head. I open my messages, my heart sinking at the sheer number of them there.

And then I blink and the world blinks with me.

When I wake, it's dark. Darker than before, at least. The torch I lit earlier has gone out. I'm not completely blind: the Energy Hearts growing from the walls around give off light of their own, and the pool of liquid Energy still shimmers even without any other light source. I shudder as I look at it. Despite everything, I can still feel a draw, a temptation to touch it again. But it's not as overwhelming as before.

Still, refusing to repeat the same stupid error, I forcibly look away. I'm feeling better. A little, at least. My body is still aching, my Energy Heart is still sore, and I can sense that my hand is no less a black hole than it was before. My mind is less tired, though, and I realize how my decision-making skills have been seriously affected by my exhaustion after these fraught days. The last proper sleep I had was with Bastet and the cubs in the temporary forest shelter, after all.

Entering the trees was a decent decision to make with the information at hand, but we didn't have to *keep* going through them. We could have waited for the pursuing lizard folk to lose interest or set a trap for them if they stuck around.

Continuing through the forest meant that we then had little choice but to follow the trees' leading. I'm still glad that I had enough wherewithal to decide not to light a forest fire in the same forest we were trying to traverse, but facing the salamander was unfortunate.

Coming down into the tunnel wasn't by itself a bad idea, but the jury *is* still out on that one since I don't know if we'll be able to make it to the other side—or whether the other side will be outside the forest. The salamander's gland would have allowed me to create all the torches I needed, but choosing the option where it might come down to mutually assured destruction at any moment isn't the most sensible one. Especially since I don't know how many of those monsters might be lying in wait.

No, my biggest recent absolute *foolishness* was, of course, touching the unknown liquid. And that straight after I castigated my Bound for the same thing. A wave of embarrassment goes through me as I think of my unintentional hypocrisy. In fact, I did something even worse than them: I sensed that it was a bad idea to touch the liquid and I still couldn't stop myself.

Why couldn't I stop myself? I remember feeling the intense desire to touch it—and also the intense feeling of fear. It was like my subconscious took control of my limbs. It was . . . scary.

How do I stop it again? If it happens again. The glance I accidentally laid on the pool of shimmering liquid didn't evoke the same *need* to touch it that I felt before. Fortunately. Is it like that creature I killed in the forest? Was it trying to lure me in actively and now it isn't? Or once bitten, twice shy?

Or could it be all the leveling up I did? I don't remember how many times I did, but I remember that I increased my Willpower; could that be the reason why I can resist it now?

But none of that makes up for the fact that I made choices that have had serious consequences. Bastet almost died. I almost died. Twice. And I can sense I'm not healed. Now with more self-reflection I dread opening my notifications to find out just how badly I'm hurt.

When will I stop making stupid mistakes? I wonder morosely.

My emotional state must communicate itself to my companions completely unintentionally, because the large mass lying beside me shifts to sit upright. In the light of the Energy Hearts, I can't see any details, but I know who it is from his size and shape.

Do not chastise yourself too much: Energy calls to Energy, River tells me, accurately guessing the cause of my depression. *It's unsurprising that you felt a pull to it and that, not having any idea of what it was, you gave into the attraction. We did much the same when exposed to the Energy Hearts, if you remember.*

Yeah, but you were able to return here and harvest them without losing yourself once you became aware of it, I point out bitterly.

What called to you is many, many times more powerful than an Energy Heart. Many times more powerful even than such a number of Energy Hearts as we have here. It is unsurprising that the temptation was commensurately greater.

Then why didn't anyone else feel it? I question sourly.

We do not have Energy Hearts, he replies calmly. My brows knit together.

That makes a difference? I ask, curiosity managing to cut through my recriminatory thoughts.

A significant one, I believe. While you have been resting, I have been considering the matter carefully, and I think I have divined the reason for why you were drawn while we felt nothing but curiosity—a reverse of the situation earlier, when you desired our attention but we were too enraptured by the Energy Hearts to give it. For us, Energy is transitory, flowing in and flowing out, leaving small specks behind with every wave, and we hope that one day enough specks will accumulate to cross the threshold of Evolution and form an Energy Heart of our own. The same is not true of you, evidently. Here River hesitates. *Markus . . . do you already have an Energy Heart?*

I consider the question carefully.

"I . . . Maybe?" I answer. That glowing thing I saw inside me earlier . . . could that be an Energy Heart? It certainly looked like one.

Because if you did, it would make sense why you would not be so drawn to Energy Hearts but enraptured by the life-blood. Your being knows that you do not need to form an Energy Heart, so instead, you are attracted to what can fill it. The greater the concentration of Energy, the greater the attraction. And no other substance has a greater concentration of Energy than the life-blood of the realm.

I see, I respond, intrigued despite the situation. Touching the liquid Energy was only the last in a series of bad decisions, but it would be nice if it wasn't just because of poor judgement. Perhaps it was just lack of willpower.

I sigh. Just sitting here and moping isn't going to help anything. I look around the cavern with more purpose and spot Bastet continuing to harvest Energy Hearts. River is obviously resting for a bit, but I can see the evidence that they've been hard at work: there's a large pile of Energy Hearts in the middle of the cavern and some of the walls are starting to look a little bare.

Trying to harvest as many of them as possible is definitely high on the priority list. Everything River has told me about them indicates that they should be a great boon to my Bound and their attempts to Evolve. That can only be a good thing, surely.

After that, I still think that exploring the tunnel is a better idea than going back into the forest. There have been no indications of any other creatures here. Nothing appeared when I was screaming my head off, indicating that either there isn't any-thing here at all, or they're the kind to hide from potential threats rather than to attack them. And the tunnel itself is not dangerous to us in the same way the trees are. Assuming I can bear to walk next to the liquid without touching it, that is. I remember from Bastet's memories that part of the journey requires walking along what looks like a stream—and not one of water.

Grab me if I move even a fraction towards the life-blood, okay? I ask River and get his agreement before turning to look at the liquid.

Gazing at it, I can see the same sort of images playing within the shimmering rip-ples as I had before and can feel the attraction trying to grab me. This time, though, I'm more able to resist it. I still really, really want to touch the liquid, but my body obeys my mind and does not move. *It should be okay to walk next to that,* I decide.

"All right, everyone," I croak; my voice has just about healed enough for me to talk, but not without sounding like I'm a chain-smoker. It hurts to talk, though, so I resolve to do as little as possible until it's more healed. "Good job harvesting these things while I've been . . . unavailable. Let's get as many as we can and then keep going through the tunnel. Make sure you rest a bit too, though. We don't know what could be waiting for us at the end of it."

Are you well, Carer? Lathani asks with concern.

"No," I admit. "And I need to see what I can do about that."

Thanks for guarding me, I say mentally to Bastet and River. *I'll come and help you as soon as I can.* Bastet sends me a sense of concerned agreement.

Do you wish for any help, Mast—Markus? River asks in concern. *I do not know what I could make from the materials I have at hand, but perhaps if you tell me what ails you, I could help.*

It's fine, I say—I don't want to tell him that *I* have no idea what's wrong either. *But thanks for the offer. I'll let you know,* I say after a moment, feeling bad at my previous brusque response. He doesn't respond verbally but lifts his chin for a moment, then pushes himself to his feet and goes to work on harvesting more Energy Hearts.

As I turn my attention to the most important thing for me to do, I feel a mixture of excitement and reluctance warring for dominance. Instead of once more opening my messages and seeing the mass of notifications waiting for me, I open my status panel. My eyes widen.

CHAPTER FORTY-ONE

Consequences

Name: Markus Wolfe		Race: Human	Class: Tamer
Level: 12	Energy to next level: 7%	Energy absorption rate: 326u/hr	Energy towards debt: 75%
Intelligence	36	Mana: 334/334 (-7%)	
Wisdom	36	Mana regeneration rate: 720u/hr (-20%)	
Willpower	42+8 (+20%)	Health regeneration rate: 40u/hr (-20%)	
Constitution	19	Health: 95/190	
Strength	15	Stamina: 90/90	
Dexterity	15	Stamina regeneration rate: 150u/hr	
Class Skills: Dominate – Novice 1 Tame – Beginner 5 Fade – Initiate 1		Non-Class Skills: *Lay-on-Hands – Journeyman 1* Stealth – Novice 1 Animal Empathy – Novice 5 Meditation – Novice 3 Energy Manipulation – Beginner 2 Sensation Management – Beginner 5	

The first thing that hits me is the level I've gotten to. Level *twelve*. I was sitting at level *four* when I entered the tunnel. In one move, I've multiplied my level by three times. The sheer amount of Energy that I absorbed in such a short time must have been utterly immense.

No wonder I feel like I've been tortured. Having a few thousand volts of electricity pass through me wouldn't have felt good either.

The second surprise is just how much progress I've made on my debt. From single digits to three-quarters completed, it's a *lot* of change. And that was only a third or so of what remained after I increased my level eight times, maybe even less than that—it was hard for me to get a clear estimate considering the situation. Frankly, I'm glad it worked at all!

Between my significant progress in leveling up and my progress on my debt, it almost makes all the pain and sheer terror I went through worth it. What am

I saying? It *was* worth it, but an instinct inside me warns me that it would be an *immensely* stupid idea to try again. Not for now, at least.

The third surprising thing is the amount of Energy I'm absorbing per hour and how few percentage points I've moved towards my next level despite that. I don't know exactly how long I've been sleeping, but I'm sure it's more than a couple of hours. Even if it was only four hours, that would mean it now costs around two hundred Energy units per point! If I slept for longer, it would only increase the Energy cost. I have a feeling I'll be languishing at level twelve for a good long while. That might not necessarily be a bad thing, though—some instinct tells me that leveling up right now is a *bad* idea. And it might give my physical stats the chance to catch up a bit. They're now lamentably far behind my mental and soul ones.

In fact, two of my physical stats are less than half my lowest mental stat, something that the scholars from Nicholas's world suggested was a bad thing. Maybe that's why, despite my thought process feeling faster and smoother, it's not as much of a qualitative increase as the number of points I just ploughed into my mental stats would suggest. Or maybe it just takes some time for my mind to adjust to the change.

That said, I can't exactly complain, particularly given the fact that I've just skipped *eight* levels *and* paid off a good portion of my debt. Not to mention that I survived touching something River said most of his legends consider to be lethal.

Looking at my stats next, I nod as I go through them, though I find myself mystified at a couple of the increases. The additions to Strength (Endurance) and Dexterity are quite likely to be from the climb down here, so that's logical enough— I've been a bit distracted with everything else to notice if I had notifications waiting for me. I probably need to make more of a habit of checking my notifications automatically. I've missed too many recently.

The additional three points each to Willpower and Constitution are a different question. With what little concentration I had to spare at the time, I remember choosing to double down on the point choice I made in my last level-up. In short, that meant a whopping sixteen points each to Wisdom, Intelligence, and Willpower. I didn't touch Constitution at all, so why that's increased by three points, I have no idea. Nor do I know why Willpower has increased by nineteen points instead of sixteen. Hopefully, some answers will be in my notifications.

Looking at my pools and regeneration rates, however, I can already see some of the negative consequences of what I've done to myself.

My mana pool has a reduction of seven percent, which translates to about twenty-six points of mana. It doesn't sound too significant compared to the one hundred and sixty points of mana I've gained from leveling up, but that is two Lay-on-Hands that I won't be able to cast—if I'm still able to cast it, that is. Given the painful backlash from trying to heal my vocal cords, I can only hope that I haven't permanently messed up my ability to do magic. That would be . . . *frustrating*. In classic British understatement style.

My mana regeneration rate and health regeneration rate are a different story. For some reason, they have a full twenty percent reduction, taking a significant chunk off both rates. By this point, I should be earning fifteen mana units per minute, meaning one every four seconds or so. Instead, I'm roughly earning one unit per five seconds. It may not sound like a big difference, but when it's the life of one of my companions—or me—on the line, those extra seconds add up. Though, if put in the context of my previous mana regeneration rate of four hundred and fifty units per hour, half of what I would have access to now if I hadn't touched the Pure Energy, the net result is one of significant gain.

Fortunately, my assessment that my body is fairly undamaged is borne out by the lack of reduction to any of those stats. Though, I must have taken some sort of damage since I'm actually at half health. Not verging on dangerous territory at all—that seems to be when I'm below thirty units—but it's worrisome all the same. The reduction to my health regeneration is a bit of a blow and reveals that, indeed, the damage went far deeper than I would have ever believed possible before coming to this world. However, I have a better health regeneration rate now than I did before this whole experience so . . . take the win where I can? Scanning down the screen, I see my next surprise: two new Skills. *Sensation Management and Energy Manipulation*, I say to myself thoughtfully.

Then as I flick my eyes over my status again, I notice that my health is now sitting at ninety-four. Perhaps one of the benefits of my increased mental stats is improved recall, because I know immediately that I've somehow lost a point in health just in the time since I last looked. Checking my notifications has turned into an absolute priority. Deciding to look for whatever answers I can in my messages, I mentally trigger the message box to open. The long list of unread messages stretches beyond what I can see.

Prompted by the urgency of my dropping health, I decide to try something out that I theorize might work. Closing my eyes, I focus on my need to know whatever is affecting my health units. As I open them again, I'm greeted by a much-truncated message box. Instead of the many unread messages in front of me, I see only three. Well. Time to test whether it truly worked. I mentally select the oldest message.

Warning!
You have entered an area of high Energy density. Your level is too low to safely absorb this Energy. Time until Energy poisoning begins: 0:10:00

Next message/ Close messages

Energy poisoning? Well, that's concerning. I quickly move onto the next message.

Warning!
You are in an area of high Energy density. Your level is too low to safely absorb

> this Energy. Time until Energy poisoning begins: 00:00:00
> You are being poisoned. Your health will drop by one unit every 36 seconds until you leave the area, increase your capacity to absorb Energy safely, or expire.

> Next message/ Close messages

Well. Great. I guess that answers my question. *In an area of high Energy density . . .* I close the message and quickly push myself to my feet, eyeing the pool of Energy beside me like it's a cobra about to bite. I stride quickly to the exit of the cavern, watching my health bar in the corner of my vision carefully.

Markus? River calls from where he's harvesting Energy Hearts.

I'm being poisoned by the Energy here, I tell him tersely through our Bond since my vocal chords are still hurting too much to speak out loud. I stop at the point where the tunnel becomes the cavern and watch my health bar carefully. It drops very slightly, so I back up a little bit more until I can see the night sky above my head. Thirty seconds pass by . . . then a minute . . . then another thirty seconds. My health bar ticks up by a point. I breathe out a sigh of relief, which turns into concern a moment later as another thought comes to mind. *Bastet, River, neither of you are losing health, are you? What about the cubs? Lathani . . .* Then I remember that she can't hear me when I speak mentally. *Bastet, can you check if Lathani is okay?* Hopefully, the raptorcat manages to get the message across.

I am not losing health, River answers sounding puzzled. Equally confused, Bastet responds with a sense that she's also fine and that the cubs are as well, as far as she can tell.

I feel a little . . . odd, Lathani answers—apparently, Bastet was successful. *But it does not feel like I am injured.*

Bastet, can you suggest that she comes here with me just in case, then? I ask, frustrated with my inability to connect directly. A moment later the nunda cub joins me where I'm perched on a rock sticking out of the tunnel floor. I automatically put my hand on her and trigger Lay-on-Hands, then almost scream in pain at the feeling of fire that goes through me.

If I thought the pain was just the ache of an overused muscle, I might have continued anyway; instead it feels like I'm digging my fingers into said muscle and *yanking*. Except not in any way a physical pain. So, in short, I fear making things worse.

Damn. I frown as I shake out my hand, my jaw clenching hard. It's the worst time for my healing to go on the fritz: in the middle of an unfamiliar tunnel, where I'm getting slowly poisoned by something in the environment.

Then my frown deepens as I consider the messages I read, my mind rushing through some mental math. I pull it up again just to check it out.

It doesn't make complete sense. If I'm losing one unit per thirty-six seconds, I could only have been sleeping for a bit under two hours. I'm pretty sure I slept for longer than that—I feel more rested that I would be after around two hours of sleep. So how am I not dead yet? With my current health points, I would have less than two hours of that kind of drain before I'd be out. My health regeneration would have given me a bit more time, but not much more. Yet I still have ninety-three units left in the tank?

Logically, something must have changed between that message and now, though I'm obviously still being poisoned.

Hoping the next message might hold some answers, I move on to read it.

Congratulations!
You have increased your Wisdom, Intelligence, and Willpower over the first threshold (30). Your body is more able to cope with high Energy density.
Your level remains too low to safely absorb this Energy. You are still being poisoned. Your health will drop by one unit every 66 seconds until you leave the area, increase your capacity to absorb Energy safely, or expire.

Next message / Close messages

That explains it, then. I underwent a period of more intense poisoning, and then I increased my level and added points to my stats, which reduced the impact of the Energy poisoning. If my math is correct, that means I must have slept for around five hours, depending on how long the whole life-blood mess took.

That's a relief. Now that I'm out of the poisoning zone entirely—and I resolve to keep checking my health bar to make sure that is the case, as I don't have any sort of icon telling me when I'm poisoned—my health should be able to naturally increase a little even without my healing magic.

It also means, if my calculations are correct, that the tunnel may still be a possible route out of here: even if we leave right now, I'll still have almost two hours to play with, even without taking my regeneration into account. And since I've still got lots of notifications to go through, and my Bound are still harvesting Energy Hearts, I have the time to regenerate more health before we attempt to go through.

In fact, I might even suggest we wait until my health regenerates completely. It will take less than three hours to do so and will allow us all to rest and prepare for whatever might come next.

I communicate that message to everyone, and no one objects to taking a little bit more time. River and Bastet are particularly eager to spend more time in this place. I pull out some of the salamander meat from my Inventory for the cubs and Lathani to munch, swallowing dryly as I see them enjoy it.

Then, with three snoozing cubs pressing against my feet, I reopen my notifications from the beginning again.

Congratulations!

> You have worked hard on your Strength (Endurance) and have earned a point.
> This has been applied to your status.

> Next message / Close messages

> Congratulations!
> You have worked hard on your Dexterity (Agility) and have earned a point. This
> has been applied to your status.

> Next message / Close messages

Well, that confirms my thoughts about where the extra points to Strength and Dexterity came from: a direct result of the difficult climb down, I guess. Though, I'm a little surprised that I got offered them outright after such little relative effort. Maybe that's another effect of the high Energy density around here? Even sitting where I am I still have an absorption rate of two hundred and seventy-one units per hour.

> Warning!
> You have touched a source of Pure Energy. You are not high enough level to be
> able to directly absorb Pure Energy. Pure Energy is doing damage to your internal
> matrix. -1% to your mana regeneration rate.

> Next message / Close messages

Pure Energy, huh? Life-blood must be River's people's name for it. I suppose it's not exactly the first time they've used a grandiose name for something. Does that mean Energy Hearts aren't what the System would call them either? As for the actual content of the message . . . that doesn't sound good. But I suppose I have an indication of the reason for the reduction I saw on my stats page.

> Warning!
> You have touched a source of Pure Energy. Your soul is not strong enough to
> resist the effects of Pure Energy. Pure Energy is doing damage to your soul. -1%
> to your health regeneration rate.

> Next message / Close messages

Which explains my other twenty percent reduction.

> Warning!
> You continue to hold Pure Energy in your body. You are not high enough level
> to be able to safely contain Pure Energy. Pure Energy is doing damage to your
> internal matrix. -2% to your mana regeneration rate.

Next message? Y / N

Warning!
You continue to hold Pure Energy in your body. You are not high enough level to be able to safely resist Pure Energy. Pure Energy is doing damage to your soul. -2% to your health regeneration rate.

Next message? Y / N

The next few messages are a repeat of the two previous with the percentage increasing by one each time. The pattern is evident, and the twenty percent reductions are explained. I flick through the messages, just skimming them to make sure that there's no new information.

So, whatever I did damaged my "internal matrix" at the same time as it damaged my soul. What is this internal matrix, and how can I fix it? And is it even possible to fix my soul? Something to think about later when I'm safe.

Congratulations!
You have tried to manipulate Pure Energy with mana. You have created a connection with Pure Energy.

Next message / Close messages

I'm not sure what there is to congratulate about that, I mentally tell the box bitterly. I can only think that this came as I first connected with the Pure Energy. Considering that it then tried to kill me or eat me or whatever, I wouldn't exactly consider it a *good* thing.

Warning!
Pure Energy is draining you of mana, health, and stamina. If all of these values reach 0, you will die.

Next message / Close messages

Yeah, I got that. Such *helpful* messages. Much like the time with the wolvezard, if I had spent my time checking my messages rather than reacting to the situation, I would *definitely* be dead. Though, does the message mean that even if I only had stamina remaining, I would still stay alive? *Hmm. Probably not something to experiment with . . .*

Congratulations!
You have earned a Skill: Energy Manipulation

Next message / Read Skill description / Close messages

Energy Manipulation
For being able to forge a connection with Pure Energy, survive the initial contact, and even exert some control over it while being too low level to reasonably expect such an outcome, you have earned a new Skill. Manipulating Pure Energy will be slightly easier for you, and your capability will improve with every rank. Manipulating new subforms of Energy will be significantly easier. Manipulating Energy in your body will be significantly easier. Manipulating subforms of Energy you could already control will be significantly easier.

Next message / Close messages

That description is a little different from any other I've come across before. It doesn't seem to indicate which stats it's attached to, for one. And its estimate of how much it will help me is . . . vague. I guess I'll have to find out just how it affects my use of magic later—at least, I'm assuming that magic is some form of Energy. I might be wrong, of course.

The fact, though, that I earned a Skill for resisting the Energy's attempts to drink me dry and then creating a connection with it simply highlights how lucky it is that I survived.

Warning!
Your Core is overfull and is under strain. Please level up before your Core's structural integrity is irreparably compromised.

Next message / Close messages

It seems I was right. Energy Heart *is* River's people's poetic term. I don't have an Energy Heart. I have a *Core*. Though, I suppose it's possible that Energy Hearts and Cores are actually different. Maybe Energy Hearts are what beasts earn and Cores are what come with the Class stone? Either way, it appears that my Core may fulfil the same function as an Energy Heart: storing Energy. Or mana. I'm not sure what the difference is between those, if there is any.

Either way, clearly that's what was so uncomfortably full when I channeled such a huge amount of Energy into it. Knowing now that there was enough Energy in that small amount in my hand to push me up eight levels and make seventy-five percent progress towards paying my Energy debt, I'm not at all surprised. I'm just grateful that it started off slowly: if it had all rushed into my Core at the speed it was using at the end, I reckon my Core would have exploded without me being able to do anything about it. Though, I do wonder why it started slowly and then sped up. It couldn't have been that it was trying to give me a chance, could it? Or is it something to do with my leveling up? Or even to do with this Skill? Or something completely different.

My thoughts are racing, and all I know is I'm so grateful that, somehow, I was able to access the level-up notification without having to go through all these other messages. I wouldn't have had time to do anything about it, otherwise. Given that I was also able to access the messages about me being poisoned without going through everything in between, I wonder if I've discovered a new way to deal with large numbers of notifications. Something else to explore later.

Congratulations!
You have advanced a Skill past Beginner. Meditation is now Novice 1. Your connection to the world around you has improved, and you are more able to enter a calm state even when you are emotionally perturbed. You are also more able to overcome emotions in order to improve the clarity of your thoughts while in Meditation. Due to an increased rate of Energy consumption, your receptivity to your surroundings while in Meditation has increased. As a result, your Energy absorption rate when engaging in Meditation has increased from 5% to 10% for each level in this Skill that you have past Novice. This is in addition to the 45% increase that you earned while this Skill was ranked as Beginner. This will automatically divert into refilling your mana pool at a rate increased by the same percentage as your Energy absorption rate.

Next message / Close messages

Emotionally perturbed? I say to myself incredulously. *Sure, we can call "absolutely panicked and convinced I was about to die" emotionally perturbed.* I shake my head disbelievingly. Apart from that, it's a pretty good upgrade and probably helped save my life if that bonus to the clarity of my thoughts played a part. As for the bonus to my absorption rate, which was a result of improving my "connection to the world around me," that should come in useful.

Congratulations!
You have earned 2 Skill points. Would you like to see the selection of your available Skills or save the Skill points for later?

Skill list / Bank

I bank my points for now. I'm expecting to also get Skill points at level ten and have more Skills to choose from; no point in spending time on my list until then.

The next few notifications consist of warnings about my Core being overfull followed by a couple that explain the reduction to my mana capacity.

Warning!
You have sustained damage to your Core. Your capacity to store mana is consequently reduced until your Core is restored. -1% to your mana capacity.

Next message / Close messages

Each time the message repeats, it shows another percentage point lost to my mana capacity. I'm up to three percent lost by the time a different message appears. At least this one's a bit more positive. It's another message about a Skill gain, this one for Sensation Management. As before, I choose to read the Skill description.

Sensation Management
Not many have been exposed in quick succession to the extreme heights of pain and pleasure that you have. As a result, you have gained a tolerance of and control over both. You can choose to reduce or enhance either pain or pleasure at will. The amount by which you can choose to reduce or enhance both feelings increases with Skill level and Willpower. Other sensations can be affected according to your Constitution stat level. With higher Wisdom levels, it is possible to affect the pain or pleasure felt by others.

Next message / Close messages

An interesting Skill. I'm grateful for it, frankly. The amount of pain I was in was bad enough; if it had been worse, I might have been unable to keep going, and that would have killed me. I don't miss the mention of affecting the pain or pleasure felt by others—I'm sure that could come in handy, though I can't help my mind from automatically thinking that both torturers and courtesans probably value this Skill highly.

There are another couple of notifications about my Core being overfull and about to explode. Not literally, perhaps, but that's certainly what it felt like. There's also another of the notifications about my Core being damaged, which takes the percentage loss to my mana capacity up to five. Then I get the notification I'm waiting for about Skill points. Clearly, this is when I reached level ten.

Congratulations!
You have earned 4 Skill points. Would you like to see the selection of your available Skills or save the Skill points for later?

Skill list / Bank

Eagerly, I choose to view the Skill list. I'm expecting a nice long list of at least eight potential Skills to appear, so I'm surprised when that's not the case. My surprise turns into dismay as I read the message.

> Error.
> Your internal matrix is compromised. Available Skills are inaccessible until this is restored to full functionality.
>
> Next message / Close messages

Well, that's a blow. I was really looking forward to seeing what I had available. Now I'll have to wait until I've "restored" my "internal matrix," however I'm expected to do that. At least, I hope that I'll be able to restore it; if it's something that will have to wait until I'm in Nicholas's world to heal, I'm stuffed.

At least it doesn't appear to be an exception to *all* new Skills—Sensation Management and Energy Manipulation prove that. It just appears to be an issue with gaining Skills from my Class, which is frustrating enough.

My mouth in a thin line, I push my sudden disappointment to the side and move on—what else can I do?

> Achievement awarded: Survivor
> For facing a situation that you had less than 0.1% probability of surviving, yet still finding a way through it, you have proven your tenacity and steadfastness. You have gained +3 points to Willpower and +3 points to Constitution.
>
> Next message / Close messages

Apparently, this is the last one. I'm grateful. I've got enough to think about from all the other messages. I'm still a little surprised that there's nothing in the memories I got from the System lore stone that talks about achievements considering I've earned three in just a few days. By this point, though, my capacity to feel surprise seems to be rather worn out. At least I have an explanation for the extra points to Willpower and Constitution. It would be good to keep the description for later reference, and I wonder idly if I can pin messages or something.

Having seen the tiny probability of survival, I suddenly feel like the luckiest bastard out there. I'd much rather take reductions to my mana, mana regeneration, and health regeneration than be dead! And, looking on the bright side, I just got eight levels and a whole lot of payment towards my debt out of it. In comparison to all the other ways I've almost died, this one is most definitely the best, even if it was also the most painful and risky.

After closing the message, I notice I now have another tab at the top of my screen: I always had "status screen" and "messages," but now I have "achievements." *Huh.* I flick over to it. Survivor is at the top, but Steadfast I and Risky Innovator are there too. Wait, is this in response to my thoughts about being able to see the message about my achievement later? If that works, maybe I can try to get something about my Bound. It's part of my Class, isn't it? Certainly, it would be useful to have some sort of information about their health states, their progress towards Evolving, that sort of thing.

As if my screen was just waiting for me to think of such a thing, a new tab flicks into being labeled "Bound." Right. It seems like my interface is a lot more customizable than I thought it was. Good to know. Or is it that it becomes easier to customize over time? I remember when even getting my health, stamina, and mana bars to fix themselves in the corner of my vision was a struggle.

Ideas start making themselves known, but once more, I decide to think about them later. After managing to get my bars to have a little number in them, that is. I open my newest tab and give a thoughtful hum as I see the information there.

CHAPTER FORTY-TWO

Consideration

I take a quick moment to glance over my Bound tab. The information available is quite simplistic but useful: it puts numbers to things I was never able to properly quantify before. The HR worker in me is satisfied—being able to measure progress and development in numerical form was a big part of my job before all of this.

Bound – Dominate – "Bastet"
Health units: 486/650
Mana units: 50/50
Stamina units: 280/280
Progress to Tier 2: 82%
Lifespan remaining: ~1y 6m

Bound – Dominate – "River"
Health units: 830/830
Mana units: 16/70
Stamina units: 300/300
Progress to Tier 2: 46%
Lifespan remaining: ~34y

Bound – Tame – "the bird"
Health units: 120/120
Mana units: 75/75
Stamina units: 190/190
Progress to Tier 2: 31%
Lifespan remaining: ~16y

Interesting, very interesting. The first thing I note is that I seem to be rather shortchanged in stats! At least, I was when I arrived here. I started with a mere sixty mana and forty health. Even if I'd been at peak human performance, I probably wouldn't have had much more than a hundred and twenty in either. The only one of my Bound who has stats as low as that in health is the bird! Mana in general isn't nearly as high, but even Bastet has fifty points to start with. They all still outclass me in stamina, though—apart from the bird, who has the same size pool as I do.

At least I can say that my current situation is better than that in health and mana. Considering I've made significant investment in Intelligence, I can live with the fact that my health pool is still pretty small in comparison with Bastet or River: my mana is several times either of their pools. After all, I can just cast a healing spell on myself if I'm injured. At least, I *normally* can. Dread goes through me at the thought I dare not voice even to myself that I might have lost that capability.

Still, I suppose River's and Bastet's bigger pools make sense. No wonder River wasn't too badly damaged by the salamander's fire where I got my side half melted off; no wonder it took so long to heal Bastet when she was almost dead those two times. And it seems that I didn't even fully heal her, as she's still missing a good third of her health pool. But I remind myself that I was able to kill the telekinetic Pathwalker with a single blow, which caved in her skull—a big health pool means nothing to certain injuries.

Seeing that Bastet apparently only has just over a year left in lifespan is a little shocking. She *did* say she was old . . . but I can't imagine her not being by my side. Feeling melancholic at the thought of losing someone else I've gotten close to, I flick away the information and return to the "real" world.

Unwilling to move and wake up the three raptorcat cubs currently snoozing against my feet or the nunda now dozing against my side, and still feeling far too fatigued myself, I close my eyes. I tell myself it's only for five minutes, that I'll get up and help Bastet and River to harvest more Energy Hearts in a little bit. But I think a part of me knows I'm just lying to myself.

When I blink my eyes open, I see a crocodile-mawed creature standing above me and shout as I roll sideways and grab for my knife.

Hey! I hear an annoyed voice say in my mind at the same time as several irritated and sleepy chirps reach my ears. I blink at them as I struggle to think through the traces of a dream where I was running away from creatures that morphed every moment from crocodilian to tentacled. I felt like I was running through mud, barely staying ahead of the enemies chasing me.

But that was just a dream. We got away from the tentacled beast, we got away from the lizard folk, and we beat the salamander. It's just my mind playing tricks on me again.

"Sorry," I say, a hint of a flush going up my neck, then push myself upright while trying to avoid looking directly at anyone. Suddenly, I realize that my voice is still scratchy but not painful anymore—the benefit of natural regeneration in a magical world.

You seemed troubled, River offers warily.

"It's fine," I tell him. "I'll come and help you harvest the Energy Hearts."

We've done as much as we can reach. Apparently, he's willing to go with the change of topic.

"All right," I reply briefly before patting each of the cubs in nonverbal apology for disrupting their sleep. Then I head back towards the entrance to the cavern. A quick glance at my health bar reveals that I must have slept for another couple of hours: it's almost full again.

Looking around, I spot several large piles of the Energy Hearts near where my Bound have been working. Sure enough, most of the walls only have traces of where the Energy Hearts used to be. The Energy Hearts I see still on the walls are probably more trouble than they're worth to get at, trapped as they are in various crevices and up above my head.

"Okay, guys. Are you all ready to leave once I've grabbed these Hearts? Have you eaten and rested?" I feel guilty for napping on the job while they both worked.

I have rested as much as I will be able to in such a place, River says. The feeling over the Bond is once again that of calm on the surface and a maelstrom underneath. I dare not probe any further. Not here, not now.

Bastet also sends me a sense of tiredness but a preference to get out of the place now that the Energy Hearts have been harvested. Lathani just wants to go join her mother, predictably. I do check with her that she will be fine traveling through the tunnel; I'm still concerned that she seems to be having some sort of reaction to it.

I'll be fine, she tells me impatiently. *I am not hurt, and my feeling of oddness has not changed since entering this place again. I do not think it is getting worse.*

Ultimately, I have to admit that going through the forest is probably even more risky than the tunnel.

I start loading Energy Hearts into my Inventory from one of the piles and continue working my way steadily around the room. Interestingly, it seems like there's a limit on the number of Energy Hearts that can fit in one slot: about a hundred approximately fist-sized ones in each. Clearly, the limit to each slot isn't based on number, as I fitted *significantly* more firewood into a slot than that. Not to mention a good half ton of clay and loads of salt, so it's not about physical space either. Maybe it's to do with the amount of Energy in them? At least I don't have to worry about space, though—with the number of Inventory slots I've just gained all in one fell swoop, I'm not likely to run out of room anytime soon.

By the time I finish loading in the last of the Hearts, I have four slots filled up and a fifth partially filled. Not bad for a few hours of work!

"Did you keep doing this throughout the whole time I was sleeping?" I ask River curiously.

Of course, he answers, as if it should never have been in doubt. When he feels my surprise, he continues. *This is an unprecedented opportunity; spending time on another task would seem a waste.* Now that definitely makes me feel bad about sleeping . . .

"Perhaps we can come back," I offer, "and get the last ones that are too awkward to get out now? Or maybe they will regrow."

Perhaps, River agrees, doubt tinging his mental message, *though places of opportunity such as this rarely go unguarded for long.*

True. But even though it almost killed Bastet, the salamander still came off worst from our confrontation. Who's to say that we wouldn't be able to gain access again. *And maybe even find a way to use the Pure Energy safely,* a sneaky voice in my mind suggests.

I push *that* thought firmly to the side—it might be a good idea if I had the right method, but finding that method is going to be fraught with danger. While the potential of Pure Energy makes the effort worth it, I need to make sure that I approach the attempt with a lot more consideration than what happened this time.

I do consider coming back earlier for Energy-absorption purposes, though. That's significantly less dangerous but still offers huge potential benefits. As long as I'm not being poisoned, that is, or can heal myself of the poison's effects. And as long as we don't need to travel through the vine-strangler forest to get here. An idea for a later time.

While I was packing up the Energy Hearts, I noticed that there have been some changes to my Bonds. Or not the Bonds themselves, but my ability to touch and interact with them. I'm now able to pinpoint exactly where my two Bound are in the cavern, to the point where I could find them if otherwise deprived of senses. I even have a vague sense of where the bird is, though the distance reduces the accuracy there. As for touching the Bonds themselves, where previously it felt like I was wearing gloves, even if they were thin ones, I now feel like I'm touching a braided sinew cord bare-handed.

There's a big difference. I have so much more understanding of my two Bound, and their Bonds, that were formed with Dominate. I can feel their feelings with clarity, and I sense that I could invade their thoughts with a simple flex of will. If the latter seems morally dubious, it's nothing to the other things I realize I could now do with the Bond.

With just a moment's thought, I could impose pleasure—or pain. I could use the Bond to puppet my Bound like a marionette, controlling their every move and refusing them any agency at all. Even if I didn't go that far, I sense that any command I might give while gripping the Bond would be impossible to refuse, regardless of my tone of voice or how much attention I'm paying.

I can also sense that the more I might wrap my Bound in chains, the easier it would become for them to resist me. Their stats aren't included in the information I have about them on my screen, but I reckon that if their Willpower stats were stronger than mine, I would be unable to exert full control over them. Not that I'm intending on doing anything of the sort; in fact, the idea makes me feel a little sick. It's everything I feared after Dominating Spike: a slavemaster's tool. The only reason I used the Bond recently to give commands was because I feared that I wouldn't be able to get them away from the Energy Hearts in any other way. The only difference between the two Dominate Bonds is that Bastet's is thicker—built, I suppose, from time and shared experience.

The difference is even more clear between the Bonds I hold for Bastet and River and the one I hold with the as-yet-unnamed bird. Although I can sense her location somewhere above us and touch on her emotions, I sense that I cannot touch her thoughts without explicit permission. The Bond is significantly more two-sided and my ability to affect it unilaterally far more limited.

In fact, I can only affect it on my side of things: I can block access so she wouldn't be able to communicate with me or touch my emotions. I can block my own location from her, or indeed, broadcast it. I can send a message to her, but I cannot ensure that it is received. In short, it rather reminds me of an instant messaging feature, except with added emotional connection. Needless to say, I can sense that any attempt of mine to impose my will on hers would be met with a quick refusal and probably a blockage or severance of her side of the Bond.

It's all very interesting, but putting the last of the Energy Hearts into my Inventory marks the end of the time I have to ruminate. It's time to explore this tunnel, which will hopefully take us through to an area not covered by vine-stranglers.

I pull out the torch I lit earlier and quickly set myself to relighting it. It takes a bit of convincing, but finally, I'm holding the branch in the air with a flickering flame on one end. If nothing else, it will serve as a canary in the coal mine and let us know if we're running out of oxygen.

Then, checking that we haven't left anything behind, we head towards the other exit of the cavern. As we pass the Pure Energy, I'm unable to avoid casting a glance at it. *One day,* I promise myself. One day I'll be able to harvest the immense potential in that substance without a ninety-nine point nine percent chance of dying.

But today is not that day, so I force myself to shift my gaze instead to the hole in the floor that is our path out of here.

"Okay, everyone, let's get moving."

CHAPTER FORTY-THREE

A Killer by Themselves

I climb carefully through the gaping void in the floor once the cubs are in the sling against my chest again. I'm pretty sure they've put on a growth spurt since we've been in here—they're packed more tightly than ever and not happy about it. Maybe they have grown: if creatures in this world Evolve from Energy, what's to say the cubs don't grow from it as well?

Bastet has already jumped down and is holding the torch in her mouth, allowing the flickering light to partially illuminate the rock below. It reflects off the flowing stream of glittering Pure Energy that covers at least two thirds of the tunnel floor. There's enough space on either side of the stream to walk, but we'll all have to be careful. At least it's easy to see.

Every time I look at it, I'm tempted once again to dip my hand in it, to step into it, to submerse myself. Close to such a large quantity, the temptation is almost irresistible. I avoid glancing at it as much as possible.

My toes finally touch the surface of sloped rock, and I slowly release my white-knuckle grip on the hole's edge. As predicted, the height of the tunnel is just a bit too low for me; I'll need to keep slightly bent to be able to walk. It's better than the tunnels we had to travel through to reach the salt cave, though. I cast a glance down the tunnel in each direction.

Not far upstream—if one can call it that when the substance only vaguely moves in a specific direction—the tunnel narrows significantly, the stream seeming to be held tightly within the walls of stone. Downstream, the tunnel extends for a longer distance before narrowing down significantly again. *What could have caused this conveniently sized walkway?* I wonder to myself.

Pulling myself from my thoughts, I help Lathani down. The cubs are already slung on my chest, but the almost-cub didn't feel too comfortable climbing down like Bastet. Especially not since she saw what barely touching the liquid did to me in the cavern. I do regret that she had to see that: she's been uncharacteristically quiet and subdued ever since.

When I carefully lift her down, she takes especial care not to go anywhere near the pearlescent liquid, pressing herself against the tunnel wall instead. I'm not going to complain about her keeping herself safe. I do take a moment to give her a reassuring head rub. She sends me a wordless communication of mixed emotions.

I'm unsurprised that fear and longing for home make up a good portion of them, though I regret that the careless, innocent cub is no more.

It's okay, Lathani, I try to project to her soothingly. I hope it gets through—we don't have a Bond, but the nunda cub is naturally telepathic and seems to understand everything else going on. *Once we're out of here, it should be a quick trip back to your mom.* She clearly must get at least the sense of my message, as her response is just as wordless and equally as mixed.

She's already told me about her fears that her changed appearance will cause Kalanthia to abandon her, so I'm not entirely surprised. There's little to say to them except what I have already: she will always have a place with me, and I doubt that Kalanthia will abandon her for aging more quickly than expected.

With the rest of the party in the passageway, River climbs down to join us. Much as I did, he slowly lowers himself from the edge of the hole by his hands. Gym bunnies, eat your heart out. If I'd had the stats then that I have now, I would have been doing chin-ups one-handed and press-up claps with my index fingers.

The moment of marveling at the differences is over and we get moving, all of us eager to be out of this place. Bastet is first, moving a little ahead so that we'll have some warning if something decides to attack. Progress for the rest of us is much slower. River, Lathani, and I all edge along the tunnel wall, but Lathani has a much easier job of it being closer to the ground and having four legs. River's job isn't much harder, since the roof of the tunnel is high enough that he can walk upright. I'm the one who's slowing down the pack.

We don't have to go far, but everyone in the group is tense, which makes even minutes feel as long as hours. Worse, I notice my health dropping faster: I'm losing a point every ten or so seconds instead of every sixty-six. I don't need to check my newly nagging notifications to know that the Energy poisoning has increased. I feel very vulnerable without being able to cast a Lay-on-Hands to top my health up.

Roughly halfway along the tunnel, there's an abrupt narrowing. Bastet just jumps through it, the hole in the center vaguely circular. Somehow, she manages to shift her angle in midair—it was probably a flap of her wings that provided enough impetus to push her back towards the bank rather than into the stream of Pure Energy, but it happened too fast for me to see in this dim light. The rest of us have to take it more slowly.

Somehow, we all manage to get through without touching the dangerous substance running beside us, though there is a close call when Lathani slips as she is scrambling over the rocky obstacle.

I automatically reach to catch her, but that puts *me* off balance a little. I think it's only my increased number of points in Dexterity that prevent me from splashing headfirst into the stream—I'm almost certain that would have killed me.

The rest of the tunnel seems to take three times as long as the first bit, even though logically I know it's only about twice the length. Finally, though, we reach the junction with the other tunnel. Here, it's almost a reverse process of the previous junction.

Bastet is already in the tunnel above, waiting for us to arrive. She reassures me that she hasn't detected any other creature since we've been apart. I pass Lathani up to her, then pull myself up and release the cubs from their entrapping sling. Maybe it's not the best idea, but I'm not keen on them continuing to scratch my chest to pieces. I'm already losing enough health units from the Energy poisoning!

Last of all, River pulls himself up too. He needs a bit of a hand due to his shorter stature, which, though useful while passing through the low tunnel, makes it harder for him to get out of it.

We keep going through the tunnel until I notice that my health is no longer dropping. Then we pause for a short time to rest and eat again since we all feel the need. The darkness of the tunnels makes it difficult to know just how long we've been traveling. It could be an hour; it could be a day. The tunnels would appear the same either way.

Biting my lip, I push myself to my feet as the same claustrophobia that I felt before descends on me again.

"Come on, everyone," I tell my group. "We're not making progress sitting here." A flicker of guilt goes through me when I see Bastet's stiff fatigue as she pushes herself to her feet and River's sigh as he stands up. But the sooner we're out of here, the sooner we can rest properly.

Moving once more, we trudge along the tunnel. It meanders one way, then the other. Always sloping, but some bits are steeper than others. Walking is boring. I would say that's a good thing—boring means nothing is jumping out at me to eat my face or any other parts—but at this point, the interminable walls are a killer by themselves; if this goes on too much longer, we'll all be sleepwalking our way into something's mouth.

Even Bastet's seemingly unflagging stamina is worn thin. She's stopped trotting forwards and back; instead, she trudges forwards only a little faster than us and pauses to let us catch up when she gets too far ahead. Lathani is slung over River's shoulders. After she started swaying drunkenly from tiredness and almost walked into a wall a couple of times, my Bound picked her up of his own accord. She was snoring within a few moments. Only the cubs have any energy, but fortunately, they're wary enough due to the unfamiliar environment to not need too much herding.

As for River, he's much like me: he's kept going by just concentrating on putting one foot in front of the other. He's tired, and I'm still feeling extremely fragile, like each of those steps could rattle something essential loose in me. We're in very poor shape for any sort of confrontation, which of course means that one is surely inevitable.

The first sign that the end may be near is when I realize that the way ahead is just a little lighter than the rest of the journey has been. Reaching the bend, I get my first sight of daylight in what feels like forever, even if it was only probably a day at the most. My heart quickens in my chest in excitement, and my feet instinctively pick up the pace despite my fatigue.

I look around at River. The light has come back into his eyes, and he's moving with more enthusiasm too. Bastet is silhouetted against the light as she hurries back to us. At first I think it's the joy of being back in the light, but when I feel her go right from tired to fully alert, I realize it's something else. The mental equivalent of an adrenaline rush passes over the Bond between us and makes me straighten up, my senses sharp.

What is it? I ask her sharply, choosing to speak mentally in case my voice will alert whatever it is—voices in this tunnel echo far too much.

She sends a sense of uncertainty and the feeling that we're approaching the den of some powerful predator. It's not scent, I don't think, but some other sense . . . which I suddenly realize I can actually use myself now. It must be since I increased my mental and soul stats, or maybe it's just because whatever creature lies up ahead is powerful enough to get through even to me. Either way, I frown as I understand what she's talking about. It's some sort of foreboding presence, one that warns of death if we approach closer.

Right, I accept grimly. *What do you think, River?* I turn to my other Bound. He's doing the lizard-man equivalent of frowning.

Something is wrong, he replies slowly. Turning his head slightly, he seems to concentrate. I wait, impatient but not wanting to interrupt his thought process. *I don't think it's real.*

What do you mean?

The presence is strong . . . but only surface deep. It's like it's an . . . imprint. And it's days old. I can't sense much more than that—I'm not like one of the Pathwalkers—but I don't think we have much to fear. Not from that, anyway. Though, there is another scent on the breeze, one that instinct tells me deserves our caution. I shall go ahead and scout, if you wish.

Sure, but be careful, I agree, only half my attention on him. Another scent? A different one from the original threat? *Bastet, can you smell it?*

She sniffs the breeze even as River moves cautiously forwards and drops into Stealth or whatever his equivalent is. He doesn't fade from view the way Bastet does, but he sort of . . . blurs. Certainly, he becomes harder to spot, especially when not moving.

Bastet doesn't seem to have caught the scent of it, whatever it is, so we just watch River move away from us and around the bend, where I can still feel him but can't see him any longer. Then, suddenly, whatever it is comes towards us more quickly than it departed. River drops his stealth as he comes back around the corner, his expression grim. At the same time, Bastet stiffens next to me and lets out a low growl.

Danger? I send to them both. Bastet's growl just grows louder. River sends back grim agreement, and I brace myself for the worst.

CHAPTER FORTY-FOUR

Poison

Bracing myself for news about another fire-breathing salamander—or worse—I'm surprised when it's not that at all.

The aura is indeed old. A powerful predator was here at some point not too long ago, but at least a few days. It left a mark—to warn others away, would be my guess.

Then why did you say there was danger? And why is Bastet reacting like this? I ask, still tense.

Because there is. Just not from the creature that left the imprint.

What is it, then? In response, River sends a picture instead of explaining verbally. It's the first time he's sent me a memory like that. Bastet does it all the time, but River doesn't. I'm interested to note that his eyesight is very good; the clarity is better even than Bastet's. He can also see more colors than either of us, which makes my brain hurt as it tries to process information it has no reference for.

I quickly focus on the content of the image rather than all the incidental details—I don't want to accidentally give myself an aneurysm.

The image sent shows a group of creatures lounging around the entranceway of the cave. They've clearly made a temporary den of the first few meters of the cave, but it's strange that they haven't chosen to go further in. Can they also detect the imprint of the predator and don't want to risk it? But then why make their home in the cave mouth? I move on, not able to answer the question and not wanting to spend more time on it. Especially since I recognize the creatures in question: lizogs.

I remember the first time I came across lizogs. It was the day I met Bastet. Well, the same day I formed my Bond with her. I don't count the time her pack chased me across the forest as a "meeting." Kalanthia had slaughtered Bastet's family, leaving their bodies to litter the ground. Predictably, the dead bodies lying around attracted scavengers—lizogs, who happened to come while Bastet and I were fetching the cubs from where they were hiding in a cave.

The creatures are relatively small, their heads only reach just above my knee. But what powerful heads they have: heavy jaws full of sharp teeth and the crushing power to bite through bone. They're like moving tanks with heavily muscled bodies and thick tails.

Last time I killed them by causing an avalanche of stones to land on their heads. Even then, one out of five survived the rockslide.

Although they're not fast, they're superb trackers; once they catch our scents, it'll be game over if we can't get away from them. Which means that we *definitely* need to get out of this tunnel since getting chased here will just see us back in the middle of the vine-stranglers again—jumping back into the pan from the fire. As for just running through them or trying to sneak through them with stealth, the problem is that we need rest: we don't want a pack of lizogs on our heels for the rest of the journey back.

Perhaps I could sneak through and lure them away? But that would require me to get through them and then also be able to get *away* from the whole pack following on my heels. Too risky. And I don't want to ask Bastet to do something like that either. River probably wouldn't be much better as a choice than I would.

Which leaves dealing with them here and now in some way. There look to be more than ten lizogs against the three of us. Four, if I count Lathani; I'm not counting the cubs—they'd become a snack for the lizogs very quickly. But it's not a great idea given that we're all tired and have had enough of fighting.

Any ideas? I ask my two Bound tiredly, sending Bastet the picture of what River saw. Bastet sends back a strong opinion that we should run for our lives. *Yeah, but that's just putting off the problem until later,* I point out, explaining the thoughts I had previously.

Bastet and I go back and forth on a couple of ideas, mostly ones I already thought about and dismissed.

Finally, we're interrupted when River comes up with an alternative suggestion.

One of the first things I learned when I started my apprenticeship was about poisons. Identifying them, treating them . . . and making them. My people often coat our weapons in a type of poison that targets stamina . . . He trails off, and I remember how Kalanthia was affected by some sort of attack on her stamina; that's why we're in this mess to begin with.

Go on, I tell him. I'm wary, but if this can get us out of our current situation, then I'm all ears.

Essentially, we have two versions, and we usually create a hybrid for our Warriors. One poisons the stamina currently in our target's body, and one poisons the body's ability to reproduce stamina. Combined, it renders our targets helpless. The poison's ability fades over time, though, and how fast depends both on how much poison entered the target and the target's healing ability. The image of Kalanthia collapsed next to the stream and her labored mental voice flash through my mind. I wonder how much poison she must have taken to cause such a strong and long-lasting effect. But the fact that this weapon was used against her shouldn't mean that I can't use it against my own enemies.

I hope you're raising this to tell me that you have some with you, I tell River dryly. *Because if you've given me this whole spiel only to tell me that you're missing some key ingredients, I'm not going to be happy.* Amusement tinged with the slightest apprehension comes across the Bond from his side.

I have ingredients for the first poison, the one that affects the stamina currently in the target. I am missing a few key ingredients for the second, though.

I shrug.

Hopefully, that will be enough. How do you poison the target? Does it just need to enter their bloodstream?

We generally stab our prey with spears, yes, he confirms. I think fast. Although River does have a spear, it's probably not the best approach. At least not without some other additions. Spears mean getting in close to those bone-crunching jaws, and I don't currently have my healing magic available. I think fast. I've got an idea but need to check whether it's possible.

Wait here, I tell my companions and then activate Fade. Stealth, of course, is already active—it basically always is unless I intentionally turn it off. Creeping forwards, I hope that the lizogs' excellent sense of smell won't pick up my scent. At least we're downwind; if we had been upwind, we would probably have already been attacked.

Taking my time to tiptoe almost soundlessly down the tunnel, I stick closely to the walls like River did. As I move, the vague sense of something waiting for me becomes stronger. There's the impulse to run, to escape the danger waiting up ahead with its maw open wide, but thanks to knowing that this is just an old imprint, I'm able to ignore it.

Reaching the end of the tunnel, I realize why the lizogs haven't come any closer: they probably can't. Or maybe they just don't want to bother.

The tunnel is almost closed with piles of rubble, creating a barrier that is probably difficult for them to climb over—I didn't get the impression from our last battle that lizogs would be particularly good at that. I can see where the rocks fell from: a chunk of the ceiling collapsed. It makes me very glad that such an event hadn't happened somewhere else in the tunnel to close it off completely. Or worse, while we were actually trying to travel through it.

Still, for our purposes right now, it's practically perfect! The rubble comes up to about my waist, which is slightly above River's. Bastet will be too short to do much, and I wouldn't want her on the other side of the barrier . . . but I still have an idea of the role she could play.

I creep back to the others and don't bother to hide my excitement. Even before I start speaking, I see them react to the emotion, and some of the fear and dismay leaves their postures. Even the cubs relax a bit, obviously sensing that the adults are less worried than before. When they start to play, I have to ask Bastet to rein them in a bit, though—we might have a chance here, but if the cubs catch the attention of the lizogs too early, we'll lose even that.

All right, listen up, I tell both my Bound once the cubs have been subdued. I hope Lathani will be able to listen in or that Bastet will be able to transfer the information to her—I'm still wary of announcing our presence to the lizogs prematurely. *I've got a plan.*

So saying, I outline what I was thinking and watch their reactions.

Do you think it's possible? I ask everyone, though I look directly at River: he's the one who will be providing the cornerstone of the strategy.

Hopefully, he responds tentatively. *I'm not sure I have enough ingredients for every-thing, but . . .*

Well, any you can make would help, I tell him. Honestly, it might be possible to win without River's contribution, but it would definitely be harder. Much harder, potentially. But in the end, we don't have much of a choice: my Bound both agree that this place is as close to perfect as we're going to get for a battle setting against lizogs.

With unanimous agreement to go forwards with my plan, we set to preparing as much as we can. Once more, it seems, I'm going to set a trap for lizogs. This one's going to be a little less elaborate than the previous, mostly due to not having a handy landslide nearby. Plus, with the number of lizogs River saw and the potential for there to be even more outside where he *couldn't* see, it would have to be a *massive* landslide, and in a cave, that would probably trap us in too.

River settles to the floor as he pulls off his box-backpack. He lifts the lid and removes several ingredients.

Can I watch? I ask. River wordlessly expresses surprise that I'd want to and acceptance if I do. I look on with interest as he places some plump berries into a small hollowed-out section of a branch and then uses his fingers to squish them into pulp. Into the juice he adds something that looks like a dried-out section of flesh and lets that soak. Then he takes some leaves and presses them into the container too. Finally, he uses his wooden knife to nick the underside of his wrist. Blood starts dribbling out into the container, its color a bit darker than my own.

It needs to stew for a few clicks, River tells me. I get the impression that "clicks" is a bit like minutes for me.

We wait, River patiently, me not so much. I'm tempted to go into Meditation, but just as I'm seriously considering doing it, River stirs the mixture. I realize that it's changed color a little, the red becoming darker with hints of green in the light of the torch.

It's ready? I ask.

It's ready, he confirms. I nod, grinning. Operation Lizog Massacre, commence.

CHAPTER FORTY-FIVE

Damage Dealer

They're coming," I warn everyone as I see movement at the entrance.

I raise my bow and take aim. As the first lizog enters the tunnel, I fire. It's not ideal to be shooting into the light, but the advantage is that the lizog probably can't see me as well as I can see it.

My practice with the bow is really paying off: I hit it in its throat as it lifts its head to sniff the air. That by itself is a bad wound—the bow's power and the short distance both contribute to the arrow digging in deeply.

It's not enough to finish the creature off, though. Not with the arrow stuck in there plugging the hole. Fortunately, I'm not relying on killing with a single blow.

I carefully applied the poison River made to all of my weapons, arrows definitely included. No doubt it's already running through the lizog's blood and, hopefully, affecting the creature's stamina.

Adrenaline is certainly running through my own veins, banishing tiredness. My companions are experiencing the same boost, which is giving us an edge—for now. Hopefully, we'll be done with the battle before the bill of our fatigue comes due.

For now, though, we've got incoming threats. The reptilian pit bull isn't willing to stand there and wait for death. Instead, after pausing in a moment of shock, it runs towards us with a menacing rumble. I try not to focus on it. Close quarters defense is my companions' concern right now. My job is to work the range targets.

The next lizog appears silhouetted against the light. I fire again.

The number of lizogs multiplies as they pour into the tunnel quicker than I can shoot them. Setting my teeth, I do my best to keep up, but I privilege accuracy over speed when I have to choose—my job is to affect as many of them with the poison as early as possible, and I don't have that many arrows left to do it with.

I'm aware via both peripheral vision and the Bonds of my companions and their actions.

River is the second damage dealer. He's standing behind our rocky barricade and is stabbing down at the lizogs with a spear that's also got a coating of poison. Bastet is prowling back and forth. Without any external weapon to coat with the stamina-damaging poison, her job is final defense if any of the lizogs get through the barricade.

That comes sooner rather than later. Alarm pulses from Bastet's side of the

Bond, and I quickly look over at her. I immediately see the issue and grab for the burning torch currently smoldering behind me.

The rubble wall is working very well in most places, but there's a section where the rocks are smaller and offer more of a slope than a wall. We noticed it before the fight started and took preparatory measures. Now that one lizog has realized there might be a route up to us via the slope, I put these into action.

I move towards the weak point in our defenses with my torch in front of me and quickly lean over to touch it to the stones. The salamander's explosive liquid flares up and badly scares the lizog, making it immediately turn tail, more frightened than actually hurt—for now.

It tries to bury itself among the other lizogs, but, in a happy accident, it appears to have gotten some of the liquid on its body. Where it rubs this off onto its pack-mates, they light on fire too, hissing and yelping.

The fire doesn't last long and doesn't actually do much damage. However, it *does* cause a fair bit of disturbance, which allows River to keep stabbing and me to continue firing arrows at the newcomers to the fight.

I doubt I'll get the chance to renew the salamander oil, though, so it's only a matter of time before another lizog summons up the courage to try the slope again.

With the poison, however, time is on our side. Sort of. We've also got our own effective time limit based on how long we can keep running on fumes. Still, the longer the barrier can continue protecting our legs from their bone-crunching jaws, the better.

I keep firing arrows until I reach for my stock and find it empty. I curse but am unsurprised—I haven't had the time to replenish my supply. However, I have been able to do something else. I shift further along the barrier to find my cache of spears. Well, more like javelins.

They're very rough, as they're made out of the firewood I collected in the vine-strangler forest. I only chose the pieces that were at least mostly straight, but they're still basically just sharpened pieces of wood. With poison on the heads.

The javelins don't fly very nicely, and few actually strike the lizogs at the right angle to sink far into them, but I'm pleasantly surprised at the damage done by those that do hit at the right angle—my Strength sends even the rough weapons sinking deeply into the lizogs' bodies.

Eventually, it seems like all the lizogs have joined the fight: no new one has appeared in the last few seconds. I use up the rest of my javelins by throwing them at the lizogs in the middle, the ones that are pressing their packmates forwards but are not actually in range of River's spear. By this point there must be at least fifteen of the reptilian dogs here and neither of us have really made any kills yet. That's disappointing, but not too concerning—yet.

Taking a couple of steps to the tunnel wall, I lean down to grab my own spear, another makeshift weapon created by sharpening the biggest bit of firewood I could find. Not wanting to spare the time to open my Inventory, I just replace it with the now-defunct bow, making sure that the ranged weapon is out of the way of our feet.

Stepping back up to the barricade, I start stabbing alongside the lizard-man. The difference between our physical stats is far too obvious: River's strikes pierce the lizogs' bodies with relative ease; mine do more to knock the lizogs off balance, their toughened, armored skin making my spears act like blunt weapons rather than the piercing ones they should be.

Of course, it could also be partly to do with the fact that he's got a proper flint head to his, where I've just essentially got a sharpened stick. But since I was providing ranged support at the beginning, we decided that it would make sense for him to keep the better spear.

On the other hand, my increased mental stats seem to help me identify where to strike to have the most effect. Actually *hitting* the spot dead-on is another question; I think I need to gain more points in Dexterity to improve that. But the middle of a fight isn't the time to wonder about stats.

Focusing on the task at hand, I lose myself in the river of bodies ahead of me. Honestly, the way the little light in here reflects off their dark scales really does make it look like water. When it looks like they're all pressing against the barrier, I decide that it's well past time to activate the trap.

"I'm lighting it up," I warn my Bound as I pick up a second makeshift torch and touch it to the head of our main one. They both back up a couple of steps. The lizogs surge against the barrier with renewed eagerness, perhaps thinking that their prey is running away. Not so much.

The makeshift torch is lit, so I set the main one back down, then, narrowing my eyes in focus, I throw the second torch into the mass of lizogs. It lands on the back of one reptilian pit bull, making the creature hiss in pain.

The lizog wriggles as it desperately tries to get the burning pain off it. It succeeds, and the torch drops to the ground.

With a *whoomph*, the salamander's liquid that I splashed around ignites and the whole section goes up in flames. I wasn't able to soak the entire area or the barrier, so only half of the lizogs have been caught in the trap, but that's better than it could be. It's a pity that it wasn't set off earlier when the previous lizog was burned—bad luck, I guess.

Bastet, River, and I focus back in on the fight and target the lizogs who aren't on fire. They're frenzied, though—perhaps the fire has triggered their kill or be killed instincts.

I'm broken out of my focus when a searing pain shoots up my leg, making me shout. A lizog has managed to find another way through and is crushing my leg. At least, it's attempting to crush it—while the teeth are sinking in, they aren't crunching through my bone as both of us would have expected. For a moment the lizog and I stare at each other. The lizog looks baffled: it seems to be saying, *This usually works.*

With gallows humor, I think back at it, *Well, performance issues . . .*

The moment passes, and the lizog doubles down on its attempt to bite my leg off. I bring my spear up and, with it this close, I'm able to line up a perfect angle to pierce through the lizog's eye and into its brain in a single brutal shove. Even as the light dies in its eyes, its teeth hold on tightly. I drop my spear and grip its jaws with both hands, then pull hard.

For a moment, its jaws don't shift, and I'm worried that I'm going to have to continue fighting with teeth deep in my calf. Then, as desperation increases my strength to a level I didn't realize was possible, there's a small movement. Not daring to let up for a moment, I strain, feeling my face go red.

Suddenly, a crack resonates through my forearms, and the lizog's jaws go limp.

The deep bite in my calf is painful. Before my recent experiences, I might have called it agonizing, but I find my previous understanding of agony has been put into perspective. The lizog didn't succeed in biting through my bone, but it certainly reached it with its teeth. Blood is pouring out of the wounds; I need to heal myself.

Crouching down, I put my hands around the wound, ignoring the pain of my touch. With the pressure, the blood isn't pouring out in the same way, but I can't hold back a flood with my hands alone. I reach for Lay-on-Hands as my sense of urgency builds.

I know that the last few times I tried this it didn't work, but perhaps it's healed a bit? My hopes are high, but for naught. I have to abandon the first attempt I make at grabbing for some mana as an awful pain shoots through me, worse even than the fire radiating up from my leg. If my new Sensation Management Skill is doing anything, I can't tell.

I don't want to touch that shattered glass vase again, but I have no choice. My body might be sturdy enough that lizogs can't just bite through it now, but I'm not invulnerable. My health bar, already reduced from walking next to the Pure Energy, is decreasing even further as my blood pumps out of my body. I *need* to heal myself or I'm going to bleed out here.

Gritting my teeth and going more slowly, I clumsily attempt to pull mana out of my Core manually rather than using the automatic function of the spell. It's the equivalent of using a finger and thumb to tease out some mana instead of reaching in with my fist the way I was before.

It still hurts but less so: it's more like the pressure of the hands around my leg holding in my blood than the teeth that ripped it apart. Excruciatingly slowly, I pull out a thread of mana and redirect it down my leg. I command it to heal flesh and replenish blood, and I'm relieved when it does just that.

It's painful, and the more mana that leaves my reserve, the more agonizing it becomes. I can't help but remember that most pain is a warning from the body; pushing past pain often means causing more damage to one's body. I stop directing mana as soon as my health bar stabilizes. I'm not healed, not even close to it, but it will have to do.

Panting, I open my eyes and access my Inventory to pull another half-torn shirt out. By wrapping it around my wound, I'll—hopefully—stop it from breaking open again as I move. Standing up, I bring my spear back to a ready position, but fortunately, there are no lizogs right by me. Just as well. I was awfully vulnerable just now.

Scanning the action, I look for anything that has changed since I was bitten. Bastet is grappling with a lizog not far from me. She seems to be doing fine and is using her body to block another attacker on the previously attempted slope. Now that we've used up the salamander oil I splashed onto it earlier, it's her job to guard the area. Fortunately, it seems that the narrow passageway is still limiting their numbers, so she isn't being overwhelmed. Yet, anyway.

River is stabbing away steadily, and the lizogs in front of him are looking rather worse for wear. There are fewer lizogs in general. The lack of light doesn't let me get a good head count, but I reckon that we must have cut the numbers in half already. I shift over to Bastet's area to help her out. Not wanting my other leg to get shredded too, I keep a little bit of distance from them and use the barricade to shield myself.

Unfortunately, they seem to have realized that this is the only way through to us, so the pressure of the lizogs behind is pushing the front one forwards, even as we block it. They soon gain ground on us, and I trade attacks with one while Bastet fights another.

Was that poison a dud? I wonder as I dodge the lunging bites of the lizog and at the same time try to pin it with my spear. *Maybe I should switch to my mace. I don't see any sort of stamina deprivation.*

As if my questioning were a trigger, it's not long until I start to see the poison's effects. The lizog I'm fighting suddenly starts slowing down, its attacks becoming more sluggish, its dodges less effective. I quickly find an opening and down it with a stab through its throat.

Returning to the barricade, I see that the remaining lizogs are also starting to show the effects—the ones on the business end of River's spear are particularly affected. Perhaps it just takes a bit of time for the poison to accumulate enough to overwhelm the lizogs' natural stamina regeneration. It wouldn't surprise me if they were powerhouses in that stat, along with Constitution.

When the area in front of his section goes still—some of the lizogs are attempting to flee but not getting very far—we both converge on the last two that are fighting Bastet. They're less impacted by the poison since they've probably only had a couple of wounds from poisoned weapons—for obvious reasons, we couldn't coat Bastet's claws.

Finally, the battlefield goes quiet except for the sound of our panting. All three of us are breathing heavily, Bastet particularly so. She's exhausted—I can see that by the drooping of her wings and the way she hangs her head.

Rest, I tell her tiredly. She's been the most active of all of us and needs a break.

She eyes me and asks wordlessly for meat. I grab a carcass out of my Inventory and drop it for all and sundry to eat. I'll need to check with River whether we can eat the meat of the lizogs without being poisoned ourselves.

The raptorcat tears off a big chunk of meat, then slumps back along the tunnel to join Lathani and the cubs. This time Lathani didn't protest against being stuck guarding the cubs: she's tired and at her mental limits too. She accepted without argument that we needed someone there to keep the cubs safe in case a lizog broke through our battle line.

In appreciation of both Bastet's and Lathani's efforts, I move the rest of the killer-chicken corpse closer to the little group so that they can eat freely. As for River and I, we start tiredly clearing up, collecting as many of my arrows as we can. I don't bother collecting the javelins—I could do far better in a day back at the den.

We can't stay here very long: all the blood and gore will attract other predators. Still, no point in leaving so many potentially useful corpses around.

"Will these be safe to eat?" I check with River as I approach one of the bodies.

Yes. We usually use this poison for hunting. The poison quickly loses potency once the prey is dead. That makes sense. Satisfied with the answer, I start to pile lizog corpses into my Inventory. As I'm doing it, another thought occurs to me.

"Remind me again why we didn't use this poison on the salamander?" He pauses what he's doing to look at me steadily.

I did. I took a moment to coat my weapon with the last of my preprepared poison before we engaged in battle. My eyes go wide, and I stop to stare at him.

"The salamander was that powerful?" I hadn't noticed any easily discernible effects on the massive creature, not like I'd seen with these lizogs. River shrugs.

It had an Energy Heart. I wasn't surprised that a few doses of it weren't enough to make much difference. Large creatures are already harder to take down, and ones with Energy Hearts even more so.

"No kidding," I remark as I turn back to my task. It makes me wonder just how much poison Kalanthia must have been stabbed with to have the effect on her it did. Then again, maybe it was the stronger version of the poison, the one River doesn't have with him. I simply don't consider the idea that Kalanthia doesn't have an Energy Heart, given her clear power and ability to use magic.

I try to put one of the lizogs that attempted to flee into my Inventory, and my eyebrows knit together when it doesn't work. Checking my Inventory, my frown deepens. It can't be due to lack of space. Since all those level-ups, I have more slots available than seem possible to use. Looking at the lizog's eyes, I realize the issue.

The lizog isn't dead.

CHAPTER FORTY-SIX

Surrender

My heart leaps in my chest when I see the lizog's nostrils opening and closing in quick pants. The creature is unable to move, brought as low by the stamina poison as Kalanthia was. It isn't as likely to die of it as she was, though: we only had one poison instead of the cocktail she was attacked with. As a result, only the lizog's current stamina is poisoned, not its regeneration. It will recover as soon as the poison fades from its system. That's why we had to deal with the rest of them with a blade through their throats, hearts, or brains.

But is that really what I should do here?

My inclination is to trigger Dominate. I wanted to do it last time, but the only lizog that survived the landslide had its eyes destroyed. Apparently, Dominate doesn't work without eyes to gaze into. Which, actually, is a bit of a downside to the Skill if you're facing an enemy that doesn't *have* eyes. Like that tentacled monster, the memory of which never fails to send a shiver down my spine.

Before initiating a Battle of Wills with this helpless lizog, though, I run through a mini moral checklist of whether it would be right to do so. Did this lizog attack me? It attempted to attack our group, at least—I'll count that as a "yes." Would a lizog fulfil a useful role? Given their extremely strong sense of smell, bone-crushing jaws, and clearly heightened Constitution and stamina, yes. Would this creature be in a worse position if I didn't Dominate it? Considering the situation, yes: even if we decide not to kill it, it's a pack animal that doesn't have a pack. I don't know for sure how things work here, but most animals in that situation on Earth find life difficult.

Besides, it's not like I could heal it of the poison even if I wanted to, so I'd be leaving it paralyzed in a place that stinks of blood and death. And if it somehow survived and followed our scent, we'd have to kill it then. Leaving it alive here would be potentially leaving an enemy at our backs, meaning that if I don't Dominate it, we'll probably have to kill it before we go.

Moral principles satisfied, I place the lizog down on the ground and sit down myself. I carefully don't think about what gunk might be getting on my trousers; like most of my clothes, they're little more than rags by this point.

Watch over me, would you? I ask River. *I may be out for a bit.* With his agreement coming over the Bond, I stare into the lizog's eyes and activate Dominate.

As always, the edges of my vision fade into fog; the only aspects still in color are the lizog and myself. A pressure presses down from above just as another tries to keep us apart. What is surprising this time is how *little* pressure there is.

The force impacting me from above is, frankly, negligible, and the block between the lizog and me is almost nonexistent. I sense that I could just stride across and force my will on the lizog with little more difficulty than strolling down a street. Is this the effect of my increased Willpower? It must be.

Force isn't my intention, though. I do start walking towards the lizog, but once I've gotten close enough to initiate a dialogue, I pause. Interestingly, I feel the connection form far faster than ever before. Is this another effect of my increased stats, or is this something particular to the lizog? Or is it a result of my Dominate ranking up? Honestly, there are too many possibilities to accurately identify the reason.

Pushing those thoughts to the side, I take some time to pay attention to what the lizog is communicating to me.

Fear is the first emotion. Understandable. We killed the rest of its pack and have made it a prisoner in its own body. It's not surprising that helplessness is strongly present too. And hunger. Pain. And . . . something else. I can't quite work out what it is, but I can tell that it's a lot more positive than any of the others.

There's also a hint of peace, calmness. Is this what the rank-up message for Dominate meant when it talked about calming and pacifying strong emotions as long as I'm calm? Either way, I hope it will make this negotiation easier.

"Would you like to join me?" I ask the lizog as I continue to walk forwards slowly. Not giving the lizog a chance to respond, I start my recruitment spiel. "We will be stronger together, working as a pack. I can offer you the opportunity to become stronger individually too, to face powerful foes and come out the victor." Pausing for a moment to feel out how the lizog is responding to my offer so far, I'm surprised by an immediate answer.

Yes, the lizog seems to say as its aura shifts from fear to eagerness. I'm rather taken aback. That's a quick turnaround.

"You want to join us?" I ask, stalling for time. Is it playing some sort of game? Pretending to give in only to betray us later or something?

When it responds a moment later, I realize that I'm anthropomorphizing far too much. Just like with Bastet at the start, I'm ascribing human reactions to a creature that definitely isn't. Instead of a clear and direct thought like it sent me before, this time I'm hit with a deluge of emotions and images to explain its acceptance.

It shows me lizogs tussling as pups, and the winners getting first dibs at the food. Even as adults, fights still establish the pecking order, determining access to food and to other coveted amenities. Only the lizog at the head of the pack is allowed to mate with any female he comes across, while the other lizogs are relegated to fetching food for the alpha as he waits for the resulting eggs to hatch.

I get the sense that males in the pack owe their loyalty to the strongest. The hierarchy changes whenever the alpha becomes weak or vulnerable in some way:

sickness, injury, old age. He opens himself up to a challenge, and the victor of the challenge will become, or remain, the alpha.

Apparently, thanks to having defeated all comers, I have taken the position of alpha in his mind. But then why the sudden change of emotions? My thoughts must communicate themselves to him, as the lizog quickly responds, and my mind translates the explosion of emotions and images into words.

You were an enemy. Now, you are pack. Apparently, lizogs have some sort of connection with others of the same species, female or male, same pack or different. I would have guessed it to be some smell, considering their impressive scent abilities, but given that he's now identifying me as another lizog, I have to conclude that it's some mental connection. Or soul. Whatever.

If one pack of lizogs intrudes on another one's territory, there's an obvious reaction: the two alphas fight, and the other lizogs often have their own battles alongside. If the fight is inconclusive, the invading pack will return to their own territory and lick their wounds. If one of the alphas is the clear winner, the other's pack will be absorbed into the winner's. The survivors, anyway. Territorial battles are bloody, dangerous affairs.

In the lizog's mind, this is exactly what has happened. Although he didn't identify me as a lizog before, he does now, and so he easily rationalizes the last few minutes. We, another pack of lizogs, invaded his pack's territory. There was a fight, and all the other lizogs except for him were killed. He himself was completely subdued. Clearly, that makes us the dominant pack, and as I am the alpha of the winning pack, he owes me his loyalty.

His reasoning seems a little flawed to my mind, but clearly that's how his kind works. How he identified me as the leader, I don't know. Because I hold River and Bastet's Bonds? Can he sense that kind of thing? I try to ask, but he just sends me a sense of power. I choose to move on and work out if I'm going to accept his willing—no, *eager*—surrender.

It feels like it should be obvious. The creature isn't fighting against me. If anything, he's almost *throwing* himself at me. Even the pressure between us has completely disappeared; in fact, it almost feels like there's a vacuum pulling me in. But at the same time, I have to work out whether introducing a creature that clearly needs to have a rigid hierarchy into the mix is a good idea.

In the end, I just mentally shrug. If it doesn't work out, I'll release the Bond. The lizog shouldn't be any *worse* off than he would be if I just left him here. And if he won't leave us peacefully, I'll have to kill him later.

"Okay," I say finally. "I accept your fealty." Unlike before, when the other side has had to make a gesture of submission, it seems to be *my* agreement that is required for the Battle of Wills to end—an odd experience.

The space returns back to normal, and very little disorientation accompanies the transition this time. Interesting.

"Bastet, River," I say, climbing to my feet, "meet your new packmate." I gesture at the still prone lizog—another one that will need a name. I'm less tired than I usually am at the end of a Battle of Wills, which is fortunate: I'm completely exhausted from everything else. And so are the others.

Bastet is looking a little better—the short rest did her good—but River's shoulders are slumped and his movements sluggish. They take a moment to send a greeting down the Bond, though. Since they can't contact each other directly, I have to pass on the greetings, but the lizog responds with an eager brightness he's unable to express in his body language.

Eager myself to get going and find somewhere we can *rest,* I shove the last two corpses into my Inventory along with my now unneeded torch.

"Come on, guys," I say, attempting enthusiasm but falling rather flat. "We just need to find somewhere safe enough to rest, and then we'll sleep. Then it'll be the last stretch home." Actually, I need to work out where we are. As my Bound trudge over to me, followed by Lathani and the cubs—the only ones with any energy among us—I open up my Map.

I'm grateful that we haven't gone completely in the wrong direction, though we haven't exactly gone straight home either. We must have gone underneath a large portion of the vine-strangler forest, as we're off to the northeast of the eye-shaped mass. Based on the distance, I reckon that it will be a day of hard travel to get back to Kalanthia's den, but it's definitely achievable. Once we've slept, that is.

Looking down at my newest addition to our crew, I realize that he's not going anywhere right now: the poison is still holding him under its thrall. Sighing to myself, I lean down and pick him up. He's probably about two or three times the mass of the pit bull he partially resembles, but I'm significantly stronger than I was on Earth, so it barely registers.

In fact, I can easily tuck him under one arm, which leaves the other free for a weapon. I mean, I'm hoping that I can go more than ten minutes without a fight, but past experience has often proven otherwise.

We head towards the end of the tunnel, Bastet having to chivvy the cubs along from where they've stopped to lick at a lump of spilled offal. Tasty—*not.* The feeling I get from both of my older Bound is that they are completely *done* with this underground experience. I can empathize.

The sound of bird song has never been as musical as it sounds to my ears now. The scent of the forest has never been as rich. I squint as even the dappled morning forest light overwhelms my dark-adapted eyes. All my companions are having the same issue. Apart from the lizog, of course, but he can't do much, still poisoned as he is.

As we take our first steps back out into the above world, a sharp cry rings out and a shadow passes over us.

CHAPTER FORTY-SEVEN

Grace and Deadliness Personified

I swing around as something falls from the sky, and my knife practically leaps into my hand as I do. At the last moment, both I and the falling creature check ourselves. I redirect my knife swing downwards, and the creature banks its wings to gain a little height.

The bird lands on a branch just above my head and glares down at me balefully. Disapproval and admonishment come down the Bond at me.

"You flew at us just as we finished a fight. What were we supposed to think?" I complain at her in response. The bird flips her wings and preens with an affronted air. I sigh. "Sorry for accidentally trying to attack you. Even if it *was* the most reasonable thing for me to do in that moment."

The bird stops her preening and gazes at me judgmentally. Clearly deciding that my apology is acceptable—barely—she pushes off from the branch with her strong front legs and quickly wings over to land on River's shoulder.

He looks at the bird, then at me. For all that our faces are completely different shapes, and his not having nearly the same types of muscles as mine, I can still see the deer-in-the-headlights look in his expression. Or maybe it's because of the emotions filtering over the Bond.

"Don't look at me," I tell him with a trace of mirth. "I'm already carrying something. Someone." Wordlessly, he sighs and then continues to trudge forwards. Realizing that we're currently walking without a proper destination, I look at the bird. "Do you know of a place nearby where we can rest?"

The bird cocks her head to one side, then the other. After a moment, she sends me a picture of a fallen tree. It's one of the forest giants; its trunk is probably as round as I am tall. Moreover, it obviously fell down a while ago: its trunk is mostly eaten away in the center.

"Is it close?" I check. My ally pauses for a moment and then sends me a sense of distance. It's difficult to parse since it seems to be measured more in wing beats and body lengths than anything more relatable for me, but I get the sense that it's not too far. As a bird flies, anyway. *Hah.* "Come on, then, guys," I tell my poor fellow land-bound companions.

We walk through the trees until we get to the hollowed-out log. Fortunately, much as the bird promised, it really wasn't very far; it's out of the way of the initial wave of scavengers coming to eat the leftovers of our battle, but not much beyond that. Also, while not perfect, it's a much better option than just falling asleep there on the forest floor.

Despite the time that has evidently passed, there's still a reasonably sturdy shell of wood around the outside. We can also put the cubs and Lathani further inside and have the fighters near the entrance. Plus, with us all piled in there, we're only really visible from one angle. It'll do.

I swing my newest Bound off my shoulders. He's still immobile. It makes me a little concerned, but I can see him breathing well enough. At least, I think it's well enough: it's slower than before he was Bound to me. Is that a bad sign? I check the Bond. He doesn't seem overly distressed—less than he was when we first forged the Bond, anyway.

Looking up, I see River climb into the log and lean against its wall, his spear propped next to him. It's good to see him prepared to fight if something goes wrong. I figure I'll do the same sort of thing, probably taking the other side. That way, something wanting to attack the vulnerable members of our party will have to go past all the adults first.

River, I ask, trying to direct my mental voice at him alone after seeing that Bastet has already laid her head down on her taloned front feet, the cubs cuddled against her. *How long will the poison take to wear off our newest packmate?*

Not too long, he reassures me. *It depends on how much poison entered his system, but he's already been affected for a relatively long time. He should be able to twitch soon, then the rest of his ability to move will follow.*

Okay, thanks. He nods and closes his eyes, then leans his head back against the log wall. He definitely deserves a good sleep, so I don't say any more to disturb him further.

I look at the lizog now.

If you feel like something's wrong, or the poison's not wearing off as it should, wake me by sending a feeling of urgency down the Bond. Understood? He replies with a sense of uncertainty but an acknowledgment, nonetheless. I get the feeling that he's not used to having the pack alpha pay so much attention to his well-being.

In fact, my impression is that he tries to avoid the attention of the alpha as much as possible since it almost always means that he's going to get bitten. A lizog pack definitely seems significantly more cutthroat than a raptorcat one. Strange. Anyway, not something to bother considering now. I look to the bird perched on a tree branch not far from our shelter.

Will you keep watch for threats? I ask her. She sends me a wave of reassurance as she leaps and glides from her perch to rest instead on top of the log above the entrance. *Okay, thanks,* I say, then climb into our temporary shelter.

Everyone else is already inside, asleep. Downsides of being the leader, I suppose: I need to make sure that everyone else is sorted before I can rest myself. Thankfully, I've done everything I must, so I join them, my aching body and overused mind pulling me straight into slumber as soon as my muscles release their tension.

* * *

Something's crawling on me. I brush at it, only to wince when my movement makes other creepy crawlies on me start biting.

"Ow, ow, ow," I complain as I sit up, brushing myself off frantically. Serves me right for falling asleep in a bug-infested log. Also, I can't say I'm surprised that this place has vicious insects: it has murderous *trees*.

By the time I feel free of little legs crawling all over me, I realize that everyone is staring. "Sorry, did I wake you?" Bastet is the first to answer and indicates that one of the cubs woke her a little before.

As she answers, I realize that my movement didn't hurt—besides the new bug bites, that is. My lips widen in a smile as I check my health bar and see that it's fully recovered. Obviously, we've been sleeping long enough for my passive healing to fix everything. I touch my leg, then pull off my makeshift bandage and shove the blood-stained fabric into my Inventory.

Going over my injury, I see that it's healed with only the faintest of marks remaining. Huh, interesting to see that there are *any* marks remaining—perhaps it's because the healing took some time rather than the relatively quick process of Lay-on-Hands?

Looking around, I see the lizog is sitting outside the log in a position that is so similar to a dog's watchful guard pose that I shake my head in amazement. He sends me a sense that he was already on guard and so wasn't woken. There's a hint of uncertainty in the emotions attached to the message; I wonder why, but when I reply with approval, I see his body language brighten. Maybe he just feels unsure about his place in our group? Not unexpected, I suppose. I'm distracted by Lathani's grumpy response to my original question.

You woke me *up*, says Lathani. *You looked like a beetle with half its legs torn off.*

"Thanks," I reply sarcastically.

You're welcome, she replies blithely. *I mean, I wouldn't want to be called a beetle with half its legs torn off, but maybe that's a compliment for you.* I'm not sure if she's being serious or messing with me, but I can't be bothered to try to find out.

I was already awake, River informs me. *I woke when Lathani started snoring. It sounded like a dying prey-beast*, he finishes slightly reflectively. Lathani's hackles rise.

Mother says that nunda are grace and deadliness personified; we are only seen or heard when we want to be, and then our majesty is enough to stun onlookers into sub-mission. I don't *snore.*

I would hate to be accused of lying, River answers with a solemn tone. I can't quite work out whether it's truly sincere or falsely so. *You most definitely do snore. And it was loud enough to startle me out of a lovely dream.*

No, I don't! Lathani shouts, her mental voice loud enough to make me wince. She bares her teeth and looks to be a moment away from pouncing on River, claws fully out. Although I'd probably bet on River in such a scuffle—experience wins in a roughly equal fight nine times out of ten—I decide to intervene.

"Guys, do you want to get back today or not?" I ask, my tone not loud but forceful. I've had practice in using different tones of voice to deal with a number of stressful situations. This one definitely calls for calm but firm intervention. "Because if you get in a fight, I can assure you that we won't be covering much ground due to needing to heal up."

The reminder is enough to make Lathani deflate. When River looks like he's considering poking at her again, making me suspect that he was being intentionally irritating for some reason, I give him a warning look and a jab over the Bond. Why he's deciding that right now would be a good time to tease the nunda cub, I don't know. Relief at escaping the dangers, or sorrow for what he's lost?

Fortunately, with my warning, he also deflates and looks away. "Good," I say, my tone losing its edge. "Now, does anyone want any food? We need to find a river for water." As I say that, my Tamed companion sends me a sense that there's some water not far from where we are. "Okay, change of plan. Let's go and find the water, then eat there. Agreed?" I get a round of agreements more or less verbally. Nodding in satisfaction, I make sure my mace is close at hand and we get going.

My bow is in the first slot of my Inventory: relatively easily accessible in case I need it, but not impeding my movement. I was pleased to note as I put lizog corpses into my Inventory that the arrows I wasn't able to collect automatically had gotten sorted into a different slot. I was less pleased to see that broken arrows got their own slot too; any broken arrow means hours more effort to recreate it. Then again, I suppose it's a boon if at least the heads are saved since they're the most difficult to recreate.

Against expectations, we actually manage to make it to the water source without being bothered by any other creatures. It's less of a river and more of a small pond with water flowing in and out. Not stagnant water, at least. As my companions drink hungrily, I quickly set up a small fire. It'll take a bit of time, but I have no idea where this water is coming from and don't feel like getting a stomach bug of some sort. Or parasites.

It's hard to wait, though: my mouth is dry and my throat aches for water. That said, I'm not actually as thirsty as I would imagine I'd be after so long without water. Not to mention that I wasn't exactly relaxing the majority of that time. I wonder if my increased Constitution has reduced my need for water?

I look up at the sky, then call up my Map to get my bearings. We've just walked a little northward from the tunnel to get here—I marked the tunnel on my Map before we left just to make sure I'd be able to find my way back. After all, it might have been a horrendous experience, but I can't forget that even if the Pure Energy almost killed me, I got a huge amount of benefit from the experience. And that's not even considering the Energy Hearts we harvested, which might regrow or replenish somehow.

After working out where the sun is in relation to the horizon, I determine that it's got to be into the afternoon already. The sun isn't that far from its zenith, but it's on its downward trend. We must have passed the night in the tunnels and then emerged sometime in the morning. Then slept for a while. It's been hard to estimate the time ever since I leveled so much—I haven't yet been able to determine how many percentage points towards my next level to expect in an hour, especially since my Energy absorption rate has been constantly changing.

My water's finally boiling. I take the pan off the fire and pour it into my sneleon shell, then, one-handed, I refill the wok and put it back on the fire. Blowing on the surface of the water, I wait with impatience until it cools enough for me to drink it.

It may just be boiled pond water, but to me right now, it's ambrosia of the gods.

CHAPTER FORTY-EIGHT

Home

We're almost home. I exchange glances with Bastet, and we both find our pace quickening as we recognize familiar landmarks: Here, a giant of a tree that lost its center leading shoot early on in life and has been growing slightly crooked ever since. There, a collection of rocks piled together to almost form the shape of a face when looked at from the right angle. We're less than an hour from the den. At last.

It's odd to think that, of our entire group, probably only Bastet and I recognize where we are. Lathani has most likely rarely left the den, and certainly not often enough to be familiar with the surrounding area. The raptorcat cubs are currently walking—their ability to keep up has progressed in leaps and bounds since we left— but I'd be surprised if they recognize the area after having spent most of our previous outings in a sling against my chest.

As for River, Fenrir, and Sirocco, they've never even been to the den before. I did check with River, but he wasn't part of the party that attacked Kalanthia and captured Lathani. I have to admit that I'm a little worried about the reception she will give him: she may consider him complicit despite the aid he's rendered. All I can hope is that, with him being one of my Bound, she will be as accepting as she was about the others I brought home with me. She and Bastet were enemies too when they first met.

Due to the lizog's surprisingly canine characteristics, one of the most famous wolf legends in Europe was an obvious choice of namesake. The lizog himself was rather indifferent regarding his name. It isn't something that's part of lizog culture, so he only embraced it because I wanted him to; the name itself was irrelevant.

In complete contrast to his attitude was Sirocco, previously known as "the bird." She was picky to the point of distraction. I ran out of names of goddesses linked to the wind and just started listing off other words I knew that were vaguely wind related. She liked "Zephyr" but wasn't completely satisfied with it. I kept going, but when I came up with "Sirocco" out of the depths of my memory, she sent a very clear message: the search was over.

Finally, all of my companions, Dominated or Tamed, have names. Call it a human failing, but I like to have a specific name for each of my Bound. Thinking about a creature in terms of its species just feels awkward to me after a certain point. Besides, it seems to strengthen the Bonds when I've chosen a name for my Bound.

The sun is well on its way to the horizon, but we've covered a lot of ground. After sating ourselves on water and food, we quickly set off. Despite walking for hours through the forest, we've barely seen a single other creature, let alone been attacked by one. I'm not complaining, especially without my healing Skill being available to us, but it's strange.

It's not as though the animals are not there: I've seen plenty of tracks, many very fresh. I even picked up the traces of another small pack of lizogs, which had probably only recently gone through. They didn't show hide nor hair of their presence, though.

"Is anyone aware of an event somewhere that I don't know about?" I ask trying to make a joke to cover my unease, but I suspect it's not very convincing. It's not that I *want* to be attacked, but neither do I want to walk into something the local denizens are specifically avoiding.

They're afraid, is all River says, like that explains it all. Afraid? Of us? I mean, I suppose that we're a bit of an imposing group, looked at from the outside. A lizog, a raptorcat, a human—not that the locals probably know what that means, but I'm taller than most in this area—a juvenile nunda, and a flying predatory bird. A bit different from me walking alone through the forest, I suppose.

It's odd to think of how far my little party has come in such a short time, I muse to myself as we get closer to home. It seems like a long time since I left the area with only Bastet and the cubs, even though it's truly only been a few days. We'll have to see how dynamics change once we're not under threat of attack at any moment. War and peace are very different things.

My train of thought is disrupted as a massive shape suddenly emerges from the bushes ahead of us. How she managed to hide in foliage that only comes up to approximately hip height on her at its tallest, I don't know. All I know is that a tumult of emotions breaks free at my first sight of Kalanthia.

Relief, exhaustion, fear, joy, relaxation, and emotions I cannot put a name to . . . I'm briefly overwhelmed and freeze in place for a moment, torn by wanting to give her a hug—her shoulder at least—and fearing that she'd dislike and reject it. Bastet is far less conflicted and immediately trots forwards to butt her head against Kalanthia's, the great nunda obligingly lowering herself to enable the contact. The cubs quickly follow suit.

Broken from my temporary stillness, I decide to follow them, then pause at arm's length in front of her, suddenly uncertain again. Kalanthia simply rubs her head against my torso, strongly enough that even with my fifteen stat points in Strength, I'm almost knocked over. I laugh and bury my face in her soft fur. Tears come to my eyes; the sudden release of the last few days' tension is a relief of immense proportions. I blink them back, though—I'm not going to cry from happiness, come on.

You were successful, Markus Wolfe, Kalanthia says warmly. Her tone is in no way a question: she knows we found Lathani. Is it because she knows I wouldn't have dared show my face again without the cub? Not without being significantly stronger than I am even now. Or perhaps it's just that she can smell her cub's scent on me. Or . . . How did she know we were coming in the first place?

"We were," I confirm but frown as I look around. Where is Lathani? Looking back, I spot her skulking behind River and Fenrir. "Come on, Lathani," I say encouragingly. She shifts but otherwise doesn't move. Kalanthia shifts as if she's about to go to her cub, since Lathani won't come to her. "Wait," I tell the adult nunda. "Let me speak to her." Kalanthia's massive head descends a little so it's once more level with mine.

You haven't . . . ? she asks, a growling threat in her voice.

"No!" I yelp as I realize after a moment what she's asking; I don't want to have my head bitten off. Literally. "No, it's just . . . Well, you'll see. She's a little nervous, that's all." I trot forwards a few steps before pausing and turning back to look at the giant leopard. "Just . . . don't move, okay?" I see her vibrating with tension and indecision, but with an unhappy grumble, she subsides a little. The swordlike claws scything in and out of her paws clearly say that her patience isn't anywhere close to infinite, so I'd better get my skates on.

I jog to the back of the group and crouch down next to Lathani. The juvenile nunda is pressed to the ground in the shifting shadows behind a bush with her ears back and teeth slightly bared. It's not aggression, though—nothing of the sort. She's terrified. And I'm pretty sure I know why.

"Come on, Lathani," I say quietly. "Your mom's right there. She wants to see you, greet you."

But what if she . . . ? Her voice is the equivalent of a mental whisper, barely audible despite appearing directly in my head.

"She won't. And if she does, remember what we discussed?"

Yes . . . She's silent and unmoving despite her acknowledgment. I wait for a few moments but can see Kalanthia's shifting increasing. Her patience is wearing thin.

I understand. This is her cub we're talking about. A cub who's only a short distance away, but who she's not allowed to see or go near.

"You can't hide here forever, Lathani," I tell the nunda cub. "I promise you, the tension you're putting yourself and your mother through is far worse than any outcome could be." Unless Kalanthia kills her, that is. But I reckon the possibility of that is *extremely* unlikely. It's not like Kalanthia is some dumb animal, unable to recognize her own offspring after having been away from it for an extended period of time.

Lathani doesn't respond, but I see her girding herself through her body language. With a determined air, she pushes herself to her feet and slinks towards her mother. And "slinks" is the right description: her ears are still pressed back against her skull, her tail droops low, and she looks like she's hauling herself to her execution through sheer force of will.

From a few meters' distance, I see Kalanthia take in the sight of her cub, much changed from how she was when she was taken away. *She's worried about your reaction,* I think, directing it as much as I can at Kalanthia. From the giant leopard's brief glance, I'm pretty sure that she received the message. Not that she probably needs it: if I can see how Lathani's feeling in her body language, her telepathic mother will know far more about her emotional state.

Slowly, delicately, as if she's approaching a fearful animal that she doesn't want to startle, Kalanthia steps forwards towards where her cub is once more frozen in place; even the determination that pushed her to that point was unable to make her take another step. I empathize with her: it's not easy to stare the possibility of your life being changed forever right in the face.

Kalanthia leans her head down and rubs it across Lathani. Despite growing significantly, Lathani is still so small in comparison to her mother—the head that brushes over her fur is almost half the size of her entire body. Still, I suppose it's a better relative size than being the *whole* of her body as it was before.

You're home, my cub, Kalanthia says. Her voice is projected to all of us. It must be intentional—she's far too in control of her telepathy for it to be otherwise. Whether it's meant as reassurance to Lathani that she's still considered Kalanthia's cub or as a warning for the rest of us, I don't know. Maybe both. *I'm happy to see you, no matter what changes you have undergone.*

Lathani holds her stiff posture for a fraction of a second longer, the meaning of the words perhaps taking some time to properly sink in. Then, with a strangled sound, she runs forwards to bury herself in her mother's belly fur.

The relieved chirp she makes is enough to bring those tears back to my eyes. With her still shaky grasp on her own mental projections, Lathani also sent all of us a snapshot of how she was feeling in that moment: the same kind of relief that I felt earlier, but a hundred times stronger, as her worst fear is so clearly cast aside by her mother's immediate acceptance. The scene is *beautiful.*

And then Kalanthia looks back at us and the sheer rage filling her eyes is enough to almost make my life flash before my eyes once again. She's clearly holding herself back from openly baring her teeth at us, but I'm confused as to why she's suddenly so angry. Then I see the true direction of her gaze: River.

CHAPTER FORTY-NINE

Friend

Kalanthia," I start as I step in front of the lizard-man. When those furious eyes connect properly with mine, I realize how stupid I was to have imagined she was actually looking at me before: the eye contact and mental projection behind it hits me like a blow. There are no words, just sheer emotion projected through her gaze.

When I feel wariness through my Bonds and see Bastet taking a few steps back as well, the cubs actually running back to hide behind me, I realize that it's not just me feeling this. I take a small step back involuntarily, swallowing hard. After that, though, I manage to hold my ground with sheer force of will.

I thought that I'd seen Kalanthia furious before when she thought I was trying to Tame her cub; in retrospect, she was just a little annoyed.

This . . . It's like I'm back in a Battle of Wills with the fire hose completely directed my way. Pressure beats against me trying to force me to submit, to *move*. But I won't. I *can't*.

Somehow, I know that River is only alive right now because Lathani is snuggling in her mother's fur. But even that tether is fragile and could break at any moment, leaving only me between them. I'm the one who brought River here; I'm responsible for keeping him alive.

"Kalanthia," I repeat again. "He's one of my Bound. He helped Lathani to escape. We wouldn't have made it without him." Short sentences are easier when just speaking feels like an impossible task. The pressure doesn't let up for a long moment and then the fiery emotion behind the massive nunda's eyes is banked. Not gone, never gone. Just hidden away again. I breathe properly for the first time in what feels like minutes, but was probably less than one.

Do you take responsibility for his actions going forwards? she asks. Her mental voice is forcibly calm but with the promise of explosive violence never far from it. I gulp a little.

"I do," I agree, my voice quieter than I intended. Not that it matters too much: all present have better hearing than me. "As with all my Bound," I add, just to be clear.

Then in recognition of this great deed you have done me, I shall allow the lizard-kin a reprieve this day. I shall make a decision on his fate tomorrow after all facts have been brought to light. We have much to discuss, you and I. With that vaguely threatening finish, she turns slightly to nose searchingly into her fur.

She straightens up, and I see that she has Lathani held gently within her jaws, the juvenile nunda cradled behind her mother's massive canines. Despite the growth spurt she's put on, Lathani still looks like little more than a cub dangling there. I can't imagine what she used to look like when her mother picked her up before. She was probably able to simply sit in her mother's mouth without emerging from either side at all.

I shall see you at the den, Kalanthia says before turning tail and disappearing into the forest. And I mean literally disappearing. The giant nunda reveals exactly how she manages to hunt prey despite being roughly the size of a full-grown African bull elephant: she does a Cheshire cat, displaying an ability to fade into her surroundings, and her spots are the last parts to vanish. I watch her disappear, wide-eyed. Her stealth is off the scale. I didn't realize it was even possible to vanish with such focus on her.

There's silence for a good thirty seconds after Kalanthia vanishes. We all stare at the spot where we last saw her, and I don't think I'm the only one wondering if she's still there. Once more, I'm glad that I didn't meet Kalanthia while she was hunting: I wouldn't even have known what killed me.

In the end, it's the cubs who break the silence. Although they were affected by the tension as much as anyone else, despite not understanding what was going on, they've clearly decided that the danger's over; it's time to play. The complaint of Ninja when Trouble leaps on top of her to wrestle is enough to shake us out of our stillness.

"So," I say to no one in particular, "that was Kalanthia." River, who's still standing just beside me, turns a little.

I truly believe you, he tells me, the emotions coming across the Bond showing how truly shaken he feels.

"About what?" I ask, confused.

That my people would have been doomed if I had not helped you bring the cub back. I do not think the Great Predator would have waited much longer to come searching herself.

"No," I agree, though I can't help wondering why she *didn't* come looking. Not that I'm complaining: it would have been a complete mess if we had arrived back to find her gone, especially if she had wreaked havoc in the lizard folk's village in the meantime. But we've been gone for several days, longer than Kalanthia would have expected, surely. Unless she knew something we didn't. She probably does—she's a cat, after all. Sort of. And felines seem to make a habit of knowing more than everyone else. "Anyway," I say after dismissing the thought, "let's get going."

We start moving, and Bastet falls to the back to make sure the cubs keep up. Spotting that, I order Fenrir to take her position scouting ahead. Sirocco, of course, is also scouting ahead, which means we have eyes both on the ground and in the air.

Frankly, in comparison to the way I used to have to sneak through this area, it now almost feels like it's a stroll in the park. Not completely: I'm still aware that an attack could come at any moment, but the chances are that we now have enough party members to both detect it ahead of time and deal with it when it comes. Spotting a tuft of familiar leaves, I make a happy noise. "Hold on, everyone," I say.

The rest of the cavalcade pauses briefly for me to dig up the plant. Sticking the tubers into my Inventory, I grin. *Roast potato tonight,* I think. *Ooh, with salt.* I'd almost forgotten that I have a couple of Inventory slots filled with that. It's crazy to think that we haven't been back home since going to explore the tunnel and encountering that terrifying monster.

You didn't have to do it, River tells me as we start walking again.

"Didn't have to do what?" I ask, still thinking about digging up the tubers. No, I didn't have to, but I'm tired of meat.

Stand in front of me, defend me. Oh. That's what he's talking about. I shrug, feeling a little confused.

"Why wouldn't I?" Incredulity comes across the Bond from him.

Why wouldn't you choose to step between a clearly furious powerful predator and the source of her ire? he asks with the accompanying feeling of wondering if I have a screw loose. *So much for being polite,* I remark wryly to myself.

"No," I correct him, unruffled, "why wouldn't I defend someone who has agreed to help me and who has gone above and beyond to do so. I know that you only agreed to the Bond to save your village—and we will, I promise—but with everything we've been through in the last couple of days, I can't help but feel we've become, or started to become . . . friends." It's the first time I've said the last out loud, but it feels . . . good to say. Though, I admit to being nervous about his response.

It's been a long time since I made a friend. Probably back in my university days—I don't exactly count colleagues as "friends," after all. I feel a little out of practice doing it. And maybe I'm wrong here. Maybe this is just River responding to the Bond between us. But the beginning of friendship is definitely what I feel on my side of things, and it feels good to think that maybe I can be friends with my Bound, that I don't have to be alone and starved for conversation with an equal even in this "uncivilized" world. "At least, that's how I feel. Maybe you don't feel the same," I add, nerves rolling in my belly. River is silent for a little time.

If one is in the grasp of a grunt-click-flash-of-red, an ally does not jump into the situation with him but attempts to slay the beast. Or, if the beast is too powerful to slay, offers his companion a clean death and goes to warn the village. Jumping into the grasp of the beast will merely lead to another victim, he points out eventually, side-stepping the question. Although I have no idea what he just referred to there, an image of an animal that has far too many limbs and is almost impossible to escape from once trapped comes over the Bond from his side of things. I huff in wry amusement.

"Where I come from, we have a little saying: 'Friends will pick you up from jail; best friends will be sitting in the jail cell next to you.'" River stares at me blankly.

I don't understand. What is a "jail" or "jail cell"? I shake my head. Figures the translation wouldn't work: the lizard folk probably don't have jails.

"It's a type of punishment from my world," I tell him as I send an image of a stereotypical jail cell along our connection. "Basically, it's saying that your closest friends will share both the good times and bad with you. And that's why I stepped between you and Kalanthia. I take the point that in some cases, if one person is in a bad situation, another jumping in beside them may not help. In other cases, however, they may provide moral support, companionship, or even mitigate the situation. As was the case just now. I felt it was unlikely that she would kill me, but it seemed all too likely that she would kill you."

You could not have known that. The rage . . . I sense the Bond between us shiver even though no such movement rocks his body. *I have never felt the like.*

"No, I didn't," I admit, shivering a little myself at the memory. "But from what I have experienced of her, Kalanthia is remarkably fair. I was willing to roll the dice."

But why? he demands. *I acknowledge culpability for my past actions towards Lathani.* Is this the first time he's used her name? Possibly. Unless he's used it with her directly without me being part of the conversation. *It's not like I created mischief like a hatchling; I helped do terrible things to her cub, things that will permanently affect her. In fact, you should offer me as a sacrifice to her rage tomorrow. If it will stop her from raining her wrath on my village, I will bear the cost willingly.*

I'm silent for a few moments. He's right in some ways, and it's admirable that he's willing to face the consequences of his own actions—so many are not. I feel uncomfortable as I compare my own behavior to River's standard. But as a wise man once said, "An eye for an eye makes the whole world blind." If tomorrow Kalanthia is determined to claim River's life, there's probably very little I can do to stop her, bar physically imposing myself between them again. But that doesn't mean I won't do my best to seek another solution.

Though, honestly, I'm dreading the discussion. She's right that we have much to talk about, but I don't look forward to having to argue for why Kalanthia should leave one of the participants in her cub's torture unscathed.

"Acknowledging the consequences of one's actions is important," I agree, recalling all the times I failed to do so myself and trying not to feel too much like a hypocrite, "and I have no doubt that such consequences will be part of the conversation I'm due to have with Kalanthia tomorrow. But what good does killing you do? Kalanthia will still be angry, Lathani will still be affected, and your village will still be in danger. In some ways, living with guilt is the harder option."

The words come from deep within. I took myself up to the roof because of guilt and fear. Stepping off it would have been cowardice, not bravery—an inability to face up to a thousand of my own actions and inactions. River is a hundred times braver than I was then, but even so, death isn't the answer. "If you want to make amends, we'll work something out together with Kalanthia that can actually help Lathani. And maybe, after some time, you will no longer feel guilty." I start moving again. A long moment goes by before River responds.

I consider you my friend too, he says in a voice that were it not mentally transferred directly to my brain, I wouldn't have heard. A quiet smile grows on my face that no one but the trees around me sees.

CHAPTER FIFTY

What the Doctor Would Prescribe

We climb up the hill to the den, and I can't help pausing at the top to take a deep breath. *I'm home.* It's funny to think that, but these days away have made it very clear to me that, indeed, this rough cave has made its place in my heart. I share a look with Bastet. Her eager happiness is enough to let me know that she feels the same as I do. Next, I turn to my three new companions.

"Welcome home," I tell them, a grin on my face. Fenrir looks at me, and a sense of asking permission comes through the Bond. I give it, curious about what he wants to do, and see him run off to sniff at everything. Fair enough.

Sirocco, in opposition to my other two companions, seems completely uninterested. She sends an impression of not enough trees and a preference to stay in the forest. Being Tamed and not Dominated, I don't actually have any say in the matter, so I just shrug as she wings her way back to the tree cover.

If you want to come for food, I'll be putting some out soon, I tell her. She sends me an acknowledgment of the offer but no indication of whether she'll take me up on it or not.

River takes the longest to give an opinion. His feelings are clearly mixed. It's not really surprising, considering everything. For all that Dominate has switched his focus to protecting and obeying me, his loyalties are still very much with the village that he's left behind. Why wouldn't they be, when the other lizard folk are all he's ever known? Because of that, I can understand that calling this place "home" isn't likely to come easily.

It's not what I expected from the den of the Great Predator, he finally muses. I raise an eyebrow.

"What did you expect? Something bigger?"

No, more bones, he says completely seriously. I laugh.

"The only bones Kalanthia keeps around are for Lathani to play with. She's not big on home decor, honestly. Come on, let's get settled in."

The first thing I do is to check on my beans. To my dismay, something has clearly been through while I've been away, or perhaps while Kalanthia was out of action. All five bean shoots have been massacred. Sighing with disappointment, I gloomily hope that they might recover. My hope stems from the fact that, unlike beans on Earth, samova beans have several shoots. There's the first shoot, which is the main leader, but it's not the only one; the plant itself looks more like a bush than a vine when full-grown. Fortunately, despite me not watering the patch for days, I can still see hints of green. If the plants get enough time without being eaten again, they might regrow.

"Fenrir," I call and see the lizog's head shoot up from where he's sniffing around in my erstwhile firepit. "If you smell anything around here, come and chase it off. Kill it if you can without leaving the hill top." He sends me eager acceptance of the order, then continues sniffing around.

That dealt with, I enter the cave hoping that it is in a better state than my farming attempts. Kalanthia is there, curled up with her back to the entrance. Reading the mood, I don't even greet her. I guess Lathani's there too, but I honestly can't see any indication of her presence. I have a feeling her mom's not going to let her go any time soon.

Quickly ducking into my alcove with River following, I fear the worst. Fortunately for me, the inside of the cave seems untouched. Maybe it smells so much of a massive predator that no creature around here is willing to investigate, even if they did gather the courage to come close enough to eat my samova beans.

All my stuff looks exactly like it did when I left about a week ago, at least. I haven't kept up to date with marking my days, so I've lost track a little, but I decide to quickly make note of them now. Within a short time, I'm sitting back shaking my head as I realize only five days have gone by since I was last here. It feels a lot longer.

Setting up the fire and sparking it doesn't take long, and soon its flames send flickering shadows across the room. After tucking the potato things near enough to the fire that the heat will cook them, but far enough away that they're not likely to be charred, I start preparing a new soup. After days of only meat, I'm rather sick of the taste again, so I just prepare some newly harvested pondweed and more tubers in a vegetarian stew. If my beans *do* recover, I look forward to adding them in to future soups.

While all this cooks, I start going through my Inventory. I've got a large number of corpses to deal with. Obviously lizog ones, but also the animals we hunted previously: killer chickens are the most numerous, but there's also that mini triceratops, the monkiles, the remains of those rolling woodlice things, and that nasty venomous creature from the vine-strangler forest. I'll do that tomorrow, I decide. Then I push myself to my feet with a small groan—my Bound will also be hungry. On my way out of the alcove, I almost jump as I see River standing by the entrance.

"You don't have to guard me here," I say, half joking. He snaps his jaw slightly to indicate his nervousness. Another look at the way he's positioning himself says it's because of his close proximity to the "Great Predator." "Seriously, if you're uncomfortable inside, you can stay outside." He shifts a little. I wait patiently—I'm pretty sure he wants to say something, but I'll wait for him to tell me rather than prying it out of his mind.

What am I to do here, Markus? Out there—he waves vaguely in the direction of the forest—*I knew what to do. I was guard, guide, and fighter. Here . . .* I get it. He's feeling lost. I consider the matter carefully.

"Well, frankly, I'd suggest having a break. We've all been under a fair bit of pressure over the last few days, and we've been running on very little sleep. A bit of relaxation and time to eat in order to return to a state of calmness is probably just what a doctor would prescribe. Why don't you take the time to consider what you want your role in this group to be?"

He frowns.

My role?

"Yeah, if you want to continue being the spearman, or if you'd prefer to take a different combat role. Or maybe . . . You made a big difference to the fight with the lizogs when you made the poison; if you could create potions that help us and hinder our enemies, that could be even more useful than being on the front lines." His tail sways gently from left to right and then relaxes again, a gesture I've come to understand is similar to a nod from us. "Look, come with me now. I'm going to put out some food for everyone to enjoy. Take some time to think about it and then let me know."

Very well. I have to admit, I'm a little surprised that you are giving me the choice. I assumed that you would be the one to decide my role, he points out gently.

I shrug.

"You know yourself far better than I know you; if you think you'd do best in a certain role, who am I to contradict you?" He doesn't respond, but his tail sways once more and he follows me out.

I open my Inventory and pull out the first couple of carcasses I get my hands on, then set them out in the shade for my companions to help themselves. By chance, they both happen to be lizogs—perhaps because they were the last ones to be added, they are the easiest to access. Suddenly hesitating, I turn to Fenrir.

"Is this . . . okay?" I mean, they were his pack, after all.

Of course, I should have expected the response I get: Fenrir is as practical as Bastet and his answer is complete indifference. Meat is meat, and that's all the corpses are now. Well, at least I have a good meat supply for a while, and although I'm determined to do some crafting after I—hopefully—fix my various issues, we can always go on a hunting trip if necessary.

However, between all the tasks currently facing me, my priority is definitely to sort myself out. It would be more convenient if the notifications telling me about my problems also indicated what I could do to solve them, but in the absence of that information, I'll just figure it out. I pointedly don't allow myself to entertain the possibility that what I've done to myself might be permanent.

After returning back inside, I continue organizing my Inventory. The Energy

Hearts stay inside, as does the salt. I don't know whether Energy Hearts can lose Energy if they're exposed to the air, but they seem okay in my Inventory. Similarly, salt does better when it's kept dry, so there's no benefit to pulling it out of my Inventory when I don't have to.

My torch remnants are a different story. I decide that one of my first crafting tasks will be to make a few more of them and stack them in my Inventory. My recent experience has proved that I need a few on hand at all times. In the interest of not accidentally setting curious raptorcat cubs on fire, I leave the flammable substance from the salamander in my Inventory too; I'd like to experiment with that a bit. I think I better take my own advice about having a rest now, though: I'm mentally exhausted from so many high-stakes situations. Hopefully, my upcoming discussion with Kalanthia won't count as another of those.

I finish rearranging my Inventory by basically returning my suitcases to it. I had them out because they were taking up a slot that was needed for other things, but now that I have so many unused slots, I'd prefer to keep all my precious belongings safe and close at hand.

When I'm done, my alcove looks a lot barer than it did when I entered; apart from things that need to be dried or otherwise processed, I've packed everything away. Even my crafting materials such as the snilepede legs, which I hope to use as fishhooks later. Or possibly as hooks for armor . . . *Hmm, there's a thought.*

Going through my Inventory also reminded me about the crocodile and salamander hides I still need to process. That's going to take some days, but I can get started on it tomorrow too. But first, food, and then . . . Well. The *other* thing that is constantly at the back of my mind.

After eating a satisfying meal of soup and baked tubers, I go outside to settle down. The sun is once more heading towards the horizon. Considering the length of the days, they pass pretty fast. Sitting in a nice sunny spot, I watch my companions for a moment.

The cubs are happy, playing with each other over a bone, not hungry but just having fun. Bastet is watching, more relaxed than she's been in days. Fenrir is eating, his large head buried in the body of another lizog about the same size as him. I wince and hope that he's not going to get any disease or parasites from his cannibalism. River seems to be doing what I am: sitting and basking in the sun. He, too, looks more relaxed than I've ever seen him. As for Sirocco, I can sense that she's sitting in the trees not that far away. She feels satiated, so either she came down for a bite too, or she found something in the woods that she likes.

After a few moments of peace, I open my status screen. Time to check on what's been happening there.

Name: Markus Wolfe		Race: Human	Class: Tamer
Level: 12	Energy to next level: 18%	Energy absorption rate: 26u/hr	Energy towards debt: 75%
Intelligence	36	Mana: 331/331 (-8%)	
Wisdom	36	Mana regeneration rate: 720u/hr (-20%)	
Willpower	42+8 (+20%)	Health regeneration rate: 40u/hr (-20%)	
Constitution	19	Health: 190/190	
Strength	15	Stamina: 90/90	
Dexterity	15	Stamina regeneration rate: 150u/hr	
Class Skills: Dominate – Novice 3 Tame – Beginner 6 Fade – Initiate 1		Non-Class Skills: *Lay-on-Hands – Journeyman 2* Stealth – Novice 1 Animal Empathy – Novice 6 Meditation – Novice 4 Energy Manipulation – Beginner 2 Sensation Management – Beginner 5	

As expected, little has changed. I've advanced a bit in some Skills, namely Dominate, Tame, Lay-on-Hands, and Animal Empathy. Each advanced a single level except for Dominate, which advanced two. *Because of Fenrir? I guess so. But why two levels?* I shake my head—maybe one day I'll understand this system, but it's not today.

I find my Energy absorption rate interesting. It's at twenty-six units per hour, and when I was here before, it was at thirteen units. Unless the Energy density has somehow changed, it means that something I've done since being away has dramatically changed how much Energy I can absorb—and that's not even using Meditation.

I'm now gaining as much Energy per hour here as I was in the lizard folk's village. Maybe this is the answer to how people at higher levels continue to improve— I had been wondering that when I realized how much Energy I now need per percentage, and that's only at level *twelve*. But if we are able to access more Energy the higher our level, that issue might have solved itself. Or is it not just because I've increased in level? Is it to do with my choices in stat points? Could it be to do with my increased Wisdom? Intelligence? Or something else?

Despite the increased Energy gain, my Energy store has only changed by two points since leaving the tunnel, and that also reflects all the Energy I received from helping kill off a whole pack of lizogs. Now that I'm in an area with a stable Energy absorption rate, I'll have to see how long it takes me to gain a point; that will give me a better idea of my current state.

I saw a notification earlier that informed me my Core has been damaged by another percentage point, and I can now see that reflected on my status screen. A single percentage doesn't seem like much, but it's reduced the total mana I can store by three units. I have to guess that it happened when I needed to heal myself earlier, when the lizog bit me. Clearly, I'm continuing to somehow suffer damage to my Core when I try to use magic. And I need to work out why.

Closing my eyes, I try to enter that state I found before. Time to find out exactly what I did to myself—and how to fix it.

CHAPTER FIFTY-ONE

Intricate Weave

It takes a few tries to reach the same space I somehow managed to reach during that whole debacle with the Pure Energy. Not that it takes any real effort to enter Meditation—that's easier every time I try it, especially since it ranked up. The issue is in finding the twist to make it an internal rather than external view. When I first enter Meditation this evening, I'll admit to finding myself thoroughly distracted. It's the first time I've engaged my Skill with an external view since gaining all those points, and the difference is *stark*.

Before, I saw connections spanning between me and those closest to me, as well as some vague links between other things and the world around. The connections between the vine-stranglers and the earth below was the strongest. I guess those were the trees' links to the thick Energy density of the tunnel, which explains their rapid growth. Now I realize that I was only seeing a fraction of what is present. In fact, I could probably only see a fraction of a fraction, as I doubt that I can see everything even now.

What I see as I stare with wondering mental eyes at the world around is like . . . roots. Luminous, intangible roots. Before, all I could see were the taproots, the thickest and most obvious of the plants' network. Now, I can see far more of the intricate links that stretch all around me. If they were solid, I would be unable to move because of their number. I wonder whether I could somehow gain control over the links . . . and if I could, what would happen?

Drawing from the link with River led me to drain mana and then health from him to replace my own. Which raises interesting questions about the nature of mana and health in general. I know that I can use Lay-on-Hands to replace health, but can I use health to replace mana?

But this wasn't what I started Meditating to think about. I return to trying to switch to an internal view and succeed a couple of minutes later. It turns out that it's mostly about willing myself inside myself, though that makes little sense when I put it into words. I find that, like going into a healing trance, I lose almost all sense of my physical body and become able to see the light within me, which has to be my mana. Just like when I accessed this space the first time, I am able to see a bright light at the center. This time, though, I see a network of dimmer but still bright golden threads everywhere else—except in one place: my hand, of course.

As I zoom in towards the center, the network undergoes a change. No longer does it appear to fill the shape of my body but instead becomes a spherical shape of intricate, interweaving lines. Has it changed, or have I just changed the way I'm looking at it? Or both. I can't help but feel that physical rules hold little sway in this space.

Deciding to start at the center, I zoom in further. My Core is a mini star burning like a sun within the solar system of those interweaving lines. A sun contained within a fractured glass bubble. The hair-thin lines, which create a beautiful, stomach-churning pattern, should not be there—I sense this instinctually. This must be the source of at least one of my reductions, most likely to my mana pool since that was the one affected by damage to my Core.

The sight is disturbing. I somehow *know* that if that container were to ever completely break, the center would truly act like the sun I'm likening it to and burn through me. Whether that would simply destroy my ability to use magic or actually kill me, I am uncertain, but I don't want to find out.

The light inside is a bit calmer than it was last time. Its glow is mostly constant, with a few flares every so often accompanied by a commensurate dimming afterwards. It's all still feeling very tender, but I don't feel quite as on the point of disintegration as I did back then. These are all good signs. The fact that the actual cracks in place on my Core do not seem to have improved in the time since they were created is not so reassuring. In fact, if anything, they've gotten worse. Does that indicate that the cracks have caused the reduction to my mana pool? That's the only stat that has shown deterioration.

I suppose if my Core is where my mana is stored, it would make sense that cracks to it would worsen when I access and draw out some of that mana. It would also make sense that damage to it could lead to a reduction in the amount of mana I can store. The pain I experienced when I activated Lay-on-Hands would also make complete sense in that context too. Following the same logic, if I wish to be able to cast magic without pain, I'll need to find a way of healing the cracks in my Core.

In hopes of finding inspiration on how to do this, I look at the rest of the damage. Focusing closely, I zoom in to look at the myriad filaments of light that surround my Core. They spool away from the glowing sunlike center and form an intricate weave that at first glance just looks like a single piece of unbroken fabric, barely visible thanks to the sun at the center obscuring them with its sheer brightness.

Getting closer to one of the hairs of light takes little more than a thought. It's impossibly thin, more like spiderweb than anything else. Yet I sense that it's far stronger than spider silk despite its thinness. I try to trace a thread from the Core, but I quickly lose track of it as it disappears among the mass of others. Trying to get a better view of the whole, I move back outwards again. Mentally frowning, I try to block out the light from the Core so I can actually see the details.

The longer I focus, the more I am able to see those glimmering lines weaving through the space. It's a bit like stargazing after having just left a bright room: at first, I can only properly see the most obvious threads, but over time the rest fade into view. They were always there, but it's only as my eyes adapt that I become capable of seeing them, hidden constellations of light revealed to patient eyes.

Such is the sense of discovery as slowly, bit by bit, the whole design is revealed. And what I see is an impossibly intricate design, something far beyond the capabilities of any human even to conceive, let alone make. Perhaps a computer could have, but even then, there is a life, a vibrancy to this network of threads that would surely not have been present in that case.

If the design of the mass had remained in the shape of my body, I might have thought that the lines of light were acting like the magic equivalent of blood vessels, transporting mana instead of blood cells around my body. Even when it shifted into a more spherical shape, I half expected to see some relation to my organs. My brain and heart, at the very least.

What I actually see is more like an impossibly intricate 3D mandala formed in the shape of a sphere with my burning Core at the center and multiple individual lines trailing off into the darkness around it. I move slowly around the edge of the sphere, looking at it carefully. Every position I take shows different aspects of the sphere, and slowly I start to realize that a few small areas are far more intricate than others. In fact, some areas are practically simple in comparison.

As I take my time over examining the lines, sensing that this is something important to understand, I realize that the particularly intricate areas look . . . different from the rest of the design. And certain areas are more different than others. I move around the whole of the design several times, verifying that what I noticed is correct. Finally, I'm pretty sure of my observations.

There are nine areas of particular intricacy, each self-contained. Three of them have a similar . . . character to the whole sphere. The lines move in similar patterns. They are more detailed, but they fit with the rest of it. The other six areas are different. Each of them has a different character both from each other and from the rest of the sphere.

One is full of flowing lines, which somehow manage to never intersect with each other. Another is hard to truly identify, as the lines seem to move a little every time I look at them. Another is full of dead ends, as Energy seems to double back on itself from one angle, but from another I can see that it's traveling at right angles to where it was originally. And the others are different again.

Regardless of similarity or difference to the greater sphere, I can see that each section links to the body of the weave around it. The sections that better match the character of the surrounding sphere link up with it flawlessly, their connections flowing from the center of the intricate area to the sun at the center of my being. The areas that are very different from the character of the surrounding sphere are a different story. In three of them, there are several loose ends where the line just . . . stops.

It's hard for me to conceptualize, and I doubt I'd be able to explain it to anyone.

I observe through some sixth sense that the lines aren't truly lines. I'm just identifying them as such because I can't visualize what they are. Some lines are more sounds than visible lines; others are like the brush of a hand to my cheek or a feather's touch. It's uncomfortable to think about exactly how I sense these things or what they really are. I stop thinking about it when instinct tells me that if I question too much, I will lose the ability to do it at all. I simply return to my observations instead of wondering *how* I can observe them.

Over time, I can't help but wonder whether these areas are in some way linked to my Skills. It would make sense. Three Skills are linked to my Class and therefore have to have some similarity between them, and six Skills are not, which would explain the disparity. If that's so, the corollary would be that the rest of the intricate web is somehow linked to my Class. Or maybe it *is* my Class. I'll have to think more about the possible consequences of it being one or the other.

Either way, my time spent touring the web and trying to work out what it is has been useful for also working out why I'm suffering from a reduction in both mana and health regeneration rates. There's a big obvious hole in the side of my sphere. It looks a bit like an ice cream scoop has taken a chunk out of the sphere and left fraying ends dangling in a blackness darker than any other area.

The frayed ends don't look at all healthy: the bright gold of the Core dims to blackened copper, then to nothing at all. Even if I hadn't spent so much time admiring the intricate design of the rest of the sphere, I'd know that this was wrong. Beyond the fraying connection, beyond the disturbing blackness, there's a sense of something missing. Is this what the Pure Energy did to me? Is this why I was in so much pain? It wasn't consuming my flesh but something else that is integral to my Class?

I suppose that if my theories are correct and the overarching sphere is my Class and the areas of particular intricacy are my Skills, then I suppose it might make sense that I can't choose any more Skills while I have the problem. What if a Skill needs to connect into lines that are currently ending in a frayed end? Or what if the Skill needs to be placed in the spot where there's just blackness? Or maybe I'm looking at this the wrong way. Perhaps I can't access the Skills because my Class needs to be completely present in order to be able to access my choices—a bit like computer programming, where one error may cause the whole program to engage the blue screen of death.

The problem is that identifying the source of the problem is one thing. Fixing it is something completely different.

Zooming into the space, I find myself unable to enter the blackness. If I try, I am shunted around to the closest frayed end of a connection. And if I try to enter from the direction of the sphere, I can't move past where the connection fades away into nothing. Maybe closer observation will help?

CHAPTER FIFTY-TWO

Cracked Core

'm feeling fatigued, and the sense of bodily pain is intruding even into this non-physical space. Deciding to take a short break, I withdraw back into my body. It's always a strange sensation, and there's always a moment where my body feels like an ill-fitting suit. When I'm fully settled into my physicality once more, I wince—my head feels like it's several sizes too small, and my brain is pounding in complaint at the fact.

Funnily enough, the sun doesn't seem to have moved much from where it was when I entered my inner space. I spent what felt like hours examining the sphere and the bite chewed out of it, but it seems like only a couple of hours have passed at the maximum. Is it because I existed as a mind almost separate from my physical form that my judgement of time was so inaccurate?

I take some time to eat and drink—despite having eaten not long ago, I'm *starving*. I also take a moment to loosen muscles that have stiffened up over my period of inactivity. Unlike getting stiff on Earth, my improved Constitution means that it only takes seconds of movement here for my muscles to release their tension. I continue wandering around and swinging my arms; the calm, aimless movement also serves to release mental tension, causing my headache to slowly reduce.

Probably about another twenty minutes or so later, I feel a lot better. My headache is gone, and I have significantly more energy. If mental energy had a regeneration rate, I reckon that mine would jump after eating and drinking a little and thinking of nothing. I take a moment to check on my companions—not much change there—and then return to my spot. It's not in the sun anymore, but I don't mind: the temperature is on the cooler side, but it's still pleasant. It'll get cold later, but by then I should be inside with a warm fire.

Closing my eyes, I dive back in. The sphere is waiting for me, the route to finding it easier with practice. I navigate to the area with the unnatural blackness, eager to try out something based on some fairly simple observations.

Both my Core and the filaments are the same color and seem to glitter in the same way. My Core is far brighter, but the substance seems to be at least similar. If my Core holds my mana, then does that mean the filaments are made out of mana too? I figure it's worth testing because if I'm right, then maybe I can recreate the connections *with* mana.

It seems like an impossible task. The sheer intricacy of the design is breathtaking;

to think of actually having to recreate it is daunting. However, I sensed something the last time I focused on one of the broken connections. Wanting to double-check, I zoom back into that area.

I focus on the connection, concentrating hard. Yes, I was right. There's some sort of . . . ghost connection? Like ashes showing where something was before it burned, or a fading smell in the air after someone walks past with strong perfume. It's only a little beyond the edge of the connection, but I can sense where the line used to go. If that sense continues even if—when—I manage to redraw the line, then I should be able to follow it like I'm using tracing paper.

It's a mammoth task. Truly intimidating. But I've got to do *something*. Not only are there connections hanging around in mid-air, meaning that I can't access any new Skills, but I'm increasingly sure that this kind of damage is slowly degenerative. Already, if I look at the faded end of a connection for long enough, I can see it becoming a little dimmer.

In the grand scheme of things, the damage is practically imperceptible, but if it is degenerative, I can't afford to sit around and hope that I can fix the issues in Nicholas's world.

While focusing on a single connection, I split my attention, my increased Intelligence allowing me to do that sufficiently. One half of my focus is on the faded end itself; the other half follows the line through the weave all the way back to my Core. I tease out the tiniest speck of mana that I possibly can. Due to the minuscule thickness of the connection, especially as it moves further away from the Core, even the tiniest fraction of mana I can extract makes the golden thread look like a snake that's eaten a massive pumpkin.

The bead flashes down the connection, moving by itself. It travels far quicker than I was expecting. When it reaches the end of the thread, I barely have enough time to focus on following the ashen trail of the faded end before it appears.

The thread grows by a noticeable fraction as the end extends a little more into the blackness. Even as I watch, though, the color dims back to old bronze or dim copper rather than bright gold. Still, my theory has been proven: I have a way to regenerate at least some of the connections.

My celebration proves to be premature, however. Enthused by my success, I try to grab a bigger bit of mana—with unfortunate consequences. A sharp pain goes through me, and an ominous cracking sounds as my Core shudders. I focus my attention on the glowing sun—if I had a mouth in this space, I would curse.

I stare in dismay at the glowing center of my internal web as the cracks spider-webbing around my Core expand just a little more. It's not much worse than before, but I have a feeling that it'll be reflected in my stats even so. After pulling out of the nonphysical space, I quickly bring up my status screen.

Name: Markus Wolfe		Race: Human	Class: Tamer
Level: 12	Energy to next level: 25%	Energy absorption rate: 26u/hr	Energy towards debt: 75%
Intelligence	36	Mana: 327/327 (-9%)	
Wisdom	36	Mana regeneration rate: 720u/hr (-20%)	
Willpower	42+8 (+20%)	Health regeneration rate: 40u/hr (-20%)	
Constitution	19	Health: 95/190	
Strength	15	Stamina: 90/90	
Dexterity	15	Stamina regeneration rate: 150u/hr	
Class Skills: Dominate – Novice 3 Tame – Beginner 6 Fade – Initiate 1		Non-Class Skills: *Lay-on-Hands – Journeyman 2* Stealth – Novice 1 Animal Empathy – Novice 6 Meditation – Novice 5 Energy Manipulation – Beginner 4 Sensation Management – Beginner 5	

My mouth set in a grim line, I acknowledge that my fear was, unfortunately, spot on. Once more, I've suffered a reduction to my mana capacity. The fact that I gained it when trying to repair the connection by a small fraction is not a good sign. If that continues happening, I'll reduce my mana capacity down to nothing in very little time.

Even if there were no other consequences to such an action except for losing the ability to store mana, that would put paid to my efforts to repair the intricate connections, which I suspect are my internal matrix. As it is, I suspect that causing such damage to my Core is likely to have far more serious consequences.

I sigh. Perhaps I shouldn't have tried to start with the golden threads but rather begun with the Core itself. The problem is that I still have no idea how to repair the Core, and with this clear prohibition on any sort of mana draw, I don't even know where to start.

On the positive side, I've gained proof of concept for the idea of regrowing the connections—as long as I continue to have a sense of where the connections should go, that is. Hopefully, the degeneration doesn't speed up. Another positive is that even this small action has pushed me up two levels in my Energy Manipulation Skill; raising that Skill higher should make my job easier and quicker, potentially offsetting any problems with leaving the repairs until later.

However, it does appear that I need to fix my Core before I can even attempt to repair anything else. How I do that is another question. I lean back and stare sightlessly up at the darkening sky above.

None of my companions have a Core. River seems to know what they are, if

Energy Hearts are the same thing, but he doesn't have one and seems to only know about them in the broadest of terms. Based on what had to happen to me to cause it, I suspect that someone cracking their Core while it's still in their body is not a common event. I can ask, but I can't hang my hopes on him knowing anything about it.

Kalanthia is someone else I could ask. I strongly suspect that she has a Core, and maybe she's even into the next stage, if there *is* a next stage. Whether she'll know about *cracked* cores is another question. As is whether what I have is the same as what she has. However, I really doubt she's in a sharing mood at the moment: she's currently cuddling with her cub and still giving off very distinct "Do not disturb" vibes. Interrupting her at the wrong time could prove worse than useless. Hopefully, she'll be more open to discussion tomorrow—I *really* don't want to leave it for too long if I can't work out anything myself.

For all that I never had it before coming to this world, mana has really become a major part of my life, particularly for healing myself and my companions. Considering how many times one of us has been injured or even close to death in the last week, I definitely don't want to be walking around without some way of dealing with injuries beyond slapping a bandage on it.

And what happens if I try to level up? Will it stress the Core further? Or could that actually be a way of healing it? Well, that's a while off—my Energy store isn't exactly growing fast. Actually . . . Could I be losing Energy? Is it possible? I shake my head. Too many questions that aren't much use asking. I've got a cracked Core; I need to fix it. End of.

I push myself to my feet and walk over to River, who's sitting in the shade looking a touch lost. After hesitating for a moment, I decide that interrupting him might actually be a good idea, might give him something else to think about. He looks up at me as soon as I approach, so I sit down heavily next to him. With hope in my heart despite myself, I ask River if he's ever heard of a cracked Energy Heart.

A cracked Energy Heart? he repeats doubtfully. *It's possible to grind the shards that crack off Energy Hearts to dust. My . . . Honored Herbalist does that to make her potions particularly powerful. But as far as I know, the Energy Heart just breaks away in chunks. It doesn't crack through entirely. And if it did, I have no idea what solution you could apply—putting a herbal compress on it?*

I thank him but refuse the offer of a herbal compress: I don't know if my Core is even a physical object in my body. If it is, I suspect it must be somewhere important, like inside my heart or my brain or something; there's no way I want anyone digging around in those! Plus, the whole idea sounds about as reasonable as the medieval remedy of rubbing salt into the brain to cure madness.

Well, I might as well see what I can find out today, and then I'll talk to Kalanthia tomorrow about it. Closing my eyes, I return to the trance state. This time, instead of inspecting the weave of glimmering connections that surround the Core in a glittering net of gold, I go straight for the Core itself.

At first, the bright sunlike glow is too strong for me to look directly at the mass, let alone see any details. Then, like I'm wearing a filter that blocks out progressively more of the light without changing the color, I become able to not only look at the sphere but differentiate the outer wall of it from the rest. The ever-moving sea of light within it certainly seems to indicate that it's filled with liquid. Is it Energy? Mana? The Pure Energy went straight into it before, filling it beyond its capacity. So, is it Energy? But then, I was able to control the little bit I pulled out to heal the filament, and I drew mana out of it for Lay-on-Hands. So, is it mana?

Inspecting the surface, I notice that though the cracks are deeper than the first time I saw them, they're not *that* deep—yet, at least. Maybe this is why I'm suffering "only" nine percent of damage. Each crack has spread a little with branching lines forming off them like a crack in glass. Needing to know what happens to have even a chance of finding out how to solve the issue—even if it causes me more damage— I experiment.

Already mentally prepared for the pain to go through me again, I reach gently for a bit of mana and imagine that I want to feed it along one of the connections. Moving almost in slow motion thanks to my intense focus, I see the glow brighten in one spot. It then starts bulging out from the body of the Core. Trying to put a physical description to it, I can only say that it looks like liquid oozing through a permeable solid—perhaps like blood dripping through already blood-soaked fabric.

As the drop emerges, I *see* my Core take damage. The wall shifts very slightly, and the movement, just like with glass or diamond, causes the whole structure to fracture ever so slightly more. Unlike with a true crystalline structure, however, a single fracture doesn't then lead to the whole structure losing its integrity. However, the damage isn't localized only to that spot: to my dismay, the cracks all over the surface deepen a little. Already braced for it, I feel the sharp pain again despite having barely any sensation of my body at all. Maybe it *isn't* actually a bodily pain anyway. I don't need to check my status to see that the damage has reduced my mana capacity further.

I return to my body, wanting to think about it for a while. I stand and look around for my companions. The sun is on the horizon; twilight is almost here. Bastet and the cubs are already inside the alcove, curled up. Fenrir is still on guard, and Sirocco is somewhere in the trees. River, however, is sitting and looking at me thoughtfully.

"What?" I ask, a little defensively.

You are remarkably vulnerable in moments like that, he notes. *I spoke to you, but you did not answer.* My shoulders rise defensively before I sigh and forcibly relax. He's not criticizing; he's just highlighting a weakness.

"I didn't realize it was that bad," I reply after a moment. "But thanks for letting me know." If I'm so unresponsive to stimulus, I must make sure to only go deep into myself when I'm somewhere safe. *Actually* . . . "Could you do me a favor? Try shaking my shoulder when I'm in it." He sends acquiescence over the Bond and moves towards me. I hold up a hand. "Just give me a moment."

Closing my eyes, I reenter the trance, by now able to use Meditation to find it within a few seconds. I don't try to explore anything about the intricate weave or my Core; I just wait. It seems like a long time before I feel a faint sensation of being shaken. It's like it's happening to someone else and all I'm feeling are the echoes of the sensation down a Bond or something. I open my eyes.

You felt that, then? River inquires. I nod.

"Yes. Faintly, though. If I was deep in concentration, I might not actually feel it at all. Also . . . did you wait a long time?" He tilts his head to one side.

No. Only a long breath. I nod thoughtfully. Okay, so time does move more quickly when I'm in my inner world. Interesting. And useful? Potentially. Then I realize that River said he was trying to talk to me earlier.

"What did you want to say to me when you tried to contact me and couldn't?" I ask.

I merely wished to find out where you would like me to sleep. Forgive me, I would rather not be too close to the Great Predator. Ah. Yes. Since I'm the host, I really should have sorted this already.

I take a moment to look inside the alcove with an eye to seeing how much space is left. Bastet and the cubs really don't take up much room, curled up as they are. My bed takes up a little less than half of the space. I could extend it by laying down some more clothes to cushion us from the hard, cold floor. Once more, I'm hit by a longing for a proper mattress. I shake my head to redirect my thoughts.

"Okay, so would you prefer to sleep inside in the warmth but be in an alcove off Kalanthia's cave, or sleep outside where it's colder, but you're further away from Kalanthia?" River takes some time to consider the matter.

My kind do not do well with the cold, he says finally. *And it is already chillier here than I am accustomed to at this time of year. I would prefer to be warm rather than outside in the night's chill. Could the Great Predator easily access me inside?*

I hesitate. "Well, not *technically,*" I finally say slowly. "She can't fit inside the alcove, and it would probably take a bit of swiping to get at you. But that said, she's the one who *made* the alcove, so I doubt it would take much effort to . . . unmake it." River's spikes flash in concern.

Then the Great Predator could collapse the rock upon our heads at any time? he asks nervously.

"Arguably, yes. But frankly, I don't think you'd be any safer sleeping out here," I point out a little awkwardly, since I don't have any good reassurances for his concern about Kalanthia killing us all with a cave-in. "You saw how easily she jumped out at us from the bushes; if she'd been hunting us, we'd have had little chance, and that's with all of us in a state of alertness." The colors of his spikes shift to a bright yellow that speaks of an intense fear. "But so far, she has proven as good as her word, and she said that she wishes to hear the whole of it before making any judgement.

There's a very good chance you're safe for tonight. I'll have to convince her to extend it beyond that, though."

River snaps his jaws a couple of times, then clearly forces himself to relax.

Very well. I will trust your interpretation of her character. Though, as I said before, if my death will save my village, I am willing to offer it.

"And I said that I'm going to try to find another way," I tell him, feeling a little exasperated at how he seems to have fixated on the idea of dying a martyr. Especially when I doubt that Kalanthia would be satisfied with just that. "Anyway, if you'd rather sleep inside, we can make some space for you. Otherwise, it's up to you to work out the best place to sleep out here."

No, I would prefer warmth. Resignation and fatalism come across the link between us.

"And do you usually make a bed of some sort, or do you just sleep on the ground?" He sways his tail from side to side in his equivalent of a shrug.

We often pull in some leaves to cushion the ground slightly, but it's not necessary.

"No, it's okay. If I just lay some more clothes down, we should have space. I recommend you sleep against the wall since I'm not going to bed yet." He lifts his chin for a moment.

I appreciate your kindness. Raising an eyebrow, I shrug.

"Just basic hosting, man. I wish I had a proper bed to offer, but I don't, unfortunately. Anyway, I'll join later."

Then I wish you luck with your Energy Heart, he says before briefly tipping up his chin once more and heading into the cave. I frown at his back. I'm getting a weird energy from him . . . Then something he said sparks an idea. Could that help me?

Pulling out an Energy Heart from my Inventory, I tilt it back and forth, admiring the way it picks up light in the darkening twilight. Even without the light from the Pure Energy nearby, the jewellike crystal gleams and sparkles like there are polished facets *inside* the structure. I take a moment to examine it again. Energy Heart is what River calls the Core inside me, the same as he calls this. Perhaps there are some similarities that could help me repair my own Core?

Once more catching the delectable scent, I'm highly tempted to use the one sense on it that I haven't so far. Then, deciding that it's unlikely to cause any more problems than I'm already deal with, I give in to my curiosity. I've already absorbed this stuff through my hand with no problems; why would absorbing it anywhere else make any difference? Hoping I'm not making another mistake, I dare to touch the tip of my tongue to the Core and lick it slightly.

It tastes as good as it promised, a bit like honey that has been stored in the same pot as a chili pepper—a sort of spicy sweetness, which zings through me. *Hmm, I wonder if it's possible to cook with these?* If adding shards to potions increases their efficacy, what could adding them to my meals do? Perhaps it's worth experimenting with at another time. Right now, though, I pull it away and quickly activate my status screen.

Again, there are no notifications, and my health isn't showing any sort of drop—at least *that* hasn't changed. Like last time, my Energy absorption rate has leapt back up to crazy figures. This time it's even higher: over two thousand units per hour. It lasts a bit longer this time, perhaps ten seconds.

Once more, the few units of Energy I gain are nothing to what I reckon I need to work towards another percentage point, let alone towards my next level. Still, as a proof of concept, it's interesting. And if I'd come across this thing when I was level three or four, I'd probably be benefiting a lot more from it. Then again, I'm not complaining about having jumped eight levels within a few minutes, as long as I can fix the damage it did to me.

On that note, time to see whether I can do anything with the Energy from the Heart to help with my Core.

I touch my tongue to the stone again since that seems to be the longest-lasting method, barring breaking off a shard. Then I drop back into Meditation. Almost in slow motion, I see a bead of brightness traveling along a group of threads that have their end points all in the same area. The brightness moves up the threads and then enters my Core.

I withdraw from the space and look at the Energy Heart thoughtfully. My instincts urge me to use magic to heal the cracks in my Core as I would heal an injury. The problem is that getting at the mana in my Core just creates *more* damage; unless I can outpace the damage with the healing, it won't make much sense to do it that way. But what if I can use *external* Energy?

Of course, in order to even consider that as a possible solution, I need to answer a pivotal question: can I control Energy entering my system in the same way that I control my mana?

Determined to find out, I take a good lick at the Energy Heart and sink into myself once more.

I see the wave of light rushing at my Core from the same spot as before. Zooming in closer, I try to take control of the Energy. It feels slippery, like I'm trying to grasp a bar of soap in a bath. Even when I think I've got my fingers around it, it shoots away from me. I attempt it over and over again, my attempts taking on a more frantic air as we approach my Core.

The Energy seeps through the wall around my Core and fades into it without causing any damage to the walls of it. I watch in frustration as the last of the light fades without me having been able to affect it in the slightest. But I don't give up. I sense that this may be more of a case of "not yet" than "not ever."

I return to the physical world, take another lick, then dive back into my inner world. Again, I fail. Again, I try. Again, I fail. I repeat the cycle several more times. I even break a shard off the Energy Heart in hopes that the elongated period of Energy will give me more chance to grasp a mote. It does; I still fail.

I question whether to give up on the idea or not. It is, after all, just intuition telling me that there's a path through this way; perhaps it's just my imagination wanting to see opportunity rather than a valid possible method. Then again, what other ideas do I have right now? Maybe I'll get some more from Kalanthia tomorrow, but I might as well try this one until I'm too tired to keep going. It's not like I'm using up much of the Energy Heart with each attempt.

Setting to with grim determination, I try and fail, try and fail, try and . . . succeed?

For a fraction of a moment, I manage to actually hold the slippery Energy. Then it twists free, and I lose it again. However, even that ever-so-fleeting success was enough to give me hope. I try again and again, and each time I show a little progress at improving my grasp.

When I reach the point of actually being able to grip the Energy, I next have to try to guide it the way I would guide the healing energy of Lay-on-Hands to my wounds. The Energy fights me. It's not the docile, calm healing mana that I'm used to; this is more like trying to herd cats. And, with my recent experiences looking after Trouble, Ninja, Stormcloud, and Lathani, I feel like I'm sufficiently expert in the subject to tell.

However difficult it may be, it's not actually impossible, and I start to make progress. It feels like I'm taking hours over it, but my frequent returns to the physical world prove that actually less time is passing than I thought. Less doesn't mean none, however, and the second moon is starting to rise before I manage to get any proof of whether my idea might even work at all.

When I finally manage to grasp a small part of the light rushing into my Core, redirect it to the wall of my Core, *and* succeed in controlling it enough to feed the Energy into the crack, I'm ecstatic to see the results. Almost like repairing a windscreen by filling in the crack in the glass, the Energy sinks into the crack and mends a small section of it.

Looking at the number of cracks all over my Core and the tiny section that I've spent hours trying to repair, I should be dismayed, dispirited. But I'm not—I'm ecstatic! I've successfully proven that this is a method that can be used to repair my Core without causing further damage.

I'm also tired, not just physically but mentally. Deciding that further efforts right now would probably have diminishing returns, I instead push myself to a standing position and stretch my stiff muscles. Checking my status, I'm not surprised to see that there's no change to any of my reductions; I've only made a very small change to a big problem, after all. I *have* gained two percent of progress towards my next level, though—a testament to just how many times I've had to lick the Energy Heart. The diminished size of the Energy Heart is another indicator, despite how little of it I used each time. It's probably about two-thirds of the size it was before, even though I only broke a shard off it that once, licking it all the other times. *I hope that we'll have enough for all our needs,* I think to myself with a little dismay. *And that the cave will regrow them in time.*

We might have harvested lots of the Energy Hearts, but Bastet and River deserve to have a large share in the bounty, as they're the ones who harvested the bulk of what we have. Then Kalanthia may want some for Lathani. And I want them as well for healing my Core. And perhaps my other companions would benefit from them.

Suddenly, the piles of Energy Hearts that I have in my Inventory seem far too few.

Well. Something to consider another day. For now, it's time to sleep. Heading towards the cave, I take a moment to touch my Bonds to check on my companions.

Sirocco is in the trees, her Bond sleepy, though with the sense that she would easily rouse if necessary. River and Bastet are much more deeply asleep; obviously, they feel safe enough where they are. River seems to be having some uneasy emotions, perhaps bad dreams. I try to send soothing sensations down the link, and a soft smile creeps onto my face when his emotions calm down in response. As for Fenrir, he's not far and is still wide awake. I send a questioning feel down the Bond to him wondering if he'd like to come and join us in the cave. A moment later, he comes running, his scaly hide reflecting the moonlight as he gets closer, his whole being full of excitement.

"That's a yes, I suppose," I say to him wryly. He replies with an image of the whole lizog pack piling together to sleep and a sense of wistfulness. Well, I suppose that makes sense, then. Together we head inside. River is a lump on my bed, curled towards the wall and leaving plenty of space for me. Maybe I won't need to add more clothes to my "mattress" in the end. Bastet is curled up near the fire with the cubs tucked underneath her outstretched wing.

Yawning, I use the light of the fire to get changed into some fresh clothes; these ones are smelling rather ripe. Then, almost falling into bed, I find that it simply feels good to be home. My last memory is of feeling Fenrir nestle up to my side, his simple delight enough to ease my mind into sleep.

CHAPTER FIFTY-THREE

Face the Music

The next morning, I wake up to something I haven't seen since arriving in this world: rain. Well, actually, I wake *really* needing to pee, then realize that it's because of the sound of water falling heavily outside. I quickly go to the cave mouth to watch the downpour, then stick my hand out into the rain and feel it run down my skin.

"Good thing we got home when we did," I remark to Bastet as she comes to stand at my hip and thunder rumbles overhead. She sends a feeling of distaste over the link accompanied by happiness that she's inside and away from the downpour. Fortunately, Kalanthia clearly considered the risk of flooding and the cave is designed so that rain comes off the overhang onto a space in front of me and then flows away from the cave mouth, down a slight slope. Doing my business from the doorway of the cave, I'm struck by an idea and eagerness rises in me.

On my way back to the alcove, though, I hesitate for a moment and eye Kalanthia, fully aware that we need to have that conversation. I sense an undercurrent of trepidation making River jittery. I wonder if he slept—I wouldn't blame him if he didn't.

"Kalanthia . . . ," I start quietly. A low rumble makes the air around me vibrate. Okay. Not now, apparently. "Sorry," I murmur to River. He sways his tail in his version of a shrug, trying to pretend that it doesn't mean anything. *I just don't think we should push it if she's not ready,* I explain apologetically through the Bond.

It's fine, Mas—Markus, he replies and then walks out into the rain, raising his face to the sky as if savoring the feeling. It reminds me of what I wanted to do.

Going into my alcove, I grab my soap and shove it in my Inventory. Then, walking out into the rain and a bit away from the cave, I glory in the feeling of raindrops falling upon my head. I never would have thought that I'd miss it, but it's surprisingly pleasant. When I strip off my clothes, I do shiver a little, but it's not much colder than a refreshing shower—a free one from the skies. Besides, my improved Constitution can probably cope with a bit of cold.

With some time on my hands, and tired of stinking up whatever room I'm in, I decide that it's also time to do a bit of laundry. After taking my soap out along with a pile of dirty laundry, I let the clothes start soaking in the downpour while I soap myself up.

Dirt streams off me in rivers, the accumulation of not just normal sweat, ash, and blood, but also several level-ups' worth of nasty residue. Frankly, I'm surprised the lizogs couldn't smell me, even with me being downwind! I've been an offense to my own nostrils for too long—not to mention everyone else's.

River joins me in using the rainfall as a shower, and Fenrir joins us to just have some fun, as far as I can tell. I get the feeling that Fenrir is pretty young because he's frolicking in the water like a puppy who's never seen it before.

I glory in the feeling of the dirt washing away, in the feeling of *finally* being clean. My soap is rough, nowhere near even the cheap stuff I used to buy for myself, let alone the nice smelling moisturizing type Lucy would buy and insist on us using. At the time I'd objected on the grounds of not wanting to smell like a garden, but I had secretly enjoyed the soft feeling of my hands afterwards. When she left, I went back to buying cheap soap, not even able to look at the other type for the memories and regrets they brought back to mind.

I sigh, mixed emotions filling me at the recollection. Yet, part of me is grateful for the memories, even if they can be painful. Now, without being able to see photos on my phone, my memories are the only evidence that life existed before this world. That I loved and was loved. Even if I lost it in the end, one way or another.

Pushing the thoughts away, I center myself on the present. Memories are good, but getting lost in them isn't. I look at my soap and grin humorlessly. At least it does the job, and ultimately, that's the most important thing. In this new reality, practicality far outweighs aesthetics.

Naked, I next set to cleaning my clothes, scrubbing them as best I can. There's no getting most of the stains out, not without hot water and industrial-strength detergent, but if I can at least get rid of the encrusted dirt and smell, they will be more practical. Of course, I then hit an issue of where to put them when I've rubbed away as much of the dirt as I can. After a moment of thought, I use the low bushes dotted around the hilltop as my drying racks, spreading my clothes out one by one over the plants.

By the end of my task, the bushes look rather odd, adorned with man-made garments as they are. Still, the rain should serve to rinse out the soap, and then they'll dry out when the rain stops. Either way, it's saved me a trip down to the river! I've even managed to fill my water containers just by putting them outside for a bit.

Finally, my hunger driving me inside, I return to the cave and take a few moments to drip at least partially dry just under the overhang. Once I'm not pouring with water anymore, I head back into the alcove and grab a jacket from my bed to use as a towel. *I need to make a better bed . . .* I sit down and start hungrily munching a few bits of meat and some more of my soup from last night, then pull out a carcass for my Bound—it might mean I have to clean the area later, but I won't force Bastet and the cubs out into the wet just out of a misguided desire to keep the house neat.

Finally, when we've all eaten and I feel like River's about to vibrate out of his skin, I hear the call.

Markus Wolfe, we need to talk. I wince, feeling like it's a visit to the headmaster: glad that it's finally there, but dreading it, nonetheless.

"Sure," I respond, trying to keep my emotions out of it. "Just let me get dressed, and then I'll be right out." I'm impressed at how level I've managed to make my voice, though I wonder how much Kalanthia sees through my attempts.

Very well. Do not be long, she warns, and then the sense of her presence recedes. It's interesting to notice that, actually; I was never aware of when she was "paying attention" before. And I'm sensing a lot more of her feelings now than I did before. Either that or she's making a particular effort to project them.

I quickly pull out a shirt and pair of shorts. No underwear—they're all "in the wash." It doesn't feel much like battle attire, but I could probably be wearing plate armor and still not have much chance against Kalanthia if she felt like killing me. I might as well be comfortable.

Time to face the music.

Cleansed in Blood

And then you found us, and you know the rest," I finish. Kalanthia looks at me steadily, silent for a few long moments. She's been the perfect listener to the tale of our adventures, though I've been uncomfortably aware the whole time of how tense River is, which has taken all of the joy I might otherwise have felt out of the telling.

I didn't leave anything out—not the attacks we encountered before reaching the lizard folk's village, nor the plan we enacted to retrieve Lathani. I didn't even try to hide the discovery of the Energy Heart cave, knowing that she would question their presence otherwise. I'm filled with shame as I retell how, despite being so cautious over my Bound's reaction to Energy Hearts, I still couldn't stop myself touching the Pure Energy. Retelling the battle with the lizogs and then our journey back finishes the tale.

You must have the luck of the gods. Or perhaps the favor of one. To have survived as many impossible situations as you did . . . She shakes her head as she speaks for the first time since I started. We're sitting in the cave; it's still pouring outside. The four raptorcats are also inside, and the cubs are playing happily with Lathani. I'm glad to see that the young nunda is back to her happy-go-lucky self. Lifting the burden of worrying that she didn't have a home to go back to has done her good.

"Yeah, I recognize that I was pretty lucky to survive the Pure Energy," I admit, then decide to take the bull—or nunda—by the horns. "But can't you see how instrumental River was in getting Lathani, and us, out of danger?"

I quail a little inside as Kalanthia's lips pull back to bare her teeth and a fearsome snarl rumbles through the cave. It's deep enough that I feel its throbbing within my chest more than I actually hear it. Her telepathic presence feels like an angry predator ready to strike. For all that, I don't sense that she's about to attack *me*. It's probably just as well that River is out of immediate view, though.

He may have aided her escape, but only after he helped cause her untold damage. Do you dare try to defend what he did to my cub? she demands, her voice a blast of scorching heat in my mind. I wince, hoping she's not doing any actual telepathic damage—it feels like she could be.

"I'm not defending their actions—"

You set yourself between us yesterday, you advocate for him today, and you claim not to defend him? I ignore her interruption and carry on like she hasn't said anything.

Normally, I wouldn't dare to do that, but I sense that River's life is very much in the balance. Like I said to him last night, I will do my utmost to find a resolution that will not demand his death. Not even to save his village.

"—but he helped rescue Lathani. We might not have gotten her back if he hadn't retrieved her, setting himself against his whole village in the process. And he's expressed his regret for playing any part in what happened to her. Additionally, he was probably the one with the least influence: he was not party to her initial kidnap, and I believe it was the shaman and herbalist who did . . . what they did to make Lathani . . . grow."

Grow, Kalanthia snorts, the incandescent rage in her eyes and body language fading to deep sorrow. She breaks eye contact with me as she twists around to watch her cub romping with the young raptorcats. *Do you know what they've done to her, Markus Wolfe?* She turns back towards me, the anger lighting her eyes once more. But now I can see what it truly is: a bone-deep sadness at what has befallen one she cares for immensely, and a helpless rage that she was unable to prevent it.

My heart aches in sympathy and I have to stop an automatic response to reach out to her. I know the feeling—as a parent, it must be even worse than what I went through. It's Kalanthia's duty to care for her cub; that she couldn't must eat at her like acid. The pain no doubt drives her to lash out at anyone she feels is linked to its cause. And River, much as I hate to admit it, *is* responsible, though only in small part. That doesn't mean I want to see him torn limb from limb in pointless retribution, though.

"I don't really know," I admit, answering her question. "Something about taking power from her spirit?"

That's one way of putting it, she agrees grimly. *Another is stealing the potential of the future to give power in the present.*

I frown.

"I don't understand."

Clearly, she says cuttingly, *or you would not defend one who has done this to my cub. To put it in blunt words, the lizard folk have taken the power of Lathani's Evolution, taken literal years from Lathani's life. Years she will never get back. They have used that power to fuel unnatural growth, twisting what she had before to become something that she has not yet earned. It is potent magic, and potent magic always has a grave cost.*

"How do you know?" I ask, my mouth dry. That sounds . . . serious.

It's not the first time I've seen something of this sort, Kalanthia replies, her eyes suddenly distant. Images flicker into my mind, images of darkness, of pain and fear. Of loss. And then the images are gone, like Kalanthia hadn't meant to send them and was now taking herself in hand. Or paw. Her mien firms, and her telepathic presence gives off the sense of implacability. *A wrong has been done, one that can only be cleansed in blood. Not only for the past sins, but also to prevent them from happening again in the future.*

I don't know what to say. Those images very much felt like it wasn't just seeing something similar happen; it felt like the experience was far more personal to her. And now it's happened to her cub. If I were her, I'd be raging at the world, wanting to kill everyone who did the terrible deed to her cub, and more.

She's also right about preventing this happening again in the future. From what I have learned of the lizard folk so far, I doubt they are likely to realize their error here. They don't seem to see any creature other than their own kind worthy of dignity or respect. Their intention to imprison and deprive me of basic necessities until I became willing to craft for them was proof of that, as was their attack on Kalanthia in the first place.

But I can't just step aside and let her take out that anger on River. He's my Bound; he's under my protection. And even if I manage to make him the exception to her slaughter, he's made it clear that he won't be able to just stand by and watch his village be destroyed. Heck, our initial agreement was all about him sacrificing his own freedom for the benefit of his village.

I shift in place, my mind racing. *What can I say? Is there anything I can suggest that could be a path forwards?* My mind races but comes up blank again and again.

Suddenly, a shape approaches dripping with water. I look up from my seated position: it's River. Grim determination is in his eyes and firmly present in the Bond. I scramble to my feet as I realize what is in his mind, our conversation yesterday ringing clearly through mine.

"No," I say to him firmly, though desperation rings more clearly than authority in my voice. "We'll find another way. I promise." The way my voice breaks slightly on the last word must reveal more than I'd like about my doubts. Gratitude comes across the Bond from River even as his spikes roll gently with green-tinged yellow. There's no shift to his determination, however.

Markus . . . Master, thank you. I appreciate your protection, but I must ask your permission to do this.

"I thought I asked you not to call me that?" I say weakly, some small overly optimistic part of me hoping that by diverting his attention I might be able to stop this. It was a poor attempt that goes nowhere. He ignores me and continues speaking.

I am beset with guilt and must own up to my own deeds. I played a part in Lathani's transformation; I must bear the burden of the consequences.

"The smallest part!" I object.

A part, nonetheless, he says, refuting my attempts to absolve him of blame. I grimace and look away for a moment.

"How does this solve anything?" I ask finally, my voice quiet, grief already filling me. How is a single life going to satisfy Kalanthia's rage? But yet, if River wishes to try, who am I to stop him?

River seems to sense my acceptance of his wish to do this, and although sadness rises within him as well, his determination is not diminished in the slightest. If anything, it becomes firmer.

As I said before, if my blood can wash away the sins of my village, I will sacrifice myself willingly. All I hope is that my service to you so far has been sufficient compensation for you to continue seeking a way to eliminate the threat posed to my people by the Forest of Death.

"I will," I promise him, sighing as I realize that this is going to happen whether I want it to or not. For all that he still sometimes calls me Master, that's not who I want to be to him. And if all I am is the leader of his party, then who am I to dictate what he does with his life when it doesn't put the party at risk? Even if he's hell-bent on ending it.

There's a beat of silence as he just looks at me.

After a moment, I realize that right at the beginning he talked about seeking my permission. Grumpily, I just wave my hand and then step back and cross my arms. I have a feeling that the Bond probably better communicates my mixed emotions over it all: the desire for it not to be happening at all, the sadness that it seems to be going forwards anyway, and my acceptance of his choice. Either way, my "permission" seems sufficiently communicated.

With a flash of sadness mixed with pride coming over the Bond, River lifts his chin high in the air and sends a final message to me.

It has been an honor to fight beside you, Markus Wolfe, he tells me formally. My posture softens a little as I respond.

"And you too, Runs-with-the-river." The equivalent emotion of a sad smile flashes across the Bond to me, and then he turns away. As he steps towards Kalanthia, I refuse to look away. If he's walking towards his execution, I owe it to him to watch every moment of it.

River looks so small against Kalanthia's bulk, especially with her standing. He's not much shorter than me, but his head barely comes halfway up her chest. Her jaws could end him in a moment, a single snap enough to behead him. Even if he had his spear, he wouldn't stand a chance, but he's left the spear somewhere else. Probably in my alcove.

I could stop this, even now. I can't affect Kalanthia in any way, but I could order River to run. I have to fight against my urge to do just that, but with over forty effective Willpower points, it's significantly easier to take control over my own desires.

To force River away from this path would be a betrayal. I had my chance to forbid it, to withhold my permission. But then I would genuinely have acted as his master. Now, funnily enough, I reckon that using the Bond to potentially save his life would actually be worse than forcibly Dominating him in the first place would have been. He's made a decision; to force him to act otherwise would be a travesty. Even if that means he dies today.

It's hard to stand and watch, but I imagine it must be even harder for River, standing in front of the massive predator as he is—the Great Predator.

Pausing in front of the adult nunda, easily within her attack range, he sinks to his knees with his long-toed feet splayed out awkwardly behind him, his chin raised high in the air. It's a very vulnerable pose—there's no easy or quick way out of it. I have no doubt that it was chosen exactly for that reason.

I kneel before you, Great Predator, as representative of my village and my tribe. We are guilty of crimes against your cub. Before the ancestors, I declare that I wish to make whatever small amends I can for myself and my people. He snaps his jaws slightly, his nerves clearly taking over in that one moment.

Even if I hadn't been able to read that much in his body language, the emotions leaking over the Bond would have made it clear. I'm sure that Kalanthia can also pick up on his fear despite her lack of direct connection to him.

River continues speaking. *If my blood is what it takes to assuage your rage and wash our guilt clean, I offer it freely. Even my life is yours for the taking, should that be the price of my village's salvation.*

CHAPTER FIFTY-FIVE

An Odd Binder

There's a long moment of silent stillness. The playing cubs seem to have picked up on the tense atmosphere and have ceased their play. Instead, the three raptorcat cubs have clustered around Bastet and are watching with wide eyes. Lathani took several faltering steps towards us but has now paused hesitantly a few meters away from the center of the action. Even Fenrir has approached the cave and is crouching in the mouth, seemingly trying to make himself as unnoticeable as possible while still being able to watch.

None of us dare to twitch, barely even breathing, as we wait for Kalanthia's response. Finally, she moves, lowering her head down. Using one paw, she taps at his jaw with a control that only showcases the prodigious strength she's declining to use. Her gesture encourages him to open the eyes he squeezed shut and look up. He does and she meets his gaze. I see a shudder go through his body, his jaws sagging slightly open.

What part did you play in the torment of my cub, lizard-kin? I "hear" Kalanthia's words as if from down a long tunnel. Focusing on them, I realize that I'm hearing them through the Bond: she's not projecting them to everyone, just to River. Her tone is hard and cutting in a way that I've never felt before. Even blunted by being passed through the Bond, I still sense its edges. It's only because of what I can feel from River that I realize the very nature of the Bond is designed to prevent damaging effects from passing straight through the Bond to affect the Binder.

The lizard-man is in pain, mental pain, as Kalanthia's telepathy scours his mind. I remember her once telling me that she couldn't read my thoughts; I now wonder if she *wasn't* rather than that she truly *couldn't*. Because that's certainly what this feels like: a mental attack.

My Bound reacts in exactly the same way I would have encouraged him to: he hurriedly offers up the memories of exactly how he behaved with her cub. River is clearly nowhere near the deft hand with telepathy that Kalanthia is—as he offers up the images for her perusal, he also accidentally sends them down the Bond too.

I watch images of River caring for Lathani, changing her water, giving her food . . . and making sure she drank the potions mixed by the herbalist. His care is brusque and emotionless, but for all that, it isn't rough or cruel in any way. It's clear that taking care of Lathani was a task like any other, and one he would do to the best of his abilities. That was all.

Then, although unasked for by Kalanthia, River continues by offering up further memories of pulling Lathani out of the cage, handing her out to me, then running through the village and the forest while being pursued by his people. He adds memories of spending time with Lathani as we traveled, getting to know her a little. I hadn't realized how much they had talked while I wasn't paying attention. He ends with a more vocal thought. *I didn't think of her as a feeling being who would be missed; I now realize I was wrong—we were wrong. I humbly offer myself up to your fury, Great Predator.*

With that, the razor blades of Kalanthia's attention leave River's mind. I open my eyes, not remembering when I closed them. No longer focusing so intently on the Bond, I fix my attention instead on Kalanthia. I feel the attention of my other Bound sharpen on Kalanthia as well. We all know that the next few seconds will either lead to River's salvation . . . or his doom.

The moment stretches, the tension becomes unbearable. When my lungs start clamoring, I realize that I've forgotten to breathe and quickly remedy the situation.

Finally, Kalanthia responds. Fortunately, it's not to bite the lizard-man's head off.

You were part of my cub's torment, but your Binder is correct—it was only the smallest part. The rage that was in her tone previously has cooled. It's now verging on icy, and I almost shiver to hear it, even secondhand. *You have already made some amends, and your decision to offer your life to me in recompense speaks well of you. Yet . . .* She trails off, and I feel a knot tighten in my stomach. *Yet, you are Bound, so you offer me something that is not truly yours, and I know that your Binder has expressed discontent with your choice of action.* Her tone is measured, pensive. *Markus Wolfe, what say you?*

I startle a little, not having expected her to so suddenly include me. The clarity of her voice indicates that she's intending to project to me, rather than me just overhearing it through the Bond as I was previously. Processing her words, I swallow, my throat dry, and responsibility settles heavily once more on my shoulders.

Refusing to let the weight of it paralyze me, I step forwards, my thoughts racing. I use the short time it takes me to come level with River to construct an argument I hope is good enough to save River's life.

"Not that I feel he needed to, but River has already asked for permission to offer you his life in payment for the actions against your cub. I will not stand in the way of whatever you choose—to do so would do him a disservice. However," I add hurriedly and swallow again, licking dry lips, "I hope that you will be merciful, that you will leave him his life. He is repentant and has worked hard to bring Lathani back to you. And I would miss him greatly." The formality is infectious; the whole situation has such a sense of solemnity to it that I can't help but adopt it.

You could easily replace him if I did take his life as my due. The lizard folk are numerous, she offers neutrally. I shake my head.

"Perhaps I could Dominate another lizard-kin, but it wouldn't be *River*. I cannot replace the person I've planned with, fought alongside, and conversed with.

He's more than a tool—he's a friend." I came to that conclusion yesterday while walking through the forest; I'm not going to shy away from it now.

And if I choose to leave him his life in exchange for repayment from you instead, what say you? My heart skips a beat as relief and anxiety mix inextricably. Still, there's only one answer I can give, only one answer that I can accept from myself. I look her square in the eyes, determination in my heart.

"Then that's what I would do. Of course, I hope we could work out better compensation than my own head, if only because I just rescued your cub at your request." That was, after all, exactly what I was aiming for from the beginning of the conversation. Kalanthia just looks at me curiously for a few moments.

You are an odd Binder, she says finally, *to fight so hard for your Bound when just days ago you were enemies who would have as soon killed each other.*

I refuse to break eye contact.

"It does not seem so odd to me. They do what they can for me; I do what I can for them. That we might have been enemies without the Bond is immaterial. Can you truly tell me that if you and I had met while you were hunting that you would not have killed me without a second thought?"

No, she replies, a hint of amusement in her voice. Looking away, she prods River with one of her great paws. Fortunately, her swordlike claws are sheathed. *Get up,* she orders, her voice cold once more. *Your Binder has agreed to recompense me, so I choose not to take your life in payment for your crimes against my cub. It would displease me to bring sadness to the heart of the human who has kept my cub alive twice over.* River scrambles to his feet but moves no further, determination still emanating from the Bond. I feel apprehension fill me. What is he going to do next?

And my village? he dares to ask, even though it looks like it takes every ounce of his courage to not just run away now that the reprieve has been given to him. Kalanthia lifts her lips again and snarls a little at him, but the sound is incomparable to the rumble that filled the cave earlier.

You are impertinent, she complains, though with only a slight edge, like she's unsheathing her claws to show their threat but doesn't actually intend on using them—yet. *I shall discuss your village's fate with your Binder. Now, away with you, before I regret my mercy.*

River seems to sense that's as much as he's going to get out of her without annoying her further. Either that or he finally gets the warning from our Bond, which I've been trying to send him ever since I felt he wasn't completely done.

Whichever is the case, he raises his chin to bare his throat and then walks nervously away from her. He doesn't go far, just crouches against one of the walls of the cave, but it's far enough to symbolize that he's leaving it in our hands. A sense of hopeful trust comes across the Bond, and it increases the sense of pressure I feel to find a good solution.

Kalanthia settles back to the ground and her posture relaxes a little. In response, everyone else relaxes a little bit. The cubs go back to their play, and Lathani comes over to press herself to her mother's underside. Fenrir disappears back into the rain, and I sit down. I sense that the atmosphere has changed a little: Kalanthia is now open to negotiation, where before I had the feeling she was hellbent on pursuing blood.

"What do you want in exchange for the lives of River and his tribe?" I ask bluntly. In my experience, some negotiating parties need to be approached gently, a consensus brought about more by vague implications than outright demands or offers; others benefit more from bluntness. This situation is most definitely one of the latter.

Why do you care about your Bound's village? They are not even allies of yours. In fact, I would hazard a guess that they would kill you on sight, the massive nunda points out.

"Probably," I admit. Either that or try to capture me again and use me for my crafting skills. "But they matter to him, and so they matter to me." Musing, I add a further thought, "They only mattered to me before because they hurt two beings I care about—you and Lathani. I was angry at them then for that reason. Now . . . If I seek revenge on Lathani's behalf, or stand aside while you do, I'll hurt someone else I've come to care for. So, while I'm aware that you don't *need* me to stand aside in order to do whatever you want, I hope that we can come to some agreement where everyone benefits."

I see, she says thoughtfully, cool reason now permeating the aura around her instead of the fiery and then icy fury of before. *Then let us negotiate.*

"You said that you had two concerns, I believe," I start, remembering back to what she said at the beginning. "What they did to Lathani in the first place, and what they might do in the future. Is that correct?"

It is.

"Let's start with what they did to Lathani, then. I understand that seeking the deaths of everyone even peripherally connected to the deed would be satisfying. Heck, I want to bash the head of that shaman in myself. But ultimately, it wouldn't change anything. You mentioned that what they did was to use future potential as fuel for the present. What are the consequences of that, and is there any way of repairing whatever damage was caused?" Kalanthia eyes me, hints of her previous fury returning to her aura.

The lizard folk have done my cub wrong. They have stolen years off her life. They would have done worse had you not intervened, but I do not hold what they have not done against them, no matter their intentions. However, the fact remains that they have stolen from her, and I will have restitution for that and a guarantee that they will not pursue this course—or any similar one—again. She shifts position a little. *You ask what the consequences of their actions are. It is the severe weakening, even destruction, of her foundations, something that will have significant impact both on her ability to grow her internal channels and to Evolve to the next stage. All because of the greed of a pack of wretched reptiles!*

"I see," I say, though I don't really. Channels? Foundation? Stages? I understand all these words, but not in this context. "Now, I'm not defending what they chose to do in the slightest, but I was wondering at their antagonism towards you in the first place."

What is the relevance? Kalanthia demands, a warning rumble in her throat. I swallow again but dare to push forwards a little further.

"Well, when trying to negotiate a contract, it's always helpful to have all the background information. So, in this case, is it true that you attacked them first?"

She bares her teeth at me, the rumble turning into a true growl. I don't mind admitting that my stomach clenches in fear—her canines are longer than my *head*.

They wandered into my hunting grounds and dare to claim that I was in the wrong for hunting them? Her snarl increases in volume. I pat the air placatingly, eyeing her cautiously.

"They haven't claimed anything! I was just speaking to River about the start of the hostilities. I didn't realize they'd gone into your . . . territory." Her rumbling snarl subsides and her lips droop to mostly cover her teeth.

They entered my hunting grounds and I hunted them. Like ants, more came, following the trail the previous had left. I killed them too. More and more came until, like with ants, I chose to leave rather than clear out the nest. The rumble in her chest grows a little in volume again. *Perhaps I should have—they could not have kidnapped Lathani if I had wiped out every single one of them.*

"Ah," I say, trying to do my best to project calm through my voice. That certainly didn't go where I wanted it to. "Let's put gratuitous . . . uh . . . *hunting* to one side for a moment. What do you consider to be the restitution they need to pay?"

Kalanthia stares coldly at me for a moment, murder still dancing in her golden eyes, but eventually breathes heavily and places her head on her paws, relaxing a bit.

To be blunt: Energy. To even begin to make up for what they have done, they need to help Lathani absorb enough Energy to rebuild her foundations and reach her Evolution. Even now, I do not know how badly she has been impacted—whether she would still be able to reach Evolution eventually, though at a speed that would make it difficult for her to reach the next stage in time, or whether she would never Evolve at all. Providing enough Energy to help her repair the damage and transition is the least the lizard folk can do.

I frown in confusion.

"You mean with Energy Hearts or something." Kalanthia tosses her head in her version of a shrug.

Or by offering themselves as sacrifices for her to rip their throats out and eat their flesh. At the very minimum, I require the deaths of their leader, who decided to attack me and kidnap my cub, and the other who created the concoctions that tortured my cub—preferably at my claws. For the rest, it matters not to me which option they choose.

"I reckon it'll matter to them," I mutter to myself, though I tacitly acknowledge her desire for the shaman's blood. I can't say that I have any desire to argue against that. Then I direct my words to Kalanthia again. "And River?"

He is yours, she tells me bluntly. *I shall not harm you by taking his service away from you. As for restitution, he cannot provide any that does not steal from you. I shall hold his debt in abeyance until or unless you should choose to release his Bond.*

"I hadn't thought of that," I admit after a moment of thought. I sigh and rub at my temples as a grimace spreads across my face. It's true from a certain point of view: any beast he hunts to bring back to her is one he's not bringing back to us; every Energy Heart he chooses to give to her is one less he could use himself and weakens the party as a result. Though, that point about "holding his debt in abeyance" is a bit of a threat.

I promised to release him if I couldn't find a solution to the threat of the vine-stranglers, after all. Considering I'd probably just be releasing him to his death, it doesn't really feel like an option now. Though . . . "I want to help Lathani too," I say slowly. Is there a way of satisfying everyone? "What about if we take Lathani hunting with us? That way she could both earn Energy and learn how to fight." Kalanthia gazes at me thoughtfully.

I was planning on taking her out with me, she says finally. *I can hunt and immobilize prey much more efficiently than you, I suspect.* It's a good point.

"Well, then, what about if we bring back any Energy Hearts we find? Or I can give her some of these," I suggest as I pull one of the Energy Hearts from earlier out of my Inventory.

Kalanthia perks up in evident interest.

You found these in that cave you described?

"We did. Bastet and River seem to think they would be useful for progression. Perhaps they could help Lathani?"

The giant leopard leans forwards and sniffs at the Energy Heart. The fist-sized crystal looks like a mere drop of blood compared to her massive nose.

Are all of the Energy Hearts you found the same as these?

"I think so," I say with a shrug. "They're all roughly the same color, though some are bigger and some are smaller."

Kalanthia huffs. *They are not entirely suitable for Lathani. Too many will hurt more than help—unless the lizard folk have twisted her more than I think,* she finishes darkly. She shifts into a more considering mien a moment later. *I will accept six of them in part payment of your Bound's debt. The rest must be Cores you find in beasts while hunting. Bring me nine more Cores the size of this Energy Heart and I will consider your companion's debt cleared.*

"All right, I'll do that. Thanks," I say to her gratefully, then pull out the six she's asked for. She passes her paw over the six gleaming Hearts, and they sink into the earth like they're sitting on quicksand instead of rock. I see this as the olive branch I'm sure it is.

Kalanthia has all the power here; that she is willing to negotiate and offer alternative solutions in the face of what has been done to her cub, which I still don't fully understand but accept as being hugely damaging, is more than the vast majority of people I've known would do. Most people aim to grab as much for themselves as they can. Not Kalanthia. This is a different way of negotiating, and I'm coming to think that it's a better one.

"On to the question of the rest of the village. We've discussed restitution, but you also expressed a worry about them repeating the actions." I don't say that I agree, though I do. "What sort of guarantees would you need in order to be satisfied that the lizard folk won't cause harm to Lathani in the future?" I have a feeling she wouldn't be willing to accept a verbal contract.

Apart from killing them down to the last egg? she asks archly. The worst thing is that she's only half joking—and that only because she knows I'll dismiss it as an option immediately.

"Apart from that, yes," I say with a little exasperation. Then my eyes light up as a potential solution comes to mind. "What about an oath, like you and I swore at the beginning of our acquaintance?" Kalanthia eyes me thoughtfully.

I would not be satisfied with an oath, not with creatures that have already proven their hostility. I was willing to risk it with you because I sensed that you held no ill feeling for either of us—the reverse, in fact. They are too fallible and my cub's life too precious for me to risk them willingly taking the backlash in order to carry out their plot regardless. To be fair, the oath we took has proven to be a little open to interpretation in the past. I can understand why she might not want to rely on it. *However, a solution does come to mind. One that uses your particular skill set.*

"My skill set?" I ask, a frown creeping onto my face. "What part of my skill set?" I have no Skills that could provide more surety than an oath. *Unless . . .* "You're not suggesting . . . ?" I trail off there, but it's enough for the vaguely formed images in my mind to be picked up by my canny landlady.

Yes.

"No. I'm not going to force a Bond onto a whole group of sapient creatures." My gut reaction is one of immediate rejection. Kalanthia tosses her head in a shrug.

Then don't. Wiping them out is far more certain, anyway. It means nothing to me. If anything, killing them all would be preferable to me.

"No!" I protest as I feel the fear emanating down the Bond from River. Clearly, Kalanthia is allowing everyone to hear the conversation this time.

Then this is my suggestion. I offer this other option only because you have asked me for an alternative. Conquer them or convince them, but chain them to yourself and I will be satisfied that they pose no threat to my cub.

I don't respond for a long moment, not verbally, anyway. What Kalanthia's suggesting, forcing a Bond on them . . . It's everything I feared about my Class when I first started exploring it. Everything I've concluded I can't live with myself doing. It's different if I can offer them something, or if I'd have to kill them otherwise because of the threat they offer. I doubt that the lizard folk would accept the Bond willingly—River only did so because I could offer a solution to the problem the lizard folk had with the Forest of Death. *What could I promise an entire village?* I send the whole gnarly mess over to River and let him mull over it.

In the expectation of a rejection from River, I start trying to think through other ideas that might solve Kalanthia's need for safety for Lathani.

What if we could get the lizard folk to move? Except Kalanthia already tried that when she moved dens to escape the lizard folk's persistent attacks. I doubt she'd consider it any better if the lizard folk were the ones to move, especially since they already showed how willing they are to travel to find her.

Is there another type of oath they could swear? One with stricter failure clauses, which might offer more guarantee? I rack my brains, but nothing is coming to mind. Oaths are always sworn on quantities or percentages of Energy. The worst that can happen is losing a level and the benefits it gave you if you don't have enough Energy in your store to pay the bill. Though, how that works with beasts, I don't know.

River has taken his time to muse over the proposition, but his response, when it comes, is surprising.

I think it's an acceptable solution, he answers finally.

"What?" I ask aloud sharply before returning to speaking through the Bond. *I would have thought you'd be the last one to agree to such a thing.*

Why wouldn't I? he continues with a strange equanimity.

Because . . . because they're your people. Don't you want them to be . . . free?

Of course. I also wish them to be alive. It appears to me that they cannot be both, due mainly to the choices of our leader. He sends over a sense of resignation, but he's far more accepting of this than I would be in his place.

We can find another solution! It's an empty assertion since I know full well that any other solution would need to have Kalanthia's approval, and anything with a guarantee of a similar level to either killing them or effectively enslaving them would most likely be no better than those options. River seems to know this even as he responds to me.

What solution? My silence says more than my words could have. *Master, Markus . . . I have found my servitude to be so much better than I expected. Better than I would have treated you in the same position,* he admits with shame drifting across the Bond. *I . . . With you, I believe my people will be better off than if the Great Predator comes to hunt them.*

Eternal servitude is better than death? I ask with heavy irony in my mental voice. The response I receive is accompanied by more resignation.

*Though we believe we will go to the ancestors after our deaths, we are not keen on hastening that day. The longer we live, the more chance we have of pleasing them and earning a greater place in their number. You have proven that you are willing to let me continue to fight, to continue to earn Energy in your service. You have expressed a desire for me to find a place among your group that suits me. You do not force me to do *something I am unsuited to. You do not even require me to provide a certain amount of resources to eat the food you provide, nor do you charge for your healing services.*

Of course not! I exclaim. *You're helping me—why would I require more from you than that?*

And that is why I feel that my people would be safe enough in your care. If anything, some of our weakest might even be better off in your care than they are now. This piques my curiosity, but he continues before I can ask for clarification. *Nature's law is that the strong rule, the weak serve or die. That is how it is with my people. Only the strongest achieve Evolution, so all resources, all efforts are aimed at making the strong stronger at the expense of the weak. Yet, that is not your way. It is strange, but . . . I live now only because of it. You would have to prove your strength to my people, but should you succeed in forcing them to submit, I suspect they would benefit from it. Or maybe they would not, but if the alternative is death, what is there to lose?*

I sigh. It's the "forcing them to submit" that concerns me most. But what if they are arguably better off Bound to me than not?

Of course, in a way it's academic. First of all, I don't even know if it's possible to Bind that many creatures. There was nothing in the Skill description about numbers, but surely I can't just use it on hordes of creatures. Or is that just a self-imposed limitation?

Secondly, I'm struggling to see how I could actually put this into practice, even if I did agree with it on a moral basis. I don't know how many live in the village, but I know from being there that it's a lot. Probably more than a hundred, maybe closer to two. If I don't want to kill them—which I don't, apart from the two Kalanthia has understandably put a target on—then I have to either prove to them I'm strong enough to not risk attacking—which could take a *long* time, probably longer than Kalanthia is willing to give us—or I have to somehow get each lizard-kin alone until I have enough on my side that the rest won't attack.

Perhaps I could use what I observed about the Pathwalkers' place in the hierarchy? I'll have to talk with River about practical suggestions. They did seem interested in my crafting—maybe that's an in? I send the thought to River.

The Pathwalkers might easily be interested in what you can offer them, he agrees, though with a sense of caution. *But unless you prove that you are stronger, they will not treat you as an equal. Instead, you will continue to be considered a prey-beast—a creature to be used and devoured.*

It's a little exasperating, but he should know his people best. Anyway, before I can even consider returning to deal with the lizard folk, I need to sort out my own issues with magic. It would probably help if I could increase my physical stats, maybe level up a few more times, and definitely upgrade my armor and weaponry. That should help with the "superiority" side of things and also give more examples of what I can offer them. Some more Willpower for the actual battles probably wouldn't hurt. Especially since I will be telling them at the same time that Kalanthia's going to kill both their shaman and herbalist.

With a wry sense of amusement, I realize something: despite my initial trepidation, I've clearly accepted this course of action.

"All right, I accept your terms," I tell Kalanthia with a sigh.

Good. Now, what do you desire as a boon for saving Lathani?

CHAPTER FIFTY-SIX

A Chance

Feeling a little whiplash from the abrupt change in topic, I try to redirect my mind to answer her question. I'm a little surprised that she's still offering me a boon; for some reason I was under the impression that leaving River alive *was* the boon, and I accepted that willingly. However, if she's offering something else, I'm not going to refuse.

And I know that there's one thing I'd *really* like to learn: Earth-Shaping. I almost just blurt that out as my choice but hold myself back at the last moment. Like it or not, I have bigger problems right now, which should probably outweigh my desire to learn new magic.

With a regretful sigh, I decide that I should see if Kalanthia can help me heal the damage I sustained from the Pure Energy. That's the most urgent of my needs right now, much as I hate to lose my chance to learn to do proper magic. If she can suggest a quicker or more efficient way of healing my Core, that's a more practical boon than asking to learn Earth-Shaping.

"I damaged myself when I touched the Pure Energy. It cracked my Core and seems to have . . . eaten away at the golden lines that trace around it. Do you have any suggestions?"

Kalanthia is quiet for a few moments, and my hopes fade the longer she takes to respond.

I regret to tell you that I have none, she answers bluntly. My heart sinks. *I am no healer, though I will have to try to be one for my cub's sake. You are a different question.*

"Because I'm not your cub," I conclude heavily.

Because you are human and your way of advancement is not the same as that of beasts, she corrects.

Well, that makes me feel a little better, but the result is the same: I'm back at square one. I sigh a little. At least I found *something* that works myself, even if it is a bit Energy-heavy. Maybe practice will make it more efficient?

"In which case . . ." I hesitate for a moment. "I was wondering if you could teach me . . . Well, you know that Earth-Shaping Skill you have?" She gives an amused assent. "Do you think you could teach it to me? As the boon?" I wait with bated breath. Is it too big an ask? Or is it something she can't teach? The silence stretches as Kalanthia seems to consider the question carefully.

Perhaps, she says finally. I let out the breath I was holding with a sense of disappointment. Is she refusing it? *It's not that I am unwilling,* she continues, probably responding to the thoughts I'm emitting unintentionally. *It's more that it's something I was never taught myself—I do not know if it is something I* could *teach.* Well. That's that, then, I suppose. *However,* she continues musingly, *it would be interesting to find out.* I perk up. Does that mean . . . ? *I will try,* she tells me finally. *I may not be able to teach Earth-Shaping directly, but I can try to teach you to feel the earth. It will be up to you to learn how to manipulate it, and I will offer guidance where I can.*

"Awesome, thanks!" A rush of excitement goes through me at the thought of doing *proper* magic. Yes, Lay-on-Hands is magical, and yes, several of my other Skills also use mana, but they don't *feel* as magical as making the earth move would. And I can think of several ways I can use it to make life easier or safer for me.

Then I pause as I consider something.

"I guess I'd better heal my Core first."

That would be wise, yes, she agrees with a hint of amusement.

"All right, then, if there's nothing else to discuss, I'll get right on that!"

I head into my alcove, sit down on my bed, and pull out an Energy Heart. Just as I close my eyes, I hear the quiet click of talons on the stone floor. I open my eyes again to see Bastet sitting right in front of me, looking expectant.

"What?" I ask. "Are you hungry?" I already put a carcass out. I'm sure I did.

Bastet sends a negative response, then projects an image of the Energy Heart I'm holding in my hands. I look down at it, then back at her. She sends me impatience.

I would slap myself in the face if I wasn't holding a big rocklike object. That would make me even more of an idiot.

"You want an Energy Heart?" I ask, though I barely need to do so. She sends strong agreement. It's a good idea: it's still raining, and everyone is stuck inside. Well, River and Fenrir seem happy enough to go out, but none of us are planning on going anywhere while the rain's still pouring. I'm planning on spending this time improving myself in terms of fixing my Core. What about my Bound? Though, I am wary about it. Kalanthia doesn't want Lathani having too many of them; what if my Bound have the same issues?

"Hold on a moment," I tell Bastet, then push myself to my feet and return to the main chamber. "Kalanthia?"

Yes, Markus Wolfe, the massive nunda says with a hint of amused weariness in her voice.

"Can my Bound have these Energy Hearts safely? You didn't want Lathani having too many of them, so . . ."

The key concept being "too many," she replies. *At their level, they should mix Energy sources and gain at least half as much through hunting or absorbing beast Cores as they do through natural absorption or natural Cores. But if they pay attention to their own instincts, they should know when they have reached their limits. If they say that they are fine, they most likely are.*

"All right, thanks."

Any other questions? I'm going to nap.

"Oh, always," I admit. "But I'll leave you be."

The massive leopard closes her eyes and curls up a little more tightly. I pull an Energy Heart out and give it to Bastet.

"Well, I hope you heard that," I tell her. "If it doesn't feel right, don't continue." She sends across a sense of exasperated impatience, but I also detect a trace of appreciation—like she doesn't feel I need to fuss so much over her, but she appreciates that I care enough to do so.

I see River sitting against the wall near the entrance to the cave, staring out at the rain with an unreadable expression. Not to say that most of his expressions are *readable* exactly, but even the Bond isn't helping me out much here. Not without digging down deeper than I feel comfortable doing.

"Hey, are you okay?" I ask quietly, crouching next to him. The tip of his tail flicks and the feeling of uncertainty comes across the Bond.

My village have a chance at not being destroyed by the Great Predator, but that is not the only threat facing them. I wonder how long it will be until the Forest of Death engulfs them.

"There's still a good distance between the trees and the village," I say, trying to console him. "We need to get stronger before we can do anything real to help them, but when we're strong enough, we will go, I promise. And in the meantime, perhaps you can get stronger with these." I hand him an Energy heart. "Do you need any more than this at the moment?"

He looks at the chunk of glittering red crystal and takes it gently with his clawed fingers.

Thank you, Master—Markus, he quickly corrects himself, his tone grateful and then apologetic in turn. *The Energy Hearts we harvested from the cavern will probably each take a day or a day and a half to absorb.*

"And is there any special method to do so?" I want to let my other Bound know if there is. River flicks his tail in negation.

There is no special method. They just need to stay in contact with my skin. However, the Pathwalkers have found that focusing on trying to feel the Energy moving within is the most effective method.

"Good to know," I tell him honestly. "When you've finished with this one, come and get another from me if you feel it would be safe to do so. I would put them in a pile somewhere for everyone to access, but I don't want to risk some other beast being attracted to them or stealing them."

I pat him on the shoulder and stand.

I . . . You defended me. Defended my village. Why? he asks as I'm about to walk away. I pause and look back at him.

"Well," I reply after a moment of consideration, "because you're a friend, and it would have hurt you if I didn't. Besides, potential genocidal massacre sounds like something I should be against on principle," I remark a little wryly. The fact that I would probably have been in agreement with said genocidal massacre before I got to know and like River is something I'm not totally comfortable admitting even to myself. I mean, the shaman and the herbalist are both still on my kill list, but taking the rest of the village with them seems to be going a bit too far.

But what if the Great Predator had desired your life in place of mine?

"I honestly don't think it would have come to that," I assure him. "As you heard, she feels that she owes me a boon for bringing her cub back to her. Kalanthia has proven to be someone who pays her debts. If it came down to that, I would have asked for my life as repayment of the boon. In fact, I thought that was what she was proposing until she corrected me."

Thereby passing up any other reward she would have offered. I shrug.

"Honestly, I would have helped for Lathani's sake anyway. And I'd rather you were alive." He's silent and I just smile at him before patting him on the shoulder again and walking off to speak with Bastet. If he wishes to discuss it further, we can do so later, but for me the matter is closed.

After a short conversation with Bastet and then Fenrir, where I briefly explain what River told me, I return to the alcove, close my eyes, and continue to work on my Core.

CHAPTER FIFTY-SEVEN

Quest Complete

Controlling Energy is tiring. When I feel like I've had enough for now, I decide to check my notifications—I can see there's something waiting for me.

Congratulations! You have made progress on your Quest. You have discovered the center of the Vine-Strangler Grove and encountered a guardian of unusual size and strength. You have investigated the guardian beast's lair and have discovered a stagnant pool of Pure Energy surrounded by a plethora of Energy Crystals. You have discovered that this easy access to an unusually high Energy density is the reason for the Vine-Strangler's explosive growth.	
Quest: The Vine-Strangler Grove	Quest type: Regional
Objective: Discover why Vine-Strangler Trees are growing in this location and the reason for the unusual level of Energy. (Completed) Secondary objective: Investigate the guardian beast's lair. (Completed)	
Time to complete Quest: Unlimited	
Suggested difficulty: Initiate	Reward: Rare Bronze Chest

Congratulations! You have completed all objectives on your Quest: The Vine-Strangler Grove. This Quest deals with a situation that is not yet resolved. You can choose to accept your reward now, but you may or may not then be offered the follow-up Quest. Alternatively, you can choose to accept the new Quest. This will increase the rarity of your rewards by one rank upon completion of the second Quest.
Accept current reward / Accept new Quest

Interesting, very interesting . . . I now have a difficult choice. Part of me wants to hedge my bets and take the reward now—a bird in the hand is worth two in the bush, after all. I try to see the description of the new quest, but the System doesn't seem to be willing to show it to me until I've made a decision. It feels a bit like buying a product off the internet: who knows if it will turn out as expected?

In the end, though, I decide to accept the new quest and pass up the current reward for now. Ultimately, I justify it to myself as the reward having just been a bonus. I didn't exactly go out of my way to complete the quest—the vine-stranglers made sure I had to pass through the tunnel regardless of what I wanted to do. So, if the objectives of the new quest turn out to be impossible, I haven't actually lost anything. If anything, I've gained eight levels and a whole load of Energy Hearts, which I wouldn't have had otherwise. I've also gained a cracked Core and damaged internal matrix, but I'm working on that . . .

Congratulations! You have received a new Quest. In the course of your adventures, you explored the center of the Vine-Strangler Grove and defeated its guardian. Upon investigating the guardian beast's lair, you discovered a route down to one of the Ley Lines of the planet, running unusually close to the surface. This is an undesirable situation and will lead to many consequences if it is allowed to carry on for too long.	
Quest: The Vine-Strangler Grove II	Quest type: Regional
Objective: Find the reason for the Ley Line becoming uncovered. Objective: Rectify the situation with the exposed stream of Pure Energy and return the area to its previous state.	
Time to complete Quest: 52 days	
Suggested difficulty: Journeyman	Reward: Uncommon Silver Chest → Rare Silver Chest (rarity increased due to previous rewards being passed over)

Okay, wow. A lot to take in there. I reread the notification a couple of times, just to make sure I have understood everything. So, first of all, it's now telling me that the situation is unnatural and a problem and is asking me to find out why. Completing that objective is probably key to solving the second and fixing the issue.

Interestingly, it doesn't say "secondary objective" like I saw in the previous quest notification about investigating the salamander's lair. Is that because the two objectives are separate? Or is it because both objectives are equally important?

I also note the increased difficulty level and the higher-value reward—even before I gained the increased rarity from not accepting the previous reward, it was probably still more valuable than whatever I would have gotten from a bronze chest. I suppose that if I'd decided to take the Rare bronze chest and then also managed to receive and complete the second quest, I would also have gotten an Uncommon silver chest. Well, I hope that the reward of a rarity above is worth passing up having two chests.

Lastly, and perhaps the most immediately important, is the change in the time to complete the quest: from unlimited to fifty-two days is a big jump! Is that saying that something is going to happen in fifty-two days' time? Or are changes happening that will render the quest impossible to complete after fifty-two days?

I'm very tempted to just forget about the whole thing, my curiosity about the rewards aside. I've already almost died in the area, as has Bastet . . . But unfortunately, I don't think that's an option. I need to solve the issue with the vine-stranglers regardless of the quest. I might have broken far more promises than I'd like to admit in the past, but I'm trying to change the worst parts of myself.

The best thing I can say about the situation is that at least it's a two birds, one stone kind of thing: if the vine-strangler trees are feeding on the Energy evaporating off that Pure Energy stream, then cutting them off from it should at least stop their growth, if not kill them outright.

I conclude that I need to sit down with River and talk through a number of things with him. After all, the poison he created to use on the lizogs proved its worth, which makes me curious what other concoctions he knows how to make. I can't forget that I was given two healing potions when I first entered this world; if River could make something that was even a diluted version of those, it could be a literal lifesaver. And what if he could make one that helps regenerate mana? Just as much of a lifesaver, especially since I have the choice still hanging over my head of either adapting Lay-on-Hands into a new, more combat-applicable Skill or accepting the new Skill Body-Invasion.

And even if he can't produce health or mana potions, poisons would be a useful tool, especially for creating traps or helping us against larger and more powerful beasts. In addition to my other plans for weapons, equipment, and Evolutions, there are many ways we could get stronger and more robust as a group, making all of our goals more achievable.

As I think about the quest, I realize something is bugging me a bit. Since I'm taking a break from my work with my Core, I decide to see whether Kalanthia is open to a little more conversation.

CHAPTER FIFTY-EIGHT

To Live Up to the Image

The rain stopped at some point during my Core-healing session. Although most places are still a bit damp outside, the sun is rapidly evaporating the majority of the puddles. I prod my clothes a little, finding them still pretty soaked. Hopefully, they'll be dry by tonight.

Kalanthia doesn't seem to be deterred by the damp earth and has found herself a sunny patch to rest in. Lathani is playing with the raptorcat cubs—some game similar to tag is my guess. As I approach, the giant nunda opens her eyes and looks at me.

Markus Wolfe, you have more questions? She sounds more amused than irritated, so I figure it must be a decent time to approach her.

"I was just thinking about the tunnels," I admit. "The ones leading to and from the Pure Energy stream. They . . . I don't think they were natural." Little things have added up together—the wording of the new quest, the "reason" for the exposure of the ley lines—to lead me here. I suppose it could be a natural disaster, but something tells me that it's deeper than that. And if there is a reason, there must be a creature who thought about and decided to do it.

I agree, Kalanthia says more definitely. *From what you and Lathani have shared, the tunnel that you used as an exit was most certainly created and not formed by natural causes.* Here she looks slightly uncertain. *Though, I do not believe that the creature or creatures had the same gifts as I do with earth.*

"Oh?"

The tunneling is very . . . rough, she says disdainfully. I can't help but chuckle.

"All right, so some amateur tunneled down into the Pure Energy . . . and then tunneled out?"

Kalanthia sends a feeling of negation.

The tunnel you used to access the Pure Energy was natural. Knowing the nature of Pure Energy, I suspect that it built up somehow and then exploded when the mass became too great. The fire-aspected Cores you found support that theory.

"So, the conditions Energy Hearts are in determine their aspect, and these are fire?" I ask curiously as I pull one out to examine. I can't see the fire aspect, but I trust Kalanthia knows what she's talking about.

Indeed.

"And I guess that the creature or creatures that tunneled down did so to access the Pure Energy?"

Again, Kalanthia seems uncertain. *If so, it is a far more powerful beast than I ever thought would visit this area,* she says. *And that is not good for any of us.* I frown.

"Why would it need to be a really powerful being? Couldn't you get access?"

I have never been able to find a Pure Energy stream, Kalanthia tells me firmly. *And neither has any other beast I know capable of Earth-Shaping. I suspect that there is some powerful magic in those tunnels that makes them almost impossible to detect. So, if something did detect them and dug its way far into the earth in pursuit, it must have detection skills far better than mine—and my specialty is the earth. Besides, there is its motive to consider. Pure Energy is not for everyone.*

"Why not?" I ask, my frown deepening. "I mean, yes, it almost killed me, but surely you could withstand it?"

Markus Wolfe, I do not believe you understand just how lucky you were to survive your contact with the pool of Pure Energy. Had you touched it with any greater part of your body, you would have almost undoubtedly been lost. At the base of the valley is a lake into which Pure Energy pours. It is primarily the vapor of this lake that fills the valley with Energy and makes it attractive for us to live here.

I guess that explains why Energy reduces the higher up the valley we are: the evaporated Energy has further to travel and more space to spread out.

Even beasts of my level would struggle to be submerged in water from that lake for elongated periods of time without suffering ill effects—and that is far more diluted than what you encountered. For the most powerful, however, it presents a much easier and safer way of progressing than chasing down others of similar or greater power. Nonetheless, I am surprised that you did not die or have your foundations completely ruined.

"Well, I came *very* close," I admit as I recall the achievement I received and process the idea that there are creatures Kalanthia considers to be far more powerful than herself lurking in this valley. "And if these 'foundations' are the network of channels I have inside me, then I've certainly done damage. Which is what I'm working on healing."

As you should, she agrees.

"So, you think that this beast is really powerful if they actively went for the Pure Energy?"

Precisely.

My mind has been ticking over in the background.

"Why are there no creatures fighting over the uncovered stream, though? Yes, I get it that the liquid itself is deadly for those under a certain level, but the Energy density close to it was through the roof!" The salamander guardian wasn't enough to explain that.

It is hidden underground instead of in a lake that turns into vapor under the sun's light—I would imagine that less Energy escapes to begin with. Certainly, the fact that you only started experiencing a poisoning effect practically next to the liquid Pure Energy indicates that to be the case.

"Yeah, and what's up with the fact that it was only *me* feeling the effects?" I exclaim, interrupting her. "Well, Lathani did say she felt a bit odd too." Then, seeing Kalanthia's piercing look, I deflate a little. "Sorry."

You were poisoned because despite having a Core, your foundations are terribly fragile. Why do you think so many creatures used to be drawn to you and driven to attack?

I'm taken aback by the question.

"I . . . don't know. I thought it was just something about this place. Though I've wondered at their lack of survival instinct."

It is because any beast who Evolves has a far stronger foundation than you did, and those around them sense it. It warns the beings around them that they are too dangerous to attack. Yet you had none of this aura and still had a Core that they could detect. Any Beast who had not yet reached the Core stage would have seen you as easy prey.

"I see," I say slowly, only mostly understanding. I'm actually a little happy to finally have the answer to a question that has been bugging me for ages. Instinct *was* playing a part, but the instinct to get stronger rather than the one to survive. "And now?"

Now your aura is more similar in strength to any other with a fairly new Core. As a result, those without a Core will be more cautious about attacking you. However, beware: to beasts in the Core stage, the damage your foundation has sustained is the equivalent of a bleeding wound in the side of fragile and vulnerable prey.

"So . . . I'm not on the menu for creatures *below* Core stage anymore, but for creatures *at* Core stage, I'm now their favorite appetizer?"

Essentially, she replies with amusement. I wish I could share her lightheartedness, but hearing that I've exchanged being constantly attacked by creatures for being attacked by *more powerful* creatures is more depressing than funny. Still, I suppose that this new information explains why we weren't attacked after the encounter with the lizogs. Actually, that reminds me: I should probably check whether any of those carcasses have Cores.

"Sorry," I say again after remembering that Kalanthia had been busy saying something when I broke in with my questions, "I interrupted you. Please, continue what you were saying."

Thank you, she says with a heavy weight of irony to her mental voice. *Regarding your question about why others do not seem to have discovered what you have, I suspect that the trees have been both consuming it and preventing others from coming close. Though they would not survive direct contact with the Pure Energy itself, they are well adapted to transforming Energy into growth, and they would be very interested in protecting that source.*

"That's why they're growing so quickly," I murmur. And perhaps that's why they directed me to the center in the first place: maybe the salamander was consuming more Energy than they were willing to tolerate. Or perhaps it was the fact that it was killing and eating them that the trees were unwilling to tolerate. "So, you've seen these things before?" She certainly sounded familiar with them.

I have, Kalanthia confirms, bringing my attention back to what we've been talking about. *Much deeper in the valley, however. It is a surprise to see them so far up the mountainside. Their sentience and sapience usually require them to be in a more Energy-dense area.*

"Perhaps a seed was dropped nearby by chance and happened to grow?" Isn't that how so many trees grow in odd places on Earth? Kalanthia doesn't seem completely convinced.

Perhaps.

"What?" I ask, my eyes narrowing. She gazes at me with her golden eyes as if wondering whether to reveal her thoughts or not. "Wait," I say as my own thoughts come together. "You don't think it was intentional, do you? To hide the Energy once the ley line was revealed?"

I was wondering the same, she admits. I consider the implications. If so, it's very much something premeditated—and by a creature capable of complex thought. Not a good sign, if this quest makes them into an enemy.

And speaking of complex thought, I have another question that's been playing on my mind since our discussion earlier. I figure getting it out will help me concentrate when I go back to working shortly.

"Kalanthia, not that I'm complaining, but . . . your solution to the issue the lizard folk pose . . . it gives all the power to me and no guarantees to you. Why did you suggest it?" It might be a case of looking a gift horse in the mouth, but I haven't been able to stop the question going round and round in my mind. I don't want to consider that Kalanthia might be being duplicitous, but she's certainly intelligent enough to lie to me.

It gives me all the guarantees I need, Kalanthia answers, unruffled. I shake my head incredulously.

"How? Even if I had a Bond with every single lizard-kin in River's village, how would that provide any certainty of safety for you? I mean, we have an oath, yes, but you said you're not willing to trust your cub's life to an oath; how is this situation any better?" Kalanthia doesn't answer immediately and instead stretches out her paws, yawning a little.

Markus Wolfe, I am a little peckish. Do you have a snack in that invisible storage of yours? I huff in irritation at her avoidance of the question but dig out a couple of carcasses for her. She snaps them up, gone in two bites. I pull out three more seeing as those acted merely as appetizers. *You might wish to consider not storing your kills in that space,* Kalanthia comments as she snaps up the next and crunches it between her teeth. *They offer nutritional value, but nothing more. Any Energy within them seems to have been stripped from the meat.*

"Yeah, I'm aware." I sigh. "But it's the most convenient way to carry them around."

Convenient, perhaps, but you will have to work extra hard to gain all you must through kills alone.

"Speaking of gains," I say, trying to redirect us back onto the previous topic. "Can you explain how me gaining new Bound gains you anything?"

Are you intending to turn on Lathani? she asks bluntly.

"No!" I reply immediately.

If you gained enough power to overcome me, would you do so?

"No," I reply again. Even if I could force a Bond on Kalanthia, I wouldn't. First, I've vowed to not force a Bond on any creature; second, she's part of my pack. My . . . family.

Then it hits me. *Oh. Is that why?* The nunda gives me a knowingly amused look, seeming to agree with my thoughts—I'm probably accidentally projecting them again.

"But how do you know I'm telling the truth?" I ask her with a depth of feeling that surprises me. How can she be so certain that I won't turn around and fail her when she needs me most? I have a history of doing that.

I know, she responds unhelpfully. Then, seeming to take a little pity on me, she continues. *You are the same human who saved my cub almost at the cost of his own life without even knowing anything about her. You are the same human who has played and looked after her in my absence. The same who came across me in a vulnerable condition and didn't kill me despite the fact that you would benefit from what my death could give you. The same who then agreed to rescue my cub even without any reward promised. A human who immediately pulls out untainted meat to feed me on request. I know.*

Well, I suppose if you put it like that . . .

"All right." I decide to take her entirely at face value. "I will do my best to be worthy of your trust. And thank you," I say with feeling. Oddly enough, I really do want to live up to the image Kalanthia seems to have of me.

CHAPTER FIFTY-NINE

Energy Wrangling

After my break and conversation with Kalanthia, I spend the next few hours Meditating with an Energy Heart in my hand. It's a painstaking process, but when I work out a way of continuing to absorb the Heart even while I remain in Meditation, it speeds things up.

Funnily enough, the advice that I passed on to Bastet and Fenrir from River actually comes in handy for me too. Concentrating on feeling the Energy move in my system actually means that after some trial and error, I discover how to *pull* the Energy from the Heart directly. That means a much more consistent pull, and it also means I get through the Energy Heart much quicker. While my Bound seem to all still be absorbing their first Energy Heart, I'm on my *third*.

It also teaches me something else: at least the outer parts of the tapestry around my Core are somehow connected to my extremities. I work it out because when I hold the Energy Heart with my hands, the Energy always comes from a certain area of the golden weave. When I get curious partway through and test this by holding the Heart with my bare feet, I find that the Energy consistently comes through a different set of threads. I also find that *more* Energy comes through—double the amount, in fact. Holding the Energy Heart with just the hand that didn't touch the Pure Energy reveals that I get the same amount of Energy as I do through my feet.

All this goes towards proving my theory that the weave is, in fact, my internal matrix. I suppose if I have a dead spot in the hand that touched the Pure Energy, it makes sense that my mana regeneration has been so affected.

Going to my status screen after a good few hours of working, I'm pleased to see some progress finally.

Name: Markus Wolfe		Race: Human	Class: Tamer
Level: 12	Energy to next level: 72%	Energy absorption rate: 26u/hr	Energy towards debt: 75%
Intelligence	36	Mana: 334/334 (-7%)	
Wisdom	36	Mana regeneration rate: 720u/hr (-20%)	
Willpower	42+8 (+20%)	Health regeneration rate: 40u/hr (-20%)	
Constitution	19	Health: 190/190	
Strength	15	Stamina: 90/90	

Dexterity	15	Stamina regeneration rate: 150u/hr
Class Skills: Dominate – Novice 3 Tame – Beginner 6 Fade – Initiate 1		Non-Class Skills: *Lay-on-Hands – Journeyman 2* Stealth – Novice 1 Animal Empathy – Novice 6 Meditation – Novice 8 Energy Manipulation – Beginner 7 Sensation Management – Beginner 5

All the Energy I've absorbed has made its mark: my Energy store has leaped. That would normally be a good thing, but I'm worried about what might happen if I level up with my Core still cracked. Maybe if I hit a hundred percent I should think about directing the excess Energy to my debt instead . . .

As for my progress on my Core, I'm three percent better now than I was when I started, and it took less time to get down to seven percent than it did to get to eight or even nine percent. I might still be absorbing ninety percent of the Energy from the Heart rather than using it to repair my Core but that's a lot better than the original ninety-nine percent of it. It's a relief—the more I do it, the faster and more efficient I will become.

My Energy Manipulation Skill reflects my improvement: it also leaped through the ranks from Beginner two to seven. It's all good news, but I need another break for now. It's certainly not work I'm used to doing, and like any new task, it's exhausting.

As I stand up to stretch my legs, I pull out some food and water. Looking around, I notice that all my companions seem to have Energy Hearts close by. River is sitting there with his eyes closed, as is Fenrir, who appears to have curled up around the Core and is finally inside from the rain. Curious, I pull up the tab that links to my Bound, wondering how they are coming on.

Interesting. Of course, Sirocco hasn't made any progress—she hasn't been in the cave benefiting from the Energy Hearts. Actually, that's an important consideration. Sirocco is a companion, but one who can choose to leave at any moment. Giving her Energy Hearts could mean wasting them on someone who will choose to leave when they get stronger. On the other hand, it could make her more able to help the group while she stays part of it.

Maybe I should see what my other Bound feel about it? After all, it means sharing resources with another person, so it directly impacts them too.

I checked Fenrir's stats briefly on our way through the forest, and he's made the most progress out of all my Bound. Interestingly, he's also the one who started the lowest. Similarly, River has made four percent of progress, and his starting position was lower than Bastet, who's only made two percent of progress. I guess it's similar for beasts and for humans: the further you get, the more Energy it takes to advance.

Still, if those trends continue, we should be able to get Bastet to tier two in a week or so, depending on how quickly she continues to progress. Fenrir and River are both going to take a bit longer. Kalanthia did say they needed to complement the absorption from the "natural" Cores with Energy from hunting. I'd better talk with them about it—later, though. They all look rather intent on their own meditation right now.

I sigh. I suppose that's my cue to get back to it. I've had enough of a break to be able to face more Energy wrangling, I suppose.

CHAPTER SIXTY

Contractor

The next time I surface from my Meditation, I blink a little blearily in the dazzling brightness that threatens to blind me. Looking towards the cave mouth, the cause becomes clear: the sun has moved around enough that it's shining directly into the cave. Somehow, I've passed more than half the day just sitting still and navel-gazing. I shake my head—if Dad were still around, he'd have told me to go and do something useful *long* ago.

I push myself to my feet and stretch my limbs out one by one as pins and needles erupt and then reduce far faster than they would have back on Earth. Superior blood flow, I guess.

Walking towards the cave mouth, I'm almost knocked over as Lathani darts past.

"What are you running for?" I call after her with exasperation.

We're playing hide and seek! I need to catch little sibling before she hides again! the nunda answers quickly. Apparently, it's hide and seek *and* catch, then.

Ma—Markus, River's voice enters my mind as I turn my face up to the warm sun. I've gotten a bit chilly from leaning against the stone. Maybe I should Meditate outside for my next session.

"Yes?" I respond to my Bound after a moment.

May I head into the forest? I am lacking some ingredients for a number of concoctions. I hope to explore the local area to see what I can find.

"I wanted to speak with you about that," I admit. "Have you finished absorbing the Energy Heart?" He sends a sense of negation as he tilts his head to one side.

No, but I feel that it would not be wise for me to continue for now. My . . . The Pathwalkers warn of absorbing too much Energy at one time. According to them, it can cause some sort of damage when overdone. Well, it appears that they and Kalanthia agree on *something.*

I hesitate for a moment before giving my assent, though. I know that River's used to going out in a much more dangerous area than this—our own journey proved that. Even if we don't count the vine-strangler trees, the level of creatures that we faced were significantly above that of the ones around here, the raptorcats excepted. But that doesn't stop me from being concerned about him going out *alone.*

And I don't really think that going out with my broken Core is a very good idea, especially considering what Kalanthia said about beasts of a certain level actually being attracted to me. I reckon that might be because of the Energy I discovered leaking from my Core. Just another reason to fix myself.

But I suppose that even if I don't go with him, it doesn't mean he has to go *alone*.

Bastet is currently busy looking after the cubs, but that still leaves Fenrir and Sirocco, who are available and possibly interested. I send the bird a mental message asking her to come and get back grumpy assent. I also get the sense that it will take more than a couple of minutes, as she's out hunting. In exchange for interrupting her, I apparently need to compensate her with some food. That reminds me of something else I wanted to discuss.

"I want to get your thoughts on something," I say as I intentionally push my meaning down the Bonds with all three Dominated Bound. I feel the attention of Fenrir and Bastet sharpen on me; the former comes over to sit near River and me, and the latter remains where she is for a better view of the cubs and Lathani. I then explain what I've been thinking about the Energy Hearts and Sirocco. "So, I want to know what you think. Should we respond in kind to the relationship of exchange she seems to want to engage in? Or should we include her in all things, like any of you three?"

Immediately, I get the sense that this is a bit above Fenrir's pay grade. He's more intelligent than Spike, but only in the sense of being able to communicate better. The idea of there being a hierarchy is certainly something he understands, and according to his worldview, those at the top getting all the choice bits while those at the bottom have to be satisfied with the meanest scraps is perfectly normal. However, the idea of some of the group being properly part of the group and others not . . . That's completely foreign to him. And, to be honest, it seems like it's foreign to Bastet too.

From the raptorcat, I get confusion along with the sense of "We're all pack. Why would one be treated differently than the others?" When I send her a reply that carries the idea that resources given to Sirocco would be wasted if she then chose to leave, Bastet's confusion seems to grow. For her, that's normal. Cubs are given resources and nurtured to grow, even though the males will leave or be chased out by the time they become juveniles. Those resources aren't "wasted"; they're fed into the greater whole.

I think I understand. While the resources invested in the males won't have immediate return—not like those invested in the females, who become productive members of the pack on reaching juvenile status—there is a different outcome: males chased out of the pack either die or live and grow stronger, and those who survive are the ones to have children.

Bastet has grasped something instinctively that humanity has only understood logically: survival of the fittest means that those in competition have to be the best they can be. Over generations, raising strong male cubs means an increase in the strength of raptorcats as a whole. It's an interesting perspective and makes me reconsider my approach to the dilemma.

Out of all of my Bound, River is the only one who seems able to consider the divided nature of what I'm talking about. That's probably because his own society seems to be divided between those with Cores and those without, between Warriors and Pathwalkers, and even between lizard folk and non-lizard folk. He is the last to give his point of view.

My people channel resources to the most deserving, with the reasoning that to allow precious materials to be taken by those who are likely to die anyway is a waste, he offers, a thoughtful feeling accompanying his words. *Yet . . . my encounter with you has turned what I thought I knew on its head.* I tilt my head to one side.

"Explain?" I half ask, half order as curiosity runs through me.

What I said to the Honored Pathwalkers was true: you have no natural weapons. You have no scales. Your skin is soft. Your teeth are blunt, as are your claws. For all intents and purposes, you were the prey my kinfolk saw you as. Yet it was not me who won in our confrontations. You trapped me as well as any arhast spins her web. And then, if you had wished, you could have pushed through my resistance and forced my compliance in our mental battle.

If one who is so obviously prey can do all that, then should we be abandoning nine out of ten of our hatchlings to the providence of fate before they even reach their name-day? How many marvelous minds are hiding in weak bodies? My concept of "waste" seems to be incomplete. It seems my fellow Bound are of the opinion that she should be treated as a full member of the group. I will abide by whatever you choose.

Not entirely the most helpful, but it's interesting to see how much River's worldview is changing—much like mine, really—and I feel the bond of kinship I had already sensed with him grow in strength. Well. Perhaps I should just discuss this with Sirocco herself. See whether, now we're in a better position, she wants to change the spirit of our agreement or not.

While we wait, I check with Fenrir to see if he actually wants to go out into the forest. The response is somewhat predictable: he will follow the pack. It seems that like with everything else among male lizogs, the strongest leads and the weaker follow.

"Sirocco," I say the moment she wings her way over and lands on my shoulder, a sense of hunger being pushed down the Bond towards me. "I want to know what you think about how we should conduct our agreement going forwards." She sends a sense of confusion to me colored by a tint of apprehension. Is she worried I'm about to break the Bond and betray her? Perhaps. "Nothing bad," I assure her. "I just mean . . ." I sigh and try to put what I'm getting at into words. Not that she cares about the words, but they will—hopefully—clarify my meaning enough for her to understand.

"I don't want to limit your freedom," I tell her frankly, since that seems to be the most important thing she raised in our previous negotiation. "But I'd like to know if you want to be a full part of the group or a . . . contractor."

She sends me confusion, so I try to shove the sense of each option at her. In one option, she's benefiting fully from everything the group has to offer but is fully contributing as an equal; every member is offering help when needed without any thought of repayment, only the assurance of the same thing happening regardless of who's in trouble. And more than that: dedication and commitment to the group, as long as her core tenets are not contravened.

In the other option, I offer a sense of being together yet apart, of increased freedom but reduced benefit for each side, of negotiating each interaction to ensure that things remain balanced and fair, of the freedom to leave whenever but the lack of certainty that allows emotional bonds to form, or form as strongly.

In the end, I get a sense of thoughtfulness from Sirocco's side of the Bond. She asks me for time, wishing to give the matter due consideration. I agree, of course, and pull out a chunk of meat for her to enjoy. I'm surprised when she turns up her nose—well, beak—at it.

"What's wrong?" I ask, baffled. It's salamander meat, the same thing she enjoyed eating not that long ago. Her reply answers the question for me. It's the same reason Kalanthia suggested finding some other way to store the corpses: Sirocco's not interested in meat with no Energy in it. Well, that explains a lot.

Fortunately, there's an easy answer for it. "River and Fenrir are going out in the forest. That's why I asked you to come over. I was hoping you could accompany them to help them out, if only by keeping an eye on possible dangers. I'm sure they'd be happy to share any kills with you. Would that suit?"

The scarlet and yellow-gold bird seems to consider the question for a moment before sending me a sense of assent. She pushes away from my shoulder and glides to the top of the nearest tree, sending me a sense of impatience.

"Well, looks like she's eager to go," I remark to River. Then I look at him seriously. "Take care, okay? And if there's any issue, let me know and Bastet and I will come running."

Very well, River tells me with a hint of something to his mental voice that I can't quite identify. It seems positive, so I'll take that as a win.

"Look out for River and obey him, Fenrir," I order the lizog. He sends me a sense of submissive assent, and then the two go padding down the hill. I watch them go until they disappear into the trees. I'm a little uneasy, but I think it's probably more linked to remembering Spike's death than any true premonition. I hope so, anyway.

In the end, I just push the thoughts away and go sit on a sunny, dry spot near the cave mouth. Once more taking a few minutes to rest and refresh myself, it's not overly long before I close my eyes and drop back into Meditation. I take a bit of time to examine my work so far. I can see my progress: part of my Core is now free of cracks. I haven't yet pulled out my new Energy Heart, so I'm a little surprised when I see a wave of light racing towards my Core all of a sudden.

Pulling out of Meditation, I trigger my status screen. Sure enough, I'm back up to seventy-two percent in my Energy store after temporarily dropping to seventy-one due to the Energy leak from my Core. *Where did that come from?* I wonder to myself.

Then a thought occurs. *My Bound.* Since I haven't done anything that I would expect to earn me Energy, I draw the conclusion that it came from either general absorption of the ambient Energy or from my Bound killing something.

Very interesting. That's the first time this has happened today, which proves that my Bound absorbing Energy from an Energy Heart doesn't count but killing does. And now that I've got a little group of killers together, I could be gaining Energy while crafting better weapons or better living conditions . . .

I pull my mind back from the distracted path down which it threatens to wander. I have a much more important task in front of me right now.

Sinking back into myself, I reenter what I'm starting to call my "Core space," if only to myself. There's more than just the Core here, but it's the equivalent of calling Earth's home the solar system: my Core is as dominant here as the sun is. When another flash of Energy enters my system, I use it to repair one of the cracks. To my delight, it works just as well as Energy Hearts do. That's *excellent* to know.

Remembering where the Energy entered my Core, I trace the lines back to where they begin. It's one of the densely woven areas, one of the three that seem particularly similar to the rest of the weave around. Following the golden thread as it twists through my internal matrix, I realize that it heads straight towards the edge of my Core space. And there it just . . . ends. Except that I sense it doesn't *truly* end. Instead, it just . . . goes somewhere, but somewhere I cannot follow.

Except when, suddenly, I can. And do.

CHAPTER SIXTY-ONE

Companionship

Prey. I smell it in the air: the scent of pumping blood is easy to identify. I lift my nose and scent the breeze. There. Large. Not old. Not young. Healthy. Injured. Good prey. I nudge my packmate. He looks down at me. He has much meat and many smelly plants slung over his back already. I take a few steps in the direction of the prey and release a questioning scent.

My packmate does not respond.

He is higher in the pack hierarchy than me—pack leader has made that clear. He must make the decision to follow the scent or not. He does not respond. I take another few steps and release more scent. Finally, he moves. He follows me. I release a happy scent: the hunt has been accepted.

I wrench myself back from the connection with what feels like the mental form of a gasp. *Was that . . . ? It must have been.* I pull myself out of my Core space and rub at my temples, a sudden blossoming headache thumping there.

"Ow," I whimper quietly to myself. Almost reflexively, I reach for my mana to cast Lay-on-Hands, only to remember at the last moment that I shouldn't. Doing more damage to my Core is unlikely to help my headache. I narrow my eyes as I think back to the brief impression.

The most obvious explanation is that I somehow entered one of my Bound's heads in a much more intrusive way than normal, actually detecting events through his senses and thoughts as they occurred. I would guess that I went into Fenrir's mind, based on the various cues. It's a bit invasive, but I can definitely see the utility in being able to see through one of my Bound's eyes in real time . . . as long as I can be sure that it won't cause damage to either of us, of course.

Something to consider later. For now, I know that my Bound are on a hunt once more. I should make sure that I'm ready to redirect the Energy when it arrives.

As darkness starts to fall, I sense that my Bound are on their way back. Ever since ranking up Dominate, I've started being able to get a very rough idea of how far away they are from me and of their approximate location. Their excursion has already been productive for me; any herbal ingredients or animal carcasses they've managed to collect is a bonus. When I check my status screen, I'm already down to only four percent reduction to my mana pool.

The process is going a lot faster than I thought it would. And as I check my notifications, I realize why.

Congratulations!
You have advanced a Skill past Beginner. Energy Manipulation is now Novice 1. Tasks requiring you to manipulate Energy within your Core space are now increasingly easier and faster. You have 2% reduction in Energy wastage per level in this Skill past Novice.

Close message

It's a pretty awesome improvement and helps me threefold: easier, faster, and less Energy wasted are all things I need. I do find it interesting that the description specifically says "Core space." Does that mean that I could potentially expand the Skill to help with Energy manipulation *outside* the Core space? Or would that have to be a different Skill?

I question it because what if Energy Manipulation is the key to my idea of making Lay-on-Hands able to heal from a distance? It's only a gut feeling, an instinct that tells me this might be at all possible. Well, it's not something for now, anyway. First I need to fix my Core. Then I need to fix that golden weave. *I wonder if Kalanthia has any information on that . . .*

Since I'm taking another break, I push myself to my feet and move over to where Kalanthia is enjoying the last of the sun. Her eyes are closed, but I sense somehow that she's not asleep. Still, I hesitate for a moment—I don't know if she'd appreciate being disturbed.

Ask, Markus Wolfe. I almost jump at her voice suddenly entering my mind but manage not to. Just. *You're a quicksand of curiosity today, but I'm in an indulgent mood. So, ask.*

"As I told you before, I damaged the golden lines around my Core. I know you don't have any idea how to help me with the Core itself, but I was wondering if you recognize what I'm talking about." Kalanthia cracks one eye open to regard me.

I understand your difficulties, as I have my own Energy channels around my Core. But I would have told you earlier if I had an idea of how to fix the damage you described to me.

"And I understand that, I do," I say while mentally noting that Kalanthia apparently has the same sort of thing inside her as I do—and she's obviously seen it, otherwise she wouldn't recognize my description. "Maybe," I start, thinking as I speak, "maybe if I knew what yours were like, it would be give me an idea of what I should aim for?"

There's silence for a few moments, and I turn my head to fully look at the big nunda, wondering if something's wrong.

I . . . don't think I should say. It's odd to see her hesitant, uncertain. Kalanthia and Bastet are quite similar in many ways. Both of them decide on a course of action and then do it. Kalanthia is a lot more thoughtful, whereas Bastet is more instinctual, but both are rarely hesitant. To see the giant nunda like this makes me a bit wary.

"Why not?" I have to ask, though a knot of nervous tension begins to form in my stomach.

Energy channels are generally something very . . . private, Kalanthia says finally.

"Because they're a vulnerability of some sort?"

Every being's channels are unique and say something about the being. Their strengths. Their weaknesses. Yes, giving too much information about one's channels is equivalent to announcing what needs to be done to offer a fatal attack. It is generally something only discussed with beings we trust implicitly.

"And you don't trust me that much," I conclude as I push away my reflexive sense of hurt. It's logical—we've only known each other for, what, a month? A month and a half?

Yet she's so recently said how much she *does* trust me. Heck, her alternative solution for eliminating the threat of the lizard folk *relies* on trusting me. I'm getting mixed messages here.

It's not that, Kalanthia responds sounding a little frustrated. *It's not even* you. *It's . . . I . . .* She trails off, huffs, then gets to her feet and starts pacing a little. For all her size, her movements remind me uncommonly of a caged wolf I once saw at the zoo. Walking back and forth on a worn path, which had clearly seen it do the same movements many, *many* times before. Walking because its frustration wouldn't allow it to keep still.

"I'm sorry," I say to her. "We don't have to discuss it. I didn't mean to . . ." To what? To frustrate her? To make her feel caged? What? "Make you feel uncomfortable." Kalanthia comes to an abrupt stop in front of me.

It is nothing you have done. She seems to be gaining more control over her emotions. *It is just . . . I have bad memories. Of humans. Of what they do to us.*

To me, I hear, even if it is unspoken. I knew she had bad memories; that they involve humans is both surprising and not at the same time. She knows far too much about us to have not truly come into contact with us on her world. And I know my own species well enough to know that we have a bad habit of destroying or *using* other species we encounter—heck, other humans as well—far too often. I doubt it being a different world would change that part of our nature.

"I'm sorry," I say again, "for what you have suffered. I understand why you would not wish to speak to me about something that renders you so vulnerable." I understand, but I don't know why she would then trust me with her cub's safety. Is it because, however much she wishes to protect Lathani, the cub is still separate from Kalanthia herself?

Kalanthia sighs and nudges at me with her great head. I have to put my hands on her fur to stop myself from falling over. She doesn't seem to mind; in fact, she pushes into my touch a little.

I know in my head that you are trustworthy, she says quietly. With my hands stroking a little at her fur, it feels very intimate. Like she's revealing a vulnerability to me right here and now. *But my heart is reluctant to trust again. Not with this.* I can understand that. How many of my relationship issues stem right back to my mother's death and the pain that brought me? The hurt I felt earlier vanishes. How can I blame Kalanthia for the same thing I've done?

"It's okay," I tell her softly. "I understand. I'm sorry for pushing." She doesn't reply but does relax enough to lie down again. I quickly pull my hands away from her head, not wanting to touch her if she's decided she's had enough. The nudge and look she gives me immediately after, though, reveals that she was enjoying that, thank you very much, and would like me to continue—*immediately.*

Chuckling internally at how very catlike she is, I sit close to her and continue stroking. I even dare to rub behind her massive ears lightly, my movements becoming a little firmer and more confident as she makes a sound of pleasure and pushes against me again.

We stay like that, just us two. I couldn't say for how long. Lathani is in the cave somewhere with the cubs; Bastet's keeping an eye on them all. Though, like all moments, this one has to come to an end sometime. Eventually, Kalanthia pulls away from me, and I don't try to pursue her, moving away myself.

"So, you have no ideas on how to fix my Energy channels, then?" I ask again, illogically hoping that the answer might be different this time. Madness, perhaps.

Energy channels are made from Energy. Although I have never needed to fix my channels, nor do I know of anyone who has succeeded, I would imagine the starting place to be evident.

"I guess it is." I sigh. I already tested out a method that seems like it should work. As always, though, if there's an easier or more effective way, I'd prefer to use that. But it looks like hard work is the only real answer here.

Though, Kalanthia continues thoughtfully, *I do not know how your Energy channels differ from those of a beast. You obviously start with a Core, which very few beasts do.* I wait with bated breath, but she doesn't seem inclined to expand and instead shakes her head with finality. *We will no doubt touch on these matters again when we start your Earth-Shaping lessons. Let me know when you wish to begin.*

"I look forward to them." I smile, then turn as I hear movement coming up the hill. It's River, Fenrir, and Sirocco. When I touch the Bond with Sirocco, though, I can feel that she's very nervous. I wonder why for a moment; a glance at the massive predator next to me reminds me of a likely explanation.

It's okay, I send to her down the Bond as I feel her accept my attempt to make contact. *She's not going to eat you.* Reluctance comes back at me, but I just send waves of reassurance in response. By the time my Bound come into view, I can see that she's chosen to remain sitting on River's shoulder. But I can sense through the Bond that she's ready to take flight at a moment's notice.

"Kalanthia," I say out loud. "Can I introduce you to another of my new companions?" Mentally, I try to send her a message that Sirocco's feeling very nervous and needs a little reassurance. She seems to get it—at least, she doesn't move more than just turning her head slightly.

Welcome, Sirocco, she says finally, calmly. From the surprise that comes down my Bond with the bird, I can only assume that Kalanthia is projecting to everyone. *I will not attack you as long as you do not threaten any of those under my care.* I feel a little flattered: with the words comes a little packet of impressions. Lathani, of course, is in the number one spot, but I'm also included, as are Bastet and the cubs. It seems we've grown on the nunda just as much as she's grown on me.

Sirocco seems to send something back at Kalanthia, though I only catch the barest hints of it. From those, I would guess that it is some sort of promise to behave. Either way, I send some gratitude to Kalanthia afterwards, as Sirocco feels a lot more relaxed now that the giant cat in the room has been addressed.

Indicating with my head and a mental message for my Bound to sit near the big hole that I dug for my firepit, I move towards my group and marvel at the changes within myself. When I first met Kalanthia, telepathy wasn't even something I'd believed possible. Now, I find myself picking up and transmitting messages and impressions on an increasingly regular basis.

Fenrir sits happily where I indicate, but River hesitates.

"What is it?" I ask, my eyes narrowing. Is he injured? I didn't spot anything. *Not that I can do much about it at the moment if he is,* I think to myself a touch bitterly.

I hoped to offer these carcasses to Lath—to the Great Predator's honored cub, he says a little nervously, his clawed toes shifting in the dirt.

"Oh, I see," I say, relieved. Though, I'm confused at his new mode of address for Lathani. Especially since he was calling her by her name perfectly well before. "Sure, I mean, if you three have eaten what you need, go ahead." He lifts his chin briefly to me, then strides away. Not towards where Lathani is tumbling with the raptorcat cubs, but instead towards her mother. Curious, I watch what happens.

Great Predator, I bring some sustenance for your cub, if you will deign to accept it, he offers submissively. I sense that inside he's still fearful that Kalanthia will choose to take offense at the slightest action of his that she doesn't like. Clearly, he hasn't yet been fully convinced that she will not "take her due" for his actions in the past. Or perhaps this is something linked to his culture. For all I know, offending a member higher up the hierarchy attracts a harsh social punishment even if the member herself doesn't push for it.

Choosing to respect River's privacy a little more this time, I don't dig deeply enough into the Bond to hear Kalanthia's response—she projects it to River alone. Still, I sense the relief that pours through him, and with an elongated baring of his throat, he turns to head to Lathani.

Honored cub, I have brought some food in offering to you, he says formally. Lathani pauses and a sense of confusion emanates from her. Clearly, we're close enough to be in range for her own telepathy, and she doesn't have an iota of the control her mother does.

Why are you calling me that? It's weird. I see River struggle to form a response, conflict coming very clearly across the Bond. In the end, he doesn't need to answer, as Lathani, in true cub fashion, is easily distracted. *Ooh, yummy food. Come on, little siblings. Let's eat.* The raptorcat cubs don't need any more invitation, and the three of them dig into the two carcasses that River lays down for them. I don't recognize either of the creatures, but there's *way* too much meat for cubs to eat, even if one cub is not that dissimilar in size from a full-grown leopard.

As River comes back over, the conflicted feelings still not settled, I resign myself to having to talk with him again at some point. But now is not the time.

"How did your hunt go?" I ask the three once River has crouched down with us. Fenrir sends back a sense of happiness. If I've understood the impressions he's pushing through the Bond correctly, he's eaten better today than ever before, even managing to get a few of the organs—the choicest bits, which normally only those at the top of the pack hierarchy would snaffle.

Sirocco also sends me a sense of satisfaction—it seems that she, too, had her hunger satiated. In total I had at least five influxes of Energy from the Bonds with River and Fenrir, so they must have left some of their kills behind. Interestingly, I didn't receive anything from Sirocco, so either she didn't actually participate in the fights enough to earn Energy, or her being a Tamed rather than Dominated Bound makes a difference. If it's the latter, then that may be something I should take into account if I have the opportunity to use either Tame or Dominate in the future.

It was good, reports River, answering my question. *We hunted a clawful of beasts. They are very weak here—I was surprised at how easy the hunts were. I also managed to find a number of the herbs I sought.* He looks down at the lizog next to him with a feeling of approval. *After finding the first of each type, Fenrir was very helpful in finding other examples.*

My Bound may not be able to directly communicate with each other, but they clearly still pick up a number of cues, as Fenrir realizes that River is pleased with him. A sense of happiness comes across the Bond from the lizog, and I can't help but smile at him too.

Out of all my Bound, I think that Fenrir is the most straightforward. As long as the hierarchy is clear and he has the approval of those above him, he seems to be happy. Being able to eat tasty bits of meat is evidently enough to make his day.

"I'm glad to hear that it was successful," I say after a moment. "Fenrir, River, do you want to continue absorbing Energy Hearts?" They both agree eagerly, so I hand one out to each of them. They then both beat a quick retreat, each choosing his own spot to relax and start absorbing Energy. That leaves me with Sirocco. "Have you thought about what we discussed?" I ask, noting the avaricious look in her eyes and the desire that she sends down the Bond as she gazes at River and Fenrir.

In response, she sends a sense of uncertainty and then a whole mess of other feelings and images. They are hard to parse, but with the copious amount of practice I've had, I'm fairly confident in my conclusions. Sirocco longs for companionship beyond just a "contractual" relationship, but she's fearful that more will be demanded of her than she can give. Ultimately, she wishes to have a trial period as a full member before completely deciding.

"Fair enough," I tell her with a small smile. While it's not the fullhearted dedication to the team that I might like, it's a step in the right direction. Rome wasn't built in a day, and neither is trust. If Dominate is a forced relationship that risks falling into little better than slavery, Tame risks becoming a purely contractual exchange of benefits. To move beyond either of those requires time, trust, and effort.

In honor of that, I don't hesitate before pulling out another of the Energy Hearts. What's the good of them if we don't use them to increase the power of the team, right?

"Here. Let me know when you're done with this one and I'll give you another." She sends over a feeling of gratitude and grabs it with one of her forepaws. Then she sends across a sense of uncertainty—she's not sure where to go. She's worried that if she returns to where she roosted last night, she will be vulnerable to attack. It seems like a bit of an obvious answer to me.

"Don't go anywhere," I tell her. "I mean, if you want to sleep elsewhere, that's up to you, but you're always welcome to be here. Heck, it's dry and warm inside the cave—if it rains again, you might want to consider joining us." I remember how grumpy she felt this morning after getting drenched.

She gives a noncommittal response but settles more comfortably down on the ground. Curling around the Energy Heart, she closes her eyes and clearly sets in for a session of absorption.

It's getting dark, but there will still be at least some light for another hour or so. I really should deal with River's weirdness, but I feel like I've talked way too much today. My tolerance level for conversation has definitely reduced since arriving here.

I groan as I push myself to my feet. *I'll see what he's doing,* I decide finally. *If he's busy, I'll leave him alone.* If I'm honest with myself, I would really rather he be fully occupied so I have an excuse to avoid the conversation.

CHAPTER SIXTY-TWO

Back in Business

Another day dawns. I've been working for hours already.

The higher my stats get, the less sleep I seem to need. The hours of darkness when I didn't want to risk waking my companions by moving too much were perfect to continue my current most important task.

I'm proud to say that two days after returning home, I'm within a single percent of mending the damage to my Core completely. It looks *much* healthier now, only a few hairline cracks still visible. It's taken another Energy Heart to get there, but I feel like the finish line is right in front of me. It's fortunate because even with the small boost from my reduced Energy wastage, courtesy of my newly upgraded Energy Manipulation Skill, I've absorbed enough Energy to level up once more, as crazy as that seems to me.

I still want to fully fix my Core before actually triggering the level-up, though: the chance of the remaining hairline fractures causing an issue during it is just not worth risking. For now, I'll direct the excess Energy into my debt.

In fact, I might even wait a bit longer after fixing my Core—it just feels like a waste to direct level-up points into my physical stats while they're still under twenty, but I'm equally concerned about the gap between them and my other stats growing too big. Oh well. Since I still have the debt to pay, the Energy isn't actually being *wasted*, even if I have to wait a few days.

Taking a moment to rest and eat, I idly think through the tasks ahead of me. In the end, I didn't speak to River—he seemed so focused on the Energy Heart at the time. Ultimately, I'll just keep an eye on how his behavior develops. Maybe he's just being polite. He called those Pathwalkers "honored," after all. And given that Kalanthia is probably still not all that happy with him being around, being extra polite to her and her cub is likely to do more good than harm. And although I've noticed his tendency to almost call me "Master" all the time, maybe that's just habit of some sort—he almost refers to the herbalist in the same way too. I shelve the matter as something to observe but only intervene in if it looks like there's an ongoing issue.

My other tasks are another question. There's that quest from the System, which has a countdown of fifty-two days—fifty-one now. What does that countdown mean, anyway? That I need to complete it before the time is up, or that I can only complete it on that day? Without being certain, I'll plan for the former. That way I can still wait until the end of the countdown if I'm wrong.

Kalanthia's theory that the tunnel was created by a creature even more powerful than herself makes me more than a little nervous, but I'm still determined to investigate. If it turns out the quest is too dangerous to fulfil, I can always choose not to complete it. But hopefully, if I spend some time preparing ahead of returning to that area of the mountainside, we'll be able to find a way to overcome whatever difficulty we may be presented with.

I have more reason to somehow gain control over that area than just the quest, anyway. After reaching level twelve and seeing just how much Energy it took to earn one percentage point, I was certain it was going to take ages for me to gain the Energy I needed to level up again. Yet here I am, a bare few days later, ready to level up once more—almost entirely due to the Energy Hearts and the Energy just leaking into the environment around the Pure Energy stream.

However, if the vine-stranglers are the reason why the Energy stream hasn't become a site fought over by powerful beasts, while also posing a major threat to the lizard folk village, it might be a tricky question to solve in a way that benefits both myself and the lizard folk at the same time. I can't forget that River has fulfilled his side of the bargain; I need to do the same.

I have a burgeoning idea of how to solve both objectives in one go, but that requires other steps to be put in place. Learning how to manipulate the earth from Kalanthia is a key factor. And *that* requires me to at least fix my Core and start being able to use magic again without hurting myself. It may even require me to fix the other problems the Pure Energy caused, but Kalanthia's words yesterday give me hope that I'll at least be able to start learning.

Perhaps I could use Earth-Shaping to solve both issues, though I need to fix my Core before I can even consider that as an option. And who knows how long it would take to become competent enough to make my idea feasible. But perhaps Kalanthia would be open to helping me out—for a price.

The realization that kills by my Bound generate Energy for me, whether or not I am present, is a game changer. I'm the only one who can craft out of our little band; potentially, I could stay back at the cave, practice magic and craft weapons and armor for us, and then just keep growing from the Energy I gain from the Bonds.

However, that idea also leaves me a little uneasy. While I *do* gain Energy from the Bonds, I suspect it's only a fraction of the Energy I would absorb if I was part of the kill. If I just stay back at the den and do crafting and Earth-Shaping, I have a strong suspicion that my companions will rocket in strength while I plod along. Which could lead to issues with at least some of my Bound. I'm pretty sure that Fenrir would be an issue if he suddenly started being able to overpower me. Bastet might be less of a problem: I get the impression that a raptorcat pack is a lot more cooperative than a lizog one. As for River, he *might* still be okay, even if he could overpower my Bond with his Willpower . . . but I wouldn't stake my life on it.

In short, while I am determined that increasing the power of my companions is necessary, growing my own personal power is also essential.

That's not to say that I'm not going to do any crafting. I need better armor, and that crocodile skin is still sitting in my Inventory waiting for me to work with it. Not to mention the new salamander skin that might be even better. I also want to give my tools and weapons an upgrade if I can. I haven't forgotten about the metallic glint I saw in what used to be the raptorcats' cave. If it *is* metal, that would be awesome. While my bow is still serviceable, my arrows are only flint. I remember how little damage they did to the salamander's skin. To face equally or more powerful creatures, I need better weapons.

Still, getting the metal out of the cave is not going to be easy. I'm torn between waiting until Kalanthia has—hopefully—taught me enough about shaping the earth to access the metal that way and just going now. Why go now? Because of what I see when I look at my status sheet.

In contrast to what it looked like at the beginning of my time here, my points are now heavily invested into my mental and soul stats. That's great, except for the fact that even my lowest mental stat is more than double two of my physical stats; everything I learned from the System lore stone points to that being a bad idea. The main reason is that physical limitations can impact mental limitations; I might easily not get the most out of my Intelligence or Wisdom in terms of clarity of thought or mental dexterity due to my body being lacking. And it seems that other side effects can be felt sometimes. Just another indication that maybe my stats aren't as cut-and-dried as they appeared to be at first.

If I don't want to have to dedicate any of my impending level-up points to my physical stats, I'm going to have to work to increase them naturally a bit first. Perhaps a little trip to try to harvest some metal could do just that.

Going into the forest without my Lay-on-Hands available is a bad idea. But I should manage to finish fixing my Core before the sun is far into the sky and then my Skill should be accessible again. Repairing the rest of the damage to my Energy channels is important, but not as urgent as my Core.

Satisfied I have the bare bones of a plan for the next while, I sit back with an Energy Heart in hand. Time to fix my Core completely and then go on a little trip into the forest.

The sun is only just above the trees by the time I'm finished. I pull up my status screen and gaze at it with a sense of achievement. It tells me only what I already know.

Name: Markus Wolfe		Race: Human	Class: Tamer
Level: 12	Energy to next level: 100%	Energy absorption rate: 26u/hr	Energy towards debt: 77%
Intelligence	36	Mana: 360/360	
Wisdom	36	Mana regeneration rate: 720u/hr (-20%)	

Willpower	42+8 (+20%)	Health regeneration rate: 40u/hr (-20%)
Constitution	19	Health: 190/190
Strength	15	Stamina: 90/90
Dexterity	15	Stamina regeneration rate: 150u/hr
Class Skills: Dominate – Novice 3 Tame – Beginner 6 Fade – Initiate 1		Non-Class Skills: *Lay-on-Hands – Journeyman 2* Stealth – Novice 1 Animal Empathy – Novice 6 Meditation – Novice 9 Energy Manipulation – Novice 3 Sensation Management – Beginner 5

It is immensely gratifying to see that the reduction has been removed entirely from my mana pool. Now, just to get rid of the ones affecting my mana and health regeneration rates and I'll be golden. Looking at Lay-on-Hands reminds me of the choice I still have to make there. But first, something else to test.

"Anyone got an injury I can heal at the moment?" I call. Bastet prods my arm with her paw, then nudges Storm towards me with her nose. The raptorcat cub looks disgruntled, but I see the trace of dried blood trailing down her face from her ear—an injury from a bit of rough-and-tumble, I guess.

Placing my hand on the back of her head, I activate my healing Skill. I brace for the pain of my Core cracking again but become worried as time goes on and nothing happens. Then I realize that I'm touching her with the same hand that touched the Pure Energy. Switching to the other hand, I try again.

This time I'm relieved when I feel the flow of magic down my arm, a stronger sensation than I ever remember it being before, though a tendril of worry goes through me at the implications for my damaged hand. I gently brush the dried blood away from where the small cut was and find only unblemished skin.

Just to check, I pull up my status screen. No new reduction! Wanting to be absolutely sure, I even settle back into Meditation and slip back into my Core space.

Inspecting my Core meticulously, I don't see a single crack or fracture. The outside of it is as solid and seemingly perfect as any Energy Heart, for all that my Core glows like the sun where Energy Hearts only sparkle a little. Success is a giddy feeling, and I emerge from my Meditation grinning like a loon.

"Hey, everyone! I'm back in business!"

CHAPTER SIXTY-THREE

Almost a Piece of Cake

Mixed feelings come from Bastet as we look upon the clearing that used to be her home. It's a little different from when we were last here, but despite the forest starting to reclaim it, the scars of battle are still obvious. It's only been a month or so, yet greenery is already creeping over the open ground again.

"Are you okay?" I murmur to the raptorcat, the sound deadened and muffled. Fade is active, Stealth too. It's the first time I've used either of them since leveling up so many times, and the difference is obvious. I checked with Bastet when I first activated them, and she confirmed that my scent was harder to detect, the sounds I created slightly muffled.

Since Willpower is supposed to be the deciding factor for concealment from physical senses and it's more than doubled in the last few days, that's not too surprising. I'll have to check with Kalanthia when I get back as to whether I'm any more difficult to detect with her telepathy or whatever it is she uses.

The adult raptorcat takes a few moments to respond, and when she does, it's not all that clear. Ever since the underground tunnels, I've found that her communications have been significantly easier to parse, but this one is jumbled enough to feel more like when we first forged our Bond. Longing, sadness, nostalgia, and regret are all present, but along with them are more positive emotions: pride, solidarity, a fierce protectiveness, determination.

If I had to guess, I'd say she's feeling a remarkably human sentiment of sadness about the past and her losses but pride and satisfaction in what she has now. Or perhaps that's me overly anthropomorphizing again.

"Do you want to wait here?" I ask next. The bones of her family are in that clearing, after all. Her response is a little unexpected: unhesitating desire to accompany us, to protect us. Well, maybe it's not so surprising, then. She remembers losing one family in this place; she's going to do her damnedest to make sure she doesn't lose another. "Okay."

I frown at the entrance to the cave, inexplicably wary as I scan the area. There's no evidence of a resident. No half-eaten kills, no marks of claws on trees, no depressed areas where a creature might normally lie. It all looks untouched. Yet something tells me that the cave is not unoccupied. Maybe it's just a strong suspicion based on the knowledge that prime territory like this doesn't stay empty for long.

"Do you think there's something in the cave?" I ask my Bound quietly. Three out of four immediately agree. Yes, I have the whole posse with me, bar the cubs, who have stayed with Kalanthia and Lathani. Even Sirocco is here sitting quietly in a tree and watching out for us.

She's been more approachable, less standoffish since our discussion. She didn't try to bargain for food or resources when I asked her to come with us. And her side of the Bond feels more . . . open. Relaxed. Like maybe she's not on guard against me trying to seize control of it at any moment. It's an unexpected expression of trust; one that makes me more hopeful about our future as a group.

She's also the only one who doesn't immediately agree with my suggestion. She sends me a sharper version of the same image I'm looking at and a sense of uncertainty. Clearly, even the sharp-eyed bird can't see anything amiss. However, the other three all seem confident that my instincts aren't wrong.

Fenrir sends the sense of a smell to me. It's a strange sensation: I don't actually smell the scent myself, but it feels like I did. It's strong and not something I have any hope of identifying. Bastet agrees with my feeling of something being there, but she's unsure what. River is the only one to have any idea.

I believe it is some sort of grunt-flash-of-red-click-click. Of course, that doesn't help me much either.

"Can you describe it to me?" I ask. Instead of describing, he sends me a still image. My face automatically screws up in a grimace as I see it. Another of this planet's horrors, apparently. It looks like a millipede with a stinger and massive snakelike fangs. Actually, not that dissimilar from one of the things that attacked me in my first days here, only bigger and uglier. And with a stinger, as if the creature needed *more* weapons. *I still have those barbed legs in my Inventory somewhere,* I think to myself—I really need to go through my Inventory and actually start using these things or get rid of them.

Of course, if this *is* a rematch, then I'm the one who's gained more firepower on my side: this new snilapede may have a stinger, but *I've* got Bastet, Fenrir, and River. It's also my turn to be the ambusher.

"Did you make any more of that poison?" I ask River thoughtfully.

Yes. I managed to find enough ingredients to recreate it. I didn't find a black blob, though, so I still do not have any more of the poison that attacks stamina regeneration. A black blob?

"What black blob?" I ask blankly.

An ambush predator that hides in the trees and attacks from above with a single appendage bearing poison. Oh. *Oh.* That black blob. After briefly wondering why he used my term for them, I dismiss it as some sort of translation feature. It makes a lot of sense. When I was attacked by a blob before and saved by Spike, I was completely paralyzed, unable to move—that sounds *very* like this kind of poison.

I grin. I am *completely* in favor of hunting down those bastards to provide us with sufficient poison to deal with our own enemies. Perhaps it's hypocritical to dislike the species for what they do and then use their venom to do the same thing, but I don't care. It's a dog-eat-dog world out here.

"Let's coat our weapons, then," I say to River and match my actions to words when he passes over a container. "Right," I continue, looking back at the cave from which there is still no sign of the occupant we're all convinced is present. "No way do we want to fight the thing in there. Here's the plan—let me know if you have any better ideas."

Fenrir stumbles into the clearing, blood dripping down his leg. He's limping and making low moaning noises. The creature within the cave doesn't stir but I have the sense that something is now paying attention. Fenrir stumbles over his own foot and falls to the ground, letting out a yelping noise. The sense of watchfulness increases, anticipation rising. As the seconds tick by and Fenrir stays still, only the lifting of his side giving any indication that he still lives, the tension grows.

Finally, it breaks as the creature emerges into the light. It is as we thought: a more powerful, more deadly snilapede. Where the first one had been a bit over a meter long and perhaps five centimeters thick, this one is as thick around as my thigh and at least five meters long—and the last meter is a legless stinger more like a scorpion's tail. Accompanied now by a mouthful of other sharp teeth, its fangs are the length of my hand and gleam with deadly venom. It darts forwards, its multitude of legs carrying it quickly towards the prone lizog.

However, it never gets there. As it darts forwards, it's blindsided by a raptorcat leaping out from the dip in the ground to its side, camouflage abandoned. Bastet's stealth seems to have improved a little too, perhaps due to her progress towards tier two, but her success is mostly thanks to the glacial pace she used to get closer. I was able to find her when I tried, but if I blocked out the awareness of her through the Bond, she was practically invisible. By also hiding in one of the crevices caused by Kalanthia's attack, she kept her approach concealed from the snilapede until it was too late for the creature to react.

Her attack doesn't do much damage, but it diverts the snilapede's head enough that its fangs bash into the rock instead of its hapless prey. As for said prey, I'm impressed by Fenrir's acting skills. He leaps to his feet with all signs of weakness completely absent. The small cut we made in his skin in order to allow a bit of blood out is already healed, and my Lay-on-Hands made sure he was in top condition before the play even started. He joins the fight by digging his powerful jaws into the snilapede's side and biting down hard.

River and I are not idle either. As soon as Bastet leaped, we came running into the fray with our weapons bared. I took the opportunity before joining to quickly sharpen a stick into a rough spear. It's not as good as the flint-tipped one I gave to River, but I'll replace it soon. Hopefully with a metal-tipped one, if today plays out the way I hope it will. But first, we need to clear the way.

The snilapede doesn't stand much chance against us all. Using the poison may even have been overkill. Bastet doesn't do much damage, but she's an excellent distraction. She has the speed and reflexes to be able to avoid its venomous fangs, but like with the salamander, her slashing claws are just annoying enough to keep the snilapede's attention.

Fenrir just holds on like the pit bull he resembles as his teeth slowly dig in deeper. If he manages to get through the creature's spine, it's game over for the snilapede. As for River and I, we just keep stabbing with our weapons, finding the softer spots between the snilapede's armored skin, and delivering our poison.

It's a race to see what gives first—the snilapede's stamina or its spine. Unfortunately, we've forgotten something.

I'm painfully reminded of its stinger's existence when the venomous barb pierces my side, avoiding my chitin breast- and backplate completely.

I yell in pain, but after its initial flash, it dims significantly. I can feel the venom pumping through my system. The snilapede withdraws and I just know it's going to strike at someone else. My health is dropping about a health point per second. That's not nearly enough to take me down; I just send a Lay-on-Hands running through my body and focus on the stinger.

Timing it right, I drop my spear and jump at it bodily as it prepares to strike again. I hold on for dear life, trusting my other Bound to keep the front part of the snilapede occupied.

I shift my grip when it stops flailing around quite so much to cling on like a monkey with both legs and a single hand. With the other hand, I reach for my knife and proceed to stab, slice, and saw at the chitinous tail.

Everything is a flurry of activity, but by the time I manage to detach the venomous tip from the rest of the muscle, the fight is pretty much over. I let my strong grip go and fall to the ground to see that the snilapede is on its last legs. Literally. All the legs beyond Fenrir's grip have stopped moving. Clearly, he's hit something important. The front part of the snilapede isn't looking so great either: its movements have slowed significantly, and it appears almost drunk.

With a forceful spear strike from River to the back of its head, the attacker is done.

Although everyone looks fine, if a little tired, I quickly hurry around to apply healing. I start with Bastet since she was most at risk. There's a little venom in her system—evidently, she didn't manage to avoid *every* strike—but it's still far from posing any danger to her. I clear it out anyway. No point in making her lose health she doesn't need to.

River is absolutely fine; only a few small cuts to his feet and lower legs indicate that the snilapede might have stepped on him a few times. Fenrir is completely uninjured. His position kept him away from anything but the stinger, which never targeted him.

All my Bound fine, I take a moment to clear the rest of the venom out of my own system—I couldn't do it in the fight due to needing more concentration than

I could spare at the time. Done, a grin spreads across my face, and I marvel at what we've become. A monster like that would have been really dangerous to me alone and probably pretty dangerous even if I'd had Bastet there too. But for the four of us? Almost a piece of cake.

Cleanup can wait. *Finally, time to see what's in the cave,* I think to myself with anticipation.

CHAPTER SIXTY-FOUR

Closure

Stepping tentatively towards the entrance, I check again with my companions that they don't detect the presence of anything else in the cave. After receiving cautiously negative answers from all of them, I peer into the dark hole with my spear at the ready.

As my eyes adapt a little to the light, I see that the cave is indeed empty apart from a covering of dead leaves and dry, teeth-scored bones on the rocky floor. Bedding for and detritus from the snilapede, I guess. Stepping more confidently into the cave, I drop into Fade to gain the benefits of sharper eyesight in the dim conditions.

Going to where I remember seeing a metallic glint, I'm pleased to immediately be able to identify a number of lines that look like the delta of a river running through the rock. They shine in the dim light coming in from the entrance; with my sharper eyesight, I'm even able to see the color. If I had to guess, I'd say that they're copper.

My heart sinks a little, I admit it. Copper is metal, sure, but it isn't what I was hoping for. Mixed with tin, I could make bronze, but that requires me to find the other metal. What I was really hoping for was iron—it's a lot harder than copper, and I even know a method to make a rough sort of steel, which would be great.

Still, any metal is better than no metal, and even pure copper should be an upgrade on my flint weaponry in some ways. To retrieve it, I pull out a chunk of unknapped flint from my Inventory. I've got my axe, but it's supposed to be for trees, and that needs a sharper edge than bashing some metal out of rock does.

Gripping the large lump of flint with both hands, I raise it above my head and then bring it swinging down. The reverberation stings my fingers, but I reckon the sensation is not as bad as it would have been previously—my new Sensation Management Skill may be kicking in, or perhaps it's my increased Constitution. More irritating is the fact that my flint 'pickaxe' has just cracked into several pieces in my hands.

Sighing, I tuck the shards which might be useful later back into my Inventory and brush the rest of the fragments off me where they have sprayed. Looking through my Inventory, I search for something else that might work better. Flint is hard but, clearly, not suitable. Bone is unlikely to have an effect on the rock walls. The same for the various bits of wood that's in there. Random parts of several animals is no good either. I doubt that Energy Hearts would fare any better, even if I was willing to try. Then my eyes narrow as I spot something which just might work.

Pulling a stone from my Inventory, I weigh it in my hands and examine it in the light spilling into the cave. I'm no geological expert, but it looks like it could be granite or something similar. I picked it up ages ago because it looked like it might be useful, but forgot about it until now. It's quite a big piece—more than half the size of my head. I'll definitely get a workout with this.

Raising it into the air with both hands, I swing it against the rock with a loud crashing noise.

On the upside, my chunk of maybe-granite doesn't crack into fragments like the flint did. On the downside, my single bash with the rock has little effect—that is to say, almost none. *This is going to take a while . . .*

By the time I manage to knock out my first lump of copper ore, my hands have already started to hurt and I've managed to earn half a point in Strength (Power), proving just how much force I've been using. The fact that applying the stat only cost me two percent of my Energy store is also proof of exactly how much the requirements of Energy per percentage have increased along with my level.

There has to be a better way, I decide. If I can attach a handle to this lump of rock, I'll be able to get more power out of each swing and reduce the impact carried through to my hands. Yes, it will take me a bit of time to create the implement, but it will probably save me more time than I use, both now and in the future.

Although the pitch I have with me is cold, having been left back at Kalanthia's den while I was away, I do have plenty of bark-fiber cord. Hopefully, that will be enough. If not, I'll have to melt the pitch, but waiting for it to cool will take longer than I would like.

Heading back to the clearing, I note that all my companions have been taking advantage of my absence to eat their fair share of the body. I drop Fade and see them take notice of me immediately.

Markus, we saved this for you, River says, standing and holding a dripping piece of flesh out to me. I frown in confusion, but as I get closer, it becomes clearer. I guess the snilapede was more similar to lizards than millipedes, given what the organ looks like.

"The heart?" I ask. River sends a sense of confirmation.

You asked me to save the salamander's. I thought you might like this one too.

I smile at his consideration. "Thanks. I'll set up a fire and roast it, then." I might as well do that while sorting out my new implement. I quickly set up a fire, then get the heart roasting while I search around the area for an appropriate handle.

Finding a decent-sized fallen branch that is fairly fresh, I use my axe to cut it a little down to size. I pull it over to the fire and start attempting to fix the lump of flint to the rough handle. On second thought, I pull my container of pitch out of my Inventory and set it next to the fire to melt. Even if I don't use it here and now, having melted pitch in my Inventory will be more useful in the future than cold and set pitch.

By the time the heart is cooked enough for me to risk eating it, I have made something that might do me well enough as a very primitive pickaxe. I set the tool to one side, then take the heart and cut it into bite-sized chunks. Munching away, my gaze wanders around the area. Here and there I can see whitish lumps. As I focus on them, I realize what they are: bones.

Bastet is clearly following my gaze as sadness comes from her. Without thinking, I move closer to her and start stroking her head as I would Lathani's. After the first stroke, I freeze, realizing that I've assumed she might like that kind of contact without actually asking. She seems to take a moment to consider carefully whether she likes it or not and the next moment butts at my hand, just as Lathani would have. Okay, then.

Stroking her head, I marvel at the softness of the proto-feathers covering it. Gently, I scratch at the skin underneath them, then find the flesh below her ear tufts and stroke that as well. Bastet shivers a little and then presses closer. She's warm and surprisingly light for such a large creature. Still, despite my attempts to comfort her obviously working a little, I can sense the deep grief within her.

"Do you want to bury them?" I offer after a moment of thought. Yes, I know it isn't exactly necessary—they're already bones, after all. But the purpose of burying has never been only to protect bodies from predation: it's also about letting go, offering closure. I know that all too well, even if the funeral was only the start of letting go for me.

Bastet's response is fairly indifferent. Unsurprising. Burial is perhaps too much of a human thing to suit her. *Hmm* . . . There are other traditions after death that have the same purpose as burial: spending time celebrating the loved one's life, retelling stories about their greatest successes and most dismal failures, often having a drink or a few in memory. We can't do the last, but perhaps . . .

"What about telling me about them?" I suggest. "Remembering them as they once were and saying goodbye to them for a final time?" Bastet hesitates, but I get the sense that she might actually like that, though she isn't sure how to go about it. Smiling sadly in the shared memory of grief, I push myself to my feet and go over to the closest collection of bones. "Who was this?"

Bastet joins me on taloned feet that click very softly against the stony ground. Surprisingly, River also joins, his own feelings somber. Seeing that the rest of us have moved, Fenrir joins us with a sense of curiosity—I doubt he really knows what's going on; he just doesn't want to miss out. Even Sirocco hops over, her own feelings matching Fenrir's, though with a greater dignity. Once we are all gathered around the pile of overgrown bones, Bastet begins.

Unsurprisingly, she doesn't use words. Instead, she sends me a series of still images, which I then send to everyone else. A cub gamboling and playing with a group of other cubs. A juvenile now, fluff still stubbornly clinging on in a number of places. Her first kill, her plumed tail sticking up straight in the air and wings spread wide in joy. A severe injury, which she managed to recover from, though it left a permanent scar that remained bare of feathers even after it healed. And her death, the first to be cut down by Kalanthia when she came.

Bastet's family was . . . River sends to me, his mental voice trailing off.

Killed by Kalanthia, yes, I confirm, sending the message to him privately.

And yet they seem so friendly with each other, he continues, his bafflement coming through loud and clear to me.

Bastet is very practical and saw no reason to hold a grudge against Kalanthia as long as the safety of her and her cubs was not in question. And Kalanthia has never felt any threat from Bastet. It's hard for me to understand too, I admit, *though it certainly makes things easier.*

Difficult to understand, indeed, River agrees and then falls silent. I get the sense that lizard folk may have more in common with humans than raptorcats when it comes to holding grudges. The fact that the shaman decided to come after Kalanthia's cub can't only be to do with her desiring a powerful protector, surely? I would have thought there would be plenty of easier and nearly as good targets near them. Actually, how was Lathani's spirit supposed to protect against a group of *trees,* anyway?

My thoughts are distracted by Bastet moving away to another pile of bones. One by one, she tells their stories. This one was the youngest in the pack; this one was the oldest apart from Bastet herself. This one was the last to die; this one was the first to attack. This one was missing an eye—she gives me a look at that point, which makes it very clear *who* she considers to blame for that. This one was missing an ear. When she identifies the one that most recently gave birth, only a few steps away from the cave itself, I have to be glad that the cubs aren't with us.

Not wanting to bring them back to the scene of their family's massacre was just as much part of my reasoning for not bringing them as keeping them safe was. I can't help but think that it would be a difficult experience for them to see what remains of their mother. But maybe that's just me projecting again. I quickly strangle the images that threaten to overwhelm me of the last time I saw *my* mother. *This is time for Bastet, not for me,* I remind myself firmly and concentrate back on my Bound.

When she finishes sending the final series of images as we stand around a pile of bones close to the trees, she reaffirms her attachment to us. In place of the images of past raptorcats, she sends us pictures of ourselves. It's a bit weird for me to see myself through Bastet's eyes: I look bigger, my features less defined, my hands larger, and my muscles skinnier.

River is similarly bigger, with blunter teeth and shorter claws. Fenrir is pretty much the same as he is in real life, and Sirocco is vaguer, only her claws and beak at all defined. The cubs, on the other hand, are very clearly defined, every feather almost lined with light, like they've been put through a filter to sharpen the details.

Even Lathani is there, though she is, in contrast to the rest of us, smaller than she really is and her coat is fluffier, like Bastet isn't seeing her as a juvenile yet but as the small cub she was.

The raptorcat sends a sense of belonging and contentedness along with the images, making her meaning very clear: she misses her old pack, but she has found a new one. I immediately respond with my feeling of her being my family and a dear friend. What surprises me is when the others also respond, though I have to transmit their "words" to her. Fenrir immediately sends the sense of being glad to be with his pack. River and Sirocco are more hesitant; the bird only really sends the idea of being glad to have met us and traveled a little on the road together.

As for River, the emotions he sends are rather mixed, but since they seem positive overall, I pass them on to Bastet. For a moment we all feel connected, like more than a group of mismatched beings pulled together by my Skill. And then the moment is gone.

River, Fenrir, and Sirocco return to the corpse and their leisurely meal. Bastet stays crouching down by the bones, her gaze distant, her feelings muffled. Squatting down beside my companion, I run my hand once more over her head.

"Let me know if you need anything, okay?" I tell her, then straighten up when I receive her agreement. Walking back towards the others, intending on picking up my new tool and getting back to work, my foot catches on something and I stumble. Looking down, I see an unexpected chunk of rock sticking out of the ground. Then I look a bit more closely and my eyes go wide.

Is that what I think it is?

CHAPTER SIXTY-FIVE

Hard Graft

What are the chances? I ask myself with burgeoning hope as I lean down. After using a nearby stick to dig the object out of the ground, I lift it up to inspect it. *Looks legit . . .* I place it back down on the ground and use my newest implement to break it in two, then inspect the inside. The mixed rusty red and purple makes a grin spread across my face.

"I can't believe it," I murmur out loud. My companions all send me questioning feelings, which I wave aside. My attention is taken as my newly focused eyes look around the area, spotting the iron ore rocks just randomly sticking out of the ground. Seriously, what are the chances of finding iron deposits right next to a vein of copper ore?

Well, I'm not complaining! I wanted to find iron more than copper anyway. Pulling my digging stick out of my Inventory, I set to with eagerness. Forget Bronze Age—I'm going straight to Iron, baby.

Sure, it's going to be a long old process to get these lumps of iron ore shaped into anything even remotely useful as tools or weapons, but it's going to be *so* worth it. Whether I can make them in time for my quest deadline, I don't know, but we'll see. How well learning to manipulate earth with Kalanthia goes will probably be a deciding factor since it would likely save a lot of hard graft.

Digging up lumps and piling them into a slot in my Inventory, I'm surprised when River hands me one.

Is this what you are harvesting, Ma—Markus? Checking it, I smile and add it to my stockpile.

"Yes, it is. Do you want to help me?"

Unless you wish me not to?

I shake my head. "Don't be silly. Any help would be appreciated."

We both set to work again. Funnily enough, Fenrir decides to try to help too, digging at the ground eagerly. He doesn't quite know what we're looking for—it's obvious from his various offerings of a bone, a normal rock, and a lump of dirt—but when I direct him to dig in certain areas, he helps to uncover a number of other iron ore lumps.

Whether this iron deposit was always here or it was unearthed when Kalanthia tore up the ground, I don't know. Either way, I'm very happy to have found it. Actually . . . I wonder whether being able to detect deposits of metal is something

I could learn to do with Earth-Shaping magic. Something to experiment with later, perhaps.

When I've harvested all the iron ore I can see, and a few that were revealed by Fenrir's eager digging, I stand up straight and stretch. My back is sore from all the work, so I quickly cast another Lay-on-Hands. I haven't yet earned another point in Strength, but with the amount of labor I still have to do with the crafting I have planned, I'm not worried.

Checking on my Bound, I see that they're okay. Bastet is bored and has taken up prowling around the clearing instead of lying still. Fenrir is relaxing after all his hard work. River is sending me questioning feelings, as if to ask what's next. Sirocco is still doing the same as before: sitting perched in a tree and keeping guard for us.

Even though I have iron ore now, I don't regret spending time on harvesting the lumps of copper ore. Perhaps it's a bit unrealistic, but it would be *awesome* if I could charge my phone or Kindle by creating a generator using a copper coil and an iron magnet . . . I mean, it *should* work in theory. I would need to magnetize the metal somehow and then manage to actually draw the copper into wires . . .

I'm no electronics expert, but if it's possible to light a bulb with a potato, it has to be possible to charge my phone and Kindle with an electromagnet. They don't take that much electricity, right? Whether I can do it well enough to not burn out my electronics is another question. If I use the actual chargers rather than doing it directly into the device, would that work better?

In the end, I decide to take a few more chunks of ore with me as experimentation material for when I have time. When River starts to follow me towards the cave, I stop him.

"Thanks, but it's okay. There isn't enough space in there for both of us," I explain. Seeing him look a little at loose ends, I make a suggestion. "Why don't you have a look around this area for any herbs you recognize? Just don't go too far if you do." He looks thoughtful. As I head towards the cave again, he doesn't try to join me.

Using my tool simplifies things a lot; it still takes a lot of effort and some time before I bash free a few chunks of rock that gleam slightly red. Putting them in my Inventory, I'm unsurprised when they don't stack with the iron ore. No matter.

Returning to my companions, I note that River is not present, though I see him not far away. He's harvesting a plant, so I leave him to it. While he's at it, I notice a few of those potato things nearby and take the opportunity to dig them up too.

"Ready to go?" I ask him as I finish, brushing the dirt from my hands. River agrees and we set off as a group. I've got the corpse of the snilapede draped over my shoulders like the bloodiest scarf ever. My Bound have made a good innings on the meat, but there's still more than two-thirds of it left. And I know someone else who would appreciate it. "What did you find?" I ask River curiously as we run through the forest at a pace even I, as the one with the least stamina, can keep up almost indefinitely.

A few leaves used in a number of healing poultices, some berries that are very tasty, and even some blood-root, only found in areas where there has been significant bloodshed.

Unsurprising to find it here, then, I think to myself. "What is blood-root used for?" I ask audibly.

Mostly for a herbal concoction that helps to replenish blood. River sends over a sense of uncertainty. *I believe my . . . our . . . Honored Herbalist can make a more powerful concoction, but I am unsure. Blood-root can be difficult to find, so I was pleased to be able to harvest so much here.*

Good to know. It's a pity Kalanthia wants the herbalist dead: getting access to actual magical potions that are more effective than simple herbal remedies could expand our capabilities significantly. Maybe if we had the right kinds of potions, we could even take on the powerful beast Kalanthia suspects of creating the tunnel down to the Pure Energy. And if the herbalist made concoctions to help keep Lathani alive instead of to exploit her, it would be rather poetic justice—though, since Kalanthia wants her dead, that might be moot.

We're not far away from the cave when Bastet's warning growl rings out. Her lips have lifted off her teeth and she's gone rigid. Fenrir is hissing too. I tense and look in the direction they're staring.

It still takes me a moment to spot what she has—the creature is well camouflaged against the forest. It's hard to get a proper view of what's waiting for us even now. I grip my spear more firmly and lift it off the ground in preparation to attack. I also drop the snilapede carcass to the ground. If it comes to a fight, I don't want that impeding us.

A rattling sort of hissing sound emerges from the blurred patch of forest floor before my eyes. The creature, perhaps realizing that we've spotted it, pushes itself to its feet as its camouflage flickers away. It starts prowling around us, seemingly agitated. And now that its full body has come into view, I suspect I might know why: it resembles the massive snilapede lying in a crumpled heap on the ground. Could this be its mate?

I'm confident that we can take it on: we defeated the other one, and this looks slightly smaller than the one I've been carrying. But that time we had the advantage of surprise and a battle plan. This time we're the ones taken by surprise. Though, thanks to Bastet and Fenrir's senses, at least we didn't literally walk into an ambush.

It still hasn't attacked. Its attention seems to be on the body of what's probably its mate. Perhaps we don't need to fight? Honestly, I'd rather not. We came here to get metal and we've got some. Fighting the first snilapede was necessary for that objective; this is not.

But communicating that could be a little difficult . . . *Unless . . .*

I fix my eyes on the snilapede's snakelike ones and then murmur the trigger for my Skill.

"Dominate."

The gray space around me fades into place, the snilapede at one end, me in the middle.

The pressure is strong but not overwhelming. It's more difficult than when I faced River in this position, but it's not insurmountable. I can push forwards without needing to go all out.

Why am I here? Its first recognizable "words" come shortly after I push halfway between my starting point and the snilapede. I am unable to tell whether it's male or female, and its mental speech is only slightly less blurry than Bastet's, but we're able to communicate—that's the most important thing. Interestingly, it's the first creature since River to communicate in such easily understandable projections; though, unlike the lizard-man, it's immediately obvious that the snilapede has no true understanding of language.

"You were about to attack us, weren't you?" I ask it, continuing to push forwards.

You killed my mate, it answers. Faint emotions brush against me—anger and disappointment are the most prevalent. Markedly absent is any sense of sadness. *I had not yet fertilized her eggs.* Is it angry about basically being cockblocked?

"Your mate attacked us," I tell it—him, I suppose. "She died. If you attack us, you will die too. If you turn around and don't try to attack, we won't attack you. You can live to find another mate and . . . fertilize other eggs." Then another possibility comes to mind.

The camouflage this creature has shown is pretty impressive, and he also has a stinger at the end of his tail. His appearance might make my skin creep, but that doesn't mean he couldn't be a decent part of the team. And if I'm going to send my Bound out into the forest more and more without my presence, having good fighters to replace me will be essential. We've just killed this one's mate, sure, but he doesn't seem too sad about it, just frustrated. Maybe he'd be open to a Bond as long as it doesn't prevent him from finding another female?

"If you want, you can become part of our group. There's strength in numbers, and if you find another female of your kind, you can spend time with her without any problem. Heck, we could even help to defend her if she joined the group too."

I sense other males among your numbers, he answers immediately. *Males are competition, threat.*

"Except we are not rivals but teammates. We work together to help each other become stronger. We defend against each other's weaknesses. No one can be strong in everything."

Weaknesses are advantages for a rival, the snilapede answers firmly. *Taking advantage is natural. Defending against others' weaknesses is not.*

I sigh. Looks like this one isn't going to be a good match for our group. Pity.

"Have it your way," I tell him with a hint of frustration. "I won't force you as long as you promise not to attack us."

The snilapede seems to consider that for a long moment.

I don't attack those stronger than I am, he answers finally. Satisfied, I start backing off. Once I get far enough away from the creature, the world fractures around me and color bleeds back into my environment.

I'm immediately hit by my paralysis. By this point Bastet is familiar with what's going on, but I reassure my newer Bound.

It's fine. I'll be like this for a few seconds. The snilapede promised to leave without a fight. They relax a little but remain on their guard. I approve. We can never know what might happen in this forest even if the snilapede has agreed that avoiding a fight is best. They tense even further and tighten ranks around me as the creature comes a little closer, only to head towards the cave.

River and Bastet's wary gazes seem paranoid when the snilapede simply heads away from us, his long, sinuous body following after his head piece.

Then, abruptly, we lose sight of him.

Alarm bells start ringing in my head, and I warn my Bound to be careful. Why would he activate his camouflage right now unless he meant to—

Bastet cries out as a stinger buries itself in her belly. The rest of my Bound pile in on the snilapede, his position revealed by the attack. Fortunately, the ten seconds of paralysis have worn off and I'm able to spring to my feet, using the motion to propel myself to Bastet.

Slamming my hands on her side, I immediately cast Lay-on-Hands and feel it start chasing the venom out of the hole left by the stinger and healing the flesh at the same time. It takes most of my mana pool, but Bastet is out of danger and back in the fight within less than a minute.

Standing up, I take stock of the situation. Fenrir has repeated the same tactics as before and is clinging onto the side of the snilapede with his bone-crushing jaws. River is stabbing at the creature's head with his spear, but this one is quicker than the other and his strikes keep missing.

I pull my mace from my Inventory and slam into the snilapede's tail—I don't want to repeat the mistake of forgetting about the stinger. My blow is well-timed: it crushes the monstrous creature's stinger to the ground and, by happy accident, manages to trap it under a thick tree root at the same time. I take advantage of his suddenly restricted mobility to grab my spear with two hands, leaving the mace trapping the stinger, and stab at his tail, aiming for his spine in the hope of hitting something vital like before and making his immobility permanent.

Bastet tries to take the role she had before, dancing and slashing before the snilapede, but he seems to be fixated on River. The lizard-man is obviously tiring—the speed of the snilapede's attacks is beginning to overwhelm him.

My mace is still pinning the snilapede's tail in place, so I leave it there and run up the length of his body to attack the head with my spear.

It all happens very fast. I don't even see what occurs exactly. The snilapede suddenly moves and then a hissing shriek rings through the air. River falls away and Bastet leaps in.

I draw abreast of the head and take in the situation at a glance. River's left arm has been somehow bitten off at the elbow, blood pumping sluggishly from the stump. He's fallen back, clutching it with pain and shock written across his face. At the same time, Bastet has finally managed to get a decent grip with her teeth and claws on the creature's scaled face, but his fangs and a dangerous-looking pair of mandibles hidden inside his mouth are only inches away from her flesh.

I have to make a snap decision. The snilapede is the most dangerous threat and River seems to be applying enough pressure to his arm to stop himself from bleeding out immediately.

"Hold it as tightly as you can. I'll be with you in a moment!" I yell at him as I round on the snilapede. Bastet is weighing the creature down—he can't make the fast dodges that tired River out. I don't want to stab my companion, though.

Shifting to the side, I pull out my knife and, choking up on my spear, use both weapons to stab at the snilapede's throat like a madman.

The creature writhes, his tail finally managing to pull free of the tree root and my mace—leaving the stinger behind. Fenrir releases his grip, only to bite on the other side from where I'm attacking. Even Sirocco is finally joining the fight as she flies down to scratch at his eyes.

The desperate struggle continues for a few more seconds until, finally, we get through the snilapede's spine. He suddenly goes limp, and the sounds of battle abruptly cease with him.

But not all battle has ceased. My heart in my mouth, I turn to River to battle once more—this time for his arm.

CHAPTER SIXTY-SIX

You Can't Fix It

My mana has started recovering after using most of it to help Bastet, but it's not enough. My mind races desperately until it hits on a solution that worked before. Hopefully, it will work the other way around too.

"Bastet, I need your mana!" I exclaim even as I hurry over to River and start pouring what I do have into his arm. She responds with a feeling of grim agreement—I interpret that as her saying to take what I need.

Trying to repeat what I did before when I was the one dying, I pull on the Bond I have with Bastet. Fumbling, it takes me far too long to make the necessary connection. River is going an oddly pale shade of green, his breath coming shorter, his eyelids flickering across his eyes more and more.

I can feel his pain and shock through the Bond, the way his life is dripping away with the blood that he can't stop from leaving his system. But I don't dare create a proper tourniquet—I don't know whether that would interfere with the healing magic I'm trying to use.

Then, finally, when I'm starting to fear that it only worked with River because of some species-specific reason, I succeed in pulling a tendril of mana from my raptorcat companion.

I drain Bastet's mana pool, and then, if her hiss of pain is anything to go by, I start taking from her health too. I almost stop pulling on her resources, but her determination keeps me going. She wants to save River as much as I do.

My mana pool refills, and I direct all of it into River. Pushing out the venom is the first step; healing his arm is the second. The venom dribbles out easily enough, but his arm is far more stubborn.

"Come on!" I growl at it in frustration, opening my eyes for a moment. The stump of his arm is still there, no better than it was before. I sense that the magic is eager to close up the wound, but something is stopping it from regrowing, and I have to fight with Lay-on-Hands to stop it automatically sealing River's wound forever.

After what feels like an age of struggling with it, I have to admit what was obvious from the beginning: it seems that I've hit one of the limitations of Lay-on-Hands. Healing bones is one thing, as is repairing organs. Regrowing a lost limb is something else.

But what if I can reconnect the limb he lost? His arm must be *somewhere*.

"River, where's your arm?" The lizard-man looks at me, his eyelids almost entirely closed and what is visible of his eyes clearly glassy with pain. He doesn't seem to understand what I said, so I repeat it again, pushing it through the Bond for emphasis.

In it . . . The beast. It ate it.

His disjointed thoughts are good enough for me. I order him to keep his fingers held tightly around the stump of his arm, then push myself to my feet. Whirling on the carcass of the snilapede, I kick it onto its back.

Grabbing my dagger, I slit it from its throat until halfway along its length. Every time my blade gets caught on the underbelly armor, I curse loudly. Every time my knife is too mired in guts for it to keep going and I have to saw to get it through, I growl.

Finally, once the body is open enough, I'm able to rummage inside the organs in search of River's arm. It's absolutely disgusting—the sensation makes me feel sick; the smell makes me heave a few times. But then I find it. Sort of.

Already in the first of apparently multiple stomachs, the remains of River's arm aren't in good condition. It's been partly chewed by the sharp mandibles in the snilapede's mouth, significantly ripped by the nasty teeth-like protrusions in the esophagus, and pockmarked by the acid of the stomach. My hopes take a nosedive. It looks more like a chunk of meat than an arm by this point. Two of its fingers are already lost, the others showing bone.

I try to use Lay-on-Hands on the limb itself, but the magic just washes through the flesh without making any difference. With fear filling my heart, my eyes make contact with River's.

He's even less lucid than he was earlier, the glassiness to his gaze even worse than before. I don't think he's focusing on anything. He's terribly pale too, his scales looking more gray than green, and his jaws are clamped tightly together. But still, he somehow knows I'm looking at him, still manages to sense the terrible conclusion I've come to.

You can't fix it, can you? he asks me weakly. I clench my jaw.

"I *will* fix it," I promise. Maybe the limb has to be attached to the main body to accept healing magic?

Pressing the remains of River's forearm and hand to the stump just below his elbow, I pour healing magic into the connection, willing the two to connect.

When my mana pool runs dry, I have to admit the truth. This isn't working.

I let the forearm drop. It falls to the ground with a thud, just a lump of dead meat. Maybe that's why this isn't working: it's been detached for too long. Maybe if I was quicker, maybe if I'd thought of it sooner . . . Maybe if I hadn't taken the snilapede at his word and allowed him to choose when the battle began. Maybe if I'd just forced the Bond on the creature in the first place . . .

Sighing heavily, I avoid River's eyes. I Meditate to increase the speed of my mana regeneration, then close the open wound once enough has accumulated. That's all I can do for him.

Once done, I let my hands drop, then force myself to look up at him.

"River . . . I'm *sorry*." The word doesn't feel like it's enough. Doesn't feel like nearly enough for what he's lost. I remember how I felt when the wolvezard damaged my eye enough to make me half blind. This has to be at least as bad, if not worse. So many things require two hands.

I know that there are plenty of people on Earth either born without a hand or who have to get used to the loss of one due to an accident or lifesaving surgery. But in this world, where being able to wield a weapon is the difference between fighting off an attacker or becoming dinner, it's a different story.

With his arm healed as much as possible and the rest of his wounds intact, River is still weak—he lost a lot of blood.

Blood.

"River, that plant you found earlier. Can you eat it to help with your blood loss?"

It takes the lizard-man a long moment to focus on me—he's staring at where his arm used to be, loss and desolation the only thing I can feel through the Bond. I have to repeat myself, loathe as I am to pull his attention onto me.

The blood-root . . . It is more effective in a potion . . . but it will help even raw, he answers quietly, not even looking up at me. Almost mechanically, he starts pulling the dark-red roots from his belt container. He chews them, showing no indication of whether he likes the taste or not.

After a few minutes, his color improves a little; his emotional state does not.

I don't know what's going on inside him. Many bad thoughts, I'm sure. But which ones, I don't know. Is he blaming me?

He has reason to. I misread the snilapede completely. Thinking it over, I now realize that the creature never promised not to attack us; he said that he did not attack creatures stronger than him. I, arrogantly, assumed that was an admission that we were stronger. Which we were in the end. But I didn't consider the idea that he might not acknowledge that. Or maybe he thought he had a chance because of my paralysis?

It cannot be denied that the whole fight could have been avoided if I had forcibly Dominated the snilapede. And if I hadn't activated the Battle of Wills at all, we would have been more prepared for an attack, and River wouldn't have been forced to take Bastet's role, the main reason for his exhaustion. And if he hadn't been exhausted, he most likely would still have his arm.

Well, if he wants to leave after this, I will honor that. I'll convince Kalanthia not to kill him and to let him go—I owe him that much. But, as a rustle in the undergrowth around us reminds me, sticking around here at the scene of a fight is just asking for trouble.

"Come on, River," I say gently as I stand up and offer my right arm for him to grab.

The lizard-man doesn't even look up at me.

"River, look, I'm sure you're angry with me—you have a right to be—but please, let me help you until you get your feet under you. Then you can leave if you want."

My tone is almost begging. If he doesn't want to come home with me, if he doesn't want anything more to do with me, I'll understand it. But it will tear at my heart to leave him like this.

Finally, he looks up at me, his gaze utterly hopeless. It takes my breath away. I recognize that look. I saw it in my own eyes when I stared into the mirror after losing my job. Right before I walked up to the roof of my apartment building.

He's a man who feels like he has nothing left to live for.

I am useless. You should leave me here, he tells me so quietly that if we didn't have a Bond, I probably wouldn't have been able to hear him.

"You're not useless!" I tell him firmly. "You've . . . you've lost an arm, I know. But that doesn't make you useless!"

Back in my village, my master would have rejected me from her service. I would have been left to fend for myself, to starve or be killed by a beast. Crippled as I am, that is all I'm good for, he continues, speaking numbly as if he hasn't heard me. Maybe he didn't.

I swallow and then force myself to stop stewing in my own self-recrimination. As much as I want to respect his wishes, River is clearly not in the right condition to make decisions for himself right now. I need to get him—and everyone else— home, and then we can deal with everything.

"Come on, stand up," I tell River firmly, then grasp the wrist of his good arm and tug gently until he tugs back, allowing me to lever him up to his feet. I steady him when he stumbles, off-balance. I eye the two carcasses. It seems a waste to leave them here, but I don't want to risk drawing other predators.

In the end, I decide that losing the Energy is better than losing the carcasses entirely and put them both into my Inventory.

River still looks dazed, but getting to his feet has apparently brought his awareness back to the present. Bastet is concerned, pressing against my knees and looking from me to the lizard-man. Fenrir is worried too, a constant quiet whining hiss emerging from him. Sirocco is the only one who doesn't seem to be at all emotionally affected and is more concerned about the amount of time we've been here.

As we make our way back to the den, the only communication that passes between us is to warn of potential danger.

Despite what has happened, though, I find that I'm grateful. At least River is still alive. At least my poor decisions haven't led to the death of another of my Bound, like poor Spike. Where there's life there's hope. If River will allow me to, I'm determined to show him that.

CHAPTER SIXTY-SEVEN

Concerning

Fortunately, the rest of our trip is without incident. Then again, we've had more than enough excitement to last for days.

"Kalanthia," I say as I approach the massive nunda, who's sunning herself outside. She opens one massive golden eye and regards me with curiosity. I'm unable to summon up a smile for her, though.

Yes, Markus Wolfe? Her eyes are curious. I don't respond to the silent question that I see in them and instead avoid her gaze, looking down.

"I brought these for Lathani." I reach into my Inventory and pull out the two Cores from the snilapedes. "As a start on River's debt. And she's welcome to eat some of this if she wants. It probably doesn't have any Energy in it, though." My warning is without emotion; after everything, I'm feeling rather numb myself. I pull out one of the snilapede carcasses—the first, it turns out.

Kalanthia eyes me with an unreadable look and then turns her attention to the carcass before her nose.

Ah, a liman. She noses at the corpse. *A recently Evolved one. A good find, though it would be better if it still had Energy within it. One of the Cores is from this beast?*

"Yes. The other Core is from a similar one."

Good, Kalanthia responds. *The newly Evolved Core might help stabilize the damage to Lathani's Energy channels better than others.* Looking towards the cave, I sense her communicating with someone, though I can't make out the message. When Lathani comes running out a moment later, I guess I didn't need to; being able to detect the message at all is already a step forwards compared to where I used to be. As Lathani starts to lick at the Core happily, her mother looks at me with her head tilted. *Something seems to be concerning you. Do you wish to speak on it?*

I can't help looking over at River. During our slow walk through the forest, he seemed to adapt to having less weight on one side than he's used to, but he certainly hasn't come to terms with it yet—not that I'd expect him to do so that quickly. He was utterly silent as we walked and has now slumped down with his back against the wall. My heart goes out to him. He's lost his people, his freedom, and now his arm too.

I clench my jaw and look back up at Kalanthia.

You did not come out of your battles today unscathed, she observes solemnly.

"I did. River didn't," I say bitterly. Not that I'd like to lose an arm, but the guilt claws at my stomach for being the cause of the issue and not suffering the consequences. *Like with Spike.* And the guilt deepens at the knowledge of the relief buried inside me that it didn't happen to *me*.

What happened?

I hesitate for a long moment, but as if her inviting question has opened the floodgates, I find myself unable to keep silent, the guilty knot in my throat slipping free.

I tell Kalanthia everything, not allowing myself to leave anything out—not the fact that I was the one to initiate the Battle of Wills, nor that I let the snilapede deceive me into thinking he would not attack afterwards.

When I'm done, I feel like I've vented a stomachful of poison—and now I'm waiting to see whether someone will force-feed it to me again or tip it away.

Kalanthia doesn't respond immediately. Instead, she takes her time to mull over her words. It's something that I both love and hate about her. She's so careful with her words, with her emotions. Not like me. It means that I often struggle to know just what she's thinking or feeling, but at the same time, I know that whenever she speaks, it's fully intentional and thoughtful.

You are an odd sort of Binder, Kalanthia muses. *I have said it before, and I say it again now.*

"I bet a normal one would have just bound the snilapede with no issues, nullifying the problem before it started," I say bitterly.

Most likely, she agrees. It doesn't make me feel better. *However, I have seen where that leads, and I cannot counsel that route.*

"So, what? I should risk any creature turning around and attacking us after it refuses the Bond?"

I would suggest merely being a little wiser about those you accept promises from. Those who consider strength to be above all will not be swayed by mercy but by strength. However, yes, you should always be prepared for a fight, just as you should consider whether a fight is necessary in the first place. On my part, the only true mistake I would consider you to have made this afternoon was in not recognizing that you needed to present a strong image of overwhelming power immediately after your Battle of Wills. You showed weakness when you had already seen enough to indicate that would be an invitation for such a creature to attack. Not all beasts will be the same; you have already experienced one who was not, from your tale earlier.

That's true. I hadn't thought it about that way: maybe my mistake was not in showing mercy, but in *how* I showed that mercy.

"I just wish that River didn't have to pay the price." I sigh. Kalanthia rumbles.

It is a shame for him that he is not a Shaper. If he were an Earth-Shaper, he would be able to Shape a new hand for himself. It might even be more powerful than the original.

Shaping . . . I sit bolt upright from where I've been lounging as a thought occurs to me.

I was offered something called Flesh-Shaping in exchange for giving up Lay-on-Hands—I'm almost certain of it.

You seem to have been struck by an idea, Markus Wolfe, Kalanthia observes as I open my notifications and scroll through them to find the one I want.

> You have discovered a use of your Skill, Lay-on-Hands, which is not compatible with its originating school, the Way of the Healer. Skills from this school are explicitly focused on doing no harm. You have used your Skill in a combat situation to kill your opponent. You therefore have a choice to either Evolve your Skill or Split it.
>
> Evolve
> If you choose to Evolve your Skill, you will gain access to a new area of magic: Flesh-Shaping. This will enable you to shape your own and others' flesh to your desires with or without permission. This Skill is not classed as healing magic and is, therefore, subject to different limitations and potential growth than your original Skill. Some potential aspects that you have not yet explored may therefore be lost. Functions that you have practiced and gained personal knowledge of will be retained.
>
> Split
> If you choose to Split your Skill, you will retain your original Skill and all previous progress will remain intact. You will also gain a second Skill: Body-Invasion. This new Skill will allow you to influence an opponent's body with either destruction or overgrowth by invading their bodies with your mana. Invasions with foreign mana are automatically resisted by the enemy, and this resistance must be overcome in order for the Skill to be used successfully. Intense concentration is required for this process, and mana can flow both ways over the connection.
>
> Until you make a choice, you will be limited to the use of your original Lay-on-Hands Skill. This precludes combat applications.
>
> Close messages? Y / N

"A new area of magic . . . Flesh-Shaping," I say to myself thoughtfully. I'd almost forgotten about this choice to be made. It's just as well that I've remembered it now.

What is this, Markus Wolfe? Kalanthia asks curiously.

"Well, I was hoping you might have an idea, actually," I admit. Then I explain the situation—when I went over the fight with the salamander before, I hadn't talked about such details. I do now. "And so," I finish, "I was wondering if you've ever heard of Flesh-Shaping."

I have not heard of Flesh-Shaping per se, she says thoughtfully. Before my heart can sink too much in disappointment, though, she continues. *However, there are many types of Shaping I have encountered, both personally and through encounters with other beasts. Earth-Shaping, Lightning-Shaping, Water-Shaping, Wood-Shaping, Air-Shaping, Shadow-Shaping . . .*

They are all powerful abilities that allow beasts to gain control over a certain element. For me, and for you if you succeed in learning it, Earth-Shaping allows for the manipulation of Energy within the earth. I can extend my senses through it and cause it to change shape or receive messages from it. I am stealthier when touching earth since it actively helps me to reduce my impact as I walk or run. Some substances are harder than others to manipulate, but if they are classified as "earth," they fall within my purview. Without knowing for sure, I would guess that Flesh-Shaping is much the same.

"It does state that I should be able to control mine and others' 'flesh'," I muse half to myself.

You are considering this as a potential way of regrowing your lizard-kin's arm?

I nod. "I can't heal it. My healing magic is clearly limited when it comes to regrowing limbs. But if I can manipulate flesh . . . Though, I wonder whether bones would even count as flesh."

I do not know, Kalanthia admits. *Not everything that is in the earth is under my control, it is true.* I hum thoughtfully.

"Have you heard of Body-Invasion?" I ask Kalanthia next, my gaze not moving from the text in front of me.

Only when it comes to incorporeal or semi-corporeal beings. Spirits have a nasty habit of invading the bodies of those without sufficient Willpower to defend against them, the most powerful of them able to take control of weak bodies. Some other incorporeal beings and semi-corporeal beings do not puppet others' bodies, but they can disrupt a body's functioning. Usually, a robust network of internal connections and the ability to flood them with mana when appropriate is enough to deal with such attacks. It can be difficult to defend against an invasion conducted by a far more powerful being, however.

If that's what Body-Invasion is about, then it's not immediately useful for the matter at hand. It certainly wouldn't help me get River's arm back. However, I can't make my decision based only on River, much as I want to help him.

Seen objectively, Body-Invasion could be an interesting Skill in certain contexts. Invading and puppeteering others' bodies? Or disrupting their internal connections by using mana? Potentially powerful depending on how much effect I could have on others. But I'm not sure that it's a route I'm keen on taking. I already have my Bound, after all—why would I need other bodies to puppet? And if Flesh-Shaping is capable of doing what I did to the salamander, that would suit my needs. I don't need anything fancy like internal matrix disruptions.

And, of course, I would still be limited to the current capabilities of Lay-on-Hands. Not only is this recent issue with being unable to regrow a severed limb worrying, but there's also the matter of it always requiring body contact in order to function. And I would guess that Body-Invasion would be the same. At least at the outset. But what about Flesh-Shaping? *I wonder . . .*

"Do you have to be touching the earth to affect it?" My question seems to take her a little aback.

I . . . I am unsure, she admits slowly. *Not possessing wings, I tend to always be touching the ground, so it is a little difficult to say whether I need to be or not.*

"What if you were in a tree?" I suggest. Kalanthia is silent, though I sense a thoughtfulness from her. Then, with no warning, she pushes herself to her feet in one fluid motion. She's gone before I have time to blink, bounding quickly down the slope and disappearing into the forest.

Bastet sends a questioning feel down the Bond, and I sense my other Bound staring too—even River looks up with a hint of wariness. Sirocco sends me a faintly accusing, questioning feel, as if wondering whether I offended Kalanthia somehow.

"I don't *think* so," I reply. "I'm not entirely sure why she disappeared, but I have a feeling it's to test a theory. I doubt she'll be gone for long."

She isn't, as it turns out—only a couple of minutes. Once more there's a blur of spots and then she's lying back in her position like she'd never been gone. I eye her with a hint of amusement.

"Got your answer, then?"

Indeed, she answers, her tone implying satisfaction. I have a feeling I know what she found out before she even says it. *It was harder to manipulate the earth from the canopy above it, but I was able to do so. I wasn't, however, able to affect the earth while hovering above it.*

"I thought you couldn't fly?" I can't help but ask, confused.

No. But I can jump. For some reason, the image of the massive nunda just randomly jumping again and again in the forest amuses me despite the seriousness of the situation.

"Do you know why?"

I can guess. The tree is still connected to the earth, and by standing in it, I am connected to the tree. Air seems to have no true connection to earth, and I have no true connection to air, meaning that it becomes essentially impossible for me to forge a link. If I could spend longer in the air, I might find a way, but since I'm not likely to become a bird, I see no point in trying to do it by leaping around like a cub.

"Fair enough," I agree before returning to my thoughts. So, it looks like the secret is in sending magic down connections. Which might mean that I could potentially use Flesh-Shaping in the same way and hopefully heal from a distance. But something tells me that it's not possible to use Lay-on-Hands in the same way—perhaps the name of the Skill really is descriptive of its limitations.

This choice is still a bit of a gamble. Body-Invasion isn't immediately useful but could be powerful later—maybe. Lay-on-Hands has gotten me out of innumerable sticky situations and losing that could be . . . very bad. The main benefit of the first option is that it leaves me with my Lay-on-Hands intact.

However, as I've just found out, it's not all-powerful. In fact, for something approaching the Master rank, it doesn't feel as powerful as I might expect. Nor has its scope broadened that much. It started as a healing Skill and remains a healing Skill. The main things that have changed are how much health is healed per point of mana used, the fact that I can "dive" into my patients' bodies to seek out issues, and that it's become easier to manipulate.

Good improvements, yes, but nothing as ground-breaking as some Skills the System lore stone gave me information about. Like Fireball, which a Classer was documented as having. It started as a single golf-ball-sized thing at Beginner, grew in size at Novice, and at Initiate, the immensely hot missile was able to modulate in size between a beach ball and a marble. At Journeyman, it became more interesting, when it was able to be directed to follow a single target and engulf them in flames that couldn't be put out by normal means. By the time it got to Master, a single use of the Skill had been able to target multiple people or engulf a small army in flames that burned at the rate the Classer wanted them to.

That particular user never got to Grandmaster—killed in some battle or other. However, as an example of progression, it is a very clear one. The essence of the Skill didn't change: it always used fire and mana to do damage. However, it transformed from a fairly weak Skill, which would take several casts to do much damage, to an immensely powerful one, which could change the course of a battle if well applied.

As for Flesh-Shaping . . . If Kalanthia's words about Earth-Shaping have taught me nothing else, they've shown me that anything linked to Shaping has an incredibly wide scope. Even if she says she can't affect everything within the earth, I've seen her control at least soil and stone. Perhaps she can manipulate crystals or metal. She's certainly not limited to only being able to make pits, for example. Or spikes. She can do *anything* she has the imagination and mana for—as long as it's within the scope of the earth.

That's what draws me to Flesh-Shaping, especially in light of recent events. However, it is a gamble because there's no guarantee I'll be able to heal with it, let alone heal as well as a dedicated healing Skill can—even if that Skill has proven to have its own limits.

I bite my lip. *Functions that you have practiced and gained personal knowledge of will be retained*—that's what it says in the text box about Lay-on-Hands. Surely that is proof enough that healing at least as well as I have been so far should be all but guaranteed?

But if I choose Flesh-Shaping and I'm wrong, then we'll have a major issue.

I clench my jaw and make my decision. Nothing ventured, nothing gained. That is one of the truths of this new world. If I'd just holed up in a mostly safe shelter, I wouldn't have anything I do now.

The fact is that my healing Skill has proven to be insufficient for my needs, but Flesh-Shaping might fill in that gap.

Having made my choice, I don't allow myself to second-guess it and select the option to Evolve the Skill.

CHAPTER SIXTY-EIGHT

Useless

Nothing happens, though the nagging sense of a notification appears. Returning to my messages, I see a new one waiting for me. Worry prickles at my gut, and I can't help but fear that it's bad news.

Error.
Your internal matrix is compromised. Modifying existing Skills is not possible until this is restored to full functionality.

Close message

I read the message with dismay running through me. *Have I waited too long?* If I'd made the decision when it was first presented, it would have been before the incident with Pure Energy that damaged my internal matrix. As it is, what if by the time my internal matrix is fixed, I've lost the ability to choose? If that costs River the only chance to regain his arm, I'll never forgive myself.

And that's only if there aren't consequences from *not* choosing. The best-case scenario would be if the System automatically chose an option for me, ideally what I would have chosen for myself anyway; if it chose the second option, that would be the second-best decision, I suppose.

I can't help feeling that there are other possibilities on the table, though. What if it doesn't choose either option but instead just removes combat damage from my repertoire of potential abilities? Given that it seems to have done that in the absence of my decision, I can't help but think this is a strong possibility. Or—hopefully, this is only a paranoid imagining—what if it "breaks" my Lay-on-Hands Skill entirely, rendering it completely unusable?

The last seems the least likely, but few of the more likely options are particularly desirable either. I groan and grit my teeth as I realize that fixing my internal matrix as quickly as possible is the only solution I'm coming up with for this situation.

However, I estimate that it will take me quite a while when spending a few hours on it per day. Even if I managed to fix my Core in a little more than a day, the damage to my internal matrix is more complicated and extensive; it's definitely going to take longer. Do I even have that sort of time?

I send a look over at River sitting disconsolately against the cave wall, staring into space. Even if I do have the time, that's far longer than I want to leave him as he is.

It's been . . . four days since we fought the salamander and the original message appeared. Some instinct tells me that I won't have more than that time again to choose. Maybe even less. So, probably another three days left until . . . whatever happens. Possibly four, but I wouldn't like to bank on it.

Three days . . . Is that enough? *It'd better be*, I say to myself grimly, refusing to truly consider the alternative. Now I have a path in front of me, I'm determined to see it through. If I focus purely on this task and postpone all other activities until afterwards, I might have enough time. *And there's no time like the present.*

I stand up, deciding to find a more comfortable position, only to catch Kalanthia's gaze. I remember that we were actually in the middle of a conversation.

You have an air of resolve about you, she comments. *Have you chosen which option to take?*

"Yeah," I sigh. "But it turns out that I have to finish fixing the damage from the Pure Energy before I can take it. Thanks for your help."

It was interesting for me too, she replies. *As you humans say, good luck.*

I send her a grim smile in return, not wanting to let on how stressed I actually feel.

Eager to get this over with, I stride over to River first. Crouching in front of him, I consider what to say. I don't want to get his hopes up in vain, but at the same time, I don't want him to feel there's *no* hope.

About to speak, I'm preempted by River himself.

Have you come to release me from your service? His words are lifeless, shoved into the air as if he cannot bear to hold them in his throat.

A stabbing pain goes through me, and I swallow hard.

"If that is what you wish, I will," I answer quietly. "If you truly want to go, I will not argue. But I ask you as a . . . as a *friend* if you would stay long enough for me to see what I can do to help you."

That makes River turn and look at me searchingly, his eyes full of more life and awareness than I've seen since the battle.

You . . . you wish to . . . help me?

"Of course!" I say, startled. "I can't tell you how sorry I am that I was unable to reattach your arm or regrow a new one. And though I can't guarantee that I will be able to do so in the future, there's something . . ." I hesitate. Saying more would probably get his hopes up. "Well, anyway, I'm exploring something that might allow me to do more than I currently can. But even if it doesn't, I'm sure I can make you something that would help you, like a weapon you could easily attach to your arm so you're not defenseless."

There's no way I'll be able to create the kind of prosthetics that modern medicine has begun producing on Earth, but at least if I can attach a club to his arm, he'll be able to use it for *something*. Or maybe a shield—he could control a sturdy construction of wood with the stump of arm remaining below his elbow, right?

River's staring at me. I touch the Bond between us. It's a maelstrom of emotions; fear and confusion are the most prominent.

A weapon?

"Yes. Only if you want it, though. And I can only do it if you're willing to stay for long enough for me to make it."

Stay? You . . . I can stay?

I frown. Why do I feel like we're having two different conversations here?

"You can stay for as long as you like," I say slowly. "If you wish to go, I will release the Bond."

And if I . . . do not wish? he asks just as slowly, the sense of fear in the Bond intensifying.

"Do not wish to stay or do not wish to go?" I clarify. River hesitates for a long moment before I feel him summon up his courage to respond.

Do not wish to go.

"Then you don't," I tell him carefully, my eyes fixed on his. "You stay here with us. Nothing changes except that we find a different role for you to do. One that you can do even with your arm in its current state." Unless Flesh-Shaping does what I want it to.

But I am crippled. Useless.

My frown deepens. Does he really think that I would kick him out because he lost his arm? In a battle that he only fought because of me?

"First of all, you're not useless. Going out into the forest might not be a good idea until you're more able to defend yourself, but there are plenty of things I could use a hand with—even if it's only one. We can adapt the tools and equipment so you can use them, no problem. Second of all, even if you *were* useless, it wouldn't matter. You gained your injury in a battle you shouldn't have had to fight. That was my fault. I will make sure that you're supported for as long as you want and need it."

River just stares at me with his eyes wide open, as if I'm speaking Greek. Then he slowly clicks his jaws together so his teeth tap against each other.

I am not able to offer you the service I once could . . . but this is okay with you?

It's not his fault he's finding life difficult to get his head around right now, so I try to remind him as patiently as I can. "Yes. Particularly since it's my fault you're in this situation to begin with. But as I said, the choice to stay or leave is yours. I don't want to keep you here if you don't want to be. And you don't have to choose now, incidentally. You can stay for now until you get your feet under you and then choose to leave later. You lost an *arm* in my service—your freedom is yours for the asking," I tell him earnestly, still feeling wretched about the whole thing despite Kalanthia's words earlier. Even if it wasn't the mistake I thought it was, the point is that my lack of judgement still had terrible implications for River. I *owe* him.

His gaze turns thoughtful, and the maelstrom of emotions swirling on his side of the Bond calms a little. Am I getting through to him, finally?

Then I wish to offer you whatever service I still can. I am yours to command, as ever

I was, and I do not blame you for this injury, he says finally, looking me soberly in the eyes as that fear rises again, as if I'm about to tell him that he has misunderstood.

I just dip my own head as a sense of guilty relief swirls inside me that he's not choosing to leave, that he's not turning away what little help I can give him.

"Thank you for your forgiveness," I say honestly, though not feeling that it was earned. Then again, isn't that what forgiveness is about? A mercy on the part of the wronged rather than an act earned by the wrongdoer? "Here." I pull out an Energy Heart. "If you feel up to it. Otherwise, here." I pull out a smaller carcass and place it next to him. "You need to eat to replenish the nutrients from healing."

After a few more words, I retreat to a sunny patch on the opposite side of the cave mouth and close my eyes.

Dropping down into my Core space, I once more restart the painstaking and mentally exhausting process of trying to heal the damage the Pure Energy did to me, this time working on the damaged and burned threads of my internal matrix.

CHAPTER SIXTY-NINE

An Answer to a Question

By the time I surface again, my mind feels wrung out like a wet cloth. I have a pounding headache, which actually flares when I try to use Lay-on-Hands. Checking my status, I see why: my mana is down to the single digits. The *low* single digits.

Name: Markus Wolfe		Race: Human	Class: Tamer
Level: 12	Energy to next level: 98%	Energy absorption rate: 26u/hr	Energy towards debt: 78%
Intelligence	36	Mana: 2/360	
Wisdom	36	Mana regeneration rate: 738u/hr (-18%)	
Willpower	42+8 (+20%)	Health regeneration rate: 40u/hr (-20%)	
Constitution	19	Health: 190/190	
Strength	16	Stamina: 90/90	
Dexterity	15	Stamina regeneration rate: 150u/hr	
Class Skills: Dominate – Novice 3 Tame – Beginner 6 Fade – Initiate 1		Non-Class Skills: *Lay-on-Hands – Journeyman 2* Stealth – Novice 1 Animal Empathy – Novice 6 Meditation – Initiate 1 Energy Manipulation – Novice 7 Sensation Management – Beginner 5	

At least I've made some progress. My mana regeneration rate has improved by two percent. It's a bit disappointing that it's the only one to shown any progress; I can only hope that my health regeneration will catch up in some way. If not, I really don't know how I'm going to fix it.

Two percent doesn't seem like much in what has to be about five hours, judging by how close to sunset it is now, but it's not the only gain: Energy Manipulation has also increased by two more levels, from Novice five to Novice seven. That means future improvements will only be faster and easier.

If I take five hours to fix two percent, that means fixing the rest of the eighteen percent should take at most forty-five hours. If I worked without a break, I'd be able to do that in less than two days, but that's not feasible.

First of all, I need to let my mana regenerate since that seems to be what this process uses rather than Energy. Second of all, it's highly mentally tiring. I don't want to risk making a mistake and messing things up further which means I need time to sleep.

Meditation has also increased in level, ranking up to Initiate one—hopefully, that will help with both issues. Certainly, the one hundred and thirty-five percent increase in mana regeneration I've gained from the bonuses to my Beginner and Novice levels is one reason why I've been able to do as many repairs in the last few hours as I have. I quickly navigate to the notification.

Congratulations!

You have advanced a Skill past Novice. Meditation is now Initiate 1. You have focused on developing an understanding of your inner world by manipulating your Energy channels and the way Energy and mana flow around your body. You have both damaged and repaired your Core, an endeavor few accomplish. Gain +15% to your control of Energy or mana within your Energy channels or Core space per Initiate level in this Skill.

Close message

Interesting, and a useful bonus considering what I need to accomplish here.

I sigh and rub my face with my open hand. I'm tired and need to rest. Properly. I have a feeling that I could do another few hours, but that would be the limit for me right now. So, I need to sleep, and even during daylight hours I'll need to have some time to do different things. Otherwise, I might end up drawing the Energy channels incorrectly, and who knows what could happen as a result of that? Probably nothing good.

So, reasonably, I could probably do about ten to fifteen hours per day, perhaps broken into three periods. With the recent improvements to the relevant Skills, and any future ones that will happen as I work, I figure that's a reasonable amount to aim for. That should give me enough time even if I take breaks to do other tasks and rest my mind.

Hopefully, once my internal matrix is complete again, I'll be able to do what I need to. I can only pray that repairing my health regeneration won't be necessary to make my choice about Flesh-Shaping. If so, I'm toast—and so is any hope for replacing River's arm.

At least I have an answer to a question that was concerning me: whether I'd be able to fix the threads even past their "ghost" points. As it is, I've discovered that when I extend a thread, it seems to "know" where to go next, even when all traces of its previous length are not present. So, it really is just a matter of putting in the time and effort.

But for now, I need to take a break. I push myself to my feet and trudge inside to stoke the fire. Staring blankly at the sparks and licking tongues of flame that appear as I add more fuel, I find my mind starting to relax. Sometimes thinking of nothing is soothing.

The flames dance and jump, looking like twirling and twisting sprites as they vanish only to reappear somewhere else. The snap and pop of the branches catching light is like the percussion of an orchestra that only the flames can hear.

It fills my vision: the red glow of the embers, the darkness of the branches yet to burn, the white of the fuel already turned to ash. Every so often there is a flash of color as the fire happens upon a trace element in the wood. Other than that, though, the world becomes limited to shades of red and orange, and its warmth settles inside me just as its heat warms my body.

I extend my hand towards the fire, feeling its heat intensify and start burning. It's hot against my face, and I luxuriate in its burning warmth as the chill of the encroaching night cools my back. For a moment, I wish I could become one of those carefree flames. Their lives are short, but they burn fiercely while they are present.

Then again, passion burns just as fiercely as fire, and it has never led me anywhere good. I drop my hand and the spell breaks. Once more I'm in a cave with a crackling hearth fire in front of me. Nothing more.

I need to sleep, I decide. I'm getting lost in pointless fancies. Even if my life seems to have turned into fantasy, that doesn't mean that my fire is suddenly alive in any qualitative way.

Feeding myself with food pulled from my Inventory, I check on my Bound once more. River is already slumbering on the bed, curled up around the stump of his arm. Fenrir is lying snuggled up to River, taking up even more of the bed. I hope I'll manage to actually fit on it too, what with both of them taking up the space. Bastet is curled up next to me, but she was there when I entered. She seems to have crept a little closer to me, though, as her feathers are now pressed against my leg.

I can't help but stroke my fingers through them gently. Every time I touch them, I'm surprised at just how soft they are, unlike any fur I've ever encountered. If anything, the closest comparison is those chickens that look more furry than feathered, though they *are* feathers.

Bastet shifts a little in her sleep, and I pull my fingers away hurriedly. The sleepy contentment and longing that drifts along the Bond from her side even as she snuggles closer makes me smile, though, and encourages me to continue. I lose myself in gently combing her feathers back into place, the calm action doing as much to relax me as staring at the fire has.

My eyes are drooping, unfortunately, and I finally call it an evening when my yawns threaten to split my head in two.

I'm asleep soon after my head hits the pillow.

CHAPTER SEVENTY

Slaughterhouse

Halfway through the next day, I'm more than ready for a break. I'm making progress, that's for sure, but there's only so much mana manipulation I can do inside my channels before my head threatens to explode.

I've learned something useful: the *shape* of my mana beads is far more important when healing my internal matrix than my Core. There, I just needed to feed the mana into the Core and it basically healed itself. Here, if I just feed the mana down the channel, even though it *will* extend the channel without further direction, almost all of it is wasted. I can't afford to do that—even with the help of Meditation, I doubt I'd have enough mana to do the job within my time limit.

However, if I don't just leave it up to chance and instead keep careful control over the bead of mana, less is wasted. If I change the shape from the sphere it naturally forms into an oblong instead, the amount of mana that's wasted is significantly reduced.

I was a little anxious about pursuing that idea, though, since the time it took me to learn how to control the mana sufficiently meant that I barely made any progress between waking up and halfway through the morning. The progress I've made in the last few hours, however, has more than made up for whatever I lost in the first part of the day. I've already reduced my mana regeneration penalty to fifteen percent, and three percent progress in one morning isn't bad, especially since it only happened in the last three or four hours.

It has taken its toll on my mental energy, though, both in terms of physical pain and the ability to concentrate.

Well, I accounted for the fact that I'd need breaks in my plans last night. And maybe I can use the time to be productive. I really need to do something about that mountain of carcasses that has been piling up in my Inventory; there are more resources than just meat there, and maybe even a few Cores.

Pushing myself to my feet, I look around at my Bound. Fenrir is on guard at the edge of the plateau, watching the forest below. Bastet is also on guard, but she's watching the cubs, who are playing with Lathani. I'm not sure where Sirocco is.

River . . . has been doing his best to work around his arm all morning. I've seen him and felt the frustration from his side of the Bond every time I've surfaced out of my Core space. He's been trying to deal with the plants we collected yesterday, but crushing them with a primitive-style mortar and pestle that he pulled from somewhere is hard with only one hand. He seems to have figured it out, though his position looks rather awkward: he's holding the mortar between his feet while wielding the pestle in his hand.

"Who wants to come down to the river with me?" I ask, my question immediately gaining everyone's attention. "Bastet, do you want to come? We could bring the cubs along."

When dealing with a whole load of meat, it's sensible to do it somewhere that's easy to clean up afterwards—I know from experience that butchering carcasses is a messy job. The river isn't as safe as doing it here would be, but it's definitely more convenient. Hopefully, going with at least a couple of companions will make it safer than going on my own, though.

Bastet is interested and chirps at the cubs, calling them over. Fenrir, too, perks up and trots over to me—clearly, he wants to go. It surprises me when River stands up and joins us too.

"Are you sure you want to come?" I ask, eyeing the stump of his arm dubiously. He follows my gaze, and his jaws press tightly together.

I cannot hide here for the rest of my life, he tells me firmly. *Unless you forbid me to come, I wish to join you.*

"I won't forbid you," I quickly answer, "but it only happened yesterday. I know you've been trying to get used to it, but if you join us in the forest, you may have to fight."

I still have one arm that is capable, and I am happy to wield it in your defense, Master—I'm sorry—Markus.

I hesitate. Part of me *does* want to forbid him from coming. I hate the idea that his injury might now lead to his death. But at the same time, if my hopes with Flesh-Shaping don't pan out . . . He's right. He won't be able to stay here forever, and if I can't grow him a new arm, he'll have to learn to cope. I don't get the sense that he's suicidal—not now, at least—so if he thinks he can handle it, it's probably patronizing of me to imagine that I know better.

"All right," I say finally. "Can you still wield your spear, or do you want to borrow my mace?"

At that *he* hesitates.

I am more proficient with a spear . . . But it's true that wielding one well requires two hands. If you would not mind lending me your mace, I think that might be wise.

I wouldn't have offered it if I wasn't willing to do it, and I tell him so as I hand my mace over. Since he won't be using the spear, he hands that to me—I have a couple of rough spears in my Inventory, but this is the one with a flint tip to it, so it's better. I don't have anything I can quickly transform into a shield, but when I say that to him, he dismisses it.

I will avoid being hit, he says firmly. I eye him for a moment, then sigh and give in—again, it's his life, his choice.

Everything decided, we set off. Just as we're heading towards the edge of the plateau, Lathani comes trotting up.

Can I come too? she asks hopefully. I cast a glance at Kalanthia, who's sunning herself as usual. The big nunda gives off a sense of cautious indifference, so I just shrug.

"Sure. But you'll need to stay nearby and do what we tell you to if there's danger," I warn her. She should already know the rules after traveling with us for several days, but she *is* still a cub at heart.

I understand, she tells me seriously before bouncing happily and trotting down the hill. *Come on! Let's go.* Rolling my eyes a little, I can't help grinning too. Sharing a glance with Bastet, I see the same long-suffering amusement in her eyes. The cubs, of course, have happily followed Lathani's lead and are trotting down the slope, jumping from rock to rock. The rest of us quickly follow before they run too far ahead and accidentally get themselves into trouble.

Sirocco joins us soon after we enter the forest, and we traipse to the river as an entire party—the intrepid adventurers once more. We might easily still be trying to make our way home except for the fact that we're far better rested and generally in good spirits.

After setting up by the wide stream, I soon get a process going, and the area quickly becomes reminiscent of a slaughterhouse. Between the previously butchered salamander meat and all of this, I'm not going to be going hungry any time soon. Heck, I've probably got supplies for *months*. My stockpiles are looking just as good for my various crafting objectives.

I store away as many hides as I can keep intact. Though I'm by no means an expert, at least my skills in butchery and skinning have improved since I first entered the forest. I definitely need to do some tanning. Not only do I want to turn the crocodile and salamander hides into better armor than my chitin plate, but I am seriously running out of clothes. Even though I did my laundry a couple of days ago, I'm struggling to find clothes that are fully intact. Cleaning already damaged fabric with a rough bar of soap and then laying them out over spiky bushes for the wind to blow them dry didn't exactly help on that front either. This world has really been rough on my wardrobe, and I'm resigning myself to looking like a real wild man with stitched-together hides.

To that end, I've also been keeping the brains of the creatures, as I know that they offer an important ingredient in the process.

Although it's not a priority, I *do* want to make a proper bed at some point, and the feathers I collected from the extra large killer chickens will be perfect for a mattress and pillow. The feathers from their wings will also help in making more arrows, something that *is* a priority. That several of them had Cores was an added bonus, though they were small things.

I don't collect all the bones—there are far too many. However, I do collect a few, which I'm hoping to turn into needles for my sewing needs. My companions are happy to help me dispose of the organs and chew on the choice bits of flesh happily.

It's messy, tiring, and exacting work. In fact, I even gain a point in Dexterity and Strength (Endurance) from it. I have to pay some Energy for the points, but since I don't want to level up yet, that's not a problem. In fact, if I can get my physical stats up to twenty each before leveling up, that would be ideal.

River tries to help me, but with only one hand, he's unable to get a good enough grip on the carcass to slice accurately. In the end, he, Fenrir, and Sirocco decide to go hunting in the local area. Though I have my doubts about whether that's sensible, I remind myself that if River feels he can cope with it, it should be up to him to decide. I did ask them not to go too far, though.

Well, I think to myself, looking at the blood and gore around me, *I think I'm pretty much done here.*

It's taken longer than I intended, but once I got started, I didn't want to stop. I got into something of a rhythm. A bloody, squelching, and cracking rhythm. Before we can return to the den, though, I need to put things away, and then I *really* need to go wash up.

With resources and meat now returned to my Inventory, I walk straight into the stream fully clothed. I'm glad that I took off my chitin armor earlier when it kept getting in my way.

As I wash all the blood off, a sudden and very urgent sense of warning comes from Bastet.

CHAPTER SEVENTY-ONE

The Right Thing

I whirl around with the knife I was just rinsing off now clutched in a firm grip. No attack comes; it takes me a moment to realize that I'm not the target this time.

Bastet is snarling and leaping towards the cubs, the urgent warning still emanating from her. It's not directed at me, it's directed at Stormcloud—the one in immediate danger. I rush out of the water, my sodden clothes impeding my movement more than I'd like.

Still not having seen the enemy, I take a moment to pull my spear out of my Inventory even as I stride forwards. By the time I get to the scene of the action, Bastet is already facing off with the thing. *A snake,* I realize suddenly. For once not a horrific hybrid of a snake and something else, this time it's a legless reptile with long fangs, which it's currently baring at my Bound.

Bastet sends me a feeling of alarm and a strong sense of Storm. I look over to see the cub lying limply to one side with Lathani nudging her urgently. Has she been bitten?

Rushing to her side, I pour healing magic into her. The venom is strong and is quickly ravaging her system, but the mimic's venom in the vine-strangler forest was more powerful. I have to fight to pour a lot of magic in, but soon a trickle of faintly yellow liquid emerges from the fang puncture marks.

Storm doesn't wake up immediately, but I don't have time to wait for her to do so—Bastet's still in danger.

My healing must have only taken a couple of minutes, but in a fight that's an age. Fortunately, the snake still seems completely engaged in its dangerous dance with the raptorcat matriarch, and she's still managing to keep ahead of its fangs.

Joining the fight, I quickly stab my spear at the snake. It dodges out of the way at the last moment and the blow that was intended for its head misses.

Misses the head, that is. The snake hisses loudly as the flint spear tip instead cuts a gouge across the patterned scales of its back. It turns towards me and lunges quickly. My spear is out of position, but my knife is not. I stab downwards, my weight driving the point down quicker than ever.

I don't catch its head, but I stab straight through its body and into the ground. Stuck, the snake writhes. Stepping out of range of its venomous fangs, I hesitate for a moment. While a snake could be a useful scout or weapon, the disaster that happened yesterday is very fresh in my mind.

Bastet is looking at me, her eyes narrowed, her plumed tail lashing back and forth. I get the feeling she knows what I'm considering doing.

"It could be useful," I offer defensively. She straightens and sends me a complicated series of emotions down the Bond. I interpret them to mean that she has an inherent dislike and distrust of snakes and that she doubts this will be a good packmate, but she will go with my decision, whatever it is.

I nod slowly as I step over to check on Storm. She's coming around, her system recovering after its intense shock. I shoot some more undirected healing magic into her just to make sure. Then, moving to face the snake, I look it in its poisonous green eyes.

"Dominate."

Once more in the liminal space of the Battle of Wills, I quickly walk to the halfway point between us and then stop. The resistance offered by the snake is barely noticeable, but as always, I'm uninterested in forcing a Bond. I've learned from past experience, though. If this snake doesn't want to join me, it will have to face the consequences of its ill-considered attack on my party.

Close enough for the snake's aura to touch me, I sense its anger, fear, and pain. Unsurprising. In return, I try to project calmness and peace. Only the knowledge that Storm is fine allows me to do so, but I still have to push back my anger at its unprovoked attack on us.

Slowly, I sense the creature calm down. If it were able to move, I would guess it would go from head raised, hood open, and fangs bared fully, to hood lowered and mouth closed. There is still plenty of wariness in it, though.

"Instead of fighting us, would you like to join us?" I offer, gaining an immediate rejection. The snake gives the idea of hunting alone.

"You may have hunted alone until this point, but hunting together is far more successful. If you join us, we will grow stronger together." Apparently, that isn't particularly tempting either. The snake gives off a sense of disbelief that a group of "inferior" species without even any venom could ever be more successful than itself.

"We have these." I send over a picture of the Energy Hearts we harvested. For the first time, the snake seems interested. It inquires as to whether it would have access to unlimited numbers of such items if it deigned to join our group.

"We share and share alike. Whatever one of us finds is shared with those of the group who can make use of it." I've lost the snake's interest. It gives off a strong sense that it considers its prey to belong solely to it. The legless reptile is clearly uninterested in sharing of any kind.

I don't bother trying to convince it further. Even if its small size and venom would be a good addition to the team, its attitude wouldn't. I have no interest in disrupting the team dynamics for a self-centered creature that is only going to put its own interests first.

"Your decision," I tell it with unconcealed disappointment. At least I won't need to convince either Bastet or Storm not to seek revenge. I don't even try to ask for its surrender and peaceful retreat. It clearly sees us as inferior, so, like the snilapede, I doubt it would hold to whatever agreement it might give in this space. I don't intend to make the same mistake twice.

I hesitate over pushing forwards, nonetheless, then decide not to for two main reasons. One: I still don't want to force a Bond, even with this snake—and that's true even if I didn't fear what it might do to the dynamics of the group. Two: it's pinned in place, so it's no danger to any of us until I pull my knife out, something I won't do until I'm ready to fight again.

I walk backwards until I've left the space. The weakness of failing the Battle of Wills hits me hard and I slump to the ground. Bastet sends me a feeling of concern mixed with a question.

I'm fine, I tell her, disappointment tingeing my thoughts. *It didn't want to join us and most likely wouldn't have been a good fit even if it had.* She sends acceptance down the link along with a small bit of relief. Was she worried about me Dominating it? Seeing as we have a few seconds before my weakness wears off, I quickly ask her.

She responds with several memories of losing cubs to snakes and their venom—cubs snatched when playing and bitten while sleeping. Clearly there's no love lost between snakes and raptorcats.

You know that you can object if I attempt to Bond with something you don't feel would suit our team, right? I ask her seriously even as I feel strength returning to my limbs. Bastet responds with a mix of uncertainty and gratitude proving that, no, she hadn't realized.

"Of course," I tell her. Then, briefly ignoring the still-trapped snake, I go over and give her a little sideways hug. "You've been with me since almost the beginning of my time here; you and the cubs are my family. Newcomers have to earn your approval as much as mine." She leans into me, and my heart feels warm as we share a moment together.

The pained hissing of the snake interrupts us too soon, and I move back over to it. The snake rises, its hood flaring at my approach. I fear for a moment that it might try to spit at me like a cobra, but it doesn't. Instead, it just threatens to strike; its movements are clearly impeded by the blade cutting straight through its body.

I hesitate for a moment—this is the first time I'll kill a creature with which I've touched souls. Then I harden my heart. This creature wouldn't hesitate to kill us; it attacked us without provocation. I shouldn't hesitate to do the same.

Forcing my limbs to work, I stab at it with my spear. Dodging ability limited and fangs useless against the wooden shaft of my spear, it gains wound after wound. Each slows it further until I'm able to pierce it through the head.

I feel a sense of loss, but I don't know if that's anything real or just my imagination. Either way, I don't doubt that I did the right thing for myself and the rest of my Bound. Nonetheless, all the satisfaction I gained from my work in my Core space and the processing of the bodies has drained away from me.

"Why don't you four eat this snake, benefit from its meat?" I suggest quietly to

Bastet. Someone might as well get a bit of benefit from its death. "Then let's find River, Fenrir, and Sirocco and return to the den." She moves over to press herself against me as sorrow radiates from her. For what, I don't know. Not for the snake, I don't think. And Storm is now moving again, though a little unsteadily, so it can't be for that. Baffled, I just accept the comfort her presence offers for a moment before moving.

As it turns out, we don't have to go anywhere to find the rest of our party. The four raptorcats haven't even finished eating the snake by the time the others find us.

Are you well? I felt a disturbance. River's voice entering my head makes me jump a little, but I'm happy to hear him. He must have gotten close enough for telepathy along the Bond to work.

A snake attacked Storm. The snake's dead and Storm's fine. How are you doing? I ask anxiously.

I am well. He sounds it, actually—better than he's sounded since yesterday's events. *In fact . . . Well, perhaps you should see it first,* he says with a little hint of mischief. *Or I can tell you,* he adds a little uncertainly.

No, it's fine, I say, trying to conceal my curiosity.

Not long after, I see the shapes of my other Bound approaching through the trees. Over River's shoulders is a mass that has to be seen to be believed.

CHAPTER SEVENTY-TWO

All Living Things Die

How did you take *those* down?" I ask in astonishment. *And with only a mace and a single hand at that.* I don't think I gave him any ranged equipment, and I don't see how else he could have done it. "Actually, how did you even *find* them?" Not that I'm in any way upset at the cull he seems to have enacted.

The mass River is carrying is composed of numerous black blobs. One, two, three . . . I count *five* of them slung over his right shoulder, their bulbous tails held in his hand. Walking over to him, I view them admiringly.

It was purely down to Fenrir's nose that we found them, River tells me, proudly looking down at the lizog. Fenrir seems to realize that he's being talked about and wriggles happily. His wriggles gain in intensity as I send approval down the Bond to him. *Once we found the first, it was easy for him to understand what I wanted to hunt, and he led us directly to them whenever he caught the same sort of scent.*

"So, that's how you found them. But how did you kill them?" River makes his equivalent of a shrug.

The way I was taught to: by climbing up into the trees above them and striking at the body. When I knocked a couple of them off their branches, Fenrir was helpful there too. My jaw slackens a little.

". . . How did you do that with only one arm?" I blurt out before shutting my mouth with a snap. Unfortunately, words once said can't be recalled. My insensitive question makes his sideways eyelids flicker across his eyes and his gaze go distant, but he answers, nonetheless.

I may not have a hand on my left arm now, but I can still hook the stump of my forearm or my upper arm onto branches to support myself. It was harder than with two hands, but not impossible.

"I'm sorry," I say, shamefaced.

It is an understandable question. His understanding doesn't help with my feeling of awkwardness—the reverse, in fact. I search for a way of continuing the conversation. *If you are willing to give me a little time, I wish to harvest their venom.*

"Of course," I answer immediately, then hesitate. "Are you . . . Do you want me to do it?"

River looks rather pointedly at some of the worst victims of my butchery: the massacred skins that are no more than tattered rags now.

The venom glands are a little difficult to harvest intact, he replies slowly.

"Do you think that you'd be better at it?" I ask, this time managing not to mention his missing hand. River seems reluctant to answer, perhaps fearing that I'll be offended. I search for something to say to ease the awkwardness. Then I've got it. "Do you want to use my knife? It might work better than your own." Even if his wooden one is remarkable for what it is, it's not anywhere near as good as my own blade. And with a sharper one, maybe it will be easier for him to do one-handed. River looks at me, surprise coming down the Bond.

You'd allow me to? His question is almost hesitant, and I wonder why.

"Sure. I'm done with my own harvesting." I pull it out and hand it to him, handle first. "Just don't lose it, okay," I half joke.

I won't, he promises as he looks at my tool with eagerness and no small amount of awe. He twists it back and forth, looking at how it reflects the light. I suppose I can't blame him for his curiosity: it has to be the first metal tool he's come across in his life. Still . . .

"Are you going to use it or just look at it?" I tease him. He starts and guilt comes across the link. "Look, man, I'm just joshing you," I tell him, immediately feeling bad that he took my words too much to heart. Then, scratching at my beard, I get a thought. "Actually, could you do something for me?"

Of course, River answers immediately.

"Would you be able to harvest the venom from this too? I'll help hold it for you." I pull out one corpse I haven't yet touched: the venomous predator that tried—and very nearly succeeded in—killing me while in the vine-strangler forest. Given my iffy success rate with extracting the venom glands from a couple of other carcasses in my Inventory that had them, I'm wary of starting on this carcass myself.

I'd be happy to, the lizard-man answers honestly and with no small bit of vengeful glee. Clearly, he has some bad feelings towards this sort of creature. My question must come across the link because he looks up at me and then clicks his jaws uncertainly. *I lost two of my hatching-mates to a smaller version of this creature. Even though I managed to kill it, I wasn't in time to get them back to Herbalist.*

"I'm sorry to hear that," I say softly. "You don't have to do it if it brings up bad memories." He sends negation at me.

No, I'm happy to. Each time I kill another of these, I am gratified that fewer of my kin will die to them. Harvesting and using their bodies is only right. Okay, fine. As long as he's happy.

"Looks like we'll be staying a bit longer," I tell Bastet and Lathani. "We'll need you, Fenrir, and Sirocco to keep watch in case of any other nasty surprises. Is that okay with you?" The raptorcat quickly assents, but the nunda doesn't respond. She's crouched next to Bastet with her eyes fixed on Storm, who is now playing with her siblings.

As I hold the first carcass in place for River to cut into it, I check on the young nunda. "Lathani, are you okay?" I frown as I try to remember exactly what happened with her; I even put a free hand on her flank and send in some healing magic just to check she wasn't caught by the snake too.

She seems fine. Physically speaking. But she's far quieter than she normally is.

The little one . . . She almost died. Like prey. Lathani gives off a sense of confusion and vulnerability, her mental voice soft.

"Yeah," I agree, a pang of fear going through me in memory.

But . . . she is not prey. Why did she almost die? It's almost adorable, her sorrowful confusion. What am I saying? It *is* adorable and heartrending at the same time.

"All living things die eventually. And when life is a series of battles, anyone can be a victim." She's quiet for a little longer.

I don't want to die. The admission is stark and would almost be matter-of-fact if not for the sense of tumultuous emotions she gives off.

"I don't want you to die either," I tell her plainly. "None of us here does. Your mother in particular wants you to survive and grow strong. But we can only do that if you help yourself." Seeing the opportunity to impress on her some important facts, I continue. "You've grown a lot and will start going out into the forest more and more. Pay attention, listen to your companions, and keep your senses alert. Hopefully, doing those will mean you survive to get bigger than your mama." She sends me a scathing look.

No one's bigger than Mother!

"You could be one day," I tease her. "Then River will be calling *you* the Great Predator." A sense of amusement bubbles from her, and I feel lighter for having helped her get over her funk. "Go on, entertain yourself, but don't go too far, okay? Storm is going to be fine, but only because I was able to heal her quickly enough." She assents and then goes to play with the three raptorcat cubs. I don't miss that she is keeping much more of a wary eye on her surroundings than earlier. I approve!

Once River has extracted the venom glands from the black blobs and the mimic, I tuck the rest of their bodies into my Inventory, not keen on getting completely messy again. Although I've been helping River, only my hands have gotten dirty, and I'm quick to wash them in the stream with a bit of soap.

Upon my return, my first priority is to continue repairing my internal matrix. Returning to my relatively comfortable spot in the sun, I close my eyes and drop inside myself.

The process is now very familiar to me, and I quickly make it to my Core. There, I reach with metaphysical hands into the burning sun and tease out a bead of bright light. Though still small, it's far bigger than the ones I started with at the beginning of this process—the improvements I've made to my Energy control are obvious.

Keeping control over it as it runs down one of the gleaming threads, I concentrate fiercely and press the sphere into a longer oblong shape. The process feels easier than I remember it being—perhaps my break has done me some good. Directing it to the damaged filament, I see the golden thread extend by a fraction. I'm gratified to see that it offers at least twice as much growth with each attempt than I was able to achieve yesterday.

Over the next hours, I continue experimenting, trying to work out the most effective and efficient way of doing this. In the end, I discover that both shape and speed are the most important aspects: the thinner in diameter I make the mana and the slower it emerges from the end of the thread, the more efficient it is.

Both speed and shape are as difficult to change as trying to control the Energy that rushes towards me from my Bounds' kills was at first, but the results are definitely worth it. And, like my control over the Energy, the more I practice, the better I get.

Yes! I celebrate internally as, for the first time, I manage to use about ninety percent of the mana I pull from my Core to actually repair the thread I'm focusing on. The fraction I can repair at a time has grown by at least double even since I got back to it after my trip to the river.

My enthusiasm, which had been waning, is renewed. I continue pulling mana from my Core and work hard to increase the length while compressing the width. Each time I improve the shape of the mana, my strategy is proven as the filament grows with increasing speed.

I'm filled with hope. Maybe my estimate of three days will prove to be far more than needed. Honestly, the sooner I can fix myself, the better—for me and, hopefully, for River too.

CHAPTER SEVENTY-THREE

No Real Secret

need a break," I say out loud with a sigh as I open my eyes. Time passes oddly when I'm engrossed in my Energy channels—at once syrupy like honey and ephemeral like the morning dew.

The sun has moved away from my position, but I don't move to sit in it again. Not only do I feel the need to get up and stretch a bit, but I have a strong suspicion that my skin is getting a trifle burned. Lay-on-Hands will be able to sort it, but no need to make myself worse for no reason.

I push myself to my feet, then reach up into the air and feel my back click as my numb butt cheeks fill once more with blood. I look around and check on everyone.

Kalanthia was out this morning with Lathani. They left before I even woke up, perhaps taking advantage of the dawn to hunt. They're back now, Kalanthia an obvious mountain of fur as she dozes languidly in the sun.

Bastet is the only of my Bound present and is looking after the cubs. I wasn't keen on River going out into the forest, but he seemed so determined to go that I didn't have the heart to order him to stay. Instead, I once more asked Sirocco and Fenrir to go with him and requested that he not go too far. The pulses of Energy that I've been feeling come through on occasion seem to indicate that they are being successful in their hunt despite River's disability.

I can't deny the feelings of anxiety that claw through me whenever I think about River out there, but when I busy myself, I can put them aside for a time. I can feel a message waiting for me and take advantage of the opportunity to pull my mind away from my hunting Bound.

Congratulations!
You have advanced a Skill past Novice. Energy Manipulation is now Initiate 1. You have improved your ability to manipulate Energy to affect your internal matrix. Your capacity to control mana held within your internal matrix is improved. In addition to the previous 2% Energy efficiency accorded at Novice level, you have gained +2% of Energy control per level in this Skill past Initiate while mana is within your internal matrix.

Close message

As expected, I think to myself. I'm not surprised—if my Skill *didn't* rank up soon, I would be wondering why not. Like everything so far in this Skill, the new effects aren't anything groundbreaking, but the amount they actually help is obvious in my increased speed and ease with doing what I must. I'm pleased to see that the new better control effect is in addition to the previous effect: twenty percent Energy efficiency was good, but forty percent by the time I reach Journeyman is clearly better.

I flick over to my status screen for a moment to check on the progress. *It's down to a nine percent reduction,* I say to myself with pride. At this rate, and assuming it continues to increase the way it has, I could easily be done by tomorrow. Nerves run through me as I consider how I'll once more have to psych myself up to commit to my decision. Though the intervening time since I decided to go for Flesh-Shaping hasn't actually changed my mind, the fact is that I just don't have all the information I need to feel at ease about my choice.

My stomach rumbles and I consider how hunger doesn't care about cerebral decision-making. I pull out some roast meat and a baked potato from my Inventory and gnaw on them hungrily.

The food tastes good—there's no better seasoning than hunger. I'm getting rather bored with the same three items over and over again, though. It's been more than a month, and even if I'm not exactly a foodie, I could *really* do with a change. The issue is that the whole process of testing whether a food is any good for me is so *long*. With everything that's been going on recently, I just haven't had the time.

Then again, do I need to do the whole process? It's an interesting question. The whole point of testing a food step by step and leaving time in between each test is to avoid poisoning. I've been poisoned several times by this point and I'm still here. The main difference, of course, is Lay-on-Hands.

Something that would kill a normal human being is now just a temporary inconvenience for me. Why not just go on a tasting rampage of everything offered by the forest, and if I'm poisoned, just heal it away? *Well, maybe not a rampage,* I say to myself. *Maybe more of a gourmet tasting experience.*

It's a good thought, but one that I'm only going to have time for once I've sorted out my internal matrix. Of course, by that point, I might not be *able* to do it, I realize. If Flesh-Shaping doesn't allow me to deal with poison in the same way as Lay-on-Hands, I'll be stuck testing things the way I had to before, like with the pondweed. Then again, if I lose the ability to deal with poison, I'm going to be in a lot more trouble than not being able to expand my diet.

I remind myself *again* that the notification said I would keep all previously used facets of Lay-on-Hands, which should mean that my ability to deal with poison is maintained. But that's always the issue. "Should" is not the most reassuring word when needing to make a potentially life-changing decision like this.

Wanting to distract myself, I decide to see if Kalanthia is willing to be disturbed. As I walk over to her, I eye her closed eyes uncertainly.

I feel you there, Markus Wolfe, she says in slightly irritated tones.

"Sorry," I apologize automatically. "I didn't mean to disturb you. I was just try-ing to see if you were awake or not."

That depends on what you wish to talk about.

Typical cat.

"Well, I need a break from working on my Energy channels, and I was wonder-ing if you were open to . . . teaching me something about the earth? If it doesn't require Energy or mana manipulation, that is," I add hastily. It wouldn't exactly be a break if I needed to do more of that.

Those golden eyes slowly open, as always pinning me in place for a moment with their unmistakably predatory manner.

Very well, she agrees, shifting into a sphinxlike position. *We must start with the way you consider the earth to begin with. You will not be able to use mana to manipulate it until your being is at one with it.*

Until my being is "at one" with earth? How am I supposed to do that? I wonder to myself. It's not a good start.

She gestures for me to sit, then stretches a little and yawns widely. Then she fixes her eyes back on me. I follow her instructions and rest with my back against a rock.

There is no real secret to learning to Shape the earth. No single moment where it goes from being impossible to being possible. Not in my experience, at least. Instead, it is a series of small steps.

It was an accident when I first learned to Shape the earth. And it was an accident when my mate learned to Shape lightning too. That is why I am unsure whether this can be taught at all, she admits. Hmm, Shaping lightning . . . That sounds pretty cool as well. Though Shaping earth is probably more practical, Shaping lightning would be a really awesome combat ability. I don't interrupt, though, just listen intently to her words. Kalanthia might be uncertain, but I've seen enough impossible things happen in the last two months to be at least hopeful.

Thinking back to when it all began . . . I believe that Earth-Shaping actually started simply with feeling the earth. I spent far too much time in . . . Well, it matters not. A sense of an old aching pain comes through the connection before the giant nunda cuts it off abruptly. *Suffice it to say that my time as a cub was not what I or my mother would wish. The earth was my solace. Digging my claws into its cool firmness and tearing it apart helped me express the emotions that would otherwise tear me to shreds.* The same pain twinges again, this time a fainter echo of what came before, as if Kalanthia is actively suppressing it. I feel a touch of guilt that talking about such topics is so clearly bringing up bad memories.

I learned much from the earth, Kalanthia continues. *Endurance. Indifference in the face of attack. Sheer inevitability. The earth does not defend itself; it doesn't need to. Any attack is meaningless to it. Yet, when the earth does move, little can stand against it.* True, I suppose. A landslide is a force of nature. Even a simple rockfall can only be endured, not fought.

The more I felt the earth, the more I learned from it, the more I was able to connect with it. Little by little, I became able to affect the earth. At first, it was only the little I was touching. That was enough: I escaped my captors when the earth broke the enclosure I was being held in, and it added speed to my feet as I ran from them. As my power and connection to it grew, I was able to affect more at a time and earth further from me. By the time I reached my first Evolution, I had become adept at using it and cognizant of its rules.

Earth is slow by nature, its movements small, its trust hard to win. To speed and amplify these is possible, but the more we wish to amplify it, the more mana it consumes. That is the nature of earth; I know that the nature of lightning is different—my mate and I have discussed these matters many times.

To summarize, then. You must first feel the earth, then you must connect to it. Only after that will you be able to affect it. If, after having heard my words, you still wish to try, I suggest that you make an attempt knowing that it might take much time to even begin, and knowing that it may not even be possible. After trying, if you have questions, I will do my best to answer them.

With those words, I sense that the lesson has ended for now.

"Thank you," I say to her respectfully, appreciating the effort she has made. My mind is racing, not only with the information about Earth-Shaping, but the revelations about Kalanthia's history. I won't ask any questions about it, but I can't help my curiosity from going wild.

Nonetheless, it's clearly a painful subject for her, so I forcibly direct my mind onto more fruitful topics. *Now, how do I "feel the earth."*

Without any better ideas, I close my eyes and drop into Meditation. This time I make sure I don't go into myself, figuring that I'm unlikely to succeed in feeling the earth if I'm stuck in my Core space. However, even surrounded by the almost visible connections between me and everything else, I feel lost.

The links between me and my Bound are the most obvious, of course. If I had to compare them to lights, a normal room light would highlight my connections to the world around me, but the connections between me and my Bound are more like fluorescent tubes strobing right in front of me. Impossible to miss.

However, I don't get the idea that feeling the earth will be helped by focusing on the Bonds I have with other creatures. Instead, I try to ignore them and look at the connections I have with the rest of my surrounding world.

After my official Bonds, the next strongest connections I have are with the cubs and Lathani. Unsurprising, really. My link to Kalanthia is stronger than I would have thought. I always got the sense that she tolerated more than liked me, but the connection between us is almost as thick as the one I have with Lathani. It's very different in feel, though.

Lathani's is one of dependency, affection, and even a little bit of awe. Kalanthia's is more gratitude, amusement, and yes, a little bit of affection. I feel warm inside and suspect that a smile is spreading across my body's face. Not that I feel much more than a physical inkling, as detached from bodily sensations as I am right now.

None of that is likely to help me feel the earth, though. Or is it? *Kalanthia obviously has a connection with the earth*, I muse. *What if I can find it?* Maybe learning from her own connection is a possibility.

That seems easier said than done, though. Kalanthia is *very* connected to *everything*. In fact, unlike the vine-strangler trees in the forest, which were so clearly connected to each other and the Energy source below, the area near Kalanthia is basically just a mass of light. Like an aura, perhaps. There are no filaments of connection leading outwards, or perhaps the issue is that there are too many.

It's possible that if I had higher stat points in Wisdom or my Meditation Skill was a higher level, I would be able to differentiate the connections emerging from her, but as it is, it's like looking at an intricate pointillism painting from a distance and trying to pick out the individual colors used.

So, that's not going to help. *What about plants? They've got to be connected to the earth.* Even if I don't have a whole load of vine-stranglers here, there are plenty of bushes and other plants. Even the grasslike foliage that's cushioning my seat is a plant.

My theory is correct, but it doesn't do me much good: I can vaguely see the connection between the plants around me and the earth, but it doesn't tell me anything more than that they are connected, which I already knew. I see no way of applying their connection to my own needs, and my attempts to follow the lines of light are fruitless.

Frustrated, I pull myself out of Meditation. Kalanthia looks at me questioningly.

"I'm working on it," I tell her a bit defensively.

Do not rush, Markus Wolfe, she admonishes me a little. *The earth is patient; to connect with it, so must you be.* Patient . . . yeah. I'll admit that that's not one of my strong points. I mean, I *can* be patient and hardworking and all that, but if I don't see *any* results, I'd much rather try a different way.

Still, perhaps I'm being a little impatient. This is all new to me, and Kalanthia herself said that it took a while for her to be able to do anything. I sigh and push myself to my feet.

"Thanks for the lesson," I say to the big nunda respectfully. Even if I haven't gotten any benefit out of her instruction—yet—I appreciate her willingness to give it. Kalanthia seems to sense my impatience, though.

Do not despair if you do not succeed immediately. Persevere. It may take as many days as I have claws; it might take as many months as I have spots. But the earth will not be rushed, so neither must you.

"I'll keep working on it," I promise. "My Energy channels are more urgent, though, so I'm going to work on them now."

Do what you feel is best. However, remember that even a rock too big for you to move now will never move unless you keep trying.

"I will." Thanking her again, I return to leaning against the cave wall, choosing to sit in the shade this time. I've had enough of a break; time to get back to the grind.

CHAPTER SEVENTY-FOUR

Golden Lines

I direct the mana carefully and manage to control a steady stream from my Core. Upon reaching the damaged end of the thread, it extends outwards like a shoot growing in a sped-up recording, glowing golden.

I continue focusing and directing the long oblong of mana until the last of it has been consumed; the end of the thread dims once more but is significantly further ahead than it was before. The days of pulling a chunk out of my Core and then barely being able to keep up as it shoots through my internal matrix are gone.

I feel a wave of pride as I look around at all the connections I've repaired. I swiftly push it away—pride goes before a fall, and I *really* don't want to fail at this right now.

With the steady stream of controlled mana from my Core, the damaged end of my matrix grows at a speed I wouldn't have believed possible a few days ago. I'm almost done.

Although at first I focused on only one thread at a time, I realized quickly that this wouldn't work: many of the threads are too interconnected for any one to be fully restored without the others. Since then, I've been offering equal effort to each of the myriad threads damaged by the Pure Energy. The result is that despite none of the threads being quite finished, the black space has shrunk considerably.

Though, I realize that's not quite accurate as I look critically at the area. It would be more precise to say that the golden threads have extended into the abyss. There's still a clear difference between the space they are newly passing through and the space that is around where they were never damaged.

The damaged areas, since it seems that the areas are still damaged even if I've fixed those parts of the threads, are still a dark, inky black that almost sucks my mental gaze into it. The rest of the space the threads unspool through is a much more luminous area. Not golden like the threads themselves, but more like a cloudy night sky slightly lit by the city lights below than the void of a black hole.

Still, most of the loops and intricately woven designs that were destroyed by the Pure Energy are back in place, humming and vibrating golden in the same way the rest of the weave hums and vibrates. The only ones left to do are the few that actually don't loop back on themselves. I hadn't realized, but all around my matrix are threads that just . . . end. Some are longer than others; the ones I've been working on recently are the longest of all, at least twice as long as the ones in other parts of my matrix. And I discovered that, unlike the others, it appears they can grow even longer if I put Energy into them.

I discovered it when I accidentally used some of the Energy coming in from my Bound instead of mana to finish repairing one of the long threads that extend outwards. When I repaired another of the long channels with mana alone, the difference was obvious. I don't know what the effects of extending these fibers will be, but I'm rather curious to find out—not now, though. Right now, I need to just finish sorting out my internal matrix so I won't have to find out what happens if I don't make a choice about my Lay-on-Hands Skill.

In the end, it's taken me the full three days to sort out my internal matrix. I realize now that my initial estimates would have been *way* off if not for all the bonuses I got from the relevant Skills leveling and ranking up.

When I see on my status screen that I've finally gotten rid of that penalty to my mana regeneration rate, I actually stand up and whoop loudly.

Having finally fixed my internal matrix, I eagerly open up my notifications. I'm a little disappointed that I haven't gotten any sort of achievement for what I've just been doing. Isn't fixing the damage Pure Energy wreaks on an internal matrix worth anything? Then again, I suppose it *was* self-inflicted. That said, I got an achievement before from surviving the experience . . . Maybe I shouldn't be greedy.

I open my messages and eagerly search for the notification that I've seen twice before now. Refusing to second-guess myself, I make my choice, interested to see what will happen to my Core space when I Evolve a Skill.

Only, nothing happens.

Evolve Skill, I direct my System a second time. *Evolve Skill!*

A pit opens in my stomach as fear grabs at my throat. *Am I too late?*

I dive into my Core space and navigate over to the dense collection of lines that instinct tells me represent Lay-on-Hands. It's vibrating in a way that at first makes my heart leap in hope—perhaps the process just took a bit of time to start?

But as the vibrations continue and grow, that hope becomes confusion. The vibrations don't appear to be going anywhere or changing. They're just . . . reverberating.

Until slowly, little by little, the reverberations begin having an effect. The lines start shifting slowly but inexorably. Perhaps this is how it Evolves. How would I know?

But as I watch the vibrations increase in speed and strength, I begin to have an inarguable sense that something is *wrong.* It's like I'm watching a machine that is vibrating so much that the very bolts are coming free of their positions, and I somehow know that instead of Evolving, my Skill is slowly coming apart at the seams.

Is my most paranoid imagining correct? Have I made the choice too late and doomed my Skill entirely?

I refuse to believe that. Or accept it. Though I have no physical presence in this space, I grit my teeth and glare at the Skill in question. Even if I can't get

Flesh-Shaping, I'm determined not to lose the healing magic that has kept me alive in this dangerous world.

I focus on my Skill, following the only sense of direction that I have in this space: instinct. I flood my being with the sense of what it feels like to use Lay-on-Hands, and I'm relieved when the vibrations slow slightly. But, to my growing dismay, I realize that they haven't stopped entirely, and the Skill itself is still breaking apart, though the process is slowed.

Something tells me that Lay-on-Hands has reached a point of no return. Either it Evolves or it's destroyed.

But how can I do anything about it? I managed to slow the rate of change by focusing on how Lay-on-Hands feels to use, but I've never used Flesh-Shaping! How would I know what it feels like?

My helplessness erodes my will, and the rate of the vibrations increases again as the Skill starts to break apart faster and faster.

I glare at the Skill with fear clawing at my throat. *Maybe . . . maybe if slowing down the process isn't the answer, speeding it up is?*

Not just speeding it up willy-nilly, but focusing as much on where I want to go as where I have been. If I can repair my Core and internal matrix with just force of will and mana, who's to say that I can't do the same here?

Mana. Maybe that would help too.

Pulling a chunk from my Core, I form it into the oblong that so helped me repair my internal matrix and direct it along the threads towards the dense area. Feeding it into the design, I see the whole vibrating area flash even brighter with gold, like the threads are reflecting the light of the mini sun that is my Core.

As I maintain an impression of Lay-on-Hands, with its ability to heal flesh, bones, blood vessels, nerves, to push out poison, and revitalize dying flesh, I also envision being able to Shape the flesh in a way Lay-on-Hands cannot. I imagine any cell of the body becoming like putty, able to be moved, replicated, molded, reformed. I imagine a healing Skill without limits, able to be used both to heal and to harm, to grow and to regrow, to replicate and to destroy.

I feel a connection to the dense area of threads and sense new threads growing among the design as the feeling of wrongness in the vibrations reduces. Then that whole sense fades as the mana I supplied it with is used up. Once more I'm convinced that the Skill is on the edge of being destroyed rather than developed.

But this time I know what to do.

With renewed hope, I reach into my Core and grab as much mana as I dare, then pull it towards the Skill and focus in once more. After I repeat the process a couple of times, it feels like some tipping point has been reached. I don't need to focus as much; it no longer feels like the moment I stop visualizing where I need to go, the Skill will start destroying itself again. Instead, as long as I keep it supplied with mana, the lines of my internal matrix will weave themselves into a new design.

The lines are being smoothed in some ways, sharpened in others. New lines are developed and woven together. As the process continues, it speeds up until the movement of lines becomes a golden blur. Though making sure not to fail to provide the process with enough mana, I'm mesmerized by the movement—it's better than a fireworks display.

I sense the process coming to an end as the movement slows again bit by bit and the new design reveals itself. Once it finishes, I find that the whole collection of intricate lines is bigger than it was before, taking up about half again the space.

Drifting closer, I look at the design from multiple angles. It's . . . not as different as I was expecting. Even though I held the impression of Lay-on-Hands uppermost in my mind, I was still fearful that it would change completely. That looked like exactly what was happening while I watched the lines shift and move. Tracing the result of the Evolution with my gaze, however, proves that my fears were unfounded: the center of the design looks practically unchanged from the lines that were first there.

One good thing I see, though, is that the design itself appears more . . . suited to the matrix as a whole. It's not as well suited as the designs I'm almost certain represent my Class Skills, but it's certainly closer than the other non-Class Skills. Perhaps that's a result of my efforts during the Evolution?

Figuring that I'm not going to find out much more just by looking at my internal matrix, I pull out of my Core space and go to check my notifications.

Skill Evolution!
You have gained a Skill Evolution to your Lay-on-Hands Skill. Lay-on-Hands is now Flesh-Shaping. Previous Journeyman level understanding of Lay-on-Hands has been conserved and incorporated into Flesh-Shaping. Automatic knowledge of how to heal unfamiliar damage has been removed. Full rank has not been conserved due to the wider applications of Flesh-Shaping. Journeyman 1 → Beginner 5.

Flesh-Shaping
Use mana to affect flesh by growing, molding, replicating, regrowing . . . Your limits are your imagination and your mana. Greater applications of mana will lead to greater results. If using this Skill on a being, the being must either consent to or reject your attempts. In the case of a rejection, you may still succeed if your Willpower is high enough or your mana is plentiful enough to overcome theirs. Beware: if your will or power should prove lesser, you may suffer a backlash.

Close message

I stare at the message and feel more than a little relief. After fearing that I would lose the Skill completely, I can even take the drop in rank with equanimity. I will need to make sure that the loss of the automatic healing knowledge isn't too disastrous, but the rest of it seems to be much as I envisioned.

The warning about my limits being my imagination and mana indicates that this might be a bit of a mana hog—I doubt that I've maintained the Journeyman benefit of mana efficiency that I had with Lay-on-Hands. Of course, I might be wrong. I need to test it to find out.

In fact, testing sounds like a very good idea. Hopefully, I'll be able to get rid of this gnawing fear that I've made a mistake and broken my only healing Skill.

Heading out of the cave, I observe Bastet and the cubs as my nerves make butterflies flutter in my stomach. Flesh-Shaping sounds like a much more dangerous Skill since it can be used on enemies as well as allies. What if I use the Skill incorrectly and I accidentally kill my target? Maybe I should do this on myself first, use myself as a test dummy. It would only be fair.

But I don't have any injuries, I say to myself. The stupidity of my thought hits me a moment later and I sigh. That's easy enough to rectify, though not exactly pleasant. I turn tail and go back into the cave.

Feeling my stomach rumble, I decide to kill two birds with one stone. I pull out my wok and start preparing a stew for myself. While I wait for it to heat up, I look into the flames broodingly.

I feel my thoughts being pulled towards the yawning black hole of doubt over whether this new Skill will prove equal to what I've given up. To avoid getting sucked in, I do my best to think of other matters, like what a Skill called *Flesh-Shaping* might be capable of.

I'm rather banking on all parts of the body counting as flesh—bones as well as meat. That's certainly what I visualized when holding the Skill together. What if I could strengthen my bones? Or make myself grow claws on demand? Heck, could this even be used to enable me to transform into a beast? My imagination starts going wild, and I have to pull it back forcefully before I get too excited about something I haven't yet used.

I remind myself that even if it just means I can heal my companions, I will be happy. If it can grow River's arm back, it will be better than what I had before. If all I've lost is the ability to just dump healing magic into a wound and let it do its own job, then that's not so bad—I shifted mostly away from that sort of thing a while ago. I only use it in the middle of combat when I don't have the concentration to focus on directing the magic. Ideally, my larger party will now be able to give me the space to concentrate more even in a fight.

And hopefully, I will be able to hurt enemies with it, though the mention of a "backlash" makes me slightly concerned. Is it as simple as the magic I'm using being used to damage me instead? Or could it be that the Flesh-Shaping I'm trying to perpetrate on something else would instead be perpetrated on me? I shudder a little at that thought.

Still, it might allow us to actually take down some beasts that might otherwise seem impossible. Frankly, I don't think we would have won against the salamander if I hadn't given it an aneurysm. The thing was a tank, its bulk meaning that most of our strikes were just shrugged off. One of us would have had to make a really lucky strike to open an artery in its neck or something. However, with the combat application of Flesh-Shaping, we could bypass all of that and hit it directly in its brain.

Of course, I'll probably be required to be up close and personal—right now, at least. In the future, who knows? There's no longer any requirement to touch the subject in the Skill's name, nor does it say anything about contact in the Skill description. It's something I'll have to work on.

But I'm getting a bit ahead of myself. I haven't even used it yet.

Seeing that my stew is beginning to boil, I withdraw my knife and hold it over the steam. I let the steam sterilize the blade, then pull it back after a minute or so. After giving it a little time to cool down, I hold the blade above my forearm, unease roiling in my belly.

It's a little ironic that I'm in the same position as I was the first night I was here: contemplating hurting myself in order to test a new Skill. However, as similar as the situations are, there are also many differences.

Key among those is the knowledge that even if I don't manage to heal myself with my magic, my health regeneration will do it for me. A small cut like the one I'm planning on making will be gone within an hour or so. The only reason I'm even sterilizing the blade is because I don't want to risk introducing contamination, which might complicate the healing process. With Lay-on-Hands, I wouldn't have bothered, but this new Skill is too unfamiliar to take risks.

Reminding myself of that is enough to give me the courage that I lacked the first night I was here. Without allowing myself to doubt any further, I lower the blade to touch my skin and draw it across my flesh.

That . . . doesn't hurt as much as I thought it would, I find myself saying mentally even as the blood wells up and starts trickling over my skin. Maybe my pain resistance has just increased that much? Or something in one of my stats reduces the sensation of pain? Or it could be that Skill I got that manages sensations.

Whatever it is, it's got me spellbound as I watch the stream of red blood dripping steadily onto the floor of the cave, the almost complete lack of pain making it feel like it's happening to someone else.

My fascination is broken with the sudden appearance of Bastet, concern shooting urgently through the Bond. *Maybe I should have done this outside,* I think belatedly as my eyes flick to the puddle already being created on the floor.

"I'm okay," I tell my worried guardian. "I'm just testing something." Bastet huffs as if to chide me for not warning her. Which, when I think of it, probably would have been a good idea. Anyway, I should get to my task before my health regeneration fixes it for me.

Saying the Skill name in my mind does nothing. That's the first difference from Lay-on-Hands. I remember right at the beginning, when I first arrived in this world, all I needed to do was say the Skill name mentally and then a flood of healing magic would pass through my body. Sure, I was soon able to redirect it to make it focus on the worst wounds, but even without that the Skill was able to function by itself.

Apparently, Flesh-Shaping isn't so intuitive, but I'm not nearly as much of a novice at this whole thing as I was a month ago.

I drop into my Core space, then reach inside my Core and pull out a strand of mana. With the amount of practice I've had doing this, it takes little more than a thought. I do have to stop myself from automatically feeding it into my internal matrix—that's all fixed for now.

Then I pause, slightly at a loss. My Core space is a slightly flattened sphere. It's nothing like the shape of my body. I have the mana, but I don't have any idea where to take it.

I first try feeding it into the Skill again. Nothing happens—it just flashes through both the smooth and jagged lines of the design and then out on the other side again. *Not that, then.*

I take a moment to think carefully, and another idea comes to me. *Perhaps this will work?* Trying to hold on to the bit of mana, I slowly pull myself out of my Core space.

That's easier said than done. It's a bit like trying to juggle and then, when I've got the balls flying nicely into the air, closing my eyes and trying to keep them going. Naturally, I fail the first couple of times. In fact, it takes me enough time that I have to cut myself again before I manage to finally open my eyes while maintaining control over the bit of mana.

My eyes now open, I fix them on my wound and do my best to draw the mana that I can feel more than see to the break in my skin.

The more I focus on healing from inside my body, the less connection I feel with my physical surroundings, and the more I realize that the state is remarkably similar to when I'm in Meditation. My eyes flutter closed again with the effort, and I find that I'm in some sort of halfway state. Before my eyes I can see the ghostlike lines of my internal matrix, but I'm still centered in my body and can still feel the wound in my arm. I start making real progress.

I suddenly realize that as I draw the mana towards my cut, I'm actually pulling it through the weave of my internal matrix. Maybe that's why it's so intricate: it has to touch all parts of my body. But what about the spaces between threads? Or is it not as straightforward as that?

My questions seem to be partly answered when I move closer to my wound: the Energy channels are actually moving. There were no channels that led directly to the wound before; there are now.

But instead of reaching the end of a golden thread, the closest point to the wound is actually one of the curves that bend back towards the center. I wait for a moment as I wonder if the mana will know what to do—it always has before. I'm not terribly surprised when it doesn't, though. Instead, it just sits in my Energy channel, shifting back and forth a little.

Looks like I need to direct it in some way, I muse. *But how do I get it from inside the channel to the flesh?* It's a bit like . . . an artery. The section of flesh needs blood, but the liquid is held within arteries. So, what does the body do? Use capillaries to transport the blood to everywhere it needs to go. I need to do something like that.

But how? Do I need to create more Energy channels? Surely not. If I did, I would have needed to do that every time I healed myself with Lay-on-Hands, and I'm pretty sure that didn't happen—there's no evidence of it. Heck, if Kalanthia's words are anything to go by, not everyone has Energy channels, yet I've never had an issue healing anyone. I need to think about this in a different way.

Am I overthinking it? After learning about the internal matrix, has my thinking become too rigid? Is it less like blood in an artery and more like nutrients in the gut? I try to relax a little and focus less on my internal matrix and more on just . . . directing the magic to my wound, like I used to with Lay-on-Hands.

Elation flashes through me as, without any difficulty, it works. The mana passes out of my Energy channel without any resistance and diffuses into the blackness beyond. The next difficulty then comes from keeping the Energy together and not letting it diffuse too far—if I relax my concentration, I'm sure it will just vanish into my flesh.

Keeping it together isn't too difficult, however, and I move my mana towards where I sense the wound lies. In this state I can't see it, of course. Not that I can technically see *anything* here—it's all about feeling things through some extra sense or something.

My mana saturates the area around the wound, which I realize is already more than half healed again. While faster healing is a massive bonus, right now it's a bit annoying: I'd rather injuring myself was kept to the minimum, thanks. I fill it with my intention to heal the wound.

It does nothing.

I try to focus again on it healing me, applying my will to it as strongly as I can.

Still nada. I frown. What am I missing here? Then I think back to the Skill description. It talked about the automatic knowledge being lost but that I would retain any knowledge I'd already gained. *Does that mean . . . ?*

This time, instead of just willing it, I tell it *how* to heal. It's not that different from what I did with my eye at the beginning, though I'm a little more detailed this time. Even though I've never studied medicine, never even thought of becoming a doctor, I suddenly realize that I know how things work here. I know about how the cells need to knit back together, how the capillaries need to match back up to carry my blood where it needs to go.

I understand the differences between the various types of tissue that have been cut through and how to feed magic into them to hasten the natural healing process. I know how to use mana to pull things together and rebind them. I know how to remove any foreign bodies and neutralize any potential infections. I know how to smooth the surface so that not even a scar is left.

Almost feeling like I've fallen into a dream, I put my knowledge into practice. I'm more of a tailor than a doctor, using delicate threads of magic to make an unbroken whole of a piece of fabric that was sliced through.

When I reemerge from my Meditative state, settling back into my body, I find that I'm staring at my arm. My bloody, yet completely uninjured arm. With a suddenly shaking hand, I wipe away the remnants of blood covering the wound. Not a scratch can be seen.

I breathe a sigh of relief even as my head starts to throb like a dwarven smith is hammering away inside it, nausea warning me of low mana reserves. *I can still heal.*

Of course, having discovered that now means I need to *practice.* Taking that much time and mana to heal a simple cut isn't good enough. But it's a start. A hope. And that's more than I had before.

CHAPTER SEVENTY-FIVE

Flesh-Shaping

A few hours of practice later and I've improved in both speed and accuracy when healing myself. Knowing that I can do so is all well and good—and honestly, it does take a massive, selfish burden off my mind—but now I need to make sure that it's not only *my* flesh I can shape. After all, what the description made clear is that this isn't a dedicated healing Skill in the same way that Lay-on-Hands was.

And for that, I'm going to need volunteers.

I consider for a moment perhaps getting Bastet to bring me a "volunteer"—some little bird or beast she could catch. But then I remember what it said in the Skill description about backlash and decide not to risk it. Not that I think a little mouse is likely to be able to overcome my will or mana, but the desire to survive is a powerful one, and if I have no idea what I'm doing, it doesn't matter how much stronger I am. A mouse can topple a giant if the giant is already barely balanced.

Which means that I'm going to have to ask my closest companion if she minds me hurting her so I can test my healing on her. I swallow thickly at the thought. Feeling cowardly, I decide to eat my stew first. *I'm hungry anyway*, I think, justifying the delay to myself.

My attempts to heal myself took longer than I thought, as my stew has boiled for long enough for the vegetables to become soft. The meat could do with longer to truly become tender, but I'm hungry enough not to care.

I take my wok outside and use my wooden spoon to eat from it, blowing on each spoonful thoroughly to avoid burning my mouth. Unsurprisingly, I soon have four pairs of plaintive eyes sitting in front of me and begging wordlessly for "yummy meat."

I groan audibly.

"You guys are vultures, you know that?" I grumble, but the eyes just intensify their adorable pleading. Lathani is the worst of them. She knows all too well what she's doing, and she knows that, even as big as she is now, I still can't say no to those eyes. "Fine. I'll give you each a couple of bits. Mind you don't burn yourselves on them, now," I warn, pulling chunks of meat out of my stew and setting them before the "ravenous" felines. From how they go at the food, I might have thought they hadn't eaten in days when I know very well that they stuffed themselves first thing this morning.

I look into my wok, which only holds a few bits of meat now, and practically growl at the four felines when they look up hopefully, licking their lips. "No more. Mine."

I put all my effort into ignoring them and eating my food, and they eventually give up and go to play.

When my wok is empty and my stomach full, I no longer have any excuse to avoid this.

"Bastet?" I ask. She lifts her head and looks at me, tilting it questioningly. I chicken out. "Are any of you injured? Scratches, thorns in the feet, bruises, anything like that?" I cross my fingers in hope. I *really* don't want to take my knife to one of them. Unfortunately, she sends me a feeling of negation. My heart sinking in my chest, I try to summon up my courage to ask.

Just then, Sirocco soars over to land near me. She looks rather satisfied with herself. I stand up—her presence can only mean one thing. Sure enough, I see River's head coming up the slope.

"Welcome back," I say, smiling at the bird, then stride towards the other two. Reaching River and Fenrir just as they crest the plateau, I greet them too. "Did you have a good hunt?" I ask, looking them over anxiously. Though I see blood on both of them, most of it appears not to be their own.

Passable, Ma—Markus, River answers, though he seems dissatisfied. Fenrir doesn't. He's relaxed and comes over happily to rub his dirty head against my knee. I reach down to scratch his neck and he sends pleasure over the link between us.

"You don't seem happy about it," I observe. River's gaze flashes involuntarily to the stump of his arm. I notice that the club we tried to tie onto it is now in his right hand. "It came off?"

In the middle of a fight. He sighs, then continues as he sees my anxiety. *I was not in danger. Fenrir defended me until I could pick it up in my hand.*

"But it didn't work the way we wanted." He agrees silently.

I eye him carefully, weighing up whether to speak or not. Noticing that he has a couple of open wounds, I decide to start with that.

"So, my healing Skill has changed a little," I say casually, deciding not to tell him just how much it's changed—I don't want to either scare him or give him false hope. "Do you mind if I test it a bit on your wounds?"

River looks at me as surprise comes across the Bond, yellow flashing in his spikes.

You do not need to ask. I would not refuse you anything, least of all an offer to heal me.

"But I will when I can," I answer gently, once more reminded that he and I need to have a proper talk about his attitude—it's far too servile for me. In truth, I still don't want to be his master, no matter how he still struggles to call me by my name. But not now. "Anyway, are you hungry?"

He indicates that he's not and then lays a carcass down, which he brought back with him. We sit down together.

"All right, you need to tell me exactly how everything feels, especially if it hurts.

In fact, if it hurts, interrupt me. Right now, I'm just going to try to move some of my mana from me to you and then control it in your body." I try not to think about how that could be misinterpreted; fortunately, River doesn't seem to.

Instead, he just tilts his chin up and sends agreement over the Bond to me. *Now, how to do this?*

With Lay-on-Hands I needed to actually physically touch my target to heal them. Although I doubt that that is a requirement of the new Skill, I decide to start there.

Going into my Core space, I do the mental equivalent of frowning as I consider the situation. I see two options here. Perhaps I need to actively cause something like what happened with Fenrir: find the right connection between me and River and then send mana down it. Or maybe I should send the mana to my hand and then . . . let it seep into River's skin by osmosis?

Deciding to start with the second, as I think that might be the easier one to test, I pull four beads of mana from my Core and focus on sending them to the fingers that are touching River. With my practice earlier in this task, it's relatively easy to get the beads to the right spot, though doing four at once does test my control.

It's even harder to keep all the mana controlled once it has seeped out of my Energy channels into my flesh, but I don't see another way of doing it; my Energy channels will move close to my skin, but I sense that they won't go through it. Not the ones that curve back into the mandala, anyway. And the ones that don't curve back don't seem to move as easily as the others.

Struggling to control the cloud of mana, I focus on pushing it closer to the barrier of my skin. From my Core space, my skin feels impossibly thick, my fingers enormous. The mana moves fast, though, and would move faster if I let it. I don't, though: I fear that it would just fly completely out of control if I released my tight grip on it.

The barrier of my skin requires only a small push before it can be overcome, which is when I hit another barrier. This one holds against me for a moment before it gives way. And then I'm suddenly in a new space.

The difference is relatively subtle. The Energy has a strange feel to it, and my ability to navigate is abruptly reduced. There is no resistance, though I sense that there could be. *Perhaps because River is my Bound,* I theorize. *Or because he's consented to this.*

That my consciousness is somehow inside River is undeniable. Although I cannot sense all the details of his body, I do sense the outline of it as if it were a sort of tent around me. The differently shaped head, the clawed fingers, and the elongated, clawed feet are all hallmarks of exactly where I am.

The mana I've passed into his body via osmosis is actually easier to control in River's body than it was in mine, oddly enough. I would have expected it to be the reverse. In my own body, the mana always feels like it is eager to *go*. Whether it's zipping down my Energy channels and out of my body entirely or, once it's seeped out of the Energy channels completely, into the luminous black space, my Energy always pulls at my control like a dog on a leash.

Here, it's like that same dog is now uneasy in a new place and wants to stick close to me. I have to exert more concentration on wading through the different Energy of River's body than on holding my mana together. Still, since he's not resisting me, it's not difficult.

Curious, I start wandering around River's body with my little bead of mana, like a blood clot that has taken on a life of its own and decided to go see the sights.

As I move, I start getting more of a sense of River's body. The veins and arteries that form a network around it to deliver vital nutrients. The lungs, slightly differently shaped from my own, which do just as good a job oxygenating his blood. Better, perhaps. The heart, again, slightly differently shaped and more centrally placed than my own. The organs, mostly similar to my own but not entirely, the appendix missing and other organs added in.

I sense that after understanding comes the ability to modify, and I resolve to do this kind of scan in my own body. At the same time, I sense that my understanding is limited, perhaps due to Flesh-Shaping's current level or my knowledge of anatomy. I have no sense of how mana moves around River's body or how Energy interacts with his body to heal injuries.

Perhaps I need to study that in myself and others to be able to detect it more easily, I wonder. For once, the addition of a job to my to-do list doesn't fill me with dismay but excitement.

However, that's for another time. Right now, I need to find the wounds he has from his hunting. Eventually, I find one of the rents in his flesh, something that looks like it was made by a sharp claw swiping at him. Once I spot it, it's easy enough to identify – a sense of wrongness emanates from it.

I feed the mana into the wound while concentrating on the flesh coming together and healing, and I'm pleased to see my intentions take shape when a small part of it seals back together. Of course, it was only a relatively small amount of mana, and I seem to have lost some while exploring River's body, so just that action uses it all up.

With no more mana at hand, I find myself being pushed inexorably back to my own body. Much as I fight, I can't seem to find the same purchase on the odd Energy that surrounds me, which I've been using to navigate.

I take advantage of the fact that I'm back in my own body to grab some more mana before returning to River's body and continuing to heal the gash in his flesh.

I spend a little time just doing that—going back and forth between my body and River's to heal that one cut. It's more complicated than the slice I gave to myself: not only is it deeper, but I find evidence of foreign bodies within the wound. Actually, I don't notice those at first. It's only when I scan the wound after closing it that I realize something's wrong.

Removing the foreign bodies requires pushing them out with a drop of blood, like I have before when getting rid of venom, which in turn requires making a small exit wound for the blood to escape. I have to wonder what it looks like from River's perspective. Probably very odd—his flesh crawling together, then splitting apart for a moment to let a drop of red out before closing again.

As I continue working, I find that the magic in my control becomes easier to work with. In fact, I even start finding that it's . . . nudging me in certain ways. Like when I'm binding the capillaries together, I feel it's almost . . . helping me. Or when I manipulate the flesh to let the drop of blood out. It was me who did it, but I just had an instinct about *how* I should do it.

Pulling back to my own body, I open my eyes and look at River contemplatively. The cut is healed, but there's a problem: it took *far* too long.

Perhaps that's a bit greedy of me. When I first chose this Skill, I was worried that I wouldn't be able to heal at all. And now I'm moaning that it takes too much time? And mana. I can't forget about how more than half my mana pool went into a single relatively minor gash, which would have healed on its own without a scar.

Hopefully, practice will make perfect, and more efficient, because otherwise, my capabilities as a healer have taken a sharp nosedive. I can't spend that long healing a tiny cut. Not when I'm probably going to have to heal gashes that are ten times worse, or deal with poisoning, or perforated organs. Or a severed arm.

I look at the stump of River's arm. Even though a part of me would like to shrink away from this, to say that I need more time to practice . . . the rest of me needs to know.

"River," I say quietly, nerves forming a stranglehold around my neck that I can barely speak through.

Yes? Perhaps he realizes that something's wrong: his tone is wary, cautious.

"Listen, uh . . . I was hoping . . . I was thinking . . ." I sigh in frustration. Then, closing my eyes so I can't see him looking at me, I force the words out. "I would like to try to restore your arm."

There's silence. Dead silence.

I open my eyes and see him looking intently at me. Over the Bond I feel the faintest hint of hope, but it's quickly stifled before it has time to take root. River doesn't want to entertain false hope either.

I thought you tried that? he asks, his tone completely flat, his spikes dull.

"I did—with Lay-on-Hands. I wasn't completely honest with you earlier," I admit. "I didn't want to raise your hopes unduly. I still don't, so I will say that I don't know whether this will work. But I wasn't just trying out a new use of my healing Skill. I have a new Skill entirely, which I'm grateful can still be used for healing. And I would like to see if it can be used to regrow your arm."

Now I feel a hint of hope coming across the Bond, irrepressible. I keep my face blank. I don't want him to see the hope that I, too, hold. But maybe . . . maybe . . .

Please, he says, his tone fervent. *Please!*

"Remember, I have no idea whether this will work," I warn him.

I understand. But if there's any chance, any chance at all . . .

I nod. I completely understand where he's coming from.

"All right, I'll try."

CHAPTER SEVENTY-SIX

Dawn

Moving my hand to rest just above the stump, I pull mana from my Core and take it with me into River's body. Thanks to all the practice I've just had with this very method, it's easy enough for me to cross the boundary. I even manage to take more mana with me in one go than I could the first time I did this.

Of course, this time I'm not approaching an open wound. I closed this days ago, directly after the incident. But the scar tissue is obvious, nonetheless—I noticed it even during my previous scan of River's body. I approach it with my large chunk of mana.

The problem is that an arm is far more complex than the wound I've so recently healed. But is it really? Cells are cells. Yes, bone cells are different from muscle cells, which are different again from skin cells. But I've already had to knit together different cells. The real problem is that here, I don't have anything to connect the stump to.

I abruptly regret not keeping River's arm. It had seemed so distasteful to put my friend's arm in my Inventory at the time—what was I going to use it for? I wasn't going to *cook* it, or pull his claws out, or use his ulna for a needle. I buried it instead. I didn't think that I would be able to do anything to help River then.

Now, I doubt that it's still in a condition to be reattached—even Flesh-Shaping probably can't do anything about necrosis. And that's assuming that something hasn't gone and eaten it.

So, the success or failure of this attempt will depend entirely on whether Flesh-Shaping is capable of creating large amounts of new cells. Maybe that was why Lay-on-Hands couldn't help.

Even as detached from my bodily sensations as I am right now, I'm still capable of feeling nervous. Fortunately, I don't have any hands to shake, so I'm not worried about them causing me to do something unintentional like they might if I was a surgeon.

I decide to start with something simple: extending the top layer of the epidermis.

It takes several attempts, each failure making my hopes sink lower and lower. But I keep on trying, determined to give this as much effort as I gave to just healing with Flesh-Shaping at all. And finally, my efforts pay off. It's not easy, and this is the simplest part of the task ahead of me. But . . . it *works*: I've created a flap of skin where once there was none.

I don't know the medical names for what I'm doing, nor how they really work, like someone who's been through medical school would. Lay-on-Hands would have just healed them without my input. But with Flesh-Shaping, although I can't just leave it all up to the magic, I don't need a medical or biology degree—fortunately. As the Skill itself said, my limits are my imagination, my Willpower, and my mana.

I need intention: my desire to do something, but not just a formless desire—I can't just imagine the skin extending. No, I have to visualize *how* that will happen. I have to imagine the cells duplicating. And then I have to have the will to control the magic and make it happen.

At first, I duplicate a single cell at a time, but I quickly move onto multiple cells and then chunks of them. It still works best if I duplicate a single type of cell at a time, but I can foresee a time when I can just extend whole chunks of flesh, multiple cell types all at once.

After finding success with the different layers of skin cells, I move on to the scales that cover the skin. This is easy enough, though slightly more complicated than the layers of skin. After that, I decide to try something that I'm most concerned about: the bone.

Here, I hit more difficulty. Bone cells are very different from skin cells, and I can't just duplicate them willy-nilly. Bone isn't nearly as solid as it looks, and if I make it so, I could cause River far more issues than I solve. But I can duplicate them, so I'm determined to do that *perfectly.*

And then, once I have started figuring out the bone cells, I have to work on the muscle cells, tendons, blood vessels, and nerves. As I work, I keep a layer of skin between everything inside the body and the outside world just to ensure that there's no chance of introducing foreign bodies or causing blood loss. I soon learn how to cannibalize the skin cells as the arm grows in length.

I learn a *lot.* It's almost like the biological parts of a medical degree have been concentrated into a few hours, and on a very specific part of the body. I have to reference River's good arm and reverse the construction. I make mistakes, lots of them. Some I don't even notice until later when I come back, having learned more, and see them. I cause River pain accidentally, and then, later, I cause it on purpose when I want to test if the nerve cells are connected properly.

It takes *hours.* The sun goes down and the first moon rises before I've even made an inch of progress. We have to stop to eat and for me to rest for a bit before continuing. The second moon rises before I've gotten halfway along River's forearm, but even that is far more progress than I made in the same time before—my speed is increasing significantly with my familiarity. And with my increasing familiarity, my mana efficiency also improves.

I'm deeply grateful that I don't have to deal with his elbow joint, but that gratitude only lasts until I get to his wrist. That small section takes almost four hours by itself and requires me to take several breaks to regenerate mana and rest my mind. But by the time I get to his fingers, I'm able to do their tricky joints far more easily due to my prior experience. The rank up from Beginner to Novice in Flesh-Shaping also helps with increased finesse and mana efficiency.

When dawn arrives, the sun rising high enough above the mountain behind us to grace us with its direct rays, light glints off the scales of River's new arm, where only the tips of his claws are missing.

Exhausted beyond belief, and wanting nothing more than to tip half a cow down my throat and fall into bed, I behold my creation.

Can I . . . ? River asks, his voice hushed like his arm is something sacred, something impossibly valuable. I throw a chunk of meat into my mouth and chew on it, then use the fortitude it gives me to scan his arm for the umpteenth time.

His arm is more familiar to me now than the back of my own hand, than Lucy's smile, than the sound of the morning birdsong that trills into the air triumphantly. I check and then check again. I can't see any problems with it. I compare it to the other arm. It all looks like a mirror image. As it should: I couldn't have done this without the template of his right arm. I doubt that it's exactly what his arm was like before, but if this works, that's all that matters.

"Go ahead," I croak, withdrawing fully back into my own body.

I watch as he carefully, oh so carefully turns his arm back and forth, stretching out his clawless fingers and then closing them into a fist.

His movements gain in confidence and fluidity—the length of time he was without his arm was nowhere near long enough to cause him to lose any of the neural connections enabling him to control it. He rapidly runs through a series of movements testing both fine and gross motor control. His hand shaking, he picks up the spear laid down on the ground next to him and grips it. His grip tightens until his scales go pale green and the wooden handle of the spear creaks.

Elation mixed with joy and exhaustion comes over the Bond from his side. We probably should have done this in multiple stages but . . . I don't know. Something made me fear that if I didn't just *do* it, I would lose my confidence, telling myself that it was too difficult, that I wouldn't be able to accomplish this momentous task.

But I did. I *did.*

It's probably my own relief and sheer joy that makes me do it. A cardinal sin.

"Well, you're certainly not 'armless now," I joke. I don't even have the excuse that I'm a dad.

River stares at me for a long moment, confusion cutting through even his over-powering ecstasy for long enough that I feel prompted to explain. "You know, you didn't have an arm, so you were armless. Armless, harmless, you know?"

I color in embarrassment. Maybe wordplay doesn't translate well across the Bond.

Then River starts making an odd clicking sound. It gets louder, then becomes interspersed with grunts every so often. The Bond doesn't translate any words; instead, it just translates a feeling. Hilarity. He's *laughing.*

He laughs longer and harder than my hapless joke really deserves, but I understand why. Even greater than my own feelings, for him it is the relief of releasing his fear of life as a cripple, short-lived as it was. It's been very clear that he hasn't fully understood or believed my assurances that I would take care of him. This is the return to him of his own limb, regrown, capable of everything it had been before.

The world hasn't been put to rights. I still have an open quest, which I should probably get to. I have a forest of carnivorous trees to deal with. I have a village of lizard folk to save by convincing them to join me. And I still have a damaged soul and my own projects to work on.

But right now, I push all that aside and just appreciate the moment. I, who once stood on the edge of an apartment block contemplating that throwing myself off it was probably the best I could offer the world, have essentially given a man his life back.

So, right now, I decide to stand on the peak of the mountain and just enjoy the view.

River laughs, and I join him, the Bond reflecting and magnifying our feelings until the fear, guilt, and blame are washed away like beach sand by the waves.

Across worlds, Lord Nicholas Titanbend is preparing to leave his manor.

"Tell my groom to saddle my horse," he orders one of the servants.

"Yes, my lord," the man acknowledges, bowing and then hurrying away.

Nicholas walks towards the main doors and takes his scarf and coat from the cupboard next to them. He knows that Sarran is likely on his way but is too impatient to wait for his manservant. It's not like he's an invalid, anyway. Or one of those dainty lords, too good to even take their coats off a rail.

He snorts contemptuously at the thought, several faces coming to mind. If only the king didn't require him to play "nicely" with the other lords . . . But there is no point in thinking such things: the kingdom is in a delicate enough state as it is. There's no sense in upsetting the udja cart just to satisfy his own vanity. That would make him just as bad as one of those alara-flower lords.

The lord is already opening the doors, the heavy wood easy for him to move thanks to a combination of well-oiled hinges and his Strength stat, when Sarran appears around the corner.

A model of a manservant, as always, the other man has perfected the ability to move without making more than a whisper of sound, even to Nicholas's enhanced senses, and to be able to hurry without *looking* like he is.

"My lord, where are you off to?" asks Sarran as he stops at arm's length away from Nicholas.

"Why, do you wish to come with me?" the lord asks with an arched eyebrow.

"If my lord wishes," the other man answers levelly. About to refuse, Nicholas then reconsiders.

"In fact, yes. I do wish it. It has been too long since we traveled a road together. I'll tell the groom to saddle another horse while you get yourself changed."

"Yes, my lord," the manservant replies, bowing. He holds the position until the lord turns away, then Nicholas's keen ears catch the slightest sound to indicate his quick retreat. The lord grins to himself: though Sarran is *far* too professional to ever let on any sense of discomfort, Nicholas knows that he was more than a little perturbed at his employer's unexpected order.

The fact is that he actually *would* appreciate the company on his trip, and it *has* been a while since they've gone riding out together. Of course, it isn't in the *slightest* because of that dig about his midnight brooding two days ago.

Whistling cheerily to himself, Lord Nicholas walks along his wide driveway to the stables, which are at its end. Letting himself in, he sees the groom holding his horse, saddled and bridled.

"Sarran's coming along too, Lark," he announces. The groom, Lark, looks a little startled.

"Truly, my lord?"

"Indeed."

"Then I should go and saddle White Lightning for him, I presume," he says, a wicked grin curling at his lips and dancing in his eyes.

"Cheeky," Lord Nicholas reprimands, but the humor in his own eyes and on his lips soothes the sting. "Tease Sarran and he'll have Timar order you to help the groundsmen for a few days. Spreading the piles of material you muck out from the horses' stalls would no doubt be an appropriate response to the jest."

"That it would," the groom admits wryly. "And I have no doubts the honorable steward would support him. With your permission, my lord, I'll go and saddle Old Nala instead, then."

"Go on, then," Nicolas says encouragingly and walks forwards to take the reins. "Hello, my beauty," he says, stroking his horse's nose gently. It's been a long time since he bound this stallion as a foal, but he still remembers the joy of it. After spending weeks caring for the orphaned foal, feeding, grooming, and encouraging it, to have the young creature accept his Tame Bond had been a validation of all the effort he'd put in. All the sleep he'd sacrificed.

And even now, Tempest is still a magnificent mount, though he is starting to get on a little in years.

"But then, we both are," Nicholas sighs to himself. Tempest's strength and life has been prolonged with excellent feed, excellent care, and a good number of Cores, but even that will come to an end. The stallion's only fault is that he's never shown any sign of being able to progress to the next tier; without that, prolonging his life can only be about delaying the inevitable.

Still, for now, his beloved horse is one of his Bonded, and he takes the time to fuss over the stallion. He actually appreciates the time Sarran takes to get ready, though he's certainly going to chide his manservant about it when he appears—amicably, of course.

"Where are we going? You never said," Sarran asks once they're en route—and the obligatory joshing at him primping himself like a lord or lady bound for court has been completed.

"I wish to visit the Oracle," Nicolas answers neutrally. Sarran turns in his seat to look at him for a moment, then quickly turns back to face the front when his sudden movement threatens to unseat him.

"The one who directed you to the candidate?" he asks once he's sure he's not about to accidentally nose-dive off the side of his horse.

"The same."

"Why? If I may ask." Silence spreads between them for a few long moments. The manservant is probably giving up hope of a reply when Nicholas begins thoughtfully.

"I am wondering about the character of my candidate. To have accrued as much Energy as he did in such a short time . . . Even if his world's time moves faster than ours, it has still been much less than the year he is to be there. How did he do it? Did he kill something immensely powerful? Did he Bind the creature instead? Did he find some sort of treasure? My curiosity is driving me insane."

"And do you think that the Oracle can answer your questions?" Sarran asks, his eyebrows climbing up his head.

"The question isn't 'Can she?'," Nicholas corrects him. "The question 'Will she?' is more uncertain." He sighs. "I have brought a few items she might find interesting. I hope that at least one of them will engage her curiosity sufficiently to pay for my questions."

"Is this it?" asks Sarran, sounding like he isn't sure whether to believe it or whether to assume Nicholas is playing a joke on him. A faint hint of resignation is tucked in the wrinkles of his face, like he's prepared for the revelation that the whole story about the Oracle is just a cover for some other expedition.

Nicholas doesn't blame him. The Oracle's house is an unassuming cottage tucked into some woods just outside of their closest city. It's surrounded by flowers, and a climbing flowering vine even crawls all over the front of the house. Its blossoms fill the air with a heady fragrance.

"I felt the same way when Roland first gave me the directions," Nicholas tells him with wry amusement. "But based on my previous experience, she's the real deal. However, her requirements for payment are a little unusual."

Without saying anything more, he walks up to the door and lifts his hand to knock. Before it falls, the door opens. Clearly, it's not a coincidence, as the woman now standing in the doorway doesn't look surprised in the slightest. She could have just seen them coming through the window, but Sarran feels it isn't because of that.

"Lord Nicholas Titanbend," murmurs the lady, who looks like she absolutely fits in this quaint cottage setting and not a bit how Sarran would have imagined an Oracle to appear. "A pleasure to see you again. And Sarran Mirransson," she continues, shifting her gaze to the manservant. "A pleasure to make your acquaintance." Sarran can't help swallowing a little, his eyes going wide as he wonders just how she knows his name.

As he meets her eyes, he finds himself struck by some otherworldly quality in them. Suddenly, despite the setting, despite her appearance otherwise, he has no doubt that she is indeed an Oracle.

The Oracle looks back at Nicholas.

"I will take all three of your offered items," she announces, though he hasn't said a word or even moved to withdraw them from his Inventory. "Three items for three questions. Fair, yes?"

Nicholas can't help but chuckle a little.

"Fair indeed, my lady." A small smile teases at the corner of the Oracle's mouth, but it doesn't soften her visage at all—instead, it makes it all the more mysterious.

"Then, shall we begin?" she invites.

Inside the cozy room, Lord Nicholas takes a seat at a circular two-person table with the Oracle sitting opposite. Sarran stands at the door, falling easily into his role as manservant and, while his master is otherwise occupied, guard.

"A question each of the past, present, and future," states the oracle. "Ask your first."

Lord Nicholas thinks for a moment. The topic is obvious, but how to phrase it right is another matter.

"What was the event that caused the candidate to so quickly pay off a large portion of his debt?"

The Oracle takes a pouch, holds it within her hands for a moment, then quickly upends it.

A number of items fall out around the table and arrange themselves on the intricate design painted upon it. Bones, stones, feathers, and other objects that neither man is able to identify immediately. Murmuring to herself, she shifts some of the items off the design, tucking them back into the pouch. Others she nudges and prods before lifting her head to gaze at the lord.

"The world traveler encountered an unmissable opportunity. Like so many of those, risk was balanced with reward; he suffered greatly, but what he gained was many times the value of what he lost. Even his injury has been a boon for what he has learned from healing it."

Clear as mud, Nicholas thinks to himself, but he wasn't honestly expecting much else. Not from an Oracle. She'd been unusually direct the last time and he'd still needed to puzzle out her riddles.

Still, her answer to this question gives him some good clues. The candidate might have killed a great creature, but if so, it's likely that it was in an attempt to reach some natural treasure. *Actually, that seems rather probable. Any natural treasure is bound to be guarded by a powerful beast.* The mention of injury makes that even more likely to be the correct answer. *I'm glad I sent him Lay-on-Hands. He would probably not have survived otherwise. At least I know he is not some coward. When he saw an opportunity, he took it and did not baulk at the price he had to pay.* Satisfied with his conclusions, the lord asks the next question.

"How many Bonds does he hold right now?" It's a strategic question: the candidate's use of his Class will be key for his future success in accomplishing the task Nicholas has for him. By this point, if he has not started using his Class Skills, it spells dire things for the future. At the same time, it will be interesting to discover if he has a tendency to seek out a small group of intelligent and powerful Bonds, or a larger group of weaker and less intelligent ones.

Once more, the Oracle goes through the rigamarole of her art.

"The world traveler currently holds four Bonds, one with a sapient individual."

Nicholas's eyebrows shoot up. Though four Bonds isn't a massive number, that one of them is with a sapient individual implies that the candidate's Willpower has increased significantly—it couldn't have been more than fifteen when he was pulled through the portal. After all, sapience almost invariably increases the resistance offered in a Battle of Wills. Though, it is possible that the candidate trapped the sapient so thoroughly that it couldn't put up more than the barest amount of resistance.

He will have to hope that this isn't the case, though, as a high Willpower would *definitely* stand the candidate in better stead when he comes to this world. Of course, it could also be due to raising Dominate rapidly, but since that went along with gaining Bonds and using his Bonded, it was unlikely to be the sole reason.

Well, at least he has clearly been exercising his Class Skills one way or another, which is what Nicholas wanted to find out from his question.

"What is your third question?" the Oracle asks at a moment when his thoughts have paused—almost like she knows exactly when is best to prompt him. Which, honestly, she probably does, even though he's fairly sure she isn't able to read his mind directly. Prediction, rather, is her area of expertise.

Nicholas takes a moment to consider again, still a little shocked by the previous information.

"Will he be able to develop or learn any more Skills before he arrives?" The question is shrewdly asked in a way that the Oracle will have to confirm whether or not he will make it to the end of the year—of the candidate's local time—in order to answer the other part of it. The knowing look the Oracle gives him suggests that she's aware of his reasoning, but she doesn't argue. If anything, the glint in her eyes indicates that she's amused.

Once more she plies her trade, but this time it's different. She takes much longer over the paraphernalia than the previous two times, and a frown creeps onto her face. Nicholas waits, more than a little impatient, as she mutters to herself and nudges the items.

Finally, she shakes her head a little.

"I cannot fully answer that question." Before Nicholas can object, she holds up her hand. "It is not that I *won't*. It's that I *can't*. There is a point in the future where his fate hangs on a knife's edge, a filament bridge over a chasm. If he falls off the path, on either side lies death. All my arts cannot see further, though they can see many tribulations before this moment. Thus, I cannot say whether he will truly arrive here. However, if he does, I sense that he will have Skills in magic and arms beyond your dreams. Come to me again in a tenday and perhaps I will be able to answer the first part of your question fully." She hesitates for a moment. "In return for my inability to give you a complete answer now, do you wish to ask another question?"

Nicholas eyes her. While the greedy part of him would dearly love to milk this situation for all it is worth, an instinct warns him that he's already pushed his luck by asking a question that should probably have been two to begin with. He is playing mental games with an opponent who probably already knows his moves at least five steps in the future—the wrong move now will potentially doom him later.

"No," he says finally, trying to smile unconcernedly like the rejection means nothing to him. "You have answered my questions graciously and given me as much information as you could. You have earned your reward."

The Oracle smiles, the mystery in her eyes lightened with satisfied pleasure.

"A gentleman as always, Lord Nicholas. Then I shall give you this for free: Though I cannot see further than the precipice, all my arts tell me that it is a trial, not an executioner's block. Should he navigate his path correctly and traverse the chasm, he will be far stronger for it."

With those parting words, the two men thank the Oracle and leave, Nicholas giving her the three items he had promised.

The ride home is quiet, the two men both thinking over what they had learned that day.

End Book Status Table

Name: Markus Wolfe		Race: Human	Class: Tamer
Level: 12	Energy to next level: 100%	Energy absorption rate: 26u/hr	Energy towards debt: 78%
Intelligence	36	Mana: 2/360	
Wisdom	36	Mana regeneration rate: 900u/hr	
Willpower	42+8 (+20%)	Health regeneration rate: 40u/hr (-20%)	
Constitution	19	Health: 190/190	
Strength	16	Stamina: 90/90	
Dexterity	15	Stamina regeneration rate: 150u/hr	
Class Skills: Dominate – Novice 4 Tame – Beginner 6 Fade – Initiate 1		Non-Class Skills: Flesh-Shaping – Novice 9 Stealth – Novice 1 Animal Empathy – Novice 6 Meditation – Initiate 3 Energy Manipulation – Initiate 3 Sensation Management – Beginner 6	

Author's Note

Thank you for reading the next book in the Taming Destiny series! It's people like you who keep me writing! If you'd like to be notified of when my books launch or other versions of my books come out along with a number of other goodies, please sign up to my newsletter on my website: winterswritingcorner.com Everyone who signs up will also receive three side stories from the Taming Destiny universe as a thank you!

More side stories and advance chapters are available on my Patreon page: https://www.patreon.com/user?u=90740676

I'd really appreciate it if you could leave a review on your way out—reviews help other readers find books they like, so if you've enjoyed reading about Markus and the gang, please share the love.

I'd like to thank my Royal Road readers for helping to point out the inconsistencies and mistakes the first time around. Their comments were essential in helping to transform this work, as well as encourage me to continue writing. I'd also like to thank Podium for their hard work in turning this into a professional manuscript, audiobook (available on Audible), and print version (perhaps available in a store near you).

Thanks again. I hope you enjoyed this book and I look forward to seeing you in the next one! Markus has lots of crafting to do and a quest to prepare for.

About the Author

S. L. Winter is a writer, mother, and avid reader living in France. She first encountered LitRPG while searching for new fantasy stories to read. Although not a dedicated gamer herself, Winter was immediately hooked by the idea of fantasy worlds inspired by game rules. Three years and hundreds of devoured books later, here she is—writing her own!

RESPAWN YOUR CURIOSITY

follow us on our socials

podiumentertainment.com

@podiumentertainment

/podiumentertainment

@podium_ent

@podiumentertainment